A
TRADE IN
BETRAYALS

A
TRADE IN
BETRAYALS

Volume 3 of THE ARCIST CHRONICLES

DANIEL AUSEMA

GUARDBRIDGE BOOKS
ST ANDREWS, SCOTLAND

Published by Guardbridge Books,
St Andrews, Fife, United Kingdom.

http://guardbridgebooks.co.uk

Trade in Betrayals, A

Cover art © 2024 by Alex Storer

ISBN: 978-1-911486-91-6

*Dedicated to all those storytellers
who use their stories to create space for everyone and
topple the walls that divide us.*

THE FROZEN SEA

Jarnur

Romnai

Volcanic
Springs
Mine

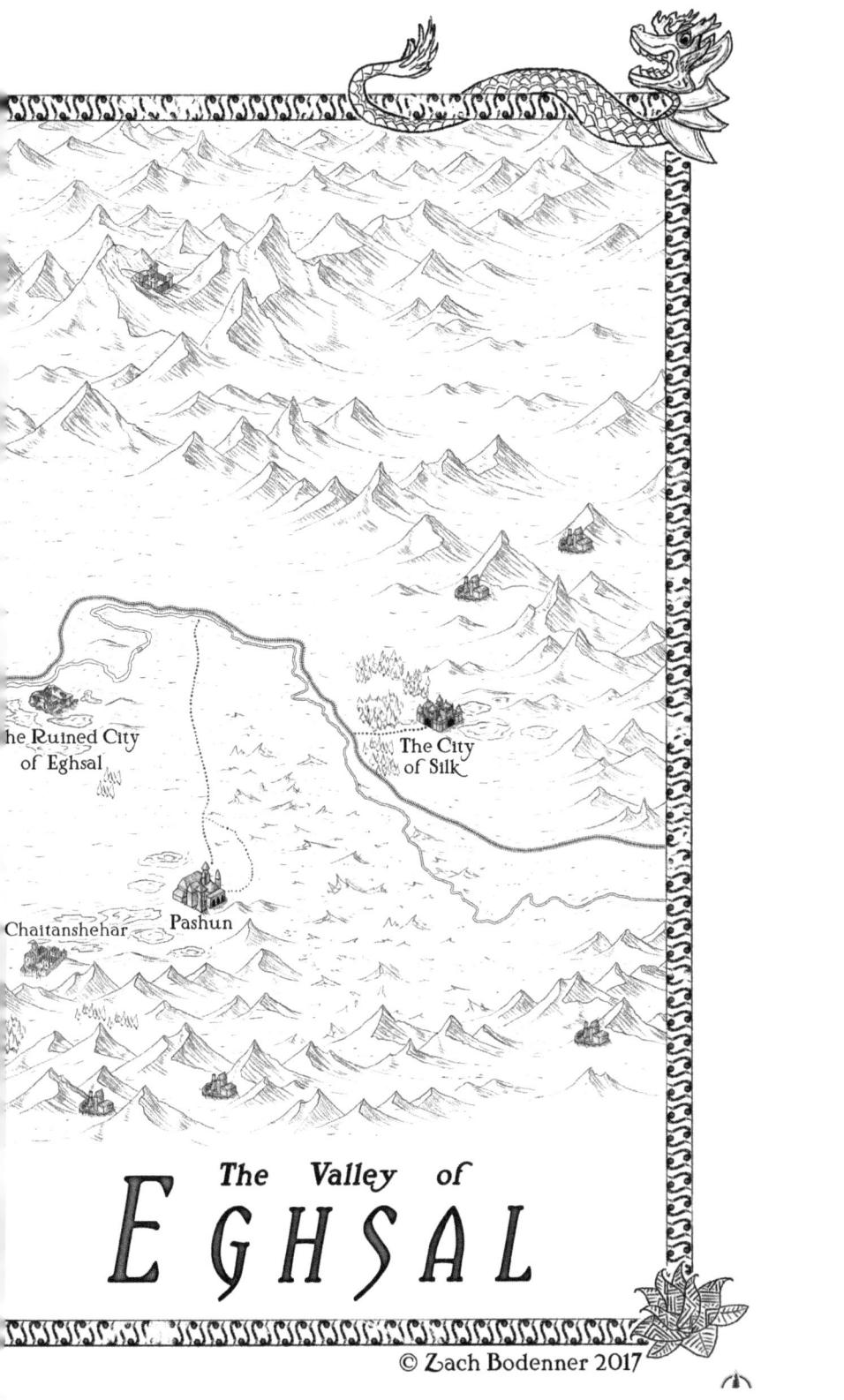

The Ruined City
of Eghsal

The City
of Silk

Chaitanshehar   Pashun

The Valley of

EGHSAL

© Zach Bodenner 2017

CHAPTER 1

A story is more than its message, a dance more than its meaning and sacred inspiration. A city is more than its walls, of course, but also more than its current residents, reaching into its past—short as those six years were for the city of Chaitanshehar—and into its future. A future that might be even shorter. Pavresh wouldn't dare venture a guess. Those six years had given promising signs, but much to worry about as well, much that left Jaritta's dream wobbly and uncertain.

Food was the biggest challenge. A blush of green spread below their slope, promising a future easing of that difficulty. Maybe, if everything worked out as they dreamed, but when had anything gone perfectly to plan? The enemies in the other cities were still a threat. It wasn't open conflict anymore, no soldiers marching across the swampland to lay siege to their city. But they were doing what they could to make the city fail, learning from Pavresh's own successes to turn the stories their citizens heard against the new city.

His concern now, though, as he led his students down the slope from the city's wall, was with the magic.

Ah, arcist magic—such power, and still so much unknown.

But like stories and dancing and cities, an arcist spell was so much more than its raw power. This was one of the key truths Pavresh tried to teach his students.

They followed in a line down a well established trail. The city wall above them was mostly intact, apart from a few places where the edge had begun to crumble. But no guards were needed to patrol it. Its doors were wide open, and a single watchtower in the center of the wall was enough, with a pair of guards keeping watch.

The defense of the city was secure because of Pavresh's old

spell, cast out of desperation five years ago—the arcist anchor of the city held, pulling them back upward into the welcoming streets. Ever since he'd secured that magic into the rocks beneath the city, its effect had pervaded the area, a nearly irresistible summons to anyone willing to join the city of Chaitanshehar, drawing them up and close and folding them into the patterns of the city. The magic made it difficult even to descend here, but the first thing he'd trained in his students was how to resist that pull for a time, how to weave a personal effect to overcome the spell's power.

They had to tell themselves a different story. As they walked down through the steep rocks, they were emissaries on an important task. As they skirted a patch of dense shrubs, they were people filling a key role for the city itself. As long as they could craft the magic to reinforce that image, to tell themselves that story, then they could manage to make the descent.

At a switchback turn, Pavresh pulled off to the side and gestured for them to continue. The path ahead was an easy slope, angling across the hillside. Some pockets of snow lingered in the shelter of the scattered rock formations and on the shaded side of the few, rugged trees. Juishika, the aging beggar woman who'd come with him from Romnai and later been among his first students, took the lead. Her clothes were little better than she must have worn back there, and new lines added wrinkles to her dark skin, but she moved with a self-assurance that would never have fit the beggar she'd been. She'd learned the magic well and scarcely counted as his student anymore, yet she insisted that she still had more to learn.

As did he, for that matter. Didn't they all? He'd trained a few others these last years, arcists who could now monitor the spell from the city while he took these newer students down to learn one part of protecting the city. None of the others he'd trained had taken to the magic as well as Juishika. And even she would soon be surpassed by some of these new, younger students.

Pavresh studied the others as they passed, tested their use of the magic.

"Tighten up your spell, Haysha. You'll tire yourself out if you spread the effect out that far." Haysha was a young student who'd come as a child with her parents from the old city of untouchables. She gave him a tight nod and pulled in her magic with a frown. She'd make a good arcist someday if she could find some kind of peace with those hard years. For now, she always struggled with bending any spell around that story of fear and flight, hunger and weariness and uncertainty. "Well done," he added as she continued down the path.

Kamlak came behind her with a smile as if to make up for Haysha's frown. He was a middle-aged man who'd learned bits of arcist magic before he arrived a year or so earlier. His spells were effective but sloppy. "You too, Kamlak. Tighten it up." His smile never wavered—what must he have been before escaping to Chaitanshehar? Probably a walla, who had to deliver food and goods all day long without letting the smile drop from his mouth.

"Yes, tisrah." He moved his hands as he adjusted his magic, unnecessary but a quirk that many self-taught arcist practitioners had somehow picked up.

Kamlak would never be great, but the city needed people like him, too: people who could maintain the spell that Pavresh had created and do the easy parts of defending the city so Haysha and Juishika and others like them could help Pavresh with the more intricate effects.

The other students passed as well, and he corrected where he noticed any struggles. They knew that they were headed down to learn how to dismantle other magic, and some worried about conserving their energy for that task. Not a terrible idea, but they needed to use enough energy on their descent to resist the city's spell.

Arcist magic was a slippery thing. Ever since he'd begun to learn the magic, he'd been able to sense when the magic was being used. Noticing more details of what people were doing and how was far more difficult, even after so many years. He did his best, guiding them where he could and mostly teaching them each to understand what they were doing beyond what he could sense.

Alarmelai, a pale-faced mumbler who'd come into the city from one of the neighboring mountains, carried her four-year-old son on her back. He'd been one of the first children born in the city, born in a place with no castes, in a city that welcomed mumblers and the people of the cities equally. She'd often struggled with the spell that let the students descend easily.

Pavresh slipped into the mumbler pidgin because it was what she found easiest. "You're doing better this time. I can tell you aren't slowing down like other times."

"Thank you, sir. It feels more right this time."

Something was strange with her magic, though. "Wait." He cocked his head and studied her through the magic. "Your son…"

Alarmelai nodded. "He's picking up on it, too. I think that was the problem before. He didn't want to leave, and that pulled me back."

A child so young… Pavresh couldn't respond as he considered what it meant to have a child growing up with arcist magic, exposed to and learning it from such an early age. It would be like a native language for him. And he wasn't the only one. Alarmelai was the only student today accompanied by a child, but Pavresh had taught a few other young parents the basics, men and women who had no choice at times but to bring their child with them to their lessons.

Someday these youths would do things with arcist magic that Pavresh couldn't even begin to imagine.

At the end of the line came Sagak. He struggled with the spell. Or perhaps it was a struggle with the fire liquor he'd been drinking the night before and even into the early morning. The city pulled him upward so strongly Pavresh almost expected to see him drawn up by force.

"Come, Sagak. You need your defense if you're going to help us today."

Help was a key word, built into the city's magic itself. It called on all the people of Chaitanshehar to help the city, to do their part to build it up. Sagak opened his eyes, reddened but with an intentness that spoke to his desire to be a part of Pavresh's students. "It's just, the magic's too strong, tisrah." The words were slurred, and he held one hand over his eyes. "All of it. We should turn it down some."

"That's the sun, Sagak. And we can't turn it down. You just have to power through."

He sniffed and squared his shoulders, and Pavresh felt the magic building around him. He clapped Sagak on the shoulder and fell in behind him as they continued on to the valley below.

The next switchback brought them beside the river. A field of scree and rockfall still marked where one of the battles for Chaitanshehar had taken place. A monument stood where the trail met the riverbank, a modest one but meaningful. Pavresh placed a hand on the roughly carved stone and built a spell of thankfulness, a spell of honoring the heroes of the past.

Skilled as they were at arcist magic, Pavresh's spell still hit his students with its full force. Several bowed their heads, and one of the men—who'd been friends with one of the people who died in the rockfall—softly cried. Pavresh felt it, too, even though he was the one casting it into magic. The emotions were real, and the story they told powerful. The battle had been before his arrival, and he hadn't known most of those who died at all. Thamiba he'd known, as a key leader of the exodus from the Eghsal ruins and the founding of Chaitanshehar, but he wouldn't say he'd known the man well. Even so, the magic brought a brief tear to his eye.

No need to make his students linger. Pavresh tamped down the magic and shepherded them onto the stairs that led beside the river. The switchbacks continued their looping descent, but this would be quicker. The stairs would be simple to destroy if anyone attacked again, but the city's enemies had changed to other tactics now that the anchor spell protected the city. New tactics that demanded the attention of Pavresh and as many students as he could train.

He wished he could find dozens more to teach every year.

At the base of the slope, there were the fields of crops. Not enough yet to feed the city, but something at least. A start for what would be there in the future. Pavresh greeted the farmers stationed here. He and the other arcists had to escort them down the slope every half dozen days or so, whenever they needed to take their turns tending the fields. Even without the full arcist training, some of the farmers were beginning to learn how to tell their own stories to let them resist the city's anchor on their own. They gave no sign down here of feeling like they ought to rush back up to the city, though Pavresh could still sense the gentle nudge of the spell from this far away.

A circle of houses beside the field was already developing its own sense of permanence. Maybe someday it would be a neighborhood of Chaitanshehar in its own right. "How are the crops?" he asked out of courtesy, not because he wanted to hear any specifics.

"Growing." The farmer swept his arms to take in the fields and then pointed to the east where the volcanic fields warmed the region. "We're pushing back the contaminated soil on the swamp side, but it's slow work."

"Good." The sulfur smell was strong down here, and not far to the east the soil became full of the same volcanic chemicals that caused that smell. It was a poison that killed any useful plants, leaving a barren land out eastward, dotted only with hardy shrubs and a few trees that were food for nothing and no one. "I pray the Fire grants us more food. We will be heading along the northern shore for a bit. We should be coming back and going up late in the day if you need us to carry anything up."

The man nodded. "I'll let you know."

The pull of the spell lessened and finally released them as they made their way along the northern edge of the swamp. They left the fields behind and felt the cold of the valley to the north, winds that competed with the lava warmth of the volcanic fields across the swamp and eastward. They walked for an hour before Pavresh felt the pull of a different magic.

"Phew. Is that what we're looking for?" Alarmelai asked with a frown on her pale face. Her son started crying, and she pulled him around to cradle him.

Pavresh nodded. The magic made him curl his lip. He wanted nothing to do with it, wanted only to turn around in disgust and leave it be. Which was, of course, what the arcist who'd created it wanted.

Thankfully, its power was much less than the power of Pavresh's spell in Chaitanshehar. Drawing on the image of the task they'd been given, adding the idea of a distasteful but necessary job, he brought his students to an old stump, overgrown with lichen and the woody brush that tolerated that land.

"Here we are," he told them. "Before we uproot it, what can you sense?"

Sagak said, "It's like a dead animal. You just want to avoid it."

Several other students nodded. Alarmelai spoke in broken Eghsal language. "It stinks. Not for real." She plugged her nose briefly and shrugged. "It's like it smells so bad it skips my nose and goes right to my brain."

"Exactly. That's the effect of it. What can you sense about the magic, though?"

Haysha leaned in close as if to see the magic with regular eyes, her frown deepening. "It's blunt. Sloppy. They don't know how to do it carefully like you teach us."

"It's true. It makes it easier to undo, at least. And I don't know if they can't or if they just found that they can do this quickly, toss up a whole bunch in a small area, and then move on. They're fast, faster than we can take them apart."

"Who are they?" asked Kamlak. "These people who make these spells. Must be someone from the other cities?"

"Must be, but beyond that..." Pavresh shrugged. "We know the names of some of the people in power in the cities and what roles they held five years ago, but communication is pretty slight these days. What makes it through is likely half rumor."

The city had its spies, but even they could only learn so

much. "When I made the spell, it was all chaos. The princes who'd claimed to rule in the name of the High Prince sent out soldiers against us. Soldiers who had previously rebelled, many of them, coming out here to prove their penance."

He'd tried to drive them away through magic. A twinge of that old fear swept through him, the way the wall of fear had sickened him, the way they'd all fled until he could undo it and create the anchor in its place.

Powerful reminders of what arcist magic could do.

"I imagine they realized pretty quickly that they needed their own arcists to counter my spell. They knew my spell would soon draw more and more people away from their influence and up to Chaitanshehar to join us. They probably worried that it would make us too powerful. As if we'd have the resources to turn around and fight them."

The idea of Jaritta sending out an army was a preposterous one, when he thought of these years of scarcity. Years of barely enough food. Years without enough metal for both weapons and farming tools. How would they possibly field an army? And yet...maybe it wouldn't be possible any time soon, but someday when he and Jaritta and the others were long gone and some other ruler led the city, would it be possible that Chaitanshehar would turn to conquering its neighbors? He had to admit that he couldn't answer that question.

Out loud he continued. "So this is what we've been talking about in our lessons. Within a few months these beacons began showing up. Crude arcist magic designed to drive people away. They aren't based on fear. Perhaps they learned something from my failure trying to harness fear. Instead they rely on disgust. A wanderer through these lands, before they ever come close enough to feel the call of welcome from our city, will encounter many of these beacons that turn the wanderer's stomach, make them sickened by the thought of our people living together."

He looked at his students. Some would have been untouchable in Romnai or Pashun. Some might have been a low-caste nefli worker or maybe a mid-caste brenil merchant, as he'd once been—technically by birth at least, though he'd never owned a shop or done anything of the sort. Some of them, perhaps, would have even been from part of the highest caste and born to power. In Chaitanshehar no one needed to know, and most people never said. And of course, he included mumblers among his students. That idea alone would turn the stomachs of many who lived in the other cities, even without recourse to magic. No doubt that disapproval was an impulse that the priests and princes had encouraged for the past five years.

The beacons were merely a last step of defense to keep the people of Eghsal from accepting Chaitanshehar as a rightful city.

"Whoever is doing this is working hard to make sure the people of the other cities despise us. There's not much we can do to counter that. But what we can do is dismantle a few of these now and then, clear a little space so that anyone who manages to get this close won't be turned back."

He gestured at Juishika. "Juishika will undo this one. Observe the way the magic responds to her so you can do the same. There should be plenty in this area for each of you to try one before we head back."

Juishika had a soft way with the magic, a way of reaching out that seemed tentative at first. She didn't move her hands at all, didn't close her eyes, which was something even Pavresh struggled to control at times. With her mind she reached in, and what had seemed cautious suddenly became definite and certain. She slipped the magical connection right off the stump as if it were a weed to be uprooted. Instantly the feeling of disgust dissipated.

"Think of it this way," he told the students. "As she's reaching out and into the magic, she's telling the stump a different story. Telling the world around it a different story about the stump."

Several were nodding, and all were looking intently at the stump that Juishika had freed of its spell.

"We're fortunate that the enemy's arcists anchor these

beacons so poorly. Usually to stumps or trees, but also to rock formations and anything they can find. But no matter what their target, the connection is always loose enough for us to undo easily."

Enough talking. He gestured with his hand for them to head out. "Stay with at least one other person, and follow the stench to other beacons. Try to copy what Juishika did."

He and Juishika strolled behind them slowly, discussing each of the students and what each would need to do next to advance their magic. The rugged land had plenty of open areas where even the brush failed to grow. Cold winds scoured the thin soil bare but for some short grasses and lichen. Pavresh could see most of the students, even as they spread out.

"Not too far out, there, Sagak," he called, and Sagak and his partner veered to the side, looking for a beacon. "He still doesn't look good," Pavresh said to Juishika.

She shook her head. "He wants to help, and he could be good, too. But..." She left the rest unsaid.

Chaitanshehar wasn't an easy place to live, and many who came had their own difficult pasts to recover from. Conquering their inner naga, as Rashul had begun calling it. Fire liquor was one way to feel like you were conquering, even if it made other parts of your life more difficult.

A sense of calm settled over him. This was a barren place, but still a good one, a welcoming one. They were in the right place, both he and his students right now and the city of Chaitanshehar itself. Sure, there were challenges. Especially the lack of food that made every winter a struggle. For a moment the sense of calm cracked as he remembered the hunger and the fear, but then the calmness returned. They were taking the right steps to overcome the hunger, doing what they could to make this place the city that the visionary Rashul and the leader Jaritta had dreamed it could be.

It was a powerful sense of calm.

An aggressively powerful calm. Only after a moment, as he thought of how the worries about hunger had been stifled so quickly, did he recognize the feeling of arcist magic. An arcist magic that was not his own.

He stiffened, alert. Beside him, Juishika was stretching her arms above her head and looking around as if for a place to take a nap. "Juishika!" he shouted.

She startled out of her distraction.

Already the magic was trying to lull him back into placidity. He used his own magic to counter it. "We need to bring the students back now."

Someone was leaning against a rock out there, trying to get comfortable. Pavresh squinted. It was a younger student, one who hadn't advanced much yet. Pavresh shouted his name, but his voice didn't carry far enough.

"Come on, something's wrong!"

He ran a short way nearer the other students in front of him, using his magic as he went to create a sense of urgency, a desperate fight for survival. Then he called again for the students. Heading the other way, Juishika called as well. Her voice cut through the air better than his, the forceful cry of the beggar she'd once been, demanding attention.

Haysha was the first to respond. She had already finished destroying one beacon. She and her partner student came running.

"Stay by me," he told them. "And help us bring in the rest."

They added their voices as a cluster of other students came hurrying over. As a group they wandered back and forth across the sparse wasteland. Kamlak stood beside his partner Sagak, who was just finishing tying off their beacon. They appeared to both be doing the work, actually. How much had Sagak's condition impeded him? They would have to confront him about his fire liquor, but not until they were safely back in the city. Kamlak's hands moved with the spell, and Sagak had his eyes squeezed shut. When they were done, Sagak opened his eyes and saw them. They both ran to meet the group.

Pavresh counted quickly. Alarmelai with her son and two other students were coming from the side, slowed down by having to carry the child. Once they made it, that would be all of them.

The other arcist's spell seemed to be gone. That or Pavresh's spell of urgency overpowered it. Pavresh took a calming breath and tried to think. Why would anyone use their magic out here in this way?

Could it have been a part of the beacon spells of disgust, triggered automatically by Juishika dismantling the first one? He'd never heard of an effect like that, but that didn't mean it was impossible. So much about arcist magic wasn't yet known that he had no idea what precisely was impossible. But wasn't it more likely that there was an enemy arcist nearby? And if so, they surely wouldn't be alone.

"We need to head back. Quickly. Some of you haven't had a chance to destroy a beacon, but we'll have to try again later. Something's not safe here."

Most of the students stared around with wide eyes, and Sagak voiced what many probably thought. "It doesn't look dangerous."

"It is. No time for questions."

If it didn't look dangerous, he'd better make it feel so. Pavresh built on his earlier spell of urgency to keep them all together and get them going as fast as they could. A sense of purpose bolstered by arcist magic could do wonders for a group this size. Not based on fear, though. The magic bolstered them much better through other emotions.

They were almost in sight of the fields when figures appeared on the rise up ahead.

Pavresh stopped.

The figures had the look of soldiers.

Pavresh carried a long mumbler knife, as he'd done since his travels among the tribes. And he had his kusti, his whip-like belt that sometimes served as protection. Neither would do a thing against true soldiers.

His hand lingered on his belt. Kusti was both the type of belt and the ritual he enacted with it. In his religious practice he used the kusti for clarity, performing a series of deliberate, contemplative movements to still worries and prepare him for whatever he needed to do. Clarity was exactly what he needed.

But no enemy soldiers would wait for him to perform kusti. He would have to rely on his own clouded thinking.

The soldiers weren't mounted, but that told him little about who they were. The wolf jati often rode mountain ponies, but they also walked great distances through the mountains. The many, fractured soldier jatis of Pashun might go either mounted on horseback or not.

Pavresh and his students huddled close together as if their closeness would protect them. He knew well that nothing in this barren land would help. Unless it was the power of their magic.

He could do it. A spell to compel the soldiers to leave his group alone. A spell to drive them aside or even turn them into Pavresh's honor guard, escorting them back to the city. But something within arcist magic resisted being used that way. It twisted the magic, from something beautiful to something nauseating. It wore away at the story Pavresh told himself of who he was and what the magic was for.

Yet to save the lives of his students... He prepared a spell in his head, not so different from the enemy arcist's beacons of disgust, one he would have to anchor within himself to force the soldiers to flee.

Then one of the soldier figures stepped forward from the rest and came across the ground between them with quick strides. Quick and efficient strides yet taut with an energy that seemed as if it might break into a dancer's steps at any moment. Pavresh knew that graceful way of walking, and he released his white-knuckled grip on his knife hilt. Valni, the former falcon jati warrior, was in charge of the safety of the city of Chaitanshehar. She'd been told of his plans and where he would be taking the students.

"Hello," he called to her. "Is all well?" He did nothing to hide the relief in his voice at finding her.

Valni waited until she was closer to answer. "Pavresh, tisrah." Like many in the city, she had a difficult time letting go of the old words of deference for those who held positions of authority. "You must get out of here. Enemy soldiers have been sighted."

"Where? Who? We haven't seen soldiers this close to the city in years."

"Not sure who. Or why they'd show up now. But it's not safe for you. We came looking for you as soon as we realized they were nearby."

Not safe for anyone, probably. Knowing Valni, she'd probably be tempted to try to engage the enemy soldiers herself. "You have some eyes out in the area to monitor them?"

Valni looked beyond him as if to see where the other soldiers were. As if itching to go and hunt them down herself. Finally she nodded slowly.

"Good. Then guide us back so no one is able to sneak around and intercept us. I'm sure they'd like nothing better than to deprive the city of most of its trained arcists."

Valni frowned and then dipped her head to his order. "You'll be safe with us, as long as we move fast."

They hurried to the crest ahead where the rest of Valni's soldiers waited. The fields spread out before them. Pavresh tweaked his spell to encourage everyone, students and soldiers alike, to keep together, keep moving, stay alert.

As they went, Pavresh asked Valni, "What do we know about these soldiers? Where did they come from?"

"They were moving fast when we caught sight of them. Coming from the northwest, so likely from Pashun. But they couldn't have been marching that fast for long, so something got them going." After a few strides in silence, she added, "Got them going straight toward where you were. It's a good thing you started back when you did."

And if he hadn't noticed how the arcist's magic tempted them to remain? Pavresh had to swallow to bring moisture back into his mouth. They'd have been caught unawares and powerless. At first he'd thought they'd happened to stumble into the path of a troop of enemy soldiers by ill luck, but clearly luck wasn't the case. Pavresh and his students had been the goal of the soldiers, their target.

The arcist, hiding somewhere in those empty lands, must have signaled where they were and then tried to keep them lazy and oblivious. And still that arcist would be hiding back there, perhaps joined by the enemy soldiers now and planning how to lure Pavresh into a new trap.

"If they're growing bolder with the magic, you may need an arcist with you, so you don't succumb to any influences."

"You've taught us how to resist," Valni said with a shrug, and it was true that she seemed to know herself so well and her role in the service of the city that Pavresh's anchor spell had little direct effect on her. "How did they know you would be there?"

The question threw another wrinkle into the image. Their enemies had known they would be heading that way, roughly at least. Perhaps they'd known that Pavresh would be there and vulnerable. Or they'd simply hoped to cripple the city's magical defenses by killing whatever arcist users were present.

Pavresh bit his lip before answering. "I've dismantled the beacons in the past. I'm sure they're aware of that fact. And I've taken other students out to dismantle them as well. Maybe I've become too predictable." He let the idea play itself out in his mind. "That's the least sinister answer, anyway."

And the more sinister? That someone had informed their enemies. Someone on the wall, watching Pavresh and his students pass through, might have sent out a message somehow. Or a farmer, that would have been easier. Down in the fields, the pull of the city's anchoring spell was much less. A person stationed there would feel less dissonance doing something that went against the city above. Some agent of Pashun might even sneak in and convince the field workers that they should inform the agent whenever someone passed through, that doing so was in the interest of the city.

None of those possibilities gave the enemy soldiers much time to prepare.

What if... No, he wouldn't even think it. But even as he told himself it was impossible, he let himself consider the idea. Maybe it was one of his students themselves. They'd known the plan, both when and roughly where they would be going. He gazed around at these people, his students. Those he'd come to know and even trust as he trained them in magic, in...power.

More than power, it was true, but what might an unknown enemy do with the power of the magic that Pavresh could teach? If the leaders of Pashun could place a traitor among his students, what else might they do to throw the city into chaos?

Far behind them, a single line of smoke trailed off toward the clouds. An enemy camp? Something more innocent? Probably his own imagination, seeing the steam from the lava fields and interpreting it as something more sinister.

But a traitor was surely more sinister than any threat lingering out there at the edge of sight. A traitor might pull everything apart and leave Pavresh with only the broken promises of arcist magic, falling through his too weak fingers.

Pavresh shivered and drew away from his students to watch them as they made their way up the stairs toward the city above.

CHAPTER 2

Jaritta met the returning arcists at the city wall. At least they all appeared to be uninjured. The terse message she'd received, rushed up the hill by one of Valni's guards, had left that question hanging unanswered.

Pavresh came straight up to meet her while the others held back, his lips pursed and eyes tight. The expression aged him. She remembered the young man at Chaitan's house, his skin copper and his features so unremarkable that he blended in wherever he was. Whether it was his age—his traveling, his experiences—or simply the fact she'd known him for so many years, he no longer seemed like someone who could disappear into any kind of crowd.

"There were soldiers."

"I heard."

"We didn't actually see them." He turned around as if to peer back across the swamp to wherever those enemy soldiers had ended up. The blush of green cropland shifted to the yellowish swampland dotted with widely spaced trees. "So we can't say who they were. But they had an arcist working for them. A skilled one. They almost caught me in their spell."

That was worrying. She exchanged a look with Azheeran, one of her fellow leaders of the city. He shrugged. Even after the spell that protected the city, he never seemed completely convinced by either the importance or the power of Pavresh's magic, probably because it had no role in the mumbler society of his childhood.

She knew well that the magic was indispensable on both counts.

"You took a terrible risk. Why didn't you have Valni or some of her soldiers with you?"

Pavresh hung his head. "I should have. If I'd known… No enemies had been seen in that area in years, though. Now I know. We won't return. Or we'll take better precautions if we do."

He would, too. Pavresh wasn't the type to promise something and then not follow through. Except if he promised to help her overthrow the ruling princes in a misguided coup. But that was long past.

"We've always suspected they had some presence out that way. Disrupting our hunting, if nothing else. But you're right, they'd never come this close." Even that disruption, coming from both the north and south of the volcanic fields, dragged the city down. She massaged her forehead for a moment and then said, "See that you are exceedingly careful next time."

Pavresh took a breath as if to profess his commitment to being careful or some other unnecessary thing. She waved a hand at the unspoken words and turned to head back toward her official chambers, a short way up the street from the wall. "For now, I imagine you could use some rest after such a tumultuous afternoon. I will summon you if you're needed for anything more."

The arcists separated to their own homes, but Pavresh stayed with her. Jaritta let him tag along to the city's main hall. In five years they'd outgrown the chambers they'd used during the original fighting. Those rooms had felt sacred, though, so she'd insisted on expanding them instead of relocating. Renovated, the outer rooms now had arched ceilings of dressed stone, supported by intricate columns of delicately carved rock. Having miners so prominent among the early citizens of the city had some benefit.

An engraving at the entrance dedicated the building to the widow Driyya, who'd been one of their leaders in the early days and had died about three years ago. As she always did on entering the building, Jaritta touched the letters of Driyya's name. *May her wisdom come to me.*

Poorma, who'd once belonged to the untouchable death jati back in Romnai, was at the room's central chair at the moment. All decisions for the city were supposed to be made by consensus among the dozen or so leaders, but sometimes one person had to make a quick or final decision for the group. That was Poorma's role at the moment.

Rashul was there as well. He was their dreamer, the one who inspired them with a vision of the future. He had no formal role, but he spent much of his time helping them to plan for a future that was unknowable and unknown.

Jaritta nodded to greet them but spoke to Pavresh. "What else can you say about those soldiers? You think they're sending out arcists with all their units suddenly?"

"This was powerful magic." Pavresh's hand shook slightly as he picked up a red plum from a bowl beside Rashul. "The people in Pashun didn't have any arcists working for them five years ago, before we created the spell here. They've obviously found someone, maybe a few even, but there were never many of us." The sneaky leader of Pashun, Mahendri, had manipulated the princes into their current arrangement. But no matter how devious he was, he couldn't summon arcists out of thin air.

Jaritta said, "You've trained a few dozen since then. They might have as well."

"Might have." Pavresh nodded. "But none of the people I've trained would be capable of a spell like that. Even back in Chaitan's place, most of the arcists who performed for the dancers probably couldn't have done that. Unless they've improved their control since then, of course. But that still means Mahendri doesn't have hundreds to throw one into every little soldier jati and unit."

"That's good, at least." The thought of an army of arcists had terrified her.

Rashul stretched and stood up. "Sounds like all the more reason to use the magic now to protect ourselves. We need to stop Mahendri before he finds some new way to use the magic."

Jaritta sighed. Rashul had been pushing hard recently for some sort of decisive action. It felt like more of a need to do something dramatic than any bigger strategy or plan. "Last month it was allying with the mumblers to invade Pashun. Now you want to magic our way in there? Even *I* know that arcist magic can't do that."

Rashul held up his hands in protest. "Nothing like that. But a targeted force of mumbler allies, aided by a wave of fear or something. We could conquer Pashun in a day. No more worries about them attacking us, plus we add all the food they grow over there. Even if most of the survivors come join us here, we still have enough to eat—"

"*Most* of the survivors." Pavresh waved his hand, still dripping with plum juice, in Rashul's face. "And we can always calculate how many we kill to make sure there's enough food, right? How callous you've grown, Rashul."

"No, that's not what I meant at all. You know me better than that."

Jaritta stepped between them. "We're not conquering anyone. Just drop that idea." A child's voice from the adjacent room carried over their noise, and Jaritta fluttered her hands to get Pavresh and Rashul to move away from her and each other. "We'll figure out about those enemy arcists later."

As she made her way through the doorway into the other room, Rashul called behind her, "Ask Chandri about the mumbler soldiers. We have stronger allies than you might think."

Then why was there so little food in the city?

In the next room, which had been converted from the original official city center into living space, Ellechandran held one child in his arms. A second sat on the floor at his feet, looking like she'd trip him if he tried to take a step in any direction. The unbaked bricks of the upper half of the room filled with a soft light from the lamps below.

Ellechandran's first wife, Chhayasheela, had divorced him amicably shortly after the city's founding. She now spent much of her time in the mountains to the south, traveling from village to village among the mumblers there. She was their primary ambassador among the mumblers.

Meanwhile Ellechandran—or Chandri, as many of the locals

called him—had stayed, becoming a main voice for those same mumbler villages within the city, helping those who joined them get settled, making sure the decisions of the other leaders did as little harm as possible to the mumblers.

But not only had he stayed, he'd fallen in love with the city's founder, scarred face and all. That fact had annoyed her at first, but only briefly. His steady presence had helped her navigate the city's growth and struggles. As she grew more familiar with his pale, mumbler features and brittle hair, dark with hints of red especially in his full beard, she'd grown to rely on him more and more as well. And now they had two young children. Two among the first generation to grow up in the caste-less city of Chaitanshehar. Heirs to Jaritta's history as both a high caste kortru and as an untouchable, and also heirs to Chandri's mumbler heritage, from the villages in the southern mountains.

Jaritta scooped baby Ovitiva from Chandri's arms and cooed at her. "She hungry?"

He nodded, so she made herself comfortable on the couch to nurse the baby.

"Tell me about the allies Rashul says we have."

Chandri sat on the floor to play with little Nataravi. He held a leaf doll out to her but focused on Jaritta. "Sheela claims we'd have plenty of support. He's right about that."

The hint of bitterness in his voice when he mentioned his first wife had almost disappeared over the years, but not fully yet. Or maybe she was merely reading that into his accent. He'd learned the language of the people of Eghsal well these past years, but he would always speak with the thick accent of his own people.

"And? What do you think of that?"

He shook his head. "Some would come. But she's too quick to trust them when they say how many fighters they would bring. And how reliable they would be. Certainly they'd rather side with us than with Pashun. The nearer the villages are to Pashun, the more reason they would have to fight against it."

But fighting wasn't what Jaritta wanted. Ruling by

conquering other lands was not what she had had in mind when she dreamed this city into existence. For a city named for the late, great Chaitan, who had walked away from his soldier jati to develop arcist magic—the very idea went against the memory of who he'd been and what he'd done.

The one thing Rashul had right was that they desperately needed food—more and better. The rugged land yielded so little. The fear of Pashun's soldiers kept their hunters close city and any potential trade routes among the mumblers equally limited. If they could trade with Pashun instead of conquering it... A vain wish, as long as the puppet master Mahendri still had his influence among the city's princes and priests.

Or as long as the city's princes and priests maintained their position above the other castes. As long as the caste system existed at all. It always came back to that, unless they could conquer Pashun and abolish the system itself entirely. Which she wasn't about to suggest. Change and progress by sword point had a way of turning back on those who imposed it. She knew enough history to recognize that.

Nataravi climbed up her knee, distracting her from the weary despair that lingered like a knot behind every thought and plan. Jaritta used her free hand to boost her daughter up to an open space on her lap. Did she look more like a mumbler or a city dweller? And if a city dweller, then what caste? Her skin color was somewhere between, and the shape of her features didn't conform obviously to one or the other or any caste or jati. Jaritta couldn't pin any identity on her. Nataravi was Nataravi—her daughter and not simply one of a type.

"What do you think, Nataravi? How will we save the city?"

Nataravi was too young to understand, too young to answer in anything beyond simple words. Even the words she knew she didn't use, but she looked over at her father and around at the room. To Jaritta it seemed her gaze took in not only the room but the entirety of the city of Chaitenshehar. Her eyes came to rest on her mother and fixed intently on her face.

As if to say that Jaritta would save it, that it was up to her in the end. She would have the help of Ellechandran and the other key figures in the city. She would have the support of the city as a whole, bolstered by Pavresh's magic spells and those of the students he was training. But it would end up falling to her to keep them all from failing.

Such a thought was surely beyond her daughter, but as soon as she pretended to put her daughter's expressions into words, she knew the words she'd chosen must be true. In the end it would be up to her to shape the city for its destiny.

Which was exactly the way she wanted it.

And exactly what terrified her.

**

Alone of the key leaders of Chaitanshehar, Datri kept herself apart. When she spoke with Jaritta or the others, she claimed that she was waiting for her husband to join her. Then she and the one-time-prince Jasfer would make a public entrance to the city's official chambers.

Jaritta doubted how sincere that claim was. Not that she doubted Datri's sorrow over not knowing what exactly had happened to Jasfer. She felt a shadow of it herself, missing the brother she hadn't seen in over a decade. But no one believed he had survived his captivity, and nothing Datri or Jaritta had done to learn the truth had uncovered any evidence that he still lived.

The real reason Datri kept to herself, Jaritta suspected, was that it gave her freedom to cultivate her network of spies and keep them loyal directly to her.

Regardless, Datri's solitude meant Jaritta had to travel to the upper reaches of the city to speak with her.

There were hungry people in the streets, their sad eyes reminding Jaritta of her past as a beggar girl in Romnai. Was she stuck allowing that same kind of hunger in this city? Hadn't she set out to create a city where that wasn't necessary? Their gazes followed her, haunted her passage through the city streets.

The houses crowded together, so different from the way

many of them had lived in the ruins of Eghsal City, spread out and each to themselves. She tried to replicate that at first, giving each person or family free choice of where and how to build. As others came they'd filled in the gaps, adding houses haphazardly with little thought for the routes through the city or any bigger picture of what the city as a whole needed.

Jaritta had to switch streets frequently because of that lack of planning, cutting backwards even to get to the next street that led in the right direction.

Datri lived in a simple house at the upslope edge of the city. There was no city wall up here. Before Pavresh's spell, the danger had all come from below and to the sides, not from above. After the spell, an upper wall certainly served no purpose. Beyond her house were only the scattered rock formations and evergreen shrubs of the mountains, with a few paths diverging among them. The city's hunters took those paths often to bring back what game they could find. When there was a chance to trade goods with the nearest mumbler villages, then the traders took those paths as well, or the mumblers themselves came to visit.

Last Jaritta knew, Datri was learning the mumbler pidgin so that she could hear rumors from the traders who came to visit, in addition to her many sources from all over the valley.

Datri must have seen her approaching, or had known to expect her. She stood in the doorway to welcome Jaritta inside. She wore a plain dress, white for mourning her missing husband. The tisane was already steeping in two gourds on a low table.

"Please, sit, sister." Datri gestured at the cushions beside the table.

Jaritta murmured, "Thank you," as she took a seat.

They were not close. If she called her *sister*, it was usually pronounced with a hint of irony, a recognition that their connection was through a man who was missing and likely dead. Datri was a decade younger than she was, but she'd aged in these past five years. Lines around her eyes added depth to her dark skin, while those eyes seemed to go deeper still, alert and intelligent but not prone to laughter. Grief and mourning and losing everything she'd known, losing the power she'd once craved above all else, they'd taken their toll, so she looked like the haggard older sister instead.

Or perhaps not *older*. If Jaritta bothered to look at herself in a mirror, she would no doubt see the effects of her own years on the streets, her years living in the ruins, the stress of founding and ruling a city, and bearing two children at a relatively late age. Not to mention the scar on her face, which had faded from its early angry look into something she rarely thought of. But it certainly didn't make her seem any younger. The splotch of red-tinted scar tissue contrasted with the smooth brown of the cheek on the other side. Likely she looked older than her years as well, in proportion with Datri's aging.

As if they were twin sisters after all.

"Have you heard any news of Jasfer?" It wasn't what she'd come to hear, but to ask anything else first would anger Datri and she might not answer the other questions.

"A locked tower in Jarnur. There's someone inside, and no one knows who."

"You think it's him?"

Datri shook her head. "Probably not. But I must learn what I can, so I'm sending someone to check. Romnai is in chaos."

"That isn't new." Jaritta sipped from the metal straw in her gourd. The tisane was hot and perfectly sweetened.

"No. It's the same as always. The new Thirty aren't accepted. Some of the old Thirty are openly opposing them. Some of the old Thirty have disappeared, just like Jasfer. The falcon jati performs penance for not stopping the High Prince's assassination by solemnly marching through the streets in rags, faces marked by ashes. And if anyone gets in their way, they strike out with all the brutal efficiency of their training. The priests declare the ashes on their faces to be sacrilegious." Datri finally took a longer breath and then drank from her tisane.

"What about Pashun? Rashul thinks we should send a force of soldiers to conquer it."

"Rashul is a fool."

Jaritta set her gourd down and leaned over the table to try to read Datri's thoughts in her face. "That may well be, but they're learning arcist magic, and at least one of them is strong enough to fool Pavresh. Rashul is concerned that the longer we wait, the more dangerous they become."

Was Datri genuinely worried for the future of the city? Or was her habitual show of cynicism and world weariness what really lay under her skin?

"I hope he is concerned. I hope we all are."

Try as she might, Jaritta could read nothing in Datri's eyes when she spoke.

"But the truth is we don't have the soldiers for it. Nor any other advantage significant enough." Datri shrugged without sloshing the tisane in her gourd. "I wish we did. Pashun may be the biggest threat to our city lasting long enough to stand on its own. Those princes can't afford to keep such a focused eye on us for much longer. They want us gone as much as we want to survive."

"They have so many little soldier jatis. You don't think we could pit one against another, get them fighting in their own streets again so they don't have time to come our way?"

"What do you think I've been trying to do these past five years?" A flash of passion passed through Datri's eyes as she said this. Pashun might not be where her husband had disappeared, but it was the leaders of the city who'd betrayed him and sent him off to a prison cell in Romnai. "And I'll keep trying, but so far their leaders have been able to keep the fights from spreading into anything serious."

Their leaders. The Prince Hrisha, who had been the mayor of the city and Jasfer's host before the coup. The disgraced Dartak, the former prince who had tried to manipulate Jaritta herself. His princely title had been stripped by the same people who convicted Jaritta to death, but Datri's intelligence indicated that he'd found a way back into the circles of power in Pashun. And behind it all, the shadowy figure of Mahendri, manipulating the factions among the leaders and among the people as well to achieve...something. Not fame—he already had more recognition than Jaritta suspected he wanted. But power, certainly. Power and an idea for how Eghsal Valley ought to be, how the castes should control everything, each in its proper place within the hierarchy of the valley.

Jaritta's city was anathema to such a view of things.

She tipped her head and sighed. What were they missing? There must be some way they could protect themselves from those reactionaries in Pashun. Some way they could convince the enemy soldiers to stay away. "We should just have Pavresh put a welcoming spell in Pashun too, make it so they have a hard time leaving."

It was a throwaway comment, not meant to be serious, but as soon as it escaped her lips she sat forward. The very idea of trying something on that scale terrified her. It seemed much more likely to destroy what work she'd achieved than to save it. And yet...

Datri put down her gourd and was looking at her hard. "Do you think it would work?"

"Well, we'd have to ask Pavresh, but..." She sat back and waved her hands at the idea. "No, we can't risk losing him. We need him to train the others, to keep our welcoming spell working. It's too big a risk."

She hadn't realized until that moment how much she relied on Pavresh being there, on his magic protecting the city. If he left on some fool's errand, the city would surely collapse right back to where it was five years earlier, a wounded and dying city oppressed on all sides, only waiting for the final strike to fell it.

"I think it's a decision that's too big for either of us to make alone." Datri turned away and began clearing the tisane from the table. "Sometimes, when the situation is bad enough, a terrible risk is the only one left to take."

Dismissed as if she were a servant in Datri's employ, Jaritta took her leave.

***

Was Datri right, that a terrible risk may be their only chance? Jaritta couldn't make that choice alone. Back in the official chambers, she summoned the other leaders of the city, those who were able to be there. Ellechandran and the girls were there, as was Rashul, though none of them had official voices in the decisions for the city. Pavresh and Poorma were there. Azheeran had gone down to visit the farms but should be back up soon. The other not-quite-official leaders who had earned their places on the not-quite-official council were there as well, representatives of the miners, the hunters, and the farmers. Juishika, who had been a beggar and was now Pavresh's student, was there to speak for the many beggars of Romnai who had come to Chaitanshehar.

In all they were ten people who would have the say in what to do. Their full count would be a dozen including Azheeran, once he made his way up the slope, and Datri. She had ignored the note Jaritta had sent asking for her presence, much as Jaritta had expected.

There were many decisions Jaritta had made for Chaitanshehar since its founding and before. The weight of this decision seemed to drag against her shoulders more than most. She took a deep breath and pictured the room at Chaitan's house—the dancers, the arcists, the musicians. It had been a beautiful combination of arts, performances that lifted the room and everyone in it away from mundane worries, to something higher that the priests could only pretend to believe in. The memory helped her forge ahead.

The air smelled like smoke. "Chandri, can you check the fireplace. Smells like something might be blocked."

While he looked into that, Jaritta explained the idea she'd had when she was speaking with Datri.

"I'm not saying this is what we should do," she said into the silence after she'd finished. "I hate the idea and hope we decide not to send Pavresh on such a quest. But I felt a responsibility to share what Datri and I discussed." She swallowed hard and realized she'd been avoiding looking at anyone directly. Catching Pavresh's eyes, she asked, "Is it…possible?"

Let it be *no*, so they could move on to other solutions.

Pavresh pursed his lips. After a moment's thought, he said, "The problem is that no one knows what's possible. Until I try it, I can't say. When I crafted this spell here, it came from desperation, remember. I don't know that I can create such an effect again."

That made sense. And hopefully made it easier to rule against the idea entirely. Jaritta nodded as if it were already decided. "Certainly not worth the risk for something so unknown, then."

"It would solve some of our biggest problems, though. I wonder…" Pavresh stared off toward the shadows of the arched roof.

Jaritta bit her lip. The more she thought on the scheme, the more convinced she became that it wouldn't work as expected, that it would open Chaitanshehar up to far more risk than it could handle.

What if he succeeded and siphoned all their people off to Pashun? What if he failed, and that failure weakened the magic itself throughout the land, exposed frailties in the spell that allowed the city to exist at all? Mahendri would be quick to take advantage of their weakness. They still knew little about the man, but over the past five years, she'd built up an image of him as a calculating genius every bit as devious as Datri but with the vast resources of the ruling princes at his fingertips.

But she also knew that she couldn't decide for Pavresh. That was not how things worked in Chaitanshehar.

While he was off in his own thoughts, Poorma spoke. "I hate to say it, but it isn't a terrible idea to explore. Even if it doesn't open Pashun up to us for direct trading, we'd be freer to hunt the land between us, north of the lava beds. We know there's game in there. And we would have more freedom trading with the mumblers if we don't have to fear running afoul of Pashun soldiers out that way."

Jaritta did her best to keep her voice even, though she wanted to shout that she was taking back her own idea. How could they seriously consider something that was much more likely to lead to disaster than success? "If we could be certain it would work and that we could get everyone back out of the city again."

"Maybe one of his students could go," Juishika said. "I don't want to say that they're expendable, because they aren't. Except compared to him, we are, in a way."

Pavresh shook his head. "None of you would have any chance of making it work at all."

"Or a smaller version, some test run in the mountains somewhere, to see if it would even be possible?"

"Maybe." Pavresh contemplated the space between him and Juishika, as if imagining what spell he might weave together. "If we have time to set it up, and you help me. Maybe several of the students, too. It's more tiring than anyone probably realizes."

The smoke smell from the hearth was growing stronger. Jaritta caught Chandri's eye. "What's wrong with the fireplace?"

Before he could answer, Azheeran slammed open the door and ran inside.

"They've lit the fields on fire!"

Everyone jumped to their feet. "What?" someone shouted.

"The Pashun soldiers. They've lit our fields on fire. Everything's burning."

Jaritta pushed past him through the doorway. The smoke in the street was thick, rising up through the city. "The food? We could put it out…"

"Gone," he said from behind her. "Burnt up, or will be soon. Not all the fields, but most of them. I doubt there'll be anything left."

Jaritta crumpled against the wall of the building.

But she couldn't give in to despair. Forcing her voice to

come out with authority, she said, "Gather everyone who can protect themselves, and let's get down there. Stop the fires, harvest anything still edible while we can. And watch for the soldiers, if they come back to fight." Valni would have to take charge of protecting them. Herding them back up the hill, if the danger grew too great.

From inside the room Poorma added, "Everyone except for Pavresh. As the current final voice, I am declaring that there is no time for him to experiment up in the mountains. He needs to plan how he will craft the spell, decide who will accompany him, and do whatever he needs to so he can carry out Jaritta's idea immediately. The city of Chaitanshehar has spoken."

A sense of dread closed in on Jaritta, and she couldn't say if it was the destruction of the crops or the risk they took sending Pavresh to Pashun. But what she knew was that she wished she and Datri had come up with a better idea to save the city.

Nataravi toddled over to balance herself against Jaritta's leg as a cloud of thicker smoke blasted up through the city, twining about them as if in mockery.

CHAPTER 3

The midmorning waves crashed over the breakwater in Jarnur with a sound like nothing Harkala had known in her years of research and field work. Louder than a steam engine. Louder than a winter storm coming over the sea. Louder than the laughter of a thousand colleagues who didn't, who *wouldn't* believe the discoveries she'd made.

She'd lived in Jarnur all her life, except when she was inland conducting her research. She'd known waves as she and her assistants built their replica boat and tested it in the calmer waters of the harbor. This sound had a different timbre, an intensity that vibrated through her.

It was nerves. She didn't need anyone else to explain that fact to her. Still, she bit her lip as another wave sent spray over the waiting ship.

"You don't think the sea's too high, Ekana?"

Ekana shook his head. "High seas are what we want. It shows the princes what our ship is capable of." Calm words, but they were belied by his own tense expression and the way his hands clenched and unclenched on the bite of rope he was holding. He was a scrawny man, but the dark-skinned hands that gripped that rope were strong.

High seas, yes, but were these too wild?

Harkala forced herself to take a deep breath of the sea air and released it slowly as the wind died momentarily. Ekana was right, they needed this kind of weather to prove their ship's worthiness to the princes. He was a good assistant and had done a master's work in getting the ship itself sea-worthy.

"All looks good inside." Sembaari waved from the gunwale where he would be stationed. It was an odd-looking ship. Sometimes she caught sight of it from the corner of her eye and thought it majestic. Other times, looking straight at it, it seemed only awkward. A stump-like protrusion near the stern had the look of a broken off mast. The sides looked too narrow for wild waves, though she knew the numbers, knew it was wider than it looked. The dimensions were off. To anyone from Jarnur it looked like a ship built by a child or an inlander, someone who didn't know fishing vessels.

Which wasn't so far off. It *wasn't* a fishing vessel, after all. It was something so much more, the result of Harkala's discovery and excavation of the remains of the ancient ships their ancestors had sailed.

Sembaari and Ekana had arrived together and taken over much of the work bringing Harkala's research to life, taking her findings and sketches and making a ship that would actually sail.

She hoped. It wouldn't sink, anyway. They'd tested it enough in the harbor to be sure of that.

When the two had first arrived, they'd been full of stories and lies about their past, of finding routes here and there to the Forgotten South and back. But the stories changed too much for Harkala to believe them, and their assistance was much worse for their attempts to continue their lies. When she'd confronted Ekana, he'd admitted they were false. Sembaari was a dark-skinned mumbler, someone who could pass as a person from the cities of Eghsal. A fascinating fact itself, but Harkala hadn't spent any of her research time on learning much about his people's history.

And Ekana was simply a local fisherman. Or maybe not *simply*. He had a history that he didn't speak of, beyond the barest outlines. Travel to Romnai, to the mountains where he'd met Sembaari, to Pashun. Those experiences haunted him. Sometimes he would fall silent in the middle of a sentence. Sometimes his body froze halfway through some action, and his eyes would gaze around him in some sort of extreme horror or remorse. But then he'd come back from it, and once he set his mind to a task, he wouldn't let go.

When he'd come back to his birth city, he'd found her and joined in on this strange and ambitious project, drawn much as she was by the idea of doing something big, of making a mark on history. He'd proven himself to be someone who would push through no matter the obstacles, with exactly the kind of single-mindedness that she needed to make her grand plans into reality.

Ever since they'd admitted the truth, they'd worked hard to earn back her trust. And now it came to this. A ship, years in the making and built on her research notes—though this final version incorporated many changes that Ekana had worked out. A ship that could sail beyond the treacherous waters that surrounded the river mouth, with its crashing waves and lines of hidden rocks.

A ship that could sail to the Forgotten South. The real Forgotten South, not some imaginary land of lies and childhood stories, of walking gods and hidden naga.

Harkala clapped her hands once to thaw them from their frozen stances. "In that case, let's go meet with the princes."

A gathering of some dozen princes sat under the shelter of a canopy at the edge of the pier. Not all thirty of the city's ruling princes, but she hoped it would be enough. The wind blew the sea spray under the canopy, and the thin, southern sun added little warmth. No doubt they would want this over with so they could find better shelter elsewhere, in time for a warming midday meal.

Harkala greeted them. "Princes. Thank you for your presence here today. You are gathered for the glory of the city, for the future, and for your own legacies. Today you will see a sight that few could dream of. A ship unlike any you've ever known."

She paused to look around at them and at the water beside them. To them she probably wasn't an impressive sight. An aging academic wrapped in plain gray, boiled wool to keep out the sea spray. But she knew that carrying herself with confidence could win them over. "I know. We are the city of Jarnur. You've known ships all your life. And great ships they are, fishing boats that can dare the nearby waves, steamships that can travel up and down the Eghsal River. For trade. For military might. You've known boats that achieved wonders, that helped create the city of Jarnur that we know today."

A horn sounded somewhere, cutting through the fog as if it needed to be recognized as well.

Harkala pushed her hair back from her face and continued. "Long ago, over five hundred years ago according to our historians, some ships landed here at the mouth of the river. I do not know how many ships there were. I do not know how many people came or what they first saw in this new land. It was an empty land, but not entirely empty. The mumblers had their villages and hunting trails. Perhaps our ancestors saw them in the distance. Perhaps fighting broke out, or maybe they met in peace and something like friendship. No one can say how that played out.

"But what we can say is that those ancestors found a way through the punishing waves. No boat, before or since, has managed to cross the waters beyond the mouth of the river. A few sea leagues out, but no farther. But those ancient people managed it. They crossed between the sea teeth, past strange currents, in between terrible waves, and until today no one has known how they did it. But we have recreated the ships—"

"Yes, we understand," a prince cut her off. "This spray is cold, and the wind isn't warm either. Can we see you launch the ship and then get inside?"

Harkala bit her tongue to keep from shouting at the prince for interrupting. When she had taken a breath, she said, "Yes, of course, tisrah."

She turned and waved an arm; Ekana and some other assistants began guiding the ship down the ramp into the water. Sembaari wouldn't be able to sail it entirely himself. It was a small enough ship as far as that went, considerably bigger than the river boats the fishermen used but not much bigger than most of the fishing boats that went out to sea. It would need an actual crew to do any real sailing. For today, he only needed to be inside as its hull touched the water so that they could declare it officially launched.

"Tisrae, princes of Jarnur." She pitched her voice to carry over even the loudest gusts of wind. "Let the princes of Romnai envy you. Let the princes of Pashun look on Jarnur with jealousy. Let all people see you, rightful rulers of this river city, and praise your wisdom and power."

The ship touched the water, displacing a wave that crested the breakwater.

"I present to you, *The Dream of the Forgotten South*, the first far voyager in the fleet of the city of Jarnur."

The princes applauded as the ship bobbed in the water. Harkala held her breath. It would stay upright, wouldn't it? They'd tested its seaworthiness, but still...

Suddenly it rolled. Harkala gasped, but a moment later it rolled back, following the natural rhythms of the water. The sea made its normal movements look violent from the pier. Ekana's calm demeanor as he directed the people holding different ropes helped to keep Harkala calm.

"I do not wish to hold you longer than necessary in this weather, tisrae. When you are prepared, please summon me to meet with you to discuss outfitting the ship and the sea journeys on which you would send it."

The princes thanked her as their cheetah jati servants gathered their possessions and escorted them, under handheld oiled canopies, away from the pier.

No one said anything more to her, no indications of how impressed they were and if they would fund her dreams of sending the ship to the Forgotten South.

"I think it went well," she told Ekana when she made it out onto the breakwater. *The Dream of the Forgotten South* still bobbed on its moorings. "Thank you, you did your part perfectly." And had she done her part well? Only time would tell. "I suppose we can't leave the ship floating here? That wouldn't be safe." A change in the waves or wind, and their precious ship would be dashed against the rocks that made up the outer edge of the breakwater.

"Climb aboard, tisrah," Ekana said, his hand an open invitation. "We'll sail around to dock. You should be on deck."

Harkala shook her head to decline. "No, I…" Then she pictured what the princes would see, if any were still watching. She pictured the view from the quays as she stood proudly on the deck of a strange and wondrous ship. Even if the princes themselves didn't see, others would. The sight of a strange and awkward ship sailing gloriously into its berth would be the story on the lips of much of the city.

"Yes, I think I will come onboard."

Ekana helped her across from the pier. Then with poles and ropes, he and all but one of the assistants guided the ship far enough away from the rocks so they could sail around to the open gap through the breakwater. One remained behind to gather up their extra gear. If she hadn't climbed aboard, Harkala would have been left standing awkwardly behind.

Good thing she'd embarked. She positioned herself in the middle of the deck near the bow. A prominent place but out of the way of anything Ekana needed to do to guide them to their berth. She breathed through her fears as the ship settled into the waves, rough and unpredictable but a familiar motion. She braced her legs in a way that every child of Jarnur grew up knowing.

Someday someone would make a statue of her in that position. The seafaring scholar. The historian hero who opened the way to the Forgotten South. Too bad the sun, now past its zenith and heading southwest into the mountains, didn't shine brighter to highlight her position. She stood straight as if she were already that celebrated statue as the ship sailed around into the calmer water of the harbor.

Right at the boundary between open ocean and harbor, a huge wave crashed into the stern of the ship. Spray soaked Harkala through, and the jolt sent her scrambling forward onto her knees. So much for a striking figure fit for a statue. She was more a bedraggled wretch, something the crew had fished out of the sea to carry home and nurse to health.

No matter. Let the sculptors recreate it as fit their style. She pushed her sopping hair out of face with both hands and stood again, perhaps not quite as arrogantly but still in a position of authority. The ship sailed smoothly into its berth among the other—the lesser—fishing vessels that were waiting out the heavy seas.

***

The Jarnur Thirty, the ruling princes of the city, were such a new institution that they had no grand assembly building like the princes in Romnai had. They met instead in a former fish market scarcely a block away from the river and all its bustle. Admittedly, the five years of use by the princes had cleared most of the stench of old fish away—inevitably some smells still wafted in from the docks and other fish markets nearby. And the stalls were cleared away, the interior made over into something more comfortable.

To Harkala, it still looked like the market it had been.

Where the chief prince presided over the room, Harkala remembered buying fresh cod. Where she waited for her turn to be called forward, she'd once bought a bucket of small lobsters that were caught in the winter months. They'd made her sick, and she'd avoided any kind of crab or lobster ever since.

A fire burned at the front of the room, a contained flame that did little to heat the space. Furnaces at the corners blew warm air in, a very welcome part of the renovations on this stormy day. And lanterns along the walls lit the space, since already the sun had ended its short path through the sky and set beyond the peaks of the mountains.

The flame at the front took prime place for its symbolism. To those who worshiped the pantheon of gods, it represented the sacred fire that even the gods served, the guiding principles for how they ruled the cosmos. To those of the splinter religion of Enshi, there were no gods serving the fire, only the fire itself, sacred source and foundation of the entire cosmos.

The fire represented and honored both religions. A safe symbol to use.

For Harkala, who left questions of religion to the priests and those who felt the need to believe, the fire she followed was neither about gods nor mystic origins but simply the truth. Or the Truth rather, the final authority and the only one she chose to bow to fully. She would seek answers and serve only the ideal of what was truthful and proven.

When she was called forward, she bowed to the flame, as expected, and faced the gathering of princes. They reclined on pillows around the room, sipping tisane and eating prawns and smoked apricots.

An easy room to tune out an unknown person speaking. She had best be brief.

"Thank you for hearing my plea, tisrae." Her voice was swallowed by the room where fishmongers cries had once echoed.

She spoke louder. "Princes of Jarnur, history is written, done, already fixed in stone. You won't hear other scholars say so, but we have no power before history. I don't mean there's nothing more to learn about it, only that what is past is dead—preserved, like the smoked apricots you are eating, but no longer living.

"And someday your rule will be past as well, but the future is waiting for you to create. You will be remembered, when this time becomes *history* for your great-grandchildren. But will you be remembered as lesser princes, subservient to the princes of Romnai and the princes of Pashun? A side note to the great or terrible things they achieve?

"Now is your chance to say, 'No!' Now is your chance to create a future where you are remembered with glory."

Harkala paused to gather herself for her request. The princes were watching her closely. Many sat forward to listen. One prince had even paused with a bite of food in the air before his lips. No one spoke to each other on the side or appeared ready to doze off to sleep.

"You have seen the ship launched, *The Dream of the Forgotten South*. Or if you missed it, you've heard of it by now, and I invite you to come see it in its berth while we are still here in Jarnur. You have already been a part of the funding for that ship, and I thank you again for your patronage.

"A ship is fun. Majestic, beautiful, glorious. But on its own it is like the past—done. A ship like our ancestors sailed, lovely. But now we need to do more. We need to sail where our ancestors sailed. To take this object and use it to forge the future of the city of Jarnur. Then history books may mention Romnai in passing, may refer to the recent rebellion and unrest in Pashun. But the focus, the great story of this age, will be the trade routes that you establish now. The discoveries that you fund."

She had them. She could see it in their bodies, in their eyes looking straight at her.

"The funding that remains is all for supplies. We don't know how long the voyage might be, so we'll want plenty of food that won't spoil. We also need goods to trade." They couldn't even know what goods would be valuable in the place they would find. Would furs be important? Precious metals? Timber? It was impossible to know. So she didn't expect the trade to be highly profitable right away, but she wanted enough to show the people they would meet what kinds of goods they could expect in return. "A variety of goods to show off this great valley and the riches of the city of Jarnur."

Harkala sketched a scholar's bow for the princes and finished with, "Thank you again, great and wise rulers of Jarnur. I look forward to working with you to create the future this city deserves."

One older prince applauded, and several spoke over each other to ask her questions. The design of the ship, the nature of goods she wanted to carry. She answered each in turn, and the questions that followed, until they tapered off into an electric silence. Not weary or bored, but ready to discuss the matter in her absence.

With one last bow toward the room's sacred fire, Harkala walked out, acknowledging the princes she passed with a simple nod.

Outside in the street, she leaned against the wall, her outward resolve collapsing into its opposite. Oh, may she never have to endure such a thing again! Scholars shouldn't have to beg for their money that way.

After a moment's respite, she pushed herself off the wall, adjusted her clothing, and headed through the evening streets toward the ship. The winds had calmed enough that the air smelled of the sea but wasn't full of spray.

Her assistants had already begun their own small party on board. Harkala climbed up the plank to join them.

"Well, what do you think they'll say?" Ekana offered her a steaming gourd of tisane.

She reached past him for a small jug of fire liquor.

"I don't even want to guess. Let's just celebrate the successful launch for now. Tomorrow I hope we'll know, one way or the other."

She took a big drink from the liquor. It burned her throat as she swallowed, burned away the taste of fear and the feeling of being judged.

"You did well," she told her assistants. "Thank you for all your work getting this ship ready." She should probably have a speech for them, but she'd given enough speeches for the day. "And soon may we enjoy the chance to sail this thing for real, out beyond the waves." To the Forgotten South, if it truly existed. To learn what manner of Truth there was to learn in distant lands.

They cheered and toasted her, and the evening dissolved into a quiet party. None of her assistants were rowdy, and those who were drinking just ended up growing quieter as time passed.

After a while, after Harkala's first fire liquor jug was gone and a second growing empty, Ekana moved to the middle of the main deck.

"I would like to dance, to celebrate this ship and declare it as sacred."

Harkala laughed aloud. "You've had too much to drink, Ekana. Don't risk falling off into the water."

He frowned and handed his gourd of tisane to Sembaari. "I haven't had anything to drink at all, nothing that would cloud my mind or make me clumsy."

Not that her thoughts were completely in order, but when she thought back through the party, it was true that she hadn't seen him with anything besides his tisane.

"I am a trained dancer and performed for the great Chaitan many times. I danced with..." His voice caught for a moment before he continued. "I danced with temple dancers. I know the right dances to commission this ship, to bless it before it journeys into the unknown."

As soon as he began dancing, Harkala swallowed her laughter. He moved with a grace she'd never noticed in all his work for her. He swept his arms low as he swayed from side to side. He spun in tight circles that ended in impressive leaps straight into the air.

There was no music for him to dance to, yet as he continued, Harkala had the sense that the waves were making music after all. Or rather that his dancing tamed and directed the sounds of the sea into real music with a rhythm and melody to match the passes, dips, and spins of his sacred dance.

The gods would surely bless this ship. The fire would bless it, the Sacred Fire of the cosmos. The engraved lines of history and truth would bless the journey they were about to undertake.

A feeling grew in Harkala, a certainty that the princes would fund them, that the ship would escape the rough seas, that they would find the Forgotten South.

As Ekana wrapped up his dance and the assistants applauded—a respectful and solemn applause—a different sound split the deep night air. A bellowing roar, answered a moment later by a second one.

Everyone rushed to the seaward side of the ship. A geyser of water shot toward the sky, bouncing the city's light back toward it. The pod of whales passed within a few ships' lengths of the end of the breakwater. The lanterns along the pier reflected off the whales' massive flanks. Another one blew a spout of water high above them.

When the whales came to the outflow of the Eghsal River, they swung outward, toward the deeper sea. Waves crashed into their sides, but not one collided with a rock or capsized.

"I think the whales came to dance for us too, Ekana," she said.

"I suppose they do," he said, his voice hushed in awe. "I've never seen them come this close to shore."

Neither had Harkala. She licked her lips, all trace of drunkenness gone from her senses, replaced by a sense of wonder that came purely from the sight of their pathway through the ocean. "They bless our ship just like you did. They bless the journey we will take." She had no doubt now of the outcome of the princes' deliberations. Of course they wouldn't deny her. They were mere playthings to the forces of truth and history and the sea. What were princes compared to whales? "And we'll take it soon, following the whales to sea."

The pod of whales dwindled into the distance until all they saw were the occasional waterspouts shooting up above the waves. Then even those were out of sight, but the deep and majestic calls of the whales still came back to shore.

CHAPTER 4

The beggar climbed down into the cesspool beside the street. Something solid had caught his eye, though he lost sight of it now that he was down here. His body ached from the climb, a crick in his back that he tried to make better by stretching, now that he could stand straight for a moment.

Sewage swirled beside his feet, but still no sign of what had drawn him down. He looked up into the snow that fell gently on his head. A dog stood at the edge of the cesspool, watching him. His dog, as much as a beggar like him ever owned an animal. His dog until the soldiers decided it shouldn't belong to him anymore. Beside the dog was one of the street gutters that trickled excrement into the pool, the end of a long trough running the length of the street where residents could dump their nightsoil and other refuse.

When he looked back at the sewage, he saw the object again. A boot? He would welcome a new pair. The geyser field beside Romnai kept the city warm for most of the year, but winter was coming. Even the geysers couldn't keep the city truly warm when the wind raced down from the north, blowing the volcanic steam away from the city. There might even be a full pair of boots swirling around in the cesspool. That would be real luck. The light was too dim to be certain, but he thought he could make out a second shape floating near the first.

It wasn't worth wrecking his current boots, worn as they were, if the new pair didn't even fit. Or proved to be as worn as his own were. He took off his boots and waded out toward the middle. The current pulled at his feet, and the bottom of the pool was slick. At least the sewage wasn't much deeper than his knees at the moment. He walked cautiously until he could reach the first boot.

It was more difficult to pull than he'd expected. When he tugged a second time, harder, the boot finally came toward him. It wasn't empty. He jumped backward and fell, landing on his backside in the sewage. A body came free, the deceased owner of the boots. It floated toward him.

The beggar couldn't recall if he was a superstitious man. He'd been...no, his mind slid away any time he tried to remember anything from before he'd been a beggar. He wasn't superstitious now, not about corpses, at least. About soldiers, sure. About the patterns of cruelty in the city of Romnai. But dead people were a common enough sight to shed any sense of dread. Still, it gave him a fright to see that body coming toward him. He scrambled to the side then forced himself to stop running.

What good was running? If the dead meant him ill, it was no worse than what the living did to him day by day.

The beggar grabbed the stiff knees of the dead man to make the corpse stop moving. He peeled the boots off and set them beside his own. They would need some cleaning before he knew if they would fit or not.

It made him sick, even more than the cesspool itself, what he did next. But a beggar couldn't be squeamish. He stripped the man's outer cloak off. It appeared to be in decent enough condition, or would be once it was cleaned up. He needed all the extra wrappings he could scavenge.

As a bonus, the cloak might still have some coins or other items of value. He wouldn't be alive today if not for things he'd found in unsavory places.

He rolled the cloak into a ball and pushed the corpse back into the swirling pool.

Climbing out wouldn't be easy. He'd have to reach up and set the boots and cloak on the edge and hope the dog would guard them until he got there. Hope that his old bones could get him up quickly enough. His muscles were strong, at least. Living as a beggar had that much to offer. Not soldier strong and not even laborer strong. He pictured the workers loading the river ships and the workers shoveling coal in the steam engines. No, he didn't have that kind of power in his muscles, but his arms had a wiry strength to them.

And he weighed considerably less than he had when he was... No, his mind slid away from that thought. Malnourishment left him with no extra fat, that much was sure.

He leaned back to see the dog. Was it still guarding his few other possessions—a begging cup, a crust of bread he'd been given earlier in the day? As he strained to set the balled up cloak near the dog, a figure suddenly stood over him. The beggar cringed back down as the dog growled at the person.

"What are you doing down there, old man?" It was a soldier. The beggar didn't recognize the insignia the man wore, but there were too many soldier jatis these days to keep track of. New splinter jatis that hadn't always been there.

Or was he remembering someplace else?

He shook his head and stared at the soldier. He should say something. Unused to using his voice, he coughed to clear his throat. "Nothing, sir. Tisrah. Just visiting. Just...looking."

"Visiting the sewers?" The soldier squinted and looked beyond the beggar toward the body spinning in the pool. "Hey, is that..."

The soldier turned as if to summon another soldier. The beggar didn't wait any longer. Grabbing both pairs of boots and the new cloak, he splashed back into the cesspool.

The corpse had been caught on a grate, but that should be easy to move aside. The beggar shoved the body away as the guard's shouts grew more urgent. Yanking on the bars of the grate made the metal squeal in protest. The dog left off its growling to whimper in response, a whimper that ended in a sharp bark. *Just scram, dog.* He made no effort to say the words through his gritted teeth. *Don't let them beat you.*

The grate came free, and the refuse that had been held back gushed through into the sewer below. Holding his breath, the beggar scrambled through as well.

From behind came cries of, "Stop! Murder!" No one would bother to follow him into the putrid chambers under the streets, not unless the dead man had been the High Prince. If there even was still a High Prince in Romnai.

After feeling around the brick walls of the low tunnel, the beggar decided that even the death of a prince probably wouldn't be enough for anyone to come here.

There was no light. The beggar waded forward a few steps and heard a sound behind him. He paused long enough to catch the whiffling snort of a dog that's gotten water on its snout. "Good girl," he managed to say, the words reverberating within the tunnel. Then with the dog half wading, half dog-paddling beside him, the beggar plunged into the darkness, crouched down so his head didn't scrape the ceiling.

He'd never been here before, not as far as he could recall. The sewer tunnels were a haphazard system that didn't serve every part of the city, and where they existed there was no common design. But he'd always been comfortable exploring new places. Always? Again his thoughts couldn't focus on anything from his earliest decades of life, but he had a loose impression—that might have been memory—of discovering passages and alleys that other people didn't know.

Some creature hissed at him, a rat's hiss, unwilling to share this luxurious home. The beggar paused, and the dog's snorts turned into a growl. The hissing moved away, along with a patter of small feet on a portion of a side tunnel that must be dry. He tried to find it, to find some place to walk more comfortably out of the current. But the ceiling came down too low.

After a time there was a glimmer of light ahead. A bigger cesspit stood at the convergence of several tunnels, not directly in that light but lit by it. Fortunately so, or he might well have fallen in. He stepped to the edge, where there was a narrow strip of brick above the sewage. Not exactly dry, but comparatively better. His feet slipped on the slime, so he put on his own, old boots. Best to save the new ones yet for when he could look them over more carefully.

The light came from one of those tunnels. The beggar stomped over to see. A ceiling had collapsed. The light was diffuse, as if it didn't come through directly. Might be an unused cellar up there, or somehow tucked in close beside a building. Hidden, either way.

This tunnel had less sewage flowing through, so he was able to keep his feet mostly dry as he made his way against the current. Fallen bricks lay below the opening. The space above had plants growing beside it. An overgrown garden, perhaps. The beggar lifted the dog up first. It squirmed but let him set it down beside the opening. Then he set the new pair of boots and the balled up cloak beside the dog.

Time to test these wiry, malnourished muscles. The beggar scrambled up to the opening, but the bricks slipped under his feet. He fell hard onto the pile. His arm throbbed, and his forehead stung. He swiped at what felt like a trickle of water above his eye, and his hand came away bloody.

Pain, but he'd known plenty of pain back when…no, the memory wriggled out of reach.

Nothing to do but to try again. He climbed the bricks more slowly, bracing himself against the far wall. The opening was higher than he'd like. He knew without trying that he wouldn't be able to pull himself up with his arms alone. He put his hands on the edge and pushed his feet against the wall. Slowly he rose, twisting his hands as he went to push upward instead of pulling.

He collapsed on the edge.

The dog came over to sniff his head. He halfheartedly batted its nose away, rolled over, and lay there as he caught his breath.

The bushes he'd noticed from below were certainly not the garden he'd pictured. They were scraggly shrubs, barely surviving in what appeared to be a narrow gap between houses. Clearly no one came this way often. He listened for footsteps or the cries of soldiers in pursuit. Nothing. No one coming after him. This cramped space between buildings was as good a place as any to examine his finds.

But first he had to sleep. Spreading the waterlogged, scavenged cloak over himself, the beggar lay down against the building and fell quickly into a fitful sleep, a sleep filled with dreams of flames and jail cells and the sulfur stench of a lava field that wasn't the geyser-filled land beside Romnai.

**

Begging was no longer the same as it had been years earlier. The beggar hadn't ever had to beg back then, when the city enjoyed the peace of the former ruling princes. But he'd known something about begging.

Somehow.

He frowned at the fragments of memories. Back then there had been many beggars. They often gathered in groups near the fancy houses along the edge of the steam beds. People hadn't *liked* beggars, even then, and the untouchables had risked kicks and worse. But there had been safety in numbers, safety in being a normal sight in the city.

Now there were few, which left him vulnerable. And the fancy places where beggars once gathered were certainly not safe.

The beggar liked to choose a place near one of the middle-caste, brenil markets. Soldiers were always around, which he didn't like, but people more often had an extra coin or a bit of food.

And most importantly, there were countless more alleys and side streets and hidden places to escape to.

He chose a smaller market today, wrapped in the cloak he'd rescued from the corpse. He had carefully cleaned the cloak so it no longer stank of sewers and death. A sulfur smell left over from the water he'd used to wash it lingered, but then that was true of the whole city, on many days. The boots had proved too small. He kept them in the hidden gap where he'd been sleeping, in case they proved useful as barter or bribery someday.

Early in the morning, he arrived as the mongers set up their stalls. He wandered through the maze of goods, the dog at his side. At times there were tempting opportunities to pilfer a bite or other good, but he never stole a thing and made sure the dog didn't touch anything either.

The risk was too great, the cost of being caught far too high. If the soldiers didn't run him off at swordpoint, the merchants would beat him to death.

Instead he made fleeting eye contact with as many sellers as he could. He didn't beg for anything, though several tossed the dog a scrap as he passed by. At least he shouldn't have to find extra food for the dog later. When the local residents and wallas arrived, he would withdraw to a place a house or two away from the market square. The sellers would remember he was there, remember that he hadn't stolen anything. And so they wouldn't send the soldiers to harass him.

Or at least he hoped they wouldn't. Not every seller felt the same kind of grudging acquiescence.

One bean seller threw a rock at him when he came too close. It bounced off the beggar's shoulder, and he skittered quickly away. Another seller, seeing it happen, glowered at the bean seller. And then turned his glower on the beggar. He tossed a dried apple near the beggar's feet as if in recompense, but his look of disapproval never wavered.

The beggar snatched up the apple before it got trampled or lost to the rats. Disapproval he could live with, and even stones to drive him away, but wasted fruit was beyond what could be borne.

The first wave of wallas came. They would be buying fast and hurrying away to make their deliveries. Most wouldn't give him a second glance, and it was rare that any of them tossed him any coin or bite to eat.

Still, he made himself a place down the street where he expected many of the wallas would pass. "Alms," he called. His voice was scratchy and hesitant. "Anything you can spare. So I don't starve. Or an extra coat on this cold day? Alms! Alms!"

Not a single walla gave him anything. In the brief calm after the mass of them left, one seller slipped down the street and gave him a tisane, already mostly cooled—pouring it into the chipped cup the beggar had found to replace the one he'd left behind. He huddled over the cup to coax the last warmth from it and drank gratefully, watching for the next passersby to beg from.

A crowd of locals trickled in over the next hours. Household staff for those with enough money, the housewives, househusbands, and grandparent housekeepers of the rest. The beggar got a few morsels and even a small denomination coin that he tied into the cloak.

The sound of marching feet came into the far side of the market square. A few merchants shouted about the disruption, but they quieted quickly.

The beggar gathered up what little he had to be ready to run. The dog sat up, its ears forward and its snout lifted.

The soldiers stayed in the market. Just as the beggar relaxed, another squad of soldiers came suddenly around the corner behind him. They marched by. One peeled off from the group and stood over the beggar.

"Clear out, old man. Find a job or starve."

The beggar drew back from the harsh words. The sentiment was seldom said out loud, though it was, no doubt, the attitude of many who passed him by. He mumbled something as he gathered himself to leave. The soldier shoved him in the back as soon as he turned to go. Catching himself, he quickly grabbed the dog to lead it away.

A growl was rising in its throat. Best not to give the soldier any cause to turn his anger on the dog.

The beggar went around a block to a new place about the same distance from the market.

The two groups of soldiers were arguing among the stalls. Maybe time to go find a different market for the rest of the day. There was a group of shoppers passing by, so he waited, calling for alms, earning a small hunk off a loaf of bread.

"Thank you," he mumbled through the bite of bread.

He hadn't been desperate to eat, but when someone gave food, they liked to see you eat it right away. Made them feel like they'd saved a starving person.

Which wasn't *that* far from the truth.

The shouting soldiers moved on in separate ways, leaving the market calm again. Not quiet, of course. The normal cries of *wares for sale* and *the last chance for a great deal* came and went in their usual ebb and flow.

As midday approached, the beggar rose and made his way toward the stalls again. There was a lull in shoppers, and the merchants sometimes had a few scraps that weren't worth holding on to for the afternoon's paying customers.

The dog again earned its share of treats. The beggar also got an old pear off one seller and the rind broken off a wheel of cheese from another. He worked on the cheese as he walked. It was hard to chew, and his teeth were far from strong. The mild flavor was scant reward for so much work.

As he rounded another stall, a cry went up. Before he'd even had time to understand what the cry was for, he smelled smoke.

He didn't wait. Smoke terrified him, though he didn't remember why. The scent made a spasm in his legs, an ache that made it hard to force them to move. He stumbled into the nearest stall as he tried to run.

The stall worker shouted at him, but he didn't look back. Let someone else sort out the falling vegetables. He needed to be away from there. The smell of smoke came from ahead and to his right. He veered left and ran into a shopper, spilling her purchases onto the ground.

He should stop and help her. He told himself he was the kind of person who would do that, who would stop and help her pick up the fallen items. Even if he hadn't been the one to make her drop them, he was the type of person who would do that. Or he used to be that person, anyway.

Not anymore. Not if there was a fire nearby. An image flashed before his mind of panicked people, of bodies running into each other to avoid the flames, to escape the smoke.

There were no flames in sight, but he couldn't shake the image. Fire was not something rational, not something he could reason with, so he jettisoned logic and the ethics he thought he should hold.

And he ran.

The dog made way for him, barking as it dashed along at his side. No one wanted to get in the way of that mongrel or of the unkempt man running beside it.

Only after passing many streets did he slow down. There were passersby here but not many. A pair of soldiers patrolling. A wallah hurrying on his way toward the river.

There was no longer any smell of smoke. Whatever fire there had been, it hadn't spread. For all he knew, the cry of alarm may have been no more than an overreaction to a cooking fire or something equally innocent. But the beggar would feel better beside the river's water.

He followed the wallah, and where the other man turned to make for the great, arching bridge over the river, the beggar kept on right to the river's edge. Old, run-down buildings stood beside the river here, their foundations recording the levels of the river's floods.

A steamship moved slowly upriver toward the bridge. It was powered by fire as well, a frantic coal fire burning at the heart of the ship. His panic had dissipated, so that recognition had no power to set him back into unreasoning terror.

The side of the ship was painted with graffiti, proclaiming that the old princes lived on. That the princes would return and restore the city to its former glory, ruling over the entire valley.

And what? That they would again let the beggars starve, let the workers waste their lives in a desperate struggle against survival. There had been soldiers in the streets back then as well, and plenty of unjust beatings. Maybe bringing the old princes back wasn't the answer to the city's violent and terrible chaos.

Not that the beggar knew what answer there could possibly be instead. Burning it all down sounded good to him, as long as he didn't have to feel the flames himself. Back to the sacred Fire that the priests blathered on about. Perhaps someday it would all be ended.

CHAPTER 5

Pavresh and the others from Chaitanshehar slunk into the city of Pashun from the bottom edge of its impressive slope. The smell of the mudpots down the slope below was overpowering. Had it always been so strong here? He couldn't recall exactly what it had been like his last time visiting. He'd spent more time outside the city, among the mumbler villages that were beyond the mines to the south.

Despite the smell, he focused his attention on the magic, building on the sense that this band of people belonged here in Pashun. They were a part of the city, nothing worth any special notice, nothing to report or even remember. It was an imperfect protection, and it kept slipping, as if something prevented it from fully taking hold. But it should give some protection, and if Chaitanshehar was going to survive, they couldn't put this off.

Pashun was a city broken, frightened. Five years before it had been divided into districts at war with each other. Pavresh didn't know what neighborhood had been part of what faction, but he could sense the fragility of the place. The streets mostly empty. The few people out moved with their faces lowered, not wanting to see or be seen except as just a forgettable part of the scenery.

A door opened as they passed, and a man called out, "We've got a fresh barrel on tap. Come inside."

"We might take you up on that in a bit," Rashul called as they hurried past.

Coincidence that he opened the door just then? Likely. A couple walking along the street behind them passed the door, and the man called out to them as well. Still, it was a sign that Pavresh's magic wasn't enough to keep them from being noticed.

"Slow down," Pavresh called out in a low voice. "We stand

out if we're rushing too much." They eased up their pace and tried to blend in enough for the magic to do the rest.

Their guide was a former miner who'd lived in Pashun as a child, before he'd been sent to work the mines. He brought them quickly up the slope from where they'd entered the city. The street lanterns were few and widely spaced.

"These are mostly lower-caste homes and shops down here," the miner said. "Or middle, maybe. The fancier houses are up higher."

Pavresh had learned what he could of Pashun from those who knew it. Valni had been sent to the city shortly before the founding of Chaitanshehar, in the service of the former High Prince. She'd wanted to accompany them, but Jaritta had forbidden it. Datri had some knowledge of how the city had changed since the princes consolidated their power. From those stories and reports, he'd already decided that there were two likely places to anchor the spell.

The seminary, near the steam bed edge of the city but farther to the south, would be a good place to make the attempt. It already had a unique hold on the people of Pashun and the unconscious ways of the city.

But the upper reaches of the city where the princes lived might work well instead. It had power simply by the fact of who lived there. The princes had preserved the central portion of the wall that protected them during the insurrection within their city. It sat high above these streets, just in front of their glamorous manors, and might give the spell the anchor he needed. Pavresh wanted to see it in person before he decided for sure.

He reached out with his magic to sense the stories the residents told themselves about their city.

"Let's go up the slope a little ways and then circle back down to the seminary, if that still seems like a good location. If you can lead us to the seminary that way?"

"We have to stay to the south of that waterway along here,"

the miner said. "As long as we do that, there are many routes, whatever roads we want to take."

The pitch of the streets was steep. They slowed to a walk and climbed up among shuttered shops and darkened houses. Rashul breathed heavily at the effort. Nothing Jaritta had said could have kept him from coming along. If they weren't going to conquer the city by force, he needed to see them make it powerless by magic.

Kamlak was along as well so Pavresh had at least one other arcist, in case that proved of any use. It had taken longer than Pavresh would have liked to decide which student would be best. Kamlak was less polished than he would have preferred, but something about the choice had fit.

Kamlak did what he could now to bolster Pavresh's spell of belonging, but even with both of them working, the effect kept slipping off, binding to them imperfectly. No cry of alarm went up, at least. Valni had chosen the other four members of their group—soldiers, as much as Chaitanshehar had people who could be called soldiers. Against the trained soldiers of the Pashun jatis, in their own city, in their own streets, Pavresh could only hope that he wouldn't need their protection.

He glanced around for anyone watching from the windows along the route. Metal bars in front of a shop offered a glimpse of what looked like cooking pots. Nothing fancy, but not terribly cheap either, as far as he could tell in the darkness. Beside that shop, a narrow door looked like it led into a walkway between buildings, or maybe a staircase up to the upper floors.

If anyone watched them pass, they didn't reveal themselves.

Their guide took them swiftly through the streets once they reached the right level. Pavresh studied the buildings up above, tried to picture if any of them would work better for his spell.

The people who lived here told stories of the mudpots, of the stink that rose up from them, of the fierce winds that blew from above to clean out the stench. That stink seemed to infiltrate even the words they used, words that lingered in arcist magic. The main city buildings were up above, the manors of the Pashun princes, the government chambers. One group of princes had declared themselves a new Ruling Thirty. Other princes didn't accept them, as the coup had given their families power over the original Thirty based in Romnai. Last he knew, those tensions hadn't been resolved, so whatever assembly building or ruling chambers either group used likely wouldn't have the official support—or arcist influence—of the seminary.

Where was the reviled Mahendri in this? In Chaitanshehar he was spoken of often and seen as a key figure in the city. But those who'd been in Pashun before the coup hadn't even known who he was. He was a figure who kept in the shadows, and as far as Datri could determine from her spies, he remained unknown to most of the people here, playing the two rival groups of princes against each other.

The miner paused at an intersection. The lights were brighter here, marking this as a key route toward the upper reaches. "You want to head up higher now? We're about halfway across the city already. It's pretty narrow at this level. So if you want to go up…"

Pavresh looked up that way one last time. The wall was there, a short segment of wall with an open gate in the middle of it. A wall no longer in use. That resonated with Chaitanshehar's wall. With Pavresh's terrible attempt at a magical wall made out of fear. How fitting to anchor it there. And yet… Was that where the power in this city was centered? When he reached out through the magic, everything felt fractured. Throughout the city, but especially up toward the princely manors. Across the street and down toward the seminary, there was more wholeness, a soothing sense of genuine influence that he could tap into. "No, let's keep on, start making our way down toward the seminary."

They crossed the bright street and wound their way through the darker streets on the other side. A pair of drunks passed by, ignoring them. Pavresh checked on their spell of anonymity and saw it loosening, so he tried to reassert that while they went.

As they quickly passed through one block, one of their soldiers hissed, "Wait."

They stopped in the darkness. It was a level road, running parallel to the steam beds below. Houses above and below crowded close, leaving little light to see by. The cobbled street felt slick beneath Pavresh's feet.

Someone coughed in the shadows, someone who wasn't a part of their team. A sheltered light came on, a candle flame perhaps. Pavresh strained to make out anything, but even the light of that flame revealed nothing. It only blinded him further so that the rest of the street was darker. He put more energy into the arcist spell to make them innocuous.

"Sorry to bother you." The man's voice caught on the words. "And please, we're no threat. You can put away your knives."

"We?" Pavresh said. "Why did you stop us?"

A woman answered, her voice scarcely more than a whisper. "Please, you're from that other city, aren't you? From the untouchable city?"

Not a chance he would answer that. Pavresh nudged the miner to get them moving again.

"We're not... I mean, we want to be on your side," the man said. "We won't turn you over to the soldiers or anything like that."

And the woman added, "You don't know how bad it is here. How long we've been watching for anyone to pass by who didn't belong."

Was it so clear that they didn't belong, despite the magic? And even more concerning, "So we just happened to pass by your home here in this alley, of all the places in the city? I find that difficult to credit."

"No, we don't, I mean, this isn't our home. I caught sight of you when you first slipped into the city. We followed you for a ways and saw you were coming through here, so we decided to intercept you."

Did that make it better that he'd managed to follow them, or much worse?

It didn't matter either way. If these two had hunting or growing skills or access to food some other way, they would be more than welcome in Chaitanshehar. And their knowledge could prove useful for Jaritta and the other city leaders. But Pavresh's team couldn't take any refugees with them on this trip.

"Make your way to the city. They'll find a place for you, if you're willing to work. But you need to leave us be." Of course, if the team was successful, then they might not *want* to leave Pashun after all. Or be able to.

"There are...things, magic stuff in the way." His voice cracked. "We can't get through."

"And that's what we hope to take care of now. Gather your family or whoever else and make yourselves ready to go. If the magic is still blocking you, figure out exactly where it's strongest. Then tell yourself a story of why you must go past, of what's so important on the other side of that magic. And then circle around that point as well as you can."

When they tried to thank him, Pavresh cut them off. "But you'll have to go on your own, and right away, because we don't know when we'll return or how."

Pavresh gave their miner guide another nudge, harder this time, to get them moving. "Let me know when we're a few blocks away." The team ran off, following their guide around a few corners back and forth to get them on a different route from the one they'd been on. Best to not risk getting caught now.

As they went, Pavresh recreated the spell to make them seem to belong, building it back up, bit by bit. They were innocents out for a stroll but also officials with a task to do. He told the story to the air, to the buildings and the streets, and let it permeate through to whatever people would be nearby.

A shroud of innocence settled over them to make people ignore their passing through.

When they came to a corner beneath an unlit lamp, they stopped and circled around Pavresh.

"I don't like that we were seen like that. That we were recognized as strangers." He paused to give anyone a chance to respond. No one did. "Any of you notice any times we might have exposed ourselves?"

"The brightly lit street?"

Pavresh wasn't sure whose voice it was, but he answered, "That was risky, but did anyone see anything specific? There or anywhere else?"

No one said anything.

"Do you think they spoke the truth? Or was it some kind of trap?" Maybe they should go back out, regroup. They could enter another night and go straight to the seminary. But it was so close now. And every day was another threat to Chaitanshehar.

"I don't see how that's a trap," their guide said. "If Mahendri were on to us, wouldn't he just send in some soldier jati to arrest us? Or kill us?

Or he'd set two soldier jatis feuding and let them be caught in the crossfire. That was the man's reputation, after all. Pavresh would have the final word, but he hated to make it all on his own. "Rashul? You think we've been noticed? Are we still safe to go forward with our plan?"

"We were never safe." Even with his voice pitched low, Rashul had a way of drawing in his listeners, of making every word seem wise and meaningful. "Safety was never what we were looking for. *Safe* would have been staying in Chaitanshehar. Or never founding that city at all. *Safe* would have been living within the castes and never challenging a thing. So, no, I don't think we're safe. But I think we can move forward and still try."

Pithy for a Rashul speech. Pavresh was about to say as much when Rashul added, "But can you sense anything more with your magic?"

"Good call," Kamlak said before Pavresh could answer. "I'm trying to do what you taught us, but I don't know it well enough."

It was an imperfect solution. Not everything that was happening left a trace in the magic of a place. But as he reached for the arcist themes, he felt a peaceful calm settle on him. Rashul was right. They were here for so much more than mere safety. Surely the divine Fire of the cosmos would protect them. It would burn a path into the fabric of creation to guide them.

Because what they were doing was important, right, just.

No fear or danger could stand against that.

"Yes. I can't promise that we'll succeed, but the timing is as good as it will ever be. And I sense no immediate threat nearby." Pavresh gestured for the miner to lead them on, and when he realized the darkness probably made the movement invisible, he said, "Take us the rest of the way. Let's make this city into one no one can escape from. That no one would choose to escape."

The streets that followed were ill lit, the buildings anonymous houses, shut tight for the night. If there were more secret bars or tisane clubs, they didn't advertise it, and no drunks wandered these streets while they passed through.

The seminary loomed above them a short time later. No one was visible around it, as far as they could see. Pavresh took a deep breath. He still felt the powerful calming effect within the magic. All would be well. Doing this here and now was the right choice. He'd seldom been so sure of himself.

He looked up and down the length of the building. This side housed the students and some families. The grand entrance was around on the lower side, but he didn't necessarily need to place the spell there. Instead he headed for the corner that pointed in toward the bulk of the city. There was a gap between two wings of the building at that juncture. Pavresh drew the magic tight around the group, making them just as certain of what they were doing as he felt.

Making them certain of their inevitable success.

At the corner, they gathered in the dark under the bulk of the seminary. Flowering fruit trees in between the two wings of the building scented the air, covering but not eliminating the sour smell of the mudpots below.

"Kamlak, come beside me, in case I need anything. Everyone else, stand guard."

The stories that lingered in that courtyard spoke of knowledge, of the gods of the pantheonic religion, of the power of the temple and its priests throughout the valley. Pavresh didn't much like that, but the calming sensation still had its hold on him.

This would work. He had accomplished it once before, and he could create a similar effect again.

Last time he'd been desperate. It had been a last-gasp effort to save the city before everyone fled for a final time. He'd been weary with the misguided spell of the day before, worn down by fear and dread. Yet he'd reached deep into the earth and anchored a sense of welcome into the rocks of the very city.

Now he was tense and afraid, but the desperation was no longer so overpowering. He was taking action for the future of Chaitanshehar and Eghsal Valley itself and not simply reacting to events as they transpired.

"Will you tell me how you do it?" Kamlak blurted. Then before Pavresh could reprimand him, he covered his mouth with his hands. "I'm so sorry. I know, I shouldn't be talking. You need to prepare." Then muttered under his breath but still loud enough for Pavresh to make out, "I'm just too anxious for this to work."

Pavresh nodded without speaking and sought the calmness he needed to weave the arcist magic into his spell.

Welcome, that was the first part of this magic. A powerful call that everyone would be welcome. Would simply putting that into the spell make it so? Pashun was far larger than Chaitanshehar and full of divisions that had existed as long as the city had. He had to reinforce that sense of welcome with ideas of the people working together, of them restoring a city broken by recent fighting into something that was better and more just than it had ever been.

Justice was a powerful marker in arcist magic. He used it to bind the sense of welcome into something more defined, something that wasn't only on the surface but undergirded the city as a whole.

What else? A common goal. The people of Pashun should feel like they were working together for something bigger than any one person. And just as in Chaitanshehar, the magic would nudge out those who refused to be a part of the vision of Pashun as something to work toward.

And to undermine the manipulator Mahendri, Pavresh reinforced the idea of unity, of the jatis, at least, working together and forming larger jatis when it made sense. Working together across castes was likely too big a change to force by magic. But perhaps the soldier jatis would join together. Or even dissolve, as their purpose for being kept separate became ever less valid.

It was ready in his mind. Now to transfer the magic into the walls and foundations around him.

Pavresh reached into the rock, but something resisted him. His mind slid off the planned anchor point, like water off oil.

He stopped and took a calming breath. So much depended on getting this right. No wonder his nerves would make it difficult to achieve. The spell had to go deep, but it had to spread wide too, to encompass the entire city and not only this building beside them.

Pavresh reached down, feeling his thoughts become surrounded by rocks, feeling the stories that held the city together. Here, deep beneath thought and awareness, this was where arcist magic worked.

He began the process of tying the uncountable strands of magic into the stone.

Again they slipped, a lace that wouldn't tie.

There must be something wrong with the rock. Pavresh reached out wider with his magic, beyond the seminary building to the foundations of the other buildings, the bedrock beneath them, and the volcanically disturbed rock just a short distance away. The spell would be less stable if he connected it there, but he had to find some way to anchor it.

As he tried for a third time to make the spell sink deep into this city, a city of enemies and innocents, a sudden calm settled on him, an arcist sense of perfect peace without any worry. A calm so deep it felt cloying. Out of the corner of his eye, he saw the soldiers he'd brought lower their weapons. The feeling made him want to close his eyes, and in the dark he couldn't be sure that his team members were all awake.

Only a deliberate arcist spell could have this kind of effect.

And only an arcist as experienced as Pavresh could hope to create such a spell.

Pavresh grabbed Kamlak to him, shaking him in case he'd succumbed to the spell. "Mahendri's arcist is here! I need you alert."

Pavresh scrambled to counter it with his own spell. He drew on the alarm of fire, the threat of an enemy drawing close, the betrayal of a place that had seemed safe. And as he worked, he shouted. "Rashul! Everyone! We're under attack. We need to flee."

"Where?" Rashul spun in a circle, and the guards and miner with them raised their weapons back up. Pavresh's spell battled with the sense of lethargy that was being imposed on them.

By the other arcist.

Pavresh turned slowly, looking for where the arcist must be hiding. Behind a darkened window in the seminary? Among the shadows in the edge of the courtyard? With so little light reaching them, it was impossible to know.

"I don't know where," Pavresh admitted. "We'll have to get moving, though. Down to the mudpots, that'll be the closest way."

And could they find their way out through that inhospitable land? This side of the lava field didn't lend itself as well to travel. Were they only trading the danger of swords and sling bullets for the danger of geysers and boiling mud?

They kept in a tight clump as they moved back to the street. Down halfway past the massive seminary's structure, a phalanx of soldiers stepped from the darkness, awaiting them.

How had they known to be here?

But then, if the arcist had known…

The Chaitanshehar soldier at the lead barked, "Back up—" His voice ended in a gurgle, an arrow through his throat. He fell to the cobbles.

The fear that washed over Pavresh had nothing to do with arcist magic.

"We have to go around," Rashul called, already moving. "There's another street across here."

Pavresh added a sense of resolve to the urgency in his magic, willing them away as fast as possible.

It was too little, too late. The enemy was too close and escape too far away.

The Pashun soldiers charged and reached them before they'd crossed the street. What light there was glinted off sword blades and knives. A step below Pavresh, Rashul—the great orator and inspiration for so much of what they'd achieved, but never a fighter—caught a blade to the ribs. Pavresh wanted to scream in anger and pain. Rashul cried out, one last time, but his voice was powerless.

Maybe it had always been powerless. Maybe his dreams were even less substantial than arcist magic or stories. Maybe they should have never listened to him in the first place. His blood splashed onto Pavresh as he crumpled around the enemy sword.

Before Pavresh could reach down beside Rashul's body or make any effort to flee on his own, someone grabbed him by the arm, and he felt a knife at his back. At the same time a voice full of authority shouted, "Enough. Weapons down!" The words came with an arcist magic sense that added force to the command, as if this was someone who commanded all authority and respect.

The few survivors from Chaitanshehar put down their weapons at their feet, and the enemy soldiers did the same. Compelled by the same magic. It would have been comic, if

Pavresh had been able to respond by fleeing the unarmed soldiers. But he was powerless to move.

"Well done," Kamlak said. His voice was no longer that of the bumbling student Pavresh had known. "You did your part perfectly, and I've learned all I needed to know."

Pavresh twisted to see his former student, but the knife kept him from turning far enough.

"I'll take this one. I may have more to learn from him. The survivors…" Even without seeing him, Pavresh could hear the way he must be shrugging in the tone of his voice. "Arrest them, I suppose. Or kill them if that's easier."

"No, don't kill them." Pavresh lurched forward, but his captor's grip held firm.

Kamlak pulled Pavresh away from the scene and whispered in his ear, "You were wrong. Mahendri sees me as his arcist. But I prefer to think of it as Mahendri is my politician."

Dragging him up the street, back toward the place where Pavresh had attempted his spell, Kamlak added in a fierce whisper, "Not that you need to tell Mahendri that, of course. Let him think me his pet."

And if he was telling Pavresh as much, then it meant he saw Pavresh as no threat. Was it because he didn't really care if Mahendri heard such a claim by way of their captive arcist? Or because he planned to have Pavresh killed before there was any chance? With Rashul dead, his team of would-be soldiers killed or captured, he fully expected that he would soon be dead as well.

He had lost. It was over, for him at the least, and quite possibly for the city of Chaitanshehar as well. He felt his body collapsing but then made himself stand upright.

If he wanted to survive long enough to warn Jaritta and help her in any way, he couldn't give up.

And the way to do that was through magic. Pavresh played on the idea of being a useful source of information. Kamlak hadn't come to Chaitanshehar to be his student only to lure him into this trap. There was no way anyone could have predicted this would happen so many months earlier.

So he'd come because he didn't know something that Pavresh did.

He needed to cling to that knowledge now. He had something Kamlak wanted. Or at the least, he knew something Kamlak used to want. He used the magic to emphasize all the other secrets Kamlak might not yet understand. The image of Rashul's body falling disrupted the spell. He pushed the memory aside for the moment and tried again. He was a wise man, some few years younger than Kamlak in truth, but he built on the image of an old sage.

Several of the Pashun soldiers had come along with them, keeping a few footsteps behind. He looped them into the spell as well, so that they would see their prisoner as valuable. No sense taking a chance of them deciding to get rid of him when Kamlak was distracted with something else.

At the place where the wings of the seminary met, they stopped.

Seemingly in a talkative mood, Kamlak spoke. "I could never quite figure out how you'd anchored that spell in the untouchable city. The best I could do was those beacons all over. And as you saw, those were too easy to undo."

They seemed to be waiting for something to happen, for someone to show up.

Kamlak scanned the night as he talked. "I learned a lot from how you taught the others to undo my spells, but it wasn't enough. Watching what you did to try to anchor the spell here, that made it all fit. I could sense the way you used the magic, even as I blocked it. I hadn't realized you could tell a stone a story like that. But now, now I think I can make it work, anchor a different kind of spell into the city. One that will make us truly powerful."

"And if you can't figure it out," a new voice came from the darkness, "then he will be right there to help you."

A figure stepped out into the little light of Kamlak's lantern.

He was a small man, entirely unimpressive at first glance. His balding head reflected the lantern light above a fringe of hair. His shoulders curved his body forward. In a crowd, Pavresh would have completely overlooked the man.

Much as Pavresh had used magic to be overlooked when spying. There was no feel of arcist magic in this man, only the natural way an average looking person tended to be ignored.

"You must be Pavresh. We have heard much of you and even lost some of our people to your handiwork." He held out his hand as if for Pavresh to shake it. "I am Mahendri. I suspect you've heard something of me as well, though I could wish I weren't so known."

Pavresh ignored the offered hand. Rashul had been killed on this man's orders. His team of soldiers and miners, people who had believed in the vision of Chaitenshehar, they were dead as well. Because of Kamlak with his deceptive simpleness, and because of this little man who'd tried to destroy the city, ever since its founding. Even after Pavresh created his spell, this little man worked to destroy them still.

Mahendri lowered his hand, but the arrogant smile never faltered. "You aren't an impressive figure."

Pavresh bit back the temptation to say he'd thought the same of Mahendri.

When he gave no answer, Mahendri said, "Good. I don't trust an impressive looking man. Too often there's nothing beneath. But you, I know how impressive you are, and I think you'll be impressed with the plans I have for this city, about the ways to make the whole valley great."

As if he would care what plans Mahendri devised, except if he could find a way to undermine them.

"But those plans come back to the spell I wish to take root here in my home city. This is why I will need you. Perhaps Kamlak can figure it out for us, but I need you so we can be sure. You will end up very rich, when everything is done."

"I'm not here to betray my city. No amount of money is enough to tempt me." In all his travels, in all the stories he'd heard and collected, he'd heard often enough how greed always turned against a person. "The magic itself cries out against such base impulses."

Mahendri leaned in close enough to be uncomfortable. His nostrils flared right in front of Pavresh's nose. "Oh, the magic. I may not be an arcist practitioner, but I know enough about it. It's all about stories, the stories you tell yourself as you're falling asleep at night."

He moved a few steps away and gestured at both Pavresh and Kamlak. "But here's a story for both of you. Once upon a time a man had a chance to choose between modest wealth and the ideals he'd learned from his grandmother's knees. Whatever those ideals were. It doesn't really matter for our story. What matters was the wealth. It was wealth to make him comfortable. And as you can guess by now, it wasn't really *once upon a time* but many. This is a story that has happened many times. Not everyone gets the chance, but more people do than you'd think.

"Some choose the ideals, and they come to regret it, if they live long enough. But most choose comfort. And I'll tell you this. After you've chosen comfort, you'll find whatever story you need to tell yourself so you can justify it. A good and honorable reason for doing what you call betrayal now." He waved his hand as if to dismiss the seminary rooms and even the bulk of the city above them. "The story is just your way to rationalize your own route to power, and it's the power of arcist magic that matters now. You'll find the story that you need in the end, one to justify everything you'll end up doing for me."

Then to Kamlak, he said, "Take him away. We'll get to work soon enough. Making the city the real power in this valley, just as the gods and the sacred fire and arcist magic itself have always intended."

CHAPTER 6

Valni paced through the burnt fields. No enemy soldiers had returned. A part of her wished they would so she could have something to fight. Worry and uncertainty offered nothing for her blades to cut, her staff to strike.

A green fuzz marked the fields they were trying to regrow. Who could say if there would be time for the crops to mature and be harvested before winter overpowered the warm air from the volcanic beds? Other fields were still only black ash. There would be no easy way to replace the food that had burned.

Not returning was a theme these days. Enemies, crops, Pavresh. His team should have returned over a twelve-day ago. They should be celebrating his success and what it would mean for the city. Or they might be lamenting his failure, making their desperate plans for how they could still survive.

But with them not returning, no one knew exactly what to celebrate and what to mourn.

She should have been allowed to go with them.

There was no way Jaritta would let her go off now to search for answers, and she was nothing if not a faithful soldier, following the commands of her superior.

Which was why she didn't ask the city leaders for permission now.

Officially she had descended to check on the damage in the fields and scout for enemy soldiers still in the area. Much as the leaders chafed at letting her wander alone on these rambles, it was a key part of her role. And a key part of her personal sanity. She still considered herself a falcon jati soldier, dedicated above all to the safety of the High Prince. But her jati had failed the last High Prince, failing to stop an assassination plot from within his own household. Others had claimed the title of High Prince since then, but none enjoyed the full support of the people of the valley. So none of them was legitimate in Valni's eyes.

While her former sisters went about Romnai in mourning—in sackcloth and anger—she performed her penance out here, in the wilds that surrounded the new city.

She served Jaritta and the leaders of Chaitanshehar as the closest thing to what a High Prince should be, but she often had to step away from the city so that the thoughts of failure didn't overwhelm her. To be gone for a few days, as she'd have to now—or a whole twelve-day by the time she went and came back—was somewhat unusual, but not unheard of. And she'd set in place all the procedures to make sure the defense of the city would be well taken care of in her absence. Just in case.

Moving away from the fields, she approached the so-called beacons that drove people away from the city. They had little effect on her. Even Pavresh's spell that drew people to the city affected her less than others. As long as she focused on her task, knew that it was what she had to do, then the magic became a distant pulse that was possible, with effort, to ignore.

She stuck to the edge of the swamp and walked fast, her long strides crossing the land quickly. The farther she got from Chaitanshehar, the fewer beacons there were. Out here the swamp poisoned most plant life, leaving a bare land of variously colored mud and strange rock formations, but it also kept the worst of the approaching winter at bay. On the other side of her route were twisted pines and scattered brush, but mostly bare land and, here and there, patches of never melting snow.

One of the last of the beacons looked like it had been torn apart, but she could still feel the magic that clung to the broken pieces, a sense of revulsion that felt like heartburn. After studying it for a moment, Valni dropped into a crouch behind a scraggly tree. She'd heard something human. A voice, a shuffle of feet, the clink of a cooking pot.

Crawling along in front of the broken beacon, she came across a hollow with a single tent and good-sized campfire. A sufficient setup for now, sheltered from the wind by the lay of the land, but not the kind of thing someone could live in through the winter.

Mumblers? No, the tent looked like something from one of the cities. She circled around and saw the sign they'd written on the side of the tent itself, a rough scrawl likely made with a charred stick. "Help. We're looking for the new city. Can anyone guide us?"

No, she couldn't. On her way back, maybe, but not now.

Except, could she leave them here? What if the weather turned worse? What if they starved?

"Hello!" she called as she stood up. She stalked down toward the tent as someone came out.

It was a middle-aged woman. No threat herself, but Valni kept her eyes moving for signs of anyone else. This did not look like someone out here alone.

The woman gave a noise like a half gasp and said, "You're from the city, aren't you? The city of outsiders? Can you help us get through?"

"Who is *us*?"

A man stepped out of the tent. "Just the two of us. We were hoping to come with more, but the man said to hurry. It looked like they were on their way to do something important."

A chill went up Valni's spine. "What man? What are you talking about?"

They told her briefly about the group they'd seen in Pashun and the instructions their leader had given for getting past the magic. "And it worked. We made it past some, but now we're turned around. We can't tell which way to go."

The timing was right. She counted back the days. They'd seen Pavresh and his group the very night they'd come to Pashun. He'd encouraged them to come and warned them that there was danger if they stayed.

Danger that had caught up to Pavresh later that same night?

"I can't guide you back. This is too urgent. But if you know how to get around the beacons, then it's easy."

"Easy when you know the land." The man looked defeated. Was it even worth it? What could a person like that bring to the city, a city so desperately in need of food and expertise?

But no, it wasn't her role to ask such questions. The city would welcome them regardless, and no one could say what vital skills or information these two might bring.

"I'll point out some landmarks. Keep them in sight, each time you get past one of the beacons, and you'll come to the switchbacks heading upward."

***

On the third day, Valni came across an abandoned soldier camp. She crept in slowly. It had been used recently. The dirt was freshly shoveled over what had been the latrine. The firepit was cool, but there were fresh logs, charred black but not burnt up and free of any settling dust that would have accumulated quickly in the area.

Valni kicked leaves aside and looked for anything worth knowing. It looked like there had been about two dozen tents. The largest one, the commander's no doubt, was only twice as big as the others. That implied a fairly low level leader. The smaller tents would have slept two soldiers in each, three if they were trying hard to limit the weight of their gear. That seemed unnecessary, with how close they were to Pashun.

So a small unit with a low-ranking commander.

They might have been the ones who set the fires to the crops. Or they might have come along afterward to monitor the city in the twelve-days since then and returned to the city more recently.

They hadn't been fleeing anything when they left the camp, but they'd still left quickly. The hasty shoveling work and the minimal attempts to hide where they'd camped spoke to a sudden but controlled departure. They were summoned back to the city, for some reason and quite quickly. Did it have anything to do with why Pavresh and the rest hadn't returned?

She headed out soon, watching for soldiers left behind. The swamp dried out as she came closer to the more concentrated lava field that was right beside Pashun. She'd crossed straight through it six years earlier. She'd skirted boiling mud and water that scalded the soil, climbed the many-hued deposits surrounding geysers, nearly fallen into calderas that pulsed with magma below. And all in all, she'd survived where she shouldn't have.

Only her soldier training, the dance-like grace of the falcon jati's fighting style, had saved her. She wasn't going to trust that it would be enough a second time. She skirted as close to the danger as she dared.

When she was finally a few hours from Pashun, she cut over into the lava bed in search of an out-of-the-way place to make her own camp. She carefully crossed a stream that hissed and spat. Then clinging to vines and rocks, she edged around an outcropping. The other side had looked promising for shelter, but it proved too exposed, so she kept going.

Around the next rise, there was a dead tree still standing. Its bleached wood looked like prime habitat for all manner of insects and rodents, but she found it clean and empty of any critters. That land couldn't support plants, so animals avoided it as well. No doubt the tree was ancient, from a time when the water table wasn't poisoned by the volcanic activity. It died when the bad water came, but survived long enough that insects didn't stick around to help it decompose.

Valni set a blanket on the ground beneath the tree's remaining roots and stretched out to sleep for a few hours. She could continue on to investigate as dusk fell.

The evening light when she woke reminded her of the time she'd first come to Pashun. That had been dawn rather than dusk, but she'd been coming through the edge of the steam beds just the same and from a similar point as she would arrive now.

There had been several soldiers camps in the wooded land in that direction, back then. She left the lava beds before the last light of the day was gone. Even away from the danger of the volcanic fields, she had to move slowly, cautious for fallen trees, the rustle of dry needles, and sentries who might be anywhere all these years later.

The night was mostly over when she noticed signs of an

enemy camp. She slowed her pace even more, watched every shadow, took each step with care. She was near the site where she'd encountered the camp years ago, stumbling lost in the dark. The soldiers by the fire then hadn't even noticed her, as she skirted around to the trail below the camp.

It had all felt…lax, she supposed was the word. Those had been soldiers with a task to do but no heavy responsibilities or significant fears. The mumblers didn't frequent the area, and wild beasts were no threat, more afraid of humans than humans were of them. The city of mumblers and untouchables hadn't even been founded. They were embroiled in the city-wide rebellion and counter rebellions, but even that had settled into a stalemate at the time, leaving them to keep watch for caravans using the trade route. A task with little real danger.

This would be different, she was sure. The tents were a lighter color than the shadows around them. Valni made out their pattern, rigid lines arranged tightly together. The fire was in a precise location, set off from the nearest tents but still close to everything. Gear hung perfectly organized, not even from the living branches that were all around, but from fallen logs that had been lashed to the trees. The opposite of lax.

This was a camp that would have more than one person keeping a careful watch, and they would be sticklers for the rules.

Valni crept back, tense for any cry of discovery.

There was no sense trying to get back to her camp in the lava beds before sunrise, so as the morning light began to creep over the mountains to the southeast, she looked for a thicker group of trees or other place to hide out. At least for the morning, until she had a better sense of what was around her. If all looked clear, she might dare to venture out later in the day.

Nothing looked promising. The lay of the land kept guiding her back toward the mudpots, thick with the smell of old eggs. She pulled her inner shirt over her mouth and walked on, now at a faster pace because of the coming light.

Where could she go?

Finally she gave up looking for a copse of trees and simply dropped down beside the steam beds. There was a low lip where the land that could support course grass dropped off to soil where nothing grew. She found a place where the chalky soil was cool and the grass above curved out. Half hidden from view, she lay there in wait.

When she'd lived in Pashun, the bells had sounded to bring in the day. Some months of the year, they rang well before the sun had risen, and other months long after. They'd also rung in the middle of the day once, a threnody for the death of the former High Prince. Valni tamped down the panic that rose as she thought of hearing the bells ring over and over.

It wasn't bells that woke the city this time. Martial trumpets broke the morning stillness, letting the people know that the day had officially begun.

There was even a sense...how to put it into words? She hadn't felt it in the ringing of the bells when she lived there, but the trumpets seemed to say that not only had the day begun but each of the people of Pashun had a task to do in response. The trumpets were a summons, a steam engine's whistle to set the people on their rigidly orchestrated tasks.

Valni knew arcist magic. Living in Chaitanshehar made it impossible to be unfamiliar with the effects of magic, the way it could manipulate people and arrange everything in a particular order.

There was magic in these trumpets. There was an arcist spell laid over the city, something perhaps as powerful as the spell that Pavresh had anchored into Chaitanshehar. It laid out a rigid order, a set of rules for the people of Pashun to follow.

She needed to stick around to better grasp what it meant for its people and what it meant for Mahendri's enmity with Jaritta's city.

And especially to understand what it meant about the fate of Pavresh and his team of infiltrators.

She crawled closer to the city, staying beside the lip of longer grasses and letting them cover her as much as they would. As she went, the arcist spell pulsed in her blood, a drumbeat calling her to march.

Remembering who she was, a falcon jati soldier in service to Jaritta and the city of Chaitanshehar, she could resist the call. She had to deliberately remember. Any thoughtless moment had her on the verge of rising up and marching straight into the city to do what must be done.

Whatever that was, she didn't know.

What had Pavresh done?

Had he cast his spell, only to find it didn't work as he'd intended? She certainly remembered the spell that had driven everyone to flee from the city when he tried to protect them through fear. He might make a mistake again. Except this military beat didn't have the feel of anything he would have intended. An unexpected side effect—that she could believe. But if he'd been trying to draw the people of Pashun toward the city and inspire them to stay nearby for the good of the city, then what did that have to do with this exacting discipline? The effects here felt deliberate.

And the signs weren't only right there in the city before her. The soldiers who'd camped close to Chaitanshehar had been summoned back at the same time. They'd left behind a casually organized camp, no doubt as fit the needs of their task. But they returned to rigidly arranged tents and camps. Valni had no way to know if they were the same soldiers out there and in the camp here, but the distinction stood out.

At just the time Pavresh's team was supposed to be creating a new spell anchored to Pashun, a unit had been summoned back, and the loosely arranged field camps had been exchanged for a perfectly spaced tent city of soldiers. A coincidence was possible...but unlikely.

Singing carried from the lower levels of the city. It wouldn't have been uncommon to hear someone break into song while they did their work, a song that rose from genuine joy or one to break the monotony of a tedious task. This, though, was a military kind of singing, many voices in unison. They sang because the singing itself was a task. Some likely found it tedious, and maybe even some found joy in singing together, but both reactions were of less importance than the simple act of joining in.

So what if it wasn't a mistake in the spell? Could Pavresh have betrayed Chaitanshehar? There was history between him and some of the others, a sense that he had betrayed them in the past, but as long as Valni had been in the city with him, she didn't think it possible that he could have done anything of the sort. He had become fully committed to the city when he came down that slope with a mass of beggars trailing along behind him. His spell was for the city, but it tied him into Chaitanshehar itself—anchored to the city, to the spell itself, and ultimately to the people there.

Valni didn't think there was any way Pavresh would turn on them and help their enemies.

After the singers fell silent, the pull of the magic drifted off. It should be permanent, like the one in Chaitanshehar. She was certain that was what Pavresh had intended with the spell he and Rashul had planned. There was no doubt this spell had weakened, just in the short time Valni had been creeping closer.

That argued against Pavresh helping the enemy. Mahendri and his arcists might be experimenting with their own version of Pavresh's spell. But for that to happen just at the same time that Pavresh and his team attempted to create their own effect, just at the time he had disappeared?

There was a connection between the two, one Valni couldn't figure out.

Over the next hour or so she continued to inch her way closer. The arcist effect grew weaker and weaker, but it still remained, a throbbing that never went away. The people of Pashun moved through the streets, up and down and along the edge of the steam beds. Did they still move with a sort of martial rigidity, or was she merely imagining that because of the power of suggestion? If anything, it looked like a city at peace, much more so than what she'd experienced years earlier.

The horse-drawn and oxen-drawn wagons came up to the city from the south, filled with ore and coal. There was a place on the road where every one of them suddenly shifted from what seemed a more relaxed way of following the road to a very precise and uniform approach. Valni couldn't see anything causing the change, but it was too regular to be simply imagination. Even this far across the face of the city, she could identify that much.

Either soldiers were stationed there and regulating the vehicles, or the magic still had some effect on that part of the city.

Closer to her, another road led away to the north, carrying goods bound for Romnai, the Silk City, and Jarnur. That route was blocked from view by the closer buildings and the lay of the land. It *used* to carry such goods, anyway. Valni didn't know how the conflict among the cities had affected such things. Some merchants, no doubt, found ways to carry the needed goods from place to place. Even in a simmering not-quite-a-war, some sort of trade surely went on.

Valni moved along parallel to the edge of the city, careful to avoid the deadly geysers and mudpots. There must be something she could observe to help answer the mystery and prepare Chaitanshehar for whatever would be coming their way next.

The trumpets sounded again through the city, as they had at dawn.

Valni stood straight up. She must get to the city and begin work on…something. She walked openly toward the steam bed edge of the city. The trumpets reverberated in her head, disrupting any attempt to think through what she should be doing. She cursed the volcanic impediments that slowed her approach to the city. Next time she wouldn't let herself get caught out there among the steam vents. She couldn't afford such carelessness when she was so desperately needed.

The trumpets ceased their glorious announcement. Valni

circled around a pool of mud and came to what looked like a more frequently used path. At last. She lengthened her stride.

Glancing down at her feet to keep from tripping on anything, she noticed a small carving in the rock. A scarab beetle.

She'd seen such a thing before. She'd been following carvings like those when she first heard the bells that mourned the High Prince's death. And later she'd followed the same route when she left Pashun.

Leaving Pashun.

It took thinking the words for Valni to come back to herself, to realize what she was doing. To remember who she was so she could resist the magic's pull.

Too late. "Hey, who are you?" A soldier's voice.

Standing at the edge of the lava field was a unit of soldiers. Were they the jati she'd known? For a moment she considered trying to bluff her way, as she'd done back then. She could learn what she needed to then, find out what had happened to Pavresh and Rashul and the others. But there was a distant drum beat that spoke of battle, of soldiers compelled to question strangers, arrest them, give them no quarter.

"What are you doing out there?"

"Looks like one of those untouchables," another said as they marched together toward her.

The time when spying was an easy lark for someone trained to fight was over.

Without giving the soldiers an answer, she turned around and ran back the way she'd come.

The scarab beetles were her guides. They marked a safe route through the lava beds. The routes were for training soldiers, so they weren't always straight or even the safest possible route, but she could be sure they wouldn't leave her at a dead end.

The pounding of feet came from the trail behind her. How many she couldn't guess. The scarabs led her on a twisting path that offered no chance to see any distance ahead or behind.

After avoiding a column of rock that looked ready to crumble beneath her weight if she leaned against it, she came to a curve that appeared to lead back toward the city. Valni glanced back. The entire squad of soldiers raced up the path toward her, three across and three by three behind them.

Leaving the path would probably be the best way to break up their organized pursuit.

She jumped over a fallen log, bleached white like the one she'd slept beneath. The colorful deposits beside a wide pool of water made the way ahead treacherous. She spared no glance back to know how her pursuers fared, but ran lightly as fast as she thought it safe.

Most likely she wouldn't be able to outdistance them. They knew the land far better than she did. She needed a place to take a stand, someplace where her training gave her the advantage. But was even that training enough to fight off an entire squad? A squad inspired and unified by arcist trumpets?

A stream flowed from the pool, lining its path with more salt-like deposits in various pastel shades. She ran beside it until it disappeared into a gaping hole in the ground. She leapt across and around the far side of that hole.

Ahead was a group of pillar-like structures with the same coloring as the pastel deposits. Maybe there she could make a stand. She dashed between two and through a short way and then stopped where two other pillars could protect her on each side, and the uneven ground promised no easy way around to get at her from behind.

The soldiers still came to her three abreast. They were no longer perfectly in lock step, perhaps because of the uneven footing, perhaps because they'd come far enough from Pashun to not feel the full effects of the spell. It still pulsed in Valni's veins, the memory of trumpets and the distant drumming, but not strongly.

Three soldiers at a time was easy. As soon as they came close enough, she stepped forward and flicked her walking staff out toward the middle soldier's head. When he flinched backward,

Valni crouched and inverted her swing, switching her grip halfway around so that the butt of the staff cracked into the leg of one of the other soldiers.

He fell, fouling up the two beside him.

Valni struck each of the other two with quick, sharp strikes. She wasn't sure if she'd killed either of them, but she didn't wait to see. She jumped back between her pillars before anyone could take aim with sling or arrow and raced through the pillars behind her. There was another pair of pillars that looked like an even better defensive position. She slowed for a moment and then ran on through.

If she tried the same tactic again, they'd simply riddle her with arrows from beyond the reach of her staff.

The pillars gave way to another stretch of open ground. A fumarole released a steady cloud of steam to one side. The air above it was so heavy it pushed the steam right back down toward the ground, forming a sort of stream of cloud-stuff, foul and brown, twisting along through the blasted rock waste. Valni swung around the other way.

A group of the Pashun soldiers stood right in her path.

A small portion of the unit chasing her that had gone around to intercept her. Only a handful, but too dangerous to fight in the open. Valni looked around wildly for any escape as the soldiers marched closer.

She edged toward the fumarole but then hung her head as if she gave up. She held up her hands in surrender, her staff still clutched loosely in one fist.

How many might she push into the fumarole before they could put up a defense? No, too risky. She was a falcon jati soldier, though, trained in a graceful form of fighting these common jatis couldn't even imagine. So as they came close to the roiling steam, she jumped toward it as well, placed her staff into the heart of the cloud, and vaulted over, pulling her staff behind her through the air.

She winced when she landed on the uneven ground and

twisted her knee awkwardly. Not enough to slow her, she prayed.

They ran toward her, but one cried out as the steam scalded his face. Valni was already running before that scream died away.

The remaining soldiers dithered on the other side of the steam. She saw one point back, around the fumarole. It would be easy for them to follow, though she had a good head start by now. The last she dared to look back they were still in the same place, as if trapped by the fear of the steam and the terror of the volcanism out here beyond any scarab-marked training route and the clear reach of the city's trumpets.

What next? She knew probably as much as she would be able to learn on her own. Pavresh's team had made it to Pashun. They'd made their attempt, but it had failed for reasons she couldn't guess. And now the city was controlled through arcist magic. What did that change mean for Chaitanshehar? Could she go back into the city and learn more? No. Leave that to Datri's spies. The real question was what she could do to prepare Chaitanshehar for whatever Pashun ended up doing. She had to assume those trumpet-controlled citizens wouldn't mean good things for the caste-less city.

Valni limped off into the mist of the lava field, seeing no sign of further pursuit as she left Pashun behind.

CHAPTER 7

Harkala took the helm of *The Dream of the Forgotten South* as they sailed through the shipyard and out beyond the breakwater. That much she could do, though she knew she was a figurehead captain and no more. Once the waves grew choppy, she handed the duty of steering over to Ekana.

A cannon, shot from somewhere above the harbor, celebrated their departure. Fishing vessels bobbed in a great crowd along the seaward side of the breakwater, bearing witness. There was even an oil fire blazing in an oversized lantern on the end of the pier, a call for the blessing of either the gods or the sacred fire. Or both, depending on the person.

The blessing of history.

A noise, a witness, and a blessing. With those three things and the supplies given them by the princes of Jarnur, they set out on this historic journey. Harkala waved to the people on the shore, waved to the boats bobbing at attention, and finally waved to the valley itself.

They were leaving the whole land behind, which felt like leaving an entire world. It shrunk behind them, as if it was never anything big, never anything important.

The crash of waves against the ship's hull forced Harkala to take her eyes away from the route they'd already taken. She needed to focus on the seas around them and the way forward. Wasn't that the way of life, anyway?

It would take them some hours to get beyond the seas plied by the Jarnur fishing vessels. They'd chosen a calm day, as calm as the waves ever were here. The wind blew lightly out to sea, and the tide would be heading out just at the time they were leaving the more familiar waters.

Harkala watched her crew as they performed their duties under Ekana's direction. She'd learned a good deal about sailing ships over the past few years and knew generally what commands to give in a calm sea like this. But she was happy to delegate the responsibility to Ekana, who'd basically grown up on fishing boats.

Sembaari was no more knowledgeable than Harkala was, relying only on what he'd learned the past few years. He was a good climber, though, and spent much of his time up in the rigging, keeping a lookout and monitoring the sails.

The others were all locals. They moved about the deck with ease, coiling rope, pulling on sails, watching for anything needing their attention. They might be accustomed to life on a ship, but this journey beyond the farthest breakers was one that had them each alert and watching for any signs of something worrying.

The ship creaked and groaned with the waves. The wind shifted but still pushed them out to sea. A flock of sea birds came beside them for a moment and shadowed their path before peeling away toward the waters to the north.

Were there better places for fishing in that direction? Maybe the Sacred Fire had sent the birds to guide her ship out of harm's way. That would be how it would go in a fable, but of course that wasn't how the real world worked, only the myths of simpler eras and people. She said nothing to Ekana, only watched as the birds circled back toward the shore.

Time passed slowly on the ocean. The sun moved as if through water, sluggish and too weak to warm them through the wind. Harkala pulled her great cloak tightly around herself.

"Breakers ahoy!" Sembaari finally called.

Harkala strained but couldn't see them yet. She took her place near Ekana.

The line of breakers were what kept the fishers of Jarnur from sailing farther. No one had crossed them, except perhaps for sailors who lost their bearings in storms and never returned. The near side was fairly well mapped, though, in the peculiar mapmaking style of the fishermen. So Ekana steered them northward a short ways to where he deemed the passage most likely to succeed.

A line of rocks caused the breakers, most of them not quite breaking the surface. The detailed maps of the fishers showed at least a single outer line of rocks and some hint of the visible reef beyond it, what seemed to be another ship-breaking cluster of rocks a short way beyond the outer barrier, a maze not built by people or gods, but the forces of water and stone. Where a gap showed between two of the rocks, their ship entered.

"Let out the drogue!" he called to the crew. This was a key part of the ship they'd built, though none of them knew exactly how it would work away from the calm waters of their many tests. The ships Harkala had uncovered from the ancient times had a peculiar arrangement near the stern, one that—if she was right in her conjectures—had held a long, buoyant device that would have dragged behind the ship to stabilize it as they passed through the rocks. They'd made theirs of sail-cloth and netting, stretched into a shape like a kite.

And now the entire crew trusted their lives to Harkala's guesswork and testing. A small boat on deck was meant as a last chance if the ship floundered. Harkala doubted it would be much better, in among those treacherous reefs, unless they ran into trouble before they'd even passed the first few sea rocks. She bit her lip as the waves crashed against each other, sending sea spray to fall like a heavy rain onto the deck.

The drogue slowed their progress, as anticipated. Their narrow hull let them fit behind a line of sea rocks without quite scraping the rocks beyond. They went slowly, the crew along the gunwales with long poles to push off the rocks at Ekana's orders. Each of them watched for any new gap to appear to let them go farther. There seemed to be no way through that next grouping. Time slowed ever further. Surely something would open up, some gods-blessed passage to guide them through. But no gap was safe enough, even for their narrow ship.

Water crashed against a rock up ahead, ending this brief back passage. Ending their attempt already.

"Maybe there's a break near there," Ekana called, pointing beside the bigger rock. His voice didn't hold out much hope.

Already Harkala could feel the failure, the reef staving in the ship's hull, the cold water crashing over their heads, pulling them all down. And history wouldn't remember them at all.

No, there must be some way forward! Other gaps farther south or north. Some overlooked way to get through.

"Ready the lifeboat," Ekana commanded, his voice too dead to carry. He repeated himself louder and added, "Just to be safe, in case we need it."

And then what? Maybe they could row themselves back through the gap they'd entered, or even find another gap small enough for the lifeboat. But would they even make it back to Jarnur?

Harkala looked out beyond the rocks toward shore. A line of fishing vessels had appeared. Waiting for them to fail. Ready to rescue them...and bring them back to Jarnur in shame.

That thought spurred her in a way the thought of death couldn't. She ran to the bow and looked down at the rocks. Then back to the rigging, where she climbed a short way up for a better view.

Nothing to be seen.

His voice resigned, Ekana called, "There's a gap back out toward shore up there. It might be tight, but we should be able to get through."

Better than wrecking.

But still a failure.

Harkala looked at the gap he'd found. It was incredibly narrow. "Are you sure—"

"We've come this far. The only way forward is to try it."

Harkala squinted. The pattern of the waves swam in and out of focus, but something drew her attention. "That still doesn't bring us back to the fishing ships, Ekana. There's another line of rocks beyond the gap."

Another line to separate them from safety. The futility beat against her. But it also meant another portion of the sea that the fishers didn't know, a new line of rocks where they might find an opening further out toward sea.

"Take it slow," Ekana said, seemingly to himself. The ship inched forward. He steered by rudder but also had two of the crew pulling on the drogue at different times to swing the ship by increments as it passed the deadly rocks. The others used their poles to ease them forward. The sails above strained and snapped as gusts rocked the ship.

"Everyone tie yourselves in!"

Harkala followed Ekana's command quickly, looping a rope behind her and across her chest before tying it to a ring in the deck. She expected Sembaari to come down and tie himself in on the deck as well, but he stayed in the rigging and secured himself directly to the ropes up there.

They came to the end. A massive rock jutted above even the highest waves, and the shoulders of the rock beneath the water made it much bigger and more deadly even than it appeared. Ekana steered them hard to starboard. Harkala found herself leaning that way, as if to help urge the ship to make the turn.

The port side scraped stone somewhere. Harkala held her breath for the sound of water rushing in.

No timbers snapped, and the scraping noise ceased as they curled through the gap and into another open channel, bounded on both sides by crashing waves.

"I see a way through!" Sembaari called from his perch. "Not much wider than we just went through, but looks clear beyond that. No shadows in the water."

With his directions, they edged between two more of the sea rocks, relying mostly on the poles to follow his instructions. The crashing waves made it impossible to see for what felt like a long time. How could Ekana guide them here? He must simply be trusting in Sembaari's description of the location of the opening in the rocks and in his ability to judge exactly where the ship was traveling.

There was again a brief scraping noise, not as bad as the last, and then the spray cleared.

Open water spread before them. The high seas at last.

Harkala's heart raced, but instead of fear it was with relief.

"We've made it through! Oh, excellent work everyone! Thank you. And *Dream of the Forgotten South*, thank you as well!"

Ekana only shook his head. "We haven't made it through yet. Only through the part we already knew. It's the unknown rocks ahead that may be the worse threat." He pointed toward more sea spray and the white peaks of distantly breaking waves.

While her heart sank, he added, "But this was an excellent start, and we need to rest from that. Keep the net out, set all our sea anchors, and furl the sails." As the crew set to work lowering the anchors, he said, "And get what sleep you can manage out here. We'll all need to be alert for what's to come."

***

After a brief rest taken in turns, during which the ship bobbed on the waves while scarcely moving, they raised the sails and made their slow way westward. The sun set with them still approaching another line of breaking waves ahead.

"Drop the sails again," Ekana commanded. "All lanterns out. When you're awake, you're watching for any change. In how close the rocks are, in waves, in wind."

Staying awake was easy at first, with nerves tingling and every thought on where the rocks were and how the ship sat in the water, how high the waves, how fast the wind. She looked constantly from one anchor line to another then back at the net.

When the adrenaline faded, all this extra attentiveness left her drained. She tried to record an account of their passage in her field book, but her pen kept trailing off across the pages. Her eyelids drooped, snapping open when salt spray splashed her face. After that she paced the deck until her watch was over.

When morning came, they had drifted back, closer to the rocks than Ekana liked. He'd been one of the two who were last on watch, so he had no one to blame but himself. That didn't stop him from shouting at everyone as they got moving.

They pulled the anchors nearest the rocks and brought up the sails, and the ship began drifting away from danger. Just as Harkala breathed more easily, the ship jolted, and she fell forward. There was an awful shrieking sound of the hull scraping against something beneath them. Then with another shuddering jerk, it sailed free.

"Sembaari, watch for anything in the water!" Then Ekana gestured to Harkala. "Take the wheel, Captain. I'm going below to look at the damage."

Harkala steered them slowly away from the rocks, alert for any hidden dangers that Sembaari might miss. There was a shadow in the water, and she nearly spun the wheel to avoid what she feared was another rock. But then the shadow twisted on itself and swam sedately away, its single fin cutting the surface of the water.

What a fool to think she could be in charge of an expedition like this. Jumping at shadows! If she'd turned to avoid that, she would have probably run them straight into one of the real rocks. She gritted her teeth and stared forward. Quick thinking and quick action were important, but she had to force herself to not react to mere nothings.

Ekana returned, his face grim.

"What's it look like?"

He shrugged. "Holding, for now. I placed a brace there to be sure." He took the wheel from her and shaded his eyes with one hand. "One of our fishing vessels would have been filling with water by now. Not a flood, maybe, but at least leaking. I don't understand why it works, but this design of the ancients is holding up better than I expected."

The design of the ancients. *Her* design. She allowed herself a brief smile, then asked, "What was it, could you tell?"

"Submerged rock. I saw that before I even went below. A ridge of some kind, under the surface but not far enough below." He shook his head. "Sembaari should have seen it. That's his job."

They had easy sailing for a while after that. Ekana even had them pull in the drogue for half the morning. Always in front of them was that other line of breaking waves, taunting and warning them. What openings there were, if any, was a mystery. The waves seemed to froth out in the ocean beyond that point.

Harkala ate a meal of hard tack and cheese followed by a small, shriveled fruit that one of the crew claimed was a ward against sickness on board a ship. She didn't taste any of it.

Ekana steered them northward where the spray looked somewhat more muted. They slowed around mid-morning as they came near the spray of the breakers. No rocks reached above the surface of the water, but there was no question that they lay just beneath it, ready to tear the ship to pieces.

Ice floated around them, little chunks here. Harkala knew from stories that farther north the ice chunks grew until they filled almost the entire sea. A ship, even one designed to survive these difficult waters, wouldn't do much good in such a place.

Sembaari kept his lookout from the rigging, and another of the crew dangled a rope from the bow to check for any obstructions.

"Not seeing much from here." Sembaari called down. "The reef is almost solid."

Their route on this side of the breakers began curving back toward Eghsal, so Ekana turned the ship around before the space was too small for such a maneuver. For several hours they continued south, skirting the edge of the reef. It swung out away from shore, which seemed like a good sign. Maybe they wouldn't even need to cross it. They could just sail due south from here.

That hope ended shortly after when a promontory appeared at the horizon, cutting them off that way. It looked like an island, but apart from one peak covered in seabirds, most of it was submerged. That underwater portion spread out to meet with the various rocks, to both the east and west, as if the island was simply an overgrown portion of the same geography.

"It comes to this," Ekana announced. "We're committed this far, so we might as well see it through. Find us a way past, Sembaari."

"I think there might be one, actually. There's a trough of deeper water not too far from that peak."

"Lead the way, then. Or rather, tell me where." Ekana steered the ship, following Sembaari's instructions.

Deeper blue water opened up before them, marking the trough Sembaari thought he'd seen.

"What's the mark?" Ekana asked. "Is it real?"

The crewman Neelar bent over the rope. "It is getting deeper." A moment later he added, "And still deeper. We have plenty of depth here. I might run out of rope."

"It's pretty narrow," Ekana said.

Harkala traced the line of deeper blue out beyond the breakers. It promised a pathway, a route to the Forgotten South. "What choice do we have now?"

Ekana gave a grudging nod. "Brace yourselves, everyone. And tie in. We'll take it slow and hope the braces below hold if we do scrape."

And if not? At least this time they had land close by. Hardly a space to live, and likely insufficient water and food to survive on. Still, it felt better to risk wrecking here than far out to sea where even the strongest swimmer wouldn't stand a chance of reaching shore.

Harkala tied herself to the metal ring on the deck and waited. The spray that fell on the edge of her cloak turned to frost.

Birds from the peak rose in a huge mass, squawking at their passage. A few came out far enough to investigate them, landing in their wake. They scavenged for food in the waters disturbed by their passage. No doubt the drogue turned the water in a way that brought many sea organisms to the surface. Harkala spared the thought to wish them well, to hope they found the food they needed. Then she took her eyes away from them and watched the trough narrow around their little ship.

Ekana took them as near the center as they could. Sembaari pointed out a protrusion just below the surface on one side, so they squeezed by on the other. Harkala gritted her teeth, but there was no scraping sound this time.

The waves crashed to starboard against a rock they couldn't see. They crashed to port against the island, farther away but still a threat because of the submerged shelf that sloped outward.

She was so sure they would scrape at some point, that she didn't at first believe they'd made it through. There must be more, must be some deadly rock yet ahead. But the ship pulled past the last line of the reef and skirted the island. All she could see was the sea—endless waves and emptiness with no sign of other reefs or dangerous shoals as far as the horizon.

Beyond that horizon, the South. The Discovered South. So soon, so close. Maybe many days and many sea leagues away, but they'd done it. They'd escaped the Eghsal Valley and could finally learn what there was to discover of the lands and seas beyond its known limits.

As they tacked toward open sea away from the island, another cloud of birds took flight. They flashed in the weak sunlight, all whites and blacks and grays. They flew toward the ship and descended right on the drogue where it dragged through the water.

"Pull it in!" Ekana commanded.

The birds squealed and complained to each other, a cacophony that made it impossible to think. Harkala unhooked herself and rushed over to help the crew haul on the frame of netting and sailcloth as fast as they could.

A bird with its foot caught came squawking over the railing. Harkala twisted the rope to release the bird. As soon as it was free, it flew straight at her. Harkala dropped the net and covered her head with her arms as the bird flew away.

The birds kept pecking at the ropes as they pulled it in, finding the creatures caught in the fibers. Harkala ran at the birds to shoo them away while the rest of the crew kept pulling. They finally got it out of the water and the birds away. Many returned to the island. Others bobbed in the waves behind them, and a significant number still circled above the ship.

"How badly is it damaged?" Ekana asked. "Here, Harkala. You take the helm. I'll inspect it."

There were no obstacles ahead, so Harkala simply kept them going straight. Ekana spent a long time examining the net, and without it to brake them, they sped along as fast as they'd sailed since their launch. The birds fell back one by one and returned to their barren rock home.

The wind remained from the east, picking up. They scudded along southwestward before it, the sails bulging out due west. Harkala scanned the horizon for storms or signs of any distant, unknown islands. Nothing visible yet. For all they knew, there might be many islands in the area, or they might sail south for days and see nothing, only the shoreline of their own southern mountains.

And when would *those* open up to allow the ship to come close to shore? Nobody had any idea where that would be or what they would find. Harkala thrilled to imagine it.

"Not destroyed at least," Ekana finally declared. "I wouldn't want to head back through rocks like those we've been through without mending it. It might disintegrate if we leave it in the water long. But if we need to use it briefly, we should be able to."

Harkala saw some weakened points where holes in the sailcloth had opened up. Seaweed draped from the net where the birds hadn't picked it clean. The ropes were beginning to freeze. That might make for a more difficult time getting it into the water, if they needed it fast. Harkala didn't feel especially cold, though, and some of the ice appeared to be dripping from the nets, melting rapidly. A breath of warmer air here swept over them.

"Why are we going west now?"

They weren't. They were heading... Harkala looked ahead again. They did seem to be swinging around to the west. The sails bellied straight ahead. "I guess the wind got behind us.

I'm sorry." She turned the wheel, but the ship didn't change direction.

"Here, let me." Ekana took over and spun the wheel hard. The ship jerked for a moment as if trying to obey, but then it kept on curving around to the west. In fact, they were heading more north than west now, entirely the opposite direction from the Forgotten South.

"What's happening?"

Ekana grimaced and turned the wheel back. "Check the sea. I think we're caught in a current."

Harkala looked over the edge, but the waves told her nothing. They were a jumble, some swept up by the wind, some at cross ways to it.

"I'll try to steer us out, but I have no idea how wide this current is."

A current from the south carrying warmer air. When she thought the words, it suddenly fit with what she already knew. She'd always been told that was why Jarnur was warmer than the inland areas. Romnai and Pashun were only habitable because of the volcanic activity beside them. The Silk City as well. Jarnur had none of that to warm it, but it did have the air currents over the ocean. And now they were caught in the accompanying water current.

How wide must such a current be to bring that much warm air?

Ekana was steering them back to the west. Trying to.

"We'll never get out of it going this way, Ekana. Take us east to escape it." They might have to cross the current again to go south, but if so, they could choose a better place and a better angle and be prepared. If they kept battling here, she could see that they would simply be swept along into the icy northern seas.

"We've made it this far. I won't turn back." Ekana's jaw clenched as he hauled on the wheel. He made the words *turn back* into some sort of curse, something more than the resignation she'd heard back before they made through the first line of breakers. "I can get us through."

He had a strange look in his eyes, as if a touch crazed by what was happening. She'd never seen him like this before.

"Ekana. It doesn't mean turning back. We just need to get out of the current."

He didn't seem to hear her. As if to himself, he muttered, "Put your hand to the wheel, you have to see it through. Even if things go bad."

A chunk of ice sloshed away from the bow. Bigger chunks bobbed up ahead. The current was warm, but it cut into frozen seas, and they couldn't risk ending up there. A piece of ice the size of their lifeboat floated into their path ahead and then turned in the direction they were going. But not as fast as them.

"Step aside, Ekana. I'm taking the wheel."

As if the crew would back her against him, a knowledgeable sailor. As if she had any real hope of getting them out of the current, except for a hunch.

Sembaari leaped down from the rigging and approached them. What was he going to do, lead a mutiny, tie her up? She certainly didn't have the physical strength to face down even a single member of the crew. But instead he held his hands out toward Ekana in a calming motion and spoke words in a language Harkala didn't know.

Ekana's hands clenched even harder, and he avoided looking at either of them, but after a moment his shoulders drooped, and he took a step back, offering to let her take over without releasing the wheel until she was ready to hold it.

The helm wrenched at her arms when he did let go, nearly knocking her to the deck. She braced her legs and wrestled it to the starboard. The current fought her. She let the ship run north on its own and then tried again to ease them away from the current.

She had it. She could feel the ship beneath her starting to escape. Just a moment more.

"Rock ahead!" Sembaari called.

Harkala panicked. She couldn't steer in this. She should do something with the sails, but she didn't know what. More sails? Lower them? She tried again, pulling harder on the wheel, just a little farther to starboard. She tried to will it over.

And they passed it by, whatever it was. Harkala didn't spare a moment to look. The prow was again swinging back into the current, so she angled eastward once more, where the chunks of floating ice bobbed in place—colder water and dangerous for that fact, but calm and still. Just then, the current took its revenge on her. The stress on the rudder was too much. It cracked, snapping the connection to the helm.

The current grabbed hold of the stern and spun it, inexorably. Harkala tried vainly to steer away from it, but the wheel did nothing.

The ship sailed north and west, out of control, away from everything she had hoped to discover.

Away from the still-forgotten South.

CHAPTER 8

Hunger pangs were supposed to make a person stronger. Jaritta knew it wasn't true when she thought the matter over. She had plenty of experience with hunger. A beggar on the streets of Romnai, an untouchable in the ruins of old Eghsal City, a refugee crossing the wilderness to this new city. So she well knew how hunger could make your body slow and your mind unreliable.

But even so, a part of her wanted to wear her hunger as a sign of pride. Going without food proved her commitment to the city of Chaitanshehar. It proved how she put the citizens of her city ahead of her own comfort. But starving did her no good, not herself, not her nursing daughter or the rest of her family, and not the people of her city.

"Fine," she answered her consort Ellechandran's worried urging. "I *will* eat, honest I will." She took a small cake made of crushed nuts, seeds, and dried fruit. It was sweet and crunchy, and she savored its flavor, making it last as long as she could. Savored the way Chandri watched her eat, the concern for her clear in his eyes. It still felt strange that someone would love an untouchable. "But I need to know what the status of our food is."

"I've been telling you—"

"No, I need to *see* the stores we have left and see what we're bringing in on a typical day."

Chandri picked up Nataravi and swooped her through the air for a moment before gesturing for her to follow him. "Come, then. You can see what there is."

Jaritta carried Ovitiva on her hip and followed.

There were no protests in the streets. At least she had that to console herself with. Her people were hungry, but they weren't rioting. She and the other leaders had been forthcoming with the people about their challenges. They'd seen the smoke of the fields below. Most even knew someone who had rushed down to try to salvage what food they could. The city was small, and the people knew and trusted her. They remembered the history and were a part of it.

There would come a day when most of that wasn't true. If the city lasted another decade, another generation, would they have grown to the size of Pashun and Romnai? Would people begin to forget the past so soon? Would they mistrust the stories and reports they were given?

If that happened, then Pavresh's spell might still prevent any protests. It wove people into a vision for the city's future, made them feel a part of the ideal city they were building. And if that meant no protests...by coercion? Jaritta couldn't say if that *was* for the best. Maybe they would come to regret Pavresh's magic and how it affected everyone in the city.

Chandri led the way into a cave not too far upslope from their chambers. The city had come together haphazardly, and the caves had been one of the things that made this site attractive. Someday they'd likely build an entrance around the cave mouth so that it seemed more like just another building. For now it was an open gash in the face of the city, and yet scarcely stood out amidst the disarray.

Huge wooden bins filled the back wall of the cave. Jaritta breathed a sigh of relief at the sight. Food was tight, but at least they had some staples left to get them through until they could harvest more. There should be lentils in one, rice in another. She'd observed the careful preservation techniques of the mumblers as they taught the people of Chaitanshehar to dry out their berries and vegetables even when the sun's rays were too thin for the task.

Her mouth watered at the thought of honey-dried mango and salted slices of dried squash. Even the leaders of the city hadn't eaten such foods for months.

The first bin held rice. Some rice. She could see the bottom of the bin in one place, and even where the rice came higher along the sides, it didn't fill much of the space.

"That's...not very much."

She leaned over the second, and this one was much fuller. Red lentils, one of the crops that had been spared the soldiers' fire attack. Jaritta ran her fingers through them, letting them spill down when she lifted her hand back up. "Something, at least. And filling." Though it was difficult to make a satisfying meal on lentils alone.

The next bin was empty. A few dried up leaves lay on the bottom, and those might be useful for adding a peppery flavor to other foods. They would have originally been wrapped around nuts or mixed into bread dough, but all that was gone from the bin. The nuts wouldn't even have come from the fields. They were harvested on the slopes up above the city and traded for with the mumblers.

"Why is *this* one so empty?"

"Demand." Chandri reached his long arm in and pulled a leaf up. It cracked, and he handed a piece to Nataravi then offered the rest to Jaritta. "Everyone wants the nuts to make their dishes."

Nataravi made a face at the sour flavor of the plain leaf but ate it anyway. Jaritta knew she should do the same, so she dutifully took it and chewed. Its flavor was mostly gone, and it made her thirsty more than anything.

The rest of the cave had smaller stores as well. Jars of oil sat on one shelf, and spices hung from the ceiling to dry. A smaller cave partially cut off from the first felt colder. Hanging from its ceiling were a handful of dried or drying carcasses. Deer meat mostly, enough venison to feed a few people, but so little for an entire city.

She leaned against Chandri and waited for his solid presence to hold her up, to remind her she wasn't alone. He hugged her with his free arm.

"And this is everything?"

"Well, every family is encouraged to keep some stores in their own dwellings. And their own gardens, if they managed to grow anything." Jaritta and Chandri's garden had been an embarrassing strip of plants that ended up giving almost nothing edible, despite the work Jaritta had put into it. "So we hope there's more than this throughout the city."

"But not a lot more," Jaritta finished for him. "Not anywhere near enough." They made their way back to the cave entrance in silence. No guard at the entrance. In theory, the arcist spell made that unnecessary. Stealing from the common stores went against the ideal of working toward the success of the city.

But that was theory. When hunger became strong enough, would any magic spell hold? She would have to give that some thought.

"I want to see the fields now." She hadn't attempted to descend the slope in ages, and the girls never had. "I suppose we'll need to have an arcist to help us go down. Do you think the girls are safe with us? Or should we leave them with someone here?"

Chandri tousled Ovitiva's curly hair as he considered, then said, "Leave them. Maybe with Azheeran's family? We'll make sure we're not gone too long."

Jaritta might have picked Poorma, who was her old friend from Chaitan's, but she agreed. It was typical of Chandri that he thought of a mumbler family to babysit. And equally typical of Jaritta, she supposed, that her first thought was someone from Romnai.

A short time later, the beggar-turned-arcist Juishika was leading the two of them down the switchbacks below the city wall. Azheeran, who had decided to accompany them while his family watched the girls, descended with them. The ground below was dark with the charred remains of the fields. A faint sheen of light green just teased at the edges of her vision, but wherever she looked directly, all she could see was ash.

When they met up with the more direct stairs, Jaritta said, "Let's continue on the switchbacks. I want a better chance to see it all laid out below us."

Back and forth they went, and Jaritta studied the fields the whole way. Not a mature plant to be seen. Even the pine trees to the north had been scarred by the fire. Blackened remains that might have been trees gave way to dead trunks, which gave way to the charred survivors. Already twisted by winds and dark winters, those trees stood sentinel over the fire scars.

When they finally reached the bottom, Jaritta bent to touch the seedlings. "It's the wrong time of year for planting, isn't it?" Even she knew that much, despite never working on a farm or owning a garden before coming here.

Chandri reluctantly nodded. "Yes, they won't be getting much sun soon. At least the swamp keeps them warm, so we might be able to harvest something. We chose the plants that need the least sunlight."

Doubtful. She could hear that in his voice. And even if they did, what would they do until then? This was a desperation crop, the fastest growing thing they had, but even then, with the stores they had remaining, they might not have enough to make it to harvest time.

"We need more," she said at last. "How? Where?"

Azheeran stalked among the little shoots, carefully stepping where nothing grew as he paced back and forth. "This is worse than I realized. Maybe there's more back by the old ruins."

Back in old Eghsal City? "You can't be thinking..." Jaritta couldn't even finish the words. Going back meant abandoning her dreams. Even if it was only for a short time. Even if it was only to bring back food. What if, once the magic loosened its grip, no one could find their way back?

What if no one wanted to?

"We always had fish there. And crops. Not organized like this and left untended for years now. But there may be something worth harvesting. I'll bring a sleigh and carry back as many frozen fish and other foodstuffs as we can get. Maybe we'll even meet some others of my people who might be willing to supply us as well."

Not abandoning, but she still hated the idea of anyone going back to Eghsal City, to the old familiar places. Anywhere was better than there. "We? Who all would you bring with you?"

Azheeran frowned. "I want my family to stay. There's no reason to put them through such a journey. I'll pick, let's say five or six. Strong, good travelers. We can be back before the snow begins in earnest."

Taking away some of their protection at a time when Pashun's plans were so uncertain. The news Valni had brought from that city had them all on edge, wondering what they had in store. Martial trumpets and arcist aggression. She dreaded the possibilities.

But still, it was the right move. They needed food more desperately than they needed those few extra people on hand to work, to hunt, and potentially to fight.

She was about to say as much, when Azheeran said, "Ellechandran, you would be a good and welcome part of any such band. Your keen eye might find foods we'd miss. Would you consider accompanying me and my sleigh?"

Jaritta froze.

Taking Chandri away from her? Leaving her alone with the girls? How did Azheeran even dare suggest it? And would Chandri... No, never.

She didn't dare meet his eyes or Azheeran's. For the first time in what seemed years, her hand crept up to pull the extra loop of fabric on her dress up to cover the old burn scar on her face. It was the old nervous habit, a clear sign of how deeply she was doubting herself.

Slowly, Chandri answered, as if still unsure. "I...I will do whatever the leaders of the city ask me to do. If it's what's best for the future of Chaitanshehar, then I will go."

Jaritta squeezed her eyes shut and breathed deeply through her nose to stay calm. If it were anyone else but her own consort, she would be putting the idea down instantly. But she recognized that the decision couldn't seem to come from her—not for Ellechandran's sake, and not for the sake of her status as a city leader, one who served the city instead of ruling it.

"But I would rather not. I don't wish to leave my family. And I think I can serve the city best by staying here. With them."

Jaritta still couldn't speak or open her eyes, but she reached out, knowing without sight exactly where to find him, and squeezed his hand.

Azheeran may have made some motion she didn't see, but when he spoke it was in the mumbler trade pidgin, not to exclude her since she had learned the language, but instead it seemed to create a touch of intimacy, a tenderness Azheeran seldom displayed when speaking the language of the people of Eghsal. "I understand. And I think it's a wise choice."

Jaritta cleared her throat and opened her eyes. "Thank you," she whispered. And in her mind she was thanking her husband as well as Azheeran for his tenderness and the land itself. She released a deep breath that held much more than air. "Now let's get back up to the girls."

***

The twelve-days passed slowly. Jaritta made sure her family ate no more than others and stretched what they had as much as she could. Ellechandran cooked lentils in the mumbler way, and she added other foods and flavorings to make it more familiar. Nataravi ate either without complaint. At least they didn't have to worry about her needing any special or different foods. Ovitiva had just begun to taste bits of their food from their plates—the softest lentils, some mashed up squash, and rice, kernel by kernel.

The bin full of lentils dropped noticeably, day after day. The other bins were already empty or down to scraping the bottom.

When would Azheeran return?

It was Chhayasheela who came back first, from her visits to the mumbler tribes in the south. She and a group of other mumblers were away from the city more often than not, doing the rounds to as many local villages as they could reasonably visit. Her arrival now felt like a good sign. She breezed in with a fanfare of mumbler drums and flutes—simple whistles that played only two different notes. People came to their doors to cheer, and to each house she gave a bag of food. A *small* bag of food.

Jaritta watched from in front of the city's chambers for evidence they brought more food. Great sacks of mushrooms and smoked meat, perhaps? A sled piled with mountain tubers? They appeared to have a little extra to spare but not much.

Jaritta went forward to meet Chhayasheela. Chandri walked a step behind her, and Poorma came from across the street to join them.

"Welcome," Jaritta said in the trade pidgin. "I see you've been able to bring in some food."

Chhayasheela grimaced and answered in the same language. "Not as much as I would have liked. The drums and whistles are to make it seem exciting. I was afraid people would be dejected if we didn't have some extravagance to go with it."

Most of the townspeople didn't speak the pidgin, at least not well yet, but Jaritta gestured for them to go inside before they continued the conversation. It was what she'd begun to suspect, seeing their arrival, but disappointing nonetheless.

Inside they sat on cushions in a cluster. The workers who helped in the chambers—Jaritta resisted the urge to think of them as cheetah jati servants, because Chaitanshehar didn't have servants, any more than it had the castes of the other cities—served them very watery tisane. Nothing to go with it to eat.

"First," Jaritta began, "thank you for your efforts. Every bit of food we bring in will help us get through this season. We need anything we can get."

Chhayasheela accepted the praise with a brief gesture and said, "But you want to know why there isn't more, I suppose?"

"Yes." Jaritta liked Chhayasheela. She was her husband's former wife, but they still got along well. "What have you found? Do the villages simply not have enough to trade?"

"That's part of it, for sure. The villages here survive but rarely have excess food. So I got everything I could from most of the villages I visited. Going back to them would achieve little."

"*Most* of them. So tell me about the rest. Is there a chance we could get more?"

"We just have so little to offer in exchange. We don't have food to trade or we'd be eating that. We have some metal goods, but not enough to make a big trade. Other goods? They have plenty of furs and leather. Plenty of bow strings. Sling bullets only get us so far when pebbles are free and nearly as effective. The only reason they might want more is if they're going to war."

"And I'm afraid we don't have more to offer, do we? A promise of our undying friendship probably doesn't go as far as we might like," Poorma said, shaking her head sadly. "It sounds like we're stuck going to even farther villages, hoping for better trade."

Chhayasheela was silent as if weighing her answer.

Jaritta leaned forward. "It looks like you have more to say. You have some different idea, Sheela?"

She nodded, but it was a hesitant nod. "Maybe. I mean I already said it. *Only if they're going to war.* Well, what if they're going to war?"

"You want us to attack and then offer weapons? Oh, that's not it, is it?" Jaritta leaned back in her cushion to consider what Sheela was saying. "You want us to prod them into fighting against Pashun. Doubly good for us, if we can trade them sling bullets and other weapons for the food we need now, while they harass our own enemies. It protects us later."

And went against the grand picture she had for the way their city worked. To turn themselves into a city that benefits from war? Pavresh would have spoken against it. He would have used some truth about arcist magic to show why it was wrong. But Pavresh wasn't there, and his last scheme for arcist magic had ended in uncertainty and likely disaster.

"It isn't as if they need a lot of prodding. Skirmishes with the Pashun soldiers are always happening. All they'd need would be some weapons. And they still see us as the same people as Pashun. City people have always banded together when it came to a choice between each other and the mumblers. So we would have to offer some kind of assurance that we wouldn't retaliate for attacking Pashun's soldiers, that they would have our blessing even."

Datri would say to do it. She probably wouldn't even hesitate. Use an enemy's weakness. If Datri had to distill her ethos into a single phrase, that would have been it.

And Chhayasheela wanted to do it. She tried to make it seem like this was her reluctant conclusion, but she wanted her people, her former people to take up arms and fight the people of Pashun. She couldn't completely suppress her own eagerness to spark a new front in the war with Pashun.

Jaritta couldn't respond. What would it mean for the city to be known for supporting warfare, and not only fighting but encouraging mumbler fighters to take arms against another of the cities of the Eghsal Valley? She was enough of a creation of her birth jati and culture to hesitate at that, no matter who her beloved husband was and what heritage her children claimed. But what would it mean for the city to starve? An end to everything, that was what it meant.

"I support it," she said even as Ellechandran was saying, "I don't think that's wise."

The door opened at that moment, and Datri herself came walking in. Her clothes were shapeless and dark, a far cry from her silk jati origins. The plainness seemed intended to remind everyone that she and her spies hid in shadows and were seldom seen. But it did nothing to hide the high-caste beauty of her face, careworn as it was. Light shone off her dark hair, as if she'd added tiny diamonds in among the strands.

"Ah, was I not invited to this meeting?" Her mock outrage faded in a moment behind a superior smile and a dismissive wave of her hand. "There is word from my agents in Pashun. They don't know exactly what's happening. I think there's a spell interfering with their thinking much of the time. But their soldiers are gathering in large numbers and preparing to march. Or preparing for something. No one seems to understand what."

Into the silence that followed, Poorma declared, "No better time than now to create for ourselves some well armed allies."

While they argued and discussed for over an hour longer, Jaritta knew it was already decided then. Their peaceful city would become the ones supplying weapons and assistance to the enemies of her own people.

But then, her own people were already her enemies, and the last few years of peace didn't mean the war they chose to start when she founded the city had ever really ended.

Later she tried to explain all this to Chandri, but he put his finger on her lips. "Hush. I know. I understand just like you do. This is the only way to save our city. I just don't like it, that's all." He put his arms around her and held her to him. So solid, so able to notice the things that mattered.

An idea had been teasing at the edges of her mind ever since they'd made their decision. That was the part she really didn't like, but as he stepped away from their embrace to pick up their daughter, she blurted it out. "That's why you should go with her."

"What?" He pulled Ovitiva close to his chest.

Jaritta closed her eyes. Was she really suggesting this? "Sheela *wants* to set them fighting. This isn't just her reluctantly suggesting it. She tells herself otherwise, but it's what she really wants." A new mumbler war, and Jaritta's dream city caught between sides, likely to be torn apart.

Jaritta gently took Ovitiva from Chandri and snuggled her face. "And maybe we have no choice, but I can see her going too far, committing us to a fight we'll have no way to win. That's why…" She swallowed hard. "That's why you'll need to be there."

Chandri stared at her. "But I can't leave you behind. It's just like before. Remember what I told—"

"I know, I do remember. And I don't want you to go at

all. My..." She swallowed hard. Sending him, her lover and husband, to travel with his former wife into danger and war. How had this come about? "My selfish wish is that you'd stay. But for the city, for its future, you need to go and be my voice. Keep us from committing worse acts than those Pashun pursues against us."

She couldn't speak any more. She closed her eyes over her tears and leaned into Chandri's fierce embrace. When she could get the words out, she said in a fierce whisper, "And do whatever it takes so my city doesn't starve. I don't really care what you promise, as long as it lets us survive."

CHAPTER 9

Arcist magic had no effect on metal bars. Not that Pavresh hadn't tried. He told them stories of doors that had opened by magic, folk tales of doors leading to new lands, to freedom. Nothing he did could bend them or make them swing open on their own.

If he'd had the chance, he might have convinced a guard to set him free, but his cell didn't even require a guard. Kamlak came to visit him, when necessary, usually alone and sometimes accompanying some city official asking him questions. Kamlak brought him food and water every day and brought him cleaning supplies once in a while, leaving it to Pavresh to keep his own cell clean. Sometimes he brought two gourds of tisane, which they sat and shared. It seemed a way for Kamlak to gloat, though most of the time they sipped their tisanes in silence.

Kamlak was too experienced to be tricked by Pavresh's magic.

In fact, he was far more expert than he'd let himself appear when he'd pretended to learn in Pavresh's school. He'd resisted Chaitanshehar's welcoming spell, which alone spoke to his power over arcist magic, and hidden who he was. And when he'd overheard the plans for Pavresh to go to Pashun for his ill-fated quest, he'd used magic to convince Pavresh to take him along.

That much Pavresh had put together, when he wasn't mourning Rashul and the rest of their group. Could Rashul truly be dead? His voice was still so alive in Pavresh's mind that he had a hard time crediting that truth. Yet at the same time, the images of that night left no doubt. Rashul had died, and the others had likely been killed as well. And throughout that journey across the city, Kamlak had manipulated them.

One time when Kamlak brought food, Pavresh asked, "Who taught you arcist magic, anyway?"

Some days Kamlak was willing to spend time talking with Pavresh, though it was always a condescending willingness. There couldn't be many other arcists in Pashun, and likely no one anywhere near his and Pavresh's level of command of the magic. This time, Kamlak only sneered at him. "You haven't figured out who I am yet, have you?"

Then he went on his way.

It gave Pavresh a mystery to contemplate. Should he have recognized Kamlak from some earlier time? He hadn't been at Chaitan's. There were others who used arcist magic there, others learning it from the master and discoverer of the magic. Pavresh took care to think through each of those people, men and women who had performed their magic while Namrani and others played music, and people like Indima and Ekana danced.

None of them could have aged into the devious Kamlak. Most of them had already been older, back then. The dozen years would have left a greater mark on any of them, after they were forced to flee Chaitan's house and go their separate ways.

Pavresh missed that way of using magic. It had been pure and exciting, something new and good for the city. Now Chaitan was dead, Indima stuck in her role as a sacred dancer, and Ekana twice the betrayer. And the city of Romnai, from every story he'd heard, was a ruined wasteland of soldiers in the streets and fear in the houses.

In such a setting as Chaitan's old house used to be, arcist magic could tell a beautiful story. It enhanced the dancing, twined with the music—and with Rashul's idealism, but Pavresh swallowed the lump in his throat and forced himself to set that part of his memories aside—and created an art unlike any other.

But if Kamlak was none of those artists of performative magic, what other arcists had Pavresh known? He'd learned the magic from a miner in his father's mine. He couldn't entirely picture the man any more, it was true. So many years and so many faces had come in between.

There was something fitting in the idea that Kamlak might

be the person who first trained him, as if it fit an arcist theme. The man who'd first shown him how to manipulate arcist threads, drawing on the stories the miners told each other and the fears of darkened tunnels, the threats of weakening support beams. There was an arcist completeness in the idea of the same man showing up now, as an enemy. But that didn't make it true. Pavresh was sure he would recognize the miner. And it was not Kamlak.

Pavresh paced for most of an afternoon before it came to him. When he'd spied for Prince Jasfer—the late Prince Jasfer, by all accounts—Pavresh wasn't the only arcist in their assemblies. Prince Dartak had been the charismatic spokesman for the group of princes who'd concocted a plan to crack down on the city's malcontents. One of his cheetah jati servants had used arcist magic to make the prince seem impressive and his arguments wise.

If their plot had succeeded, Dartak would have set himself up as High Prince. The cheetah jati servant could have had immense power as his advisor. Instead, Dartak had been stripped of all his power, and the cheetah jati servant... Pavresh had never bothered to wonder what became of the man. Could he have found a new way to seek power, attaching himself to Mahendri?

Pavresh held off deciding if he was right until the next time Kamlak visited his cell.

When he did, Pavresh was sure. He could see a younger version of this man attending to Prince Dartak in the Grand Assembly, serving him tisane and crumbly bits of pastry. Had he truly been cheetah jati, or only pretending like Pavresh did?

Not that it mattered anymore.

"Where has the former Prince Dartak gotten to these days?" he asked.

Kamlak answered with a brief, haughty laugh. "So you've figured it out, have you? He works for Mahendri now as well, just like I do. But we don't see each other. He's rather lower in importance these days." He handed Pavresh a gourd of tisane and took a long sip from his own.

"You've moved up in the world, then."

"True. But considering Dartak was stripped of title, jati, and caste, he hasn't done so poorly for himself. It's useful to have him out there. Those dissatisfied with the ruling princes gravitate to him. So we're able to keep tabs on such people as well as those with the power right now."

That fit what they'd pieced together in Chaitanshehar, from Datri's spies and other sources. Playing off one group against another and able to find the right people to do so, that seemed to be Mahendri's special gift. Pavresh focused on his tisane. Everything Kamlak told him could someday be useful for Chaitanshehar. But each thing also made it more certain that Kamlak would do all in his power to make sure Pavresh never left the city. All he could do was hope he'd find some way to escape. Each passing day sanded away that hope a little more.

"That's the mistake you made with the magic, Pavresh. Great teacher that you are, you didn't realize that power is the ultimate foundation of arcist magic. Not stories, not some vague sense of justice, but power."

Pavresh paused with his gourd at his lips. "I think without stories you don't have a way to uncover that power." He made it sound as if all Pavresh's journeying to learn the stories of the people of the valley had served for nothing. "I'd say the stories have shown me that much."

Kamlak stood, agitated. "I'll admit, your way of seeing the magic produces impressive results. I learned a good deal from your training, and even now I'm learning more. Watching you, analyzing the work you've done and what you tried to do here. Before, I couldn't figure some of the details out, couldn't make this city-wide spell idea work quite right. My attempts fluctuate and need me to renew them often. The way you anchored the spell so deep. Now it makes more sense—there is a kind of story in that, a trick that I was blinded to, focused too much on its power. But you're led astray when you look at the stories as primary." He paced on the other side of the cell, drinking from his straw. "The stories are one way to peek inside. But then you need to let them go. See past the narrative. Latch onto the power revealed beyond."

"Sounds like a story you've told yourself."

Kamlak stopped abruptly and said, "You want to see what arcist power is capable of, once you let go of the structures you've tried to place around it?"

Pavresh was about to answer when a strange sense of powerlessness cut into him, separating his thoughts from any control over his body. He would have fallen back, if he'd been able. Instead his body stood upright, back rigid and arms pinned to his side. Distantly he heard something like drums, as if deep inside his head. Martial drums, setting the beat for his body to move.

"Come with me," Kamlak said, and Pavresh's body dutifully followed.

He fought his own body, or tried. Nothing responded. It was a terrible feeling, a sort of death, the way his thoughts were trapped within a body that could only obey the commands of someone else. They walked out into the hallway outside the cell and climbed up a set of stairs. They came out in a portion of the seminary. Pavresh couldn't even choose to look around, but only gaze ahead, where his body faced.

Seminarians stood at attention as they passed, and without any conversation, Pavresh knew they heard the same drums he did. A regimented force came through the magic, setting each person into the proper, needed place.

As they walked out of the doorway, Kamlak said, "There's no story that will free you from this power. I've mined deeper than you ever did."

The magic prevented Pavresh from making any sort of answer. He supposed the comment was meant as a reference to his mine-owning father. A moment later, though, Kamlak led him to the plaza on the edge of the city where the wagons from the mines came in. The space was crammed full of ore-laden wagons, and a line of more wagons sat, abandoned, as far as Pavresh could see along the road.

"A month." Kamlak said with pride. "That's what this represents. A month of arcist power coordinating all the miners, and we got all the ore we'd usually mine in a year. One month! I was able to use parts of your spell for working across jati lines. And that frees up all those miners for us to make use of in some other way."

He turned and looked hard into Pavresh's magic-dominated eyes. Pavresh had no control to look away.

"I wonder what we could do with so many extra people. Each fully militarized." After letting the words sink in, Kamlak commanded, "Now back to your cell and close the door behind you. It should lock on its own. I will be back to check on it shortly."

Pavresh tried to resist the command. Through magic and force of will he tried at least to change his stride, to take a single step out of sequence. Nothing worked. In the end, he had no choice but to obey.

***

There had to be a way to counter Kamlak's control spell. Kamlak had resisted Pavresh's spell of welcome, and five years had proven just how strong that spell could be. But he'd somehow protected himself for the months that he was in the city. He'd probably had to create an overwhelming image of the undercover spy and reinforced it often. Not to mention being a murderer and betrayer. No, that had come after his time in the city. It wasn't necessarily a part of what he would have relied on to resist Pavresh's anchor.

What was the spell to counter Kamlak's militancy here? The undercover spy as well? Maybe, if he were arriving now. But a spy didn't rise up out of the dungeon. He might need a touch of that, but it wouldn't be enough.

He needed the infiltrator and the spy, and added to that, he would take the betrayer within, the servant who rises against their master. It still seemed lacking, but Pavresh resisted the urge to pile on extra narratives. Instead he sought a way to take the magic deeper, to see the magic beneath the stories.

To see the power he was currently denied.

For days he practiced. It felt powerful, and when the real drums out in the city sounded through the walls, he was able to block out the corresponding drumbeat inside his head that tried to make him follow orders.

It was too slow, though. He had to be quick, had to be able to react to Kamlak's magic as soon as he began to use it but before it took effect. Even an untrained arcist could sense when someone nearby was using arcist magic. If Kamlak walked in and Pavresh already had the spell in effect, Kamlak would simply wait outside or go away. Or maybe find some other—physical— attack that shut Pavresh's magic down before taking control.

No matter how he practiced, it felt too slow. The pieces of narrative layered in a way that made it powerful, or so he'd always understood. But it slowed down his ability to cast it. He pared the spell down to simple forms, hoping to make up the difference with this supposed strength beneath the stories.

If he could only be sure he was breaking through to that power. It all felt much the same as it always had before.

When Kamlak entered to bring him food, Pavresh ignored him. Until Kamlak showed signs of that arrogant talkativeness that came through only rarely, Pavresh didn't want Kamlak to have any clue what he was doing.

One day he entered looking tired, but instead of tossing his food in front of Pavresh and walking away, he loomed over Pavresh. Pavresh tensed, ready to resist Kamlak's magical control.

Instead Kamlak sighed and sat across from Pavresh. He had no gourd of tisane to offer Pavresh but sipped from his own absentmindedly.

"People are strange things. How did you not go crazy? The

people in Chaitanshehar, surely they didn't always do what you expected or wanted them to."

"You mean you don't have the power to compel all of them, all the time?" Maybe not wise for Pavresh to taunt him, but the words were out before he could think.

Kamlak didn't rise to the bait, only shook his head.

Pavresh tried again, more seriously though he knew the answer wouldn't make Kamlak any happier. "I guess I survived by telling myself a different story."

Ignoring the answer as well as his own question, Kamlak said, "Miners should make good soldiers, I would think. You did it in Chaitanshehar, sort of. And you did that without compelling them by magic. Instead I have soldiers who would rather be off digging through the rocks for shiny things. Well disciplined, they are, but not yet soldiers."

The reason for Chaitanshehar's success, as far as Pavresh understood such things, was that their recruits had a story, a role to fill. They were protecting their homes, protecting a vision of the future. But if he mentioned that, Kamlak might well turn that around and find some story to inspire his miners to war, telling himself the whole time that the story was secondary.

Before he could think of some other response to lay out a false trail, Kamlak continued. "Maybe it's the way some of them rebelled before. Their minds remember the punishment for those who fought, and it puts some key part of them out of my reach."

May they always stay there, Pavresh thought. May the Cosmic Fire keep them out of his reach. Out loud, he said, "If they want to be miners, you should let them mine. Maybe you could dig your way to the Forgotten South."

Kamlak's cold gaze was answer enough. "The danger is your silly city, threatening us. Don't lose sight of that."

"Chaitanshehar never threatened you, except in response to your own threats."

That claim seemed to anger Kamlak. He stood up and

slammed his gourd back down onto the table. The edges of the gourd spiderwebbed with cracks, and tisane seeped out. "You were a threat from the very beginning. You and that untouchable princess of yours. Who could stand to let such an abomination stand? You were a deeper threat than even the worst mumbler armies of the Mumbler Wars." When he headed for the door, he said over his shoulder, "Don't think I haven't felt all your playing around with magic in here. It doesn't matter." In the space between words, Kamlak did something, and Pavresh felt the arcist control cut down again into his mind. He'd had no time to use the spell he'd devised, no chance to respond.

Somewhere in the city the martial drums beat, and their echo sounded in his head, loud, commanding.

"You don't have the ability to withstand it, no matter how hard you practice."

***

What if there was a way he could shield his use of arcist magic? Pavresh tried masking it when he practiced his protective spell, but how could he use magic to hide magic? He tried focusing on keeping the effects small. It was only him, only his mind, even, that needed to be free from Kamlak's control. So he shrunk down his efforts, imagined himself working with tiny tools on a miniature surface.

Often it felt like practicing for a singing performance by singing in a whisper, the magic constrained by the effort to keep it hidden.

And he suspected it did little to hide his efforts anyway.

At least there would be no way for Kamlak to sense exactly what Pavresh was attempting with his magic. He would guess the goal, but not the precise route Pavresh would take to achieve it. So that left room for some hope. He needed that, needed some story to tell himself of how his situation might get better, somehow, someday. Perhaps he could find the right combination to quickly and effectively protect himself.

Some days he couldn't find the energy to make the effort. How small magic was, if it couldn't even get him free from this one little room. How doomed Jaritta's dreams were if a single knife to Rashul's body could end it all.

The next time Kamlak came to visit, he arrived at an unexpected time, which didn't even give Pavresh time to make the barest effort at his spell. Kamlak's control slammed down over him before the door was open.

"You...are a strange genius, Pavresh." It sounded half accusation and half mark of admiration. He held the door open and gestured for Pavresh to come, as if he could without it being a command. "Come with me."

Pavresh tried to use his counter spell, tried to make some hole or space within Kamlak's spell so he could at least have some sort of freedom. If his efforts worked, they made little difference as his body followed Kamlak.

Instead of heading outside, they climbed a bell tower in the seminary. Dust and cobwebs gathered in the corners of the stairs, demonstrating how seldom the tower had visitors. The walls were lined with plaster, and religious texts and artwork hung in frames on the walls. Probably rare but not especially valuable works, pieces the seminary leaders felt obligated to hang somewhere. A scarcely used stairway would make a perfect place to dump such works.

The belfry was open to the air, and a figure stood there in one of the openings, looking down. He didn't acknowledge their arrival, but Pavresh recognized Mahendri. The stench of the lava fields rose up from below, and the cold winds came down from beyond the city. The shape of the columns seemed to trap every stink that came up while letting the cold wind cut through unimpeded.

It wasn't the first time Pavresh had seen the shadowy leader behind the scenes. Mahendri had visited him in his cell several times and quizzed him on Chaitanshehar's defenses and other details of the city. Many of the questions had to do with Datri's network of spies, and Pavresh didn't even need to pretend when he expressed his ignorance on those matters.

A troop of people stood below. Soldiers, perhaps, lined up before their leaders sent them off to attack Chaitanshehar. There was probably some balcony below where some prominent prince would give a stirring speech before he sent them to attack Chaitanshehar. Pavresh wanted to close his eyes so he didn't have to see them, but he couldn't even control his eyelids.

"You remember what you said about our miners?" Kamlak asked.

Pavresh had no idea what he meant, but it didn't matter either way if he couldn't speak.

Kamlak shook his head as if annoyed and made a gesture with one hand. "You may talk."

Whether the hand motion had freed him or he simply hadn't tried before and didn't notice, Pavresh was able to move his jaw and open his mouth. He enjoyed the feel of that bit of freedom for a moment before answering. "Miners? What did I say."

"It was probably a comment you tossed out without thought, and that was my reaction at first too. You said to set them digging their way to the Forgotten South. Well…" He swung his arm out at the people below.

At the *miners* gathered to… To what, dig a tunnel through the mountains? Pavresh stifled a laugh he wasn't sure the magic would have allowed him to express. "They're going to dig a tunnel? To the Forgotten South?"

Pavresh tried to keep the incredulity from his face, and maybe Kamlak's control unwittingly assisted him in that. If sending the miners south kept them from attacking Chaitanshehar, what did it matter to Pavresh what they attempted?

"Maybe. To somewhere, anyway. We've all known that the mountains to the south are impassable. That hasn't stopped people from trying to cross, from wondering if there might be some pass that could get us through. The people of Pashun have especially been interested in the question, as you can imagine by our location. So we've long known the most promising routes, the places where we seem so close to breaking through. If only the snows would let up or the valleys extend a little farther."

"That's a great idea." Pavresh tried to make himself sound like he believed it. Let them waste their time tunneling wherever they wanted. "I would love to see the Forgotten South, to learn the stories of the peoples who stayed behind."

That much was genuine. He *would* love to speak to them, to try to understand how much of the history of the Eghsal Valley was real and how much had been elaborated and changed in the years since a group of people had landed at the mouth of the valley. Would the people of the Forgotten South look like the people of Eghsal, dark-skinned and dark hair, or would they be pale like most of the mumblers?

And if he could string Kamlak along into believing it was a great idea, all the better.

Mahendri turned their way at Pavresh's words and looked at them silently. He said nothing, but Pavresh could read the message in his look. He'd been captured for a purpose, to help Kamlak. Maybe Pavresh could help with this task. Pavresh's experience might smooth out whatever Kamlak's spell crafting still lacked. But as far as Pavresh had found, Kamlak's spells had no obvious weaknesses.

Kamlak continued as if unaware of Mahendri's silent message. "A route to the south. Who knows what trade that would open up. And if we control the tunnel through, well, we have the power. Don't forget that part of the equation. It's not about the story of a fabled land far away. It's about power."

The possibility seemed so remote, so full of unknowns that might turn the tables on Kamlak and his miners that Pavresh didn't worry about that facet. Give Chaitanshehar the years it would take for Pashun to dig their tunnel. Jaritta could establish the food and trade they needed. More people would come as Juishika and his remaining students dismantled the rest of the beacons. They'd become powerful in their own way in that time, in ways that Pashun wouldn't be able to overcome. Even if they achieved all that without Pavresh there to enjoy it.

"And maybe we'll make our way through one mountain to find yet another impassable mountain. So what do we do then?"

"Dig another tunnel, I suppose." This was getting even better. Kamlak's grandiose scheme would tie up Pashun's resources for generations to come at this rate.

"Not at all," Kamlak said. "You see, while we're making our way south, our soldier jatis will be training them, turning them into real soldiers as well, bit by bit instead of all at once. It doesn't take a big change to the magic to help nudge them in that direction. We may not even need to finish the tunnel before they're, all of them, ready to take on a new role."

Pavresh felt sick. Just when he'd begun to let his hopes up, this renewed threat came along to whisk the hope away. He couldn't even lean against a wall to recover. Kamlak's spell still gave him only control of his mouth and nothing more. The gorge rose in his throat without coming all the way up.

"No answer to that?" Kamlak sneered. "Give me a year. A year of digging around in the mountains, blasting rocks and training for war. Maybe you'll still be alive then, especially if I need to force you to inspire me with new ideas. I'll be sure you have a good vantage point to watch the miners march against your so-called city. Now *that* will be a sight to behold."

CHAPTER 10

The beggar and his dog sat on the train station platform as the steam engine came roaring in from upriver. Three other beggars were there as well, but he kept his distance from them. They each kept apart, in fact—beggars in groups were more likely to make bystanders nervous and soldiers suspicious than single beggars here and there. Usually trains these days were filled with soldiers. Skirmishes with Pashun and tensions with Jarnur meant a steady movement of soldiers at all times.

And soldiers were terrible for begging.

Might as well beg the geysers for a cup of cold water.

This train came from the Silk City, though. Should mean a pack of wealthy train riders, tired from the days of travel. Good marks.

You had to look pitiful enough, an urgent case but not pushy. The dog always looked pitiful, which helped. Its fur was a mix of colors and looked ragged. It squinted from a long healed wound. People often felt sorry for the mutt.

As for himself, he didn't like to draw extra attention. His face was worn with the years. Not so many, as far as being an untouchable. Most beggars had been so their whole lives. But long enough that he looked much older than he was, his hair unkempt and graying, his dark skin smudged with the dust that gets into the wrinkles around his eyes and mouth.

He wore his usual, ragged clothes, the new cloak taken from the corpse and a mismatched set of whatever other clothing he'd found along the way. He'd started out without even clothes to his name. Without even a name. Not that he wanted to think of that time. Now he had enough layers of rags to stay warm most of the time, as long as he could shelter out of the wind.

The train's brakes shrieked to a crescendo and then ceased with the train in its berth. The station master wore his brushed suit with buttons that newly gleamed. His assistants opened the doors, and he welcomed the travelers with a bow and a sweep of his hand. Whatever he said was too quiet to carry to the beggar.

The travelers climbed down shakily, ignoring the station master.

The beggar pushed his bowl out to be sure they would notice it sitting there, waiting for their gifts.

"Alms!" he called as they began to pass slowly by. The ground clearly seemed uneven to them, its stability unfamiliar after riding on such a shaking, rocking monstrosity for days. Had he ever ridden— The beggar forced the thought away. "Alms for my dog."

The first passenger glared his way. The beggar smiled back as if the glare had been meant in kindness. He'd grown used to pretending most people were friendly, even when the evidence was in the opposite direction. "Thank you, sir."

He shook the bowl, and a single coin rattled. He faced the next traveler, his smile already pasted in place."Alms. Alms to celebrate the Silk City. Alms to thank the gods for a safe travel here. You can keep your silks, but I'll take your extra food. If you insist. Alms!" His voice was as ragged as his clothes.

A few coins added their clink to his voice, and he got more food than he was expecting even. The travelers must be tired of the train food they'd been carrying. He fed his dog first, took a bite of dried fruit, and set the rest aside to eat once the travelers were past.

The silk weavers went on by in their fancy clothes, with their cheetah jati servants accompanying them. They were dressed nearly as well as their masters and looked down their noses at the beggar. He rarely got anything from servants.

After them, the workers came, loaded down with piles of silks and crates of the silk weavers' possessions. They had no hands to give the beggar anything most of the time. But most of them, when their loads weren't too cumbersome or they were coming back empty-handed for the next pile of silks, offered him something small, at least.

It was a good morning, much better than most. The other

untouchables shuffled away while the beggar struggled to his feet. His right leg had gone asleep, so he shook the tingles out and gathered up the food and coins. Eating a half-gone loaf of bread, he walked away.

He hadn't gone far when some other people descended from the train. He paused only long enough to see that they were soldiers after all. It was one pause too long.

"Hey, beggar, come back here."

The beggar stopped walking but didn't go toward them.

"We're talking to you, old man."

"I didn't do anything, tisrae." The words slurred in his mouth.

"You say something to us, beggar? Try again, I couldn't hear you."

The beggar hesitated a moment and then shuffled off as fast as he could go.

"Hey, get back here!"

There was a pounding of feet. Only one set as far as the beggar could guess. When the footsteps reached him, he huddled against the nearest wall, clutching the things he'd been given. "It's my bread," he said around a mouthful of food.

The soldier struck his cheek, and the half chewed bread flew free. "Stupid beggar. Thinks I want his bread. Now, get back over here so we can—"

The dog chose that moment to defend its master, growling for a second before snapping its jaws onto the soldier's threatening hand. The soldier shrieked in pain.

The beggar stumbled away, grabbing the dog by its neck. *Bad choice, bad choice.* He couldn't run, not fast enough to escape these soldiers. He should have left sooner. Should have known there would be soldiers on the train. Should have never come. He could have begged outside a market. Or next to the river docks. Or the temple.

But then soldiers might have been there as well. There was no place in Romnai that was safe.

When the soldier stopped his cursing, he said, "Oh now you'll get it, beggar. Get over here!"

The beggar shuffled onward, keeping his balance with one hand on the wall beside him. The dog stayed at his feet. Every step he feared he would trip on it, but they managed to make their awkward way.

Not that it would do any good. The soldiers would catch up soon enough. He resigned himself to it, wondered if they would kill him or merely beat him and leave him lying in the street. Not that he expected to survive a severe beating, the way his body ached with even the punishments of day to day life.

"Tishok," a different voice called from the train. "You're needed here. Leave that refuse be. You can carry your own gear."

The soldier chasing him was almost on his back. He snarled, a wolf's snarl, but obeyed his commanding officer. "I'll watch for you, beggar," he called as he went back to join his platoon.

The beggar and his dog turned down a side street as soon as they could, and turned again when the station was out of sight. Best not to take a chance. The soldiers might complete their officer's charge quickly and decide on some quick fun before their next assignment.

Nothing like revenge to bind a unit together.

The neighborhood near the tracks was narrow, switching soon to the riverside warehouses. Terrible for begging. But what wasn't terrible these days?

He headed for the river wharf where workers unloaded the cargo from a steamship. Not a lot in trade up the river, any more than by rail. But even in war, the people of Romnai needed fish from the ocean, and the people of Jarnur needed Romnai's grains and gourds and bales of cloth.

One dock worker tossed the beggar a leftover end of a sausage. The beggar gave it to the dog and kept walking along the wharf. There must be someplace to hide for a time, to escape the soldiers and the worries and the threats of the city.

A procession of mourners passed. The beggar stood aside,

trying to look respectful, watchful for the death jati workers that would likely follow the procession, carrying the body. But no cadaver followed, and he noticed that the mourners were all women. They wore no distinctive clothing, as if they'd cast aside special dress in their mourning, but no sorrow could hide their militant walk, their fiercely alert gaze.

The beggar avoided them. They might not belong to the same jati as the soldiers at the train station, but they were surely soldiers just the same. Women soldiers in mourning. It made him think... His mind slid away from any thought of who they were and what jati they belonged to.

He wandered upriver, looking in the shadows between the warehouses for someplace out of sight where he could rest. Where he could forget the snarl of the soldier.

Nothing came to view in that direction, so when he came to a stairway down toward the river, he descended. No boat was at anchor, so no workers were nearby. He swung around a support pillar and went in under the wharf.

It was dark and damp among the pillars. The dog growled at the darkness. Or maybe at some creature that lurked deep within. There was no responding growl or other animal noise. The beggar spread his overcoat on the wet ground and sat, leaning against one of the pillars. Let the wild animals threaten. They were less terrifying than soldiers.

The dog lay down beside him, head on paws but ears still alert.

He closed his eyes. In his dreams, a naga slithered up out of the mud. He was in the same place, resting beneath the pier, but his begging bowl sat before him, and he played some kind of instrument to draw people to give him alms.

The naga threw something into the bowl and spoke in a language the beggar couldn't understand. Then it flipped around and dived back into the river.

A second naga rose. Two more, even. And maybe others behind him, rising from the muddy darkness. His dream sight was clouded and imprecise. The nagas each dropped gifts into his begging bowl. It overflowed with food and riches.

Finally he stopped playing and reached for one of the gifts. It was a fig, candied and dusted with some kind of spice. He put it to his mouth, whispering words of thanks to the nagas who had given him so much.

Instead of the sweet spice of the fig, he tasted fire.

Flames licked at his lips and spread in an instant all over his body. The whole dark space beneath the wharf lit up with fire, and all the riches of the naga gifts were consumed. Even his begging bowl melted in the heat, as he beat at the flames to put them out, plunged his body into the mud, swallowed the wet muck of half rotted leaves to put out the fire.

He woke soaked to the skin. His mouth tasted of wet leaves and rot. There was no fire. In fact he shivered in the chill air. The dog sat exactly where it had been, but a low whimper escaped its mouth. It looked like it didn't dare move.

The beggar gathered his cloak and begging bowl and splashed out toward the stairway. There were lines in the mud of the riverbank. He couldn't identify what had made them. And he wasn't certain they hadn't been there before he'd gone in to sleep. But they looked like the marks the nagas had left in the mud in his dream.

Nagas and figs and fire. Who could say what it meant? It was his mind coming apart, his own past and the stories of childhood mixing into the fragments.

The beggar splashed cold river water on his face to clean some of the mud and clear his mind. Then he hurried away.

A true steam bath would be welcome. As if a beggar would be allowed in any real steam bath. Maybe he could find some hot spring water to clean himself without freezing. That would be the most he could hope for.

He crossed the river, looking over his shoulder the whole way over the bridge. It arced high above the water. If he was cornered by soldiers here, jumping would not be an option. Across the other side, he slipped away into the narrow streets where the lower caste people lived. Easier to avoid notice there. Soldiers still patrolled, but with so many little streets, he had a chance to slip away from sight, at least for a time.

**

Snow filled the streets of Romnai. Snowflakes were frequent most of the year, with the geyser steam rising above the city and hitting colder northern air. But usually that same steam kept the streets themselves warm enough to melt the snow. A bitter wind from the north this time swept the volcanically warmed air away from the city while also bringing in even more frigid temperatures.

The beggar—like all the beggars still in Romnai—shivered and froze. Even his sheltered spot behind the bush in the hidden walkway was too cold, so the beggar wrapped himself in everything he owned, held one arm over his head to shield his eyes from the falling snow, and trudged through the streets in search of someplace better.

Maybe it would have been better if the nagas had taken him. It was probably warm in their underwater dens. No wind, at least. No snow.

The temple would be fitting. They worshiped the Sacred Fire and always had torches and a central, holy flame burning. What better way to drive away the cold? But the thought of entering the main temple filled him with a terror he couldn't identify. What if the flames spread? What if the whole thing burned down?

There were smaller chapels scattered about the city. Most of the wealthy had their own private chapels tucked away inside their manors. Those flames would be burning, too, but he wasn't about to try to sneak into such houses. Instead he headed into the brenil, mid-caste, parts of the city.

A light shone from a chapel on one street. It wasn't a place he was familiar with. Did they welcome and feed beggars here? Or turn them away as untouchables unworthy of things like warmth and food? If he were a god, he'd have his followers welcome the beggars. But not the nagas. And probably not the soldiers, either, at least most of them. He shuffled close but found the doors locked. He knocked and peered into a window.

The inside glowed with firelight. With warmth. He pressed himself against the door, hoping to feel some of that heat seeping out. Maybe there would be food, even. The chaplain must eat sometimes. They would have to be food on hand somewhere inside. The dog whimpered as they waited.

No one came to his knock. He tried again and rattled the handle to see if it would fall open. Nothing.

Well, no sense giving up so soon. The snow lay deep along the walls. He tramped around to the side where there was a small entrance, cut down below the ground, leading to some kind of cellar or basement.

This door opened with a twist of its latch. Snow poured into a dark cellar. The beggar and his dog tumbled inside. The door wouldn't close fully anymore, with the snow in the doorway, so he pushed it as far shut as he could. If he couldn't find his way up to the warmth of the chapel above, at least this place would block the wind and snow.

Blindly the beggar made his way around the room. Two steps of a wooden staircase in one corner led up to another door. He pushed it open and saw light. The chapel from the side looked askew. He entered, shutting the door to the cool cellar, and crept to one of the benches.

Warmth. His fingers tingled as feeling returned. His feet hurt, but it was a welcome pain. He fell asleep while the melting snow dripped from his clothes to pool on the bench and spill onto the floor.

How many hours he'd slept before the chaplain came into the room and found him, he didn't know. The beggar heard the man unlocking the front door for worshipers to enter and setting up the room for their arrival. The beggar sat up, stretched. The snow that had melted from him made it look like he was some water creature who'd ended up here in this place of the sacred Fire. Maybe he was the naga from his own dreams, a creature from the Forgotten South carried up here and punished by Fire.

The chaplain jumped and swore at him. "Who… Get out. This is no place to sleep!" He chased the beggar through the benches, lamenting, "An untouchable on my benches! I'll have to clean them. Purify them. And a wet, dirty dog too? Get out, out, out!"

By the time he said the last word, the beggar had reached the front door. He ran through and into the street. It was a much warmer day already, even with the sun not yet risen. But the snow remained deep on the streets, and soldiers were on patrol.

The beggar and his dog followed the paths that were already broken through the drifts, keeping their distance from the soldiers, moving as fast as they could to keep the chill from getting its strong grasp on them again.

CHAPTER 11

The camp lay in the folds between two ridges. Ellechandran deferred to Chhayasheela as they approached, letting her move ahead alone, a few paces in front of the rest. It would be her job to establish their welcome. Nataravi would have loved to see how the tents nestled into the rocks, how the vibrant colors stood out against the gray and white of stone and snow. He missed her.

Missed his wife and baby as well, but Nataravi was the one who would have especially enjoyed seeing the hunters' camp.

Ellechandran waited with the other dozen porters and guards—all of them from one village or another. A *mumbler* village as the people of the valley cities would have called them. His former wife continued toward the camp on her own. The snow puffed outward from her netted snowshoes with each step.

Chhayasheela called from the edge of camp, hands open and spread wide.

A hunter left one tent and greeted them. Chhayasheela took care of the introductions. When she said they were from Chaitanshehar—the city of all villages as she called it in the trade pidgin—the hunter cracked a grin.

"How can you stand living in that place? Is it not a city of smelly valley dwellers and other stinks?"

"It is a city for everyone," Chhayasheela answered. "A city for anyone who wants to be part of it." She turned and looked at Ellechandran and the rest and then gestured beyond them, as if at the location of the city. "There would be room for you among us. If you wish. We could use some experienced hunters."

"No, not us. They say you bathe in the mud pots and marry the first person you see each morning." He smirked at the other hunters who were just coming out of the tents. "I'll let someone else enjoy that."

Where would they get that kind of idea? Ellechandran's eyes avoided Chhayasheela. Marrying a new person every day was not a part of their city, but a married couple separating and finding a new spouse or lover was more accepted than it had been in their old village. Well, let these hunters think what they wanted. Ellechandran didn't care. He just waited for Chhayasheela to get to the trading for food.

Instead she actually responded to the claim. "Not at all. See him over there, my first husband? He's married to a princess now, a real princess. And his daughters are princesses too."

He sketched an ironic bow while cursing her in his head. Why bother bringing that up? It felt awkward and unnecessary.

"And now his little princesses are hungry. So if you have no plans to join us, what kind of trade will you consider?"

Well, maybe not such a terrible approach. Impressive, in fact, how she brought it back around to their real purpose. He couldn't fault her after all.

The hunter took it in stride, and his bearing became more serious. "Come to our fire. We have little food to share ourselves, but we have warmth."

As Ellechandran passed him by, the hunter said very formally, "May my children grow to court your daughters."

It was similar to a traditional phrase spoken in his own village, not meant literally but as a sign of well wishing. He responded in his own language which wasn't so different from this man's, "May they grow to be great hunters. Your sons and my daughters both." It wasn't exactly the traditional saying, but close enough. No reason his daughters couldn't become hunters some day. And they might choose to court whomever they wished.

The fire was too small for everyone to gather close. Ellechandran tried to let some of the others go nearer, but he found himself nudged to the front beside Chhayasheela.

After the initial pleasantries to establish themselves and the trade they hoped for, the hunter said, "We come from a large village with many mouths to feed." He spoke a mixture of the trade pidgin with quite a few local words thrown in, but as they were similar to the words of Ellechandran and Chhayasheela's own village, they had no trouble following. "Small compared to your city, but still many for us. Yet our hunting grounds are wide and full of game this time of year. What can you offer?"

Chhayasheela also sprinkled local words into her responses, but she kept this one short. "Our assistance against the miners of Pashun."

Dead silence fell over the camp at these words. The hunter cleared his throat eventually and asked, "You would fight beside us? Against your own people?"

"Not our own people." Chhayasheela gestured at her own pale cheek and then at the people in her team, all with the characteristic appearance of the tribes and villages, not the cities. "No more than you're our people. Or maybe better to say you're both our people."

"So either way, you pick sides, send us soldiers—"

"We supply weapons," Ellechandran insisted. This was why Jaritta had wanted him along, and he would do all he could to meet her expectations. He couldn't let Chhayasheela promise them soldiers when they had so few to begin with. Though even their store of weapons wasn't huge. "And advice as well. Training in how to defend against their kind of fighting."

"Training in how to fight back—their way?"

Ellechandran nodded with some hesitation. Training was an easy slide away from joining in the battles themselves. His experiences with his young daughters—of promises being turned into something he'd never intended—warned him to be cautious in what they were promising.

Chhayasheela took over again. "Yes, training so you don't have to worry about them anymore. We can explain their tactics, help you arrange your soldiers and coordinate your attacks in ways they won't expect. How much food is that worth to you?"

"There are parts of the mountains where we don't hunt, because of them. Places with plenty of game and forage but also miners. Your training could let us enter those slopes?" He sat back on his heels as if contemplating.

For many of the villages in this part of the mountains, even to be seen by a miner was taboo, unless the villager was masked or properly prepared by the chief or elders. A deliberate fighting force would go through the preparations and wear specific fighting masks, as would a hunting band that expected to come near the mines. Even so, it was a taboo that weighed heavily on the people of these mountains. Being caught unawares could result in a person needing to go through purification rituals. Or if the situation was especially scandalous, it could lead to exile. As he and Chhayasheela well knew. Had he really been so accepting of those superstitions once? And to think of him now...

The masks themselves would be a part of their training. The local masks were often gaudy and awkward, but the villagers insisted on using them even in battle. The right kind of masks might make the Pashun soldiers afraid, if used right against small groups. Better yet, they would try to convince the villagers to accept helmets as mask substitutes, along with better armor that would still fit their mountain routes and fighting styles. A combination of the strengths of their usual way of fighting with just the right mixture of tricks and tactics from the professional soldiers in the valley—it should be worth a good deal of food, to the right villages.

They spent much of the day figuring out the details. Ellechandran made sure their group wasn't promising more than what Jaritta would find acceptable. Apart from that, he stayed out of the specifics.

The hunters would deliver food to the city itself. And they would demand what assistance Chhayasheela had promised at that point. Eghsal tactics, training in the use of Eghsal weapons, teachings on how to find the weaknesses of Eghsal-trained soldiers.

Would it be enough food? Nowhere close. The vastness of their task weighed Ellechandran down. He could only hope that a trickle of trade here and a trickle there would let them at least survive, scraped together with whatever Azheeran brought back from the north and the people of the city could scavenge from the fields.

In most situations like this, the hunters would offer some hospitality for the evening meal or the night, but they were a small band without any extra to share. So the agreements completed, the hunter excused his band. "We have some hunting to do before evening falls. Thank you for your kind trades. And may all your children grow to be princesses themselves."

The traders of Chaitanshehar took their leave to camp somewhere away from the hunters' planned hunting grounds, though it meant journeying into the darkness of the early sunset for some ways.

They lit their way with a sheltered lantern and huddled all close together in a copse of trees some hours later to sleep. With many more trades to come in the days ahead—or so he hoped.

***

As they made their way around the mountains to the southeast of Pashun, visiting as many villages and hunting bands as they could along the way, Ellechandran noticed an increase in animal movement heading up the mountains. A pack of wolves loped along the ridge above them before moving higher into the slopes. A herd of mountain sheep stood directly in their path at one point. Wild sheep were far from uncommon. Ellechandran had grown up tending a herd that was half domesticated, not that far from here. The reminder of his past made his breath come in shallow gasps, so he kept his thoughts on the animals alone. Usually sheep ignored humans. As soon as they came across this herd, though, the animals took off for an empty field above them, skittish and flighty.

Later that day, a lone wisent—a hulking animal that usually stayed in the lower elevations where there was grazing beneath the snow—stood in a wallow below them, shaking snow from the great hump on its back. Nataravi would have enjoyed seeing such a strange creature. When he made it back, he would have to describe its thick, dark fur, the head that looked too big for its body, the legs that could spur it into a sudden, unstoppable motion. Wisents could be majestic, thundering across the sparsely wooded slopes below. This one only looked lonely.

The team formed an arc to close in on the beast. Ellechandran knew that the hollow had steep sides that would trap the animal if it caught scent of them. He'd hunted deer through here. The thought made him twist to keep a look out for local hunters. The place they would likely gather was empty for now, so he forced his eyes back to the wisent. No fur was better at keeping a traveler warm than wisent fur, and the meat on a typical animal would feed many.

They would have to cut short their trading journey or use the animal in trade with a nearby village, but it might be worth that. Not *too* nearby. He glanced again to where the local hunters might gather, imagining himself among them, imagining them coming across him and recognizing who he was.

As they came closer, Chhayasheela held up her hand. "Stop. Look at its side. I can see its ribs."

It did seem like a gaunt shadow of a healthy wisent. Even its fur was peeling off, as happened in summer but might prove deadly this time of year.

"It isn't worth hunting that. Not unless we know there's a village *very* close, someplace desperate enough to give us something in exchange for it." Chhayasheela looked around the group without quite meeting Ellechandran's eye. They both knew they were very close to the village that had cast them out into exile. Would they be desperate enough to trade for a lone wisent? Were Chhayasheela and Ellechandran desperate enough to try? He'd begun to wonder if she was thinking of visiting. They might pretend they were strangers—they'd changed in the years since leaving, so they might fool some of their old neighbors.

But it was unlikely they'd escape without being recognized. Better to stay away.

Other villages in the area were widely scattered. Even in those, there would be people who had known them, people who had married across tribal lines, and people who had switched tribes and been accepted in their new homes for other reasons.

"Nothing I know of that would be worth the attempt," Ellechandran finally said.

Chhayasheela nodded. "Let's keep going, then."

His breathing came easier as they put some distance between themselves and the village.

The next day a flock of winter geese rose suddenly down the slope from them, their black and gray feathers striking against the light, snow-promising sky. The birds circled and formed an arrow shape in the air, then flew away to the west, over the ridge line of the nearest foothills.

As the group descended toward where the geese had been, Ellechandran heard a strange noise. A human-made noise.

Several others heard it at the same moment, and everyone halted.

"To shelter," Chhayasheela said after a moment. "Hide in those trees."

The trees that were available were widely spaced and unlikely to hide anyone well. They made do as well as they could. A troop of people came into view. Soldiers? Ellechandran strained to make out the details through a gap in the fallen tree where he hid.

They were dark-skinned. That only meant they weren't from a mumbler village. Would Jaritta have sent a group from Chaitanshehar out this way? Very doubtful. What purpose would it serve, when she knew he and Chhayasheela would be around this area? Which meant this troop was from Pashun.

They marched, but not like soldiers. Or like soldiers who were still learning how to move as a group. But whatever they were, they were moving up the hill toward the trading group's scant hiding place.

Behind them, an open plain of snow lay between their few trees and any promise of shelter. But a quick dash up through that snow might be their only chance to get away. The members of their squad, having grown up in mumbler villages, should know how to move silently, how to stay as hidden as possible. Difficult to imagine it would be enough here. The soldiers would surely see them and might choose to chase them down like prey.

Chhayasheela was signaling for everyone to be ready and tensed as if about to give the signal when Ellechandran noticed a rill below the trees where they hid. It angled downward but away from the path of the not-exactly-soldiers heading their way. As it went, it deepened into a gully. He couldn't see much of the stream after that, but it appeared to wind away to the north, behind and away from the path of the soldiers.

Ellechandran motioned for Chhayasheela's attention then pointed toward the stream. She frowned and studied its length. After a moment, she nodded then indicated they would head over two by two, keeping the stream between them and the group from Pashun.

Ellechandran was one of the first pair. He and Venthaian crouched low and ran, lightly where the ground was uneven. He didn't drop into the stream at the first chance, but ran along the lip until the gully was deep enough. Once that far, they jumped over the edge and into the shadows.

No cry came of being seen.

Two more came a moment later, but this time there was a cry of alarm. Ellechandran stuck his head over the edge to see what the others would do. Already three more of their own people were running toward the gully.

Two of the strangers separated from their group. These two had the look of real soldiers. They carried swords, currently sheathed, and walked with a sense of power. One had a sling in his hand—loose, but a trained soldier could still launch a stone faster than the eye could follow without needing any real time to prepare. The other had a spear or staff of some kind.

Chhayasheela sent the rest of them and came last herself.

As she made her way along the rill, she fell. Ellechandran cried out and pulled himself up to the edge of the gully. Had the soldier with the slingshot attacked? Ellechandran hadn't seen anything. He stayed in a crawl and scurried closer to her. She was moving, which was a good sign.

"Sheela," he called as he crawled. "Are you hurt? Are you shot? Where?"

"Yes. No. Just fell, twisted my ankle."

The soldiers were still coming closer. "We have to move. Can you walk?"

She shook her head but half crawled his way, favoring one leg. He reached her and put an arm around her shoulders. Taking her weight, they made it back to the gully. The soldiers had paused and were talking and pointing in their direction.

Her eyes were closed in pain, so Ellechandran spoke to the others. "We need to get as far from here, as quick as we can. We'll follow the stream down and see where it leads, but watch behind us for anyone following."

He lifted himself up to the lip of the gully and then dropped back down. The soldiers appeared to be deep in discussion. Probably whether to pursue or not. To them, the trading squad had probably appeared like nothing but a hunting band of mumblers.

Whether that made it more likely the soldiers would pursue them or less, Ellechandran didn't hazard a guess. All he knew was that they needed to get away from there.

"Let's move. The rocks might be slippery, so help each other and watch where you step." Not a time to sprain a knee of the rough rocks. They certainly didn't need to all be hobbling out of the gully when they finally found its end. If they made it that far at all. "But be as fast as you can while being careful."

***

Chhayasheela had to rely on the others more and more as they descended. Ellechandran grew worried at the pained expression in her eyes, her clenched jaw. He remembered other expressions on that familiar face, other journeys together. They took turns helping support her. She moved where she was led but gave no indication that she would be able to plan anything out or direct them.

They came out below the foothills, much farther north than they had planned to travel during their attempts at trading. This was Pashun land, miner land. They had to get away before they were discovered. A childhood of fearing the taboo of being seen, a time of living through the aftermath of breaking that taboo, and now the reality of the fight between Chaitanshehar and Pashun—all of it pushed him to flee, to get higher into the mountains as soon as he could.

Would there ever be a time when he didn't have to fear discovery by anyone?

The land above offered no easy route of escape. Going back into the gully made no sense, and elsewhere the climb would be steep, with little shelter and no obvious path to take. Less than ideal if they were all healthy. Not possible at all while trying to help Chhayasheela maneuver.

Her latest assistant, Aagathiya, helped her onto a blanket where she lay, moaning. Ellechandran bent down beside her. "We'll have to carry you, Sheela. But I'm going to take a look at it first." She couldn't even open her eyes to respond but gave him a tight nod.

Her ankle looked black with pooled blood. The skin around it was red and hot, and it was swelling against her leather boot.

He loosened the laces and pulled the top of the boot out to ease the pressure on it. There was a strange intimacy to the act, an echo of their married past mixed with a clinical, dispassionate present. He pushed the memories aside to focus on helping her. "Bring some snow," he told whoever was listening. "We'll pack it around the ankle while I put together something more for it."

While they took care of the snow, Ellechandran dug through their packs for some medicinal herbs. He should have learned where they were keeping such things, but he'd left those details to Chhayasheela. She'd always been good at organizing, much better than he was.

He found some paste wrapped in an oilcloth. When he touched it, his fingertips tingled and went numb. That should dull the pain somewhat from the outside. He set it aside with some strips of cloth for bandaging. Underneath a second oilcloth-wrapped packet, he found a bundle of kinked roots. They bent back and forth on each other like the switchbacks that led up to Chaitanshehar. He took one out and brought it to her.

"Can you chew on this?" He could steep it like the valley people steeped their tisane, but it would be stronger if she simply bit down on the root. Its woody texture alone might distract her from some of the pain, even before the effects of the root took hold.

She opened her mouth for him to put the root in. Another strange intimacy, only now the action called to mind feeding his children. His and Jaritta's children. Ellechandran waited, tense, and watched her jaw move sharply up and down. Slowly she lay her head back, as her chewing slowed down and her body relaxed.

Echoes and futures both could wait. For now his task was to keep them all safe, in a harsh land with little to offer them.

"She'll be hunting with the spirits for a time," he told the others. "I'll take a look at her ankle once more in a moment, then we should get moving from here." To somewhere. He frowned and looked upward again but still saw no good route that way.

The snow had taken down the swelling some. Ellechandran cleared it all away and dried her ankle with a soft cloth. Then he smeared the numbing paste all the way around her ankle until he couldn't feel his own fingers from the paste's effect. It made his hands too clumsy, so he had someone else wrap the bandages around the paste.

"Let's see if we can put some of the snow on again. If we

can keep it on somehow, I mean." He packed the snow against it—might as well take advantage of not being bothered by the cold on his fingers himself—wrapped it in a length of leather, and tied it loosely in place.

After getting the solid Venthaian and Aagathiya to carry her, he pointed westward along the base of the slope. "We'll have to go this way for now. I'll try to get us up higher as soon as there's a good route to follow, but watch for the miners as we go."

As they made their way along the base of the hills, Ellechandran tried to imagine what his family in Chaitanshehar would think of that world. It felt familiar to him, the furtive flight along the cold hillside, the worry that at any moment they might have to find a place to hide.

Ovitava, of course, was too young to be aware of what was happening, if she were here. Nataravi, though, would have thought it a game. For a little while. She would have liked looking around for the miners and had the eyes to spot them probably before any of the rest of them did. But she would have grown bored with it and wanted to go back up into the mountains soon. She loved the mountains.

What would Jaritta have thought? She was a driven woman. Put her in charge, and she'd plan their routes and never hesitate to do the work needed. But she wouldn't have enjoyed it. She would have simply looked ahead to their destination, pressed on as quick as they could to get the travel over with.

Which was a big part of what made her so different from his first wife. Chhayasheela was a traveler. She'd been the one who insisted on them joining the exiles and untouchables in Eghsal City, but almost as soon as they'd begun getting settled in Chaitanshehar, she'd been anxious to get moving again. She needed to see the sights along the way, wherever that way led. Seeing the same places day after day had worn her down until she'd decided to leave. To leave the city—without abandoning it, of course—and to leave him.

Their route brought them around a rock pile, and suddenly they faced the opening to a mine. Ellechandran dropped down, watching for guards, soldiers. No cries of alarm. Crouched low, he herded everyone back around the rocks, to where the mine entrance was still just in view.

Could they climb up, away from the mine? He strained his ears for the sounds of soldiers and overseers as he looked. They needed to find a way to a higher elevation, away from the Pashun mines and the places where its soldiers would be. He gestured to one of the better scouts in their group, a young woman named Gnalamani. "You're probably the most agile of us. You think you could find us a route?"

She studied the mountainside, shaking her head. It didn't look great, he had to agree, especially while carrying one of their group. But they'd stayed down at this level long enough already. Too long, in fact. If they could get past the first climb, there looked like a more level stretch for a while before they'd have to climb again.

As she edged closer to the base to look for climbing holds, Gnalamani suddenly stopped and stared at the mine. "I don't think there's anyone there."

Ellechandran spun around and studied the mine entrance. It shouldn't be closed. The mines never closed. Stopping the work at a mine was like stopping the entire city of Pashun. Or should be. And yet…

It did have a look of abandonment, and for all his straining to hear, he realized that he hadn't heard any human sounds besides their own group's. Jaritta always said he had a gift for noticing details, for realizing what this or that thing might mean. He'd been trying so hard to notice the details of the mountainside above that he hadn't paid close attention to the scene directly before them. A heavy door of some kind had been pulled across the entrance, but it didn't quite shut fully. There was snow piled in front of that door as if it hadn't moved in some days, at least.

The road that led to the mine had no traffic. No horses pulling great wagons full of ore. No masters driving a line of miners to their shift of digging. Ellechandran had seen the mines in operation when they'd gone searching for people to join the city, and he'd heard the stories of the miners after those workers had come. This didn't fit what he'd seen or imagined.

"If there's snow blown into that door, then I think we can trust no one's around." He scanned the hillside again. "But let me go check first. If we have to run, we don't want the people carrying Sheela to fall behind."

He picked Gnalamani and Aagathiya to join him and made his way cautiously to the mine entrance.

No cries or shouts of surprise. Promising. The ground beside the door was scraped, as if they'd tried to close a door that was always open and discovered it no longer fit the opening. A mound of snow had fallen inside the mine, tapering off after a pace or so.

When they pushed the door open farther it shrieked on metal hinges. There was no answering cry of alarm, within or from the wooded slope surrounding them.

Ellechandran gestured for the rest of them to come. "We'll shelter in here for now. It'll be warmer out of the wind, at least. Let's hope Chhayasheela heals quickly." And that the miners didn't return. And that their food could keep them going while stuck in this one place.

So much that could go wrong, and all the decisions falling to him. Maybe Sheela would be up again in no time. Then she could decide where to go from there. Jaritta might always need to be planning, and Chhayasheela might need to see new sights. But the one thing he *didn't* need was to be the person making decisions for matters as weighty as these.

They pulled the door back mostly closed, lit a mining lantern that had been left behind, and set up a camp of sorts a short way into the tunnel, with guards watching both the way into the mine from outside and the mysterious dark beyond them, empty of any sound of miners working, rail carts running, overseers cursing.

The silence left a good deal of room for imagination, memories of the past—of Chhayasheela and the village of their childhood, of Jaritta, of their girls—fears of the future, and stomach-growling hunger that was surely not only their own but the pangs of an entire city, waiting desperately for their return.

CHAPTER 12

Indima took a step and spun, nearly knocking over a cheetah jati servant who was hurrying through. The man opened his mouth to yell at her and then appeared to recognize who she was. He shut his mouth and was already walking away by the time Indima spun away from him.

The Silk City streets were narrow. The city itself was small enough that carts and horses were seldom needed. People walked, and people could navigate smaller streets easily.

But not if there was a dancer taking up the space.

Indima stepped over a fallen paper, one of those that might have originally wrapped a package from the market. She made the step a part of the dance, as if she'd always intended to cross the street that way.

A busier intersection made her passage more difficult. Her intent was always to make her dancing seem like it belonged in another world. She had long cultivated an image of someone touched by some other place, a place glimpsed by the people here but not really a part of the world in the same way.

Bumping into or stumbling over a passerby would undermine that impression.

Indima slowed her dance. It wasn't a sacred dance. She still danced the holy dances in the temple, but she'd freed herself from the limits that proscribed those official ones. This was her own personal interpretation, easy to adjust her speed and moves as the crowds gathered and dispersed. A pause to make a dramatic pass with her arms could shift into a sideways glide or a leap ahead with equal grace, and no one would know whether she intended the one or the other originally.

She swooped between two men and ducked to avoid a woman's moving elbow. A small boy stood beyond them, and she recognized the look in his eyes. He was planning to interrupt her as she passed him by. Spinning back, she slipped between another group of people. They moved into the space between her and the boy.

Once past the intersection, she moved faster. The tassels on her sleeves clicked against her wrists, a soft sound only she could hear. Much like the music itself, the rhythms and melodies that guided her movements—she heard it all plainly, even if it was only in her head.

She only stopped dancing when she came to her parents' house and closed the door behind her. Even then, her fingers beat a rhythm on the wall, against her side, on her wrist when all else was out of reach.

Her father's new wife greeted her, looking up from the inkpot and half-written letter lying before her. "Where did you dance today?"

Tupti was still somewhat scared of Indima, though she tried to hide it. Her mother had died three years earlier, and Tupti stepped into the picture scarcely a year ago. A good woman for her father, with her own work a step away from the silk harvesting that employed her father and most of the silk weavers in the city. She and her cheetah jati assistant coordinated with various lower ranking jatis to make sure the city and its workers had the supplies necessary to keep the city running smoothly. Sometimes one jati had extra stores of certain goods that were running low elsewhere, so they worked to smooth over such inconsistencies before they became problems.

And though it wasn't officially Tupti's role, she coordinated other matters as well, when a delicate touch needed to get a person from one jati away from a dangerous situation. Into another part of the city, perhaps, or assigned to a family that was heading away, back to Romnai.

"Across town," Indima said vaguely in answer to the question. Even in the house she kept up her facade of otherworldliness. Except that she ate when she was hungry, which was usual right after a dance.

She took a wafer of flatbread and some figs. Then when she

realized that wouldn't fill her, she spread cheese thickly onto the wafer.

"Not at the temple?" There was always a touch of disappointment whenever Tupti asked about the temple dancing. Like she couldn't imagine anyone choosing to dance outside the sanctioned confines of the temple.

The temple *was* where she'd established herself as a dancer. She continued to dance for the priests on holy days, reminding people who she was. Reminding them of the gods-touched power of her movements.

It was those times that had made her known throughout the city. The waif who danced so purely that the gods surely noticed and blessed those who viewed her. People felt the presence of the gods whenever she performed.

At first the priests had forbidden anything but the sanctioned dances. She'd gone along with their rules in public, sneaking off to hidden rooms when she needed something different. But slowly she'd built up the image of herself as a gods-touched eccentric, so full of the cosmic fire that she could add her own touches when she danced through the streets. Slowly she made each dance more and more her own, and the priests never dared to challenge her sacrilege.

The silk weavers learned to accept her unpredictable street dancing. To them, and even to her stepmother, that was who she was. Not entirely sane, but such a gifted performer that they put up with the rest of it.

It kept her honored. And famous.

And most of all, separate, alone. Who could relate to an aloof genius like that? The distance suited her. It let her remember the past, and above all it let her lose herself in the dancing.

"You had some visitors," Tupti said. "They didn't say who they were. But they left a flower for you. I set it by the southern window for the sunlight."

Indima walked through the sitting room to the southern window. It was at the end of a hallway, a poor way to plan a house when the sun was so often to the south. At least there was space for a comfortable cushion to sit in and enjoy the sunshine. A flower stand beside the cushion held eight different plants in separate pots, with room for another four. Which of the eight was a new one?

She had to look each one over to be sure. People often sent her flowers—worshipers moved by the dancing, passersby who simply appreciated the chance to observe something beautiful to break up the dark days. Most of them were already cut, a touch of color to brighten the house for a few days before they were burned. And whoever had given those flowers, the memory was cast away just as soon. She remembered each of the potted plants given to her with greater care, the eight here and the others in a room downstairs full of plants that grew beneath a glass roof.

After touching each of the plants carefully, she decided the new one was the one with pale yellow flowerlets. She smelled deeply, but its scent was already diffused, subsumed into the general smell of the room as a whole.

It wasn't a gift from a random fan, no matter what her stepmother assumed. Indima turned the pot and traced her fingers over the information lightly carved into the clay. To the eye it was nothing more than a dark colored clay, coated in something reddish brown. The message carved into that coating could only be found by touch.

Indima held a stick of incense in the candle that sat in the window. She let the fire burn up and down the sides until a good length of it was charred black. Then after brushing the coating off, Indima placed a paper against the pot. She rubbed the charred stick over the paper so that the letters could be read.

The pot told, in a coded shorthand, of the situation in Chaitanshehar. Her childhood friend Datri sent the information every few months. In fact, there were aspects of the city's situation that she knew better than most of the people who lived there, better even than some of its leaders knew, especially when it came to things an outsider might need to know to make their own way to that place. No food in the city, but that wasn't news and quickly passed over. There were strange events in Pashun, soldiers mustering...maybe. Datri wasn't entirely sure, but the city was prepared for an attack at any moment, an attack that hadn't yet come.

The rest of the message spoke of the routes to get to the city. The enemies of Chaitanshehar had worked since its founding to keep people away from the city. Most of it was magical wards that turned people back and led them to become lost. Sometimes their enemies set up soldier stations as well, and other hidden spies or obstacles to turn people away from ever reaching the city.

Datri's network of spies kept track of those stations and noted the best routes to avoid the magical traps. She knew the safe houses in each of the cities where a person might hide for a few days and get new supplies, though these days those houses seemed to have disappeared from Pashun. There were no new magical wards to confuse pilgrims to the city, and the people of Chaitanshehar had cleared some new paths as well. Datri described them as if they were locations on a kiwan board, telling where to turn and how far to travel. It was an imperfect description, but short of drawing a map, they hadn't been able to come up with a better way.

Indima committed the routes to memory, reminding herself of the older ones and learning a few new ones. They were steps in a dance, dances that she would perform in the days ahead so that the memory didn't slip away.

At the end was a final reminder, that anyone wishing to join their city please bring as much food as they could carry. She touched those words, recognizing the understated desperation that must lie behind them. Datri was not someone to beg.

After one more review of the routes, she crumpled the paper and tossed it into the flames in the fireplace of the room beside that hallway. Then she went to her stepmother's sitting room.

"Will you be eating here tonight, dear?" Tupti blotted her writing quill and set it down.

"Late," Indima said. "Shidhi can get me something to eat when I return."

"Where will you be? You know your father will ask when he returns from the galleries." He would come in smelling like the preservatives they used on the silks. Or else like fish tanks, if he'd spent the day with the fish that grew their own fibers resembling silk, fibers that might be used for clothing someday. She wasn't disappointed to miss that smell.

"Dancing," was all she said.

Tupti looked at her hard, waiting for her to say more. "At the temple?" she said finally.

Indima shook her head. "There's a square just down the street. He might even see me as he's coming in."

Lips pursed, Tupti picked her quill up again and resumed her letter writing. Stepdaughter ignored.

Suited Indima just fine.

She wore her temple dancing clothes, long and chaste silks that floated like wings beneath her arms when she lifted them, but with added bracelets that clacked as she moved.

In the square she danced the story of Chaitanshehar. She used the passes and motions of the sacred dances but combined them in different ways to tell the story of a distant city.

She danced of the dangers of the lava fields. She danced of the cold. Those could have told of any of the cities of the valley. Cold and fire, the twin dangers of Eghsal.

But then she lifted a pass from a dance to the goddess Aoso to tell how the city was new. A sequence that was meant to honor the twin gods Shemo and Humo served to retell their battles against the soldiers who wanted to tear them down. When she took a dance that was supposed to honor the laws and ways of the god Ryo, she inverted it. With arms moving in serpent-like motions, she danced of a city that welcomed the untouchables and outcasts and even the mumblers. That part of the dance almost tripped her up. She had little use for castes and had taken a lover from a lower caste once, an unthinkable crime to her family and peers. The only lover she ever missed.

But mumblers were...they were *mumblers*, different somehow. Yet they formed a part of the city as well, and Datri had never indicated any problems within the city caused by them living together. Mumblers learning the language of the people of the cities, and the people of the cities learning the mumbling language in turn. She had always been taught that mumblers couldn't speak real words because they weren't as smart as real people. Turned out, it was as false as so many other claims about the valley's past.

The dance shifted into wide steps and sweeping turns. She told of the magic wall that drew people closer. She took a quick-footed part of the celebration of the goddesses of chaos—Teja, Kiela, Maela—to tell of the magic wards the city's enemies placed in the way. And it segued into a dance of Perkwom, offering the god's protection and safety.

An invitation.

People gathered around the square—quite a crowd by now, though their suppers grew cold in their homes. They applauded. How much would they understand of the dance they'd seen?

Even in the temple, the dancers asked that question. What purpose did their participation serve in the festivals and holy days of the gods and goddesses? There was an emotional element that anyone should pick up on. The audience responded to the arc of the dances, to the joys, devastations, and honor.

In some ways that was the most important part of a sacred dance, to capture some key emotional depth to the story of that day's goddess or god. Indima aimed for the same connection in her subversive way. The emotion and excitement of founding a brand new city, the terror of being besieged and under attack, the sense of being welcomed into a new home. Those should all be felt, no matter what else the audience understood. They could read it in her face and body language.

Now her movements slowed, and she made no attempt to incorporate any familiar patterns. She tilted her upper body backward, swaying in shrinking circles. Her dance was the slow, relaxing acceptance of a hot spring pool on a cold day. That was how she imagined Chaitanshehar now, apart from the hunger. She'd never been there herself and guessed she never would, so she let her imagination of what the place could one day be dictate the way the dance resolved to its ending.

Indima came to a rest with one leg trailing behind, the other bent at the knee, and her face resting on her open hand, her whole body bending forward as if already resting in something that was still to come.

Sometimes in the temple dances there was more to what they did. If someone knew the story already, they might be reminded of the details of the pantheon in all its wrinkled complexity. Even the parts it was impossible to dance lay behind the movements, waiting for those who knew to bring it forward in their own minds.

Those who knew the story. That was a part of her attempt here as well as in the temple. The rumors of the city of untouchables were common even out here, so much deeper into the valley. So people knew of its existence, if nothing else. And the more they knew that was true, the more they would recognize as she danced.

When she stood, she gazed around the square at her audience. Some of them would seek her out later. That was the real reason for her dances. Let the priests think it was simply a harmless indulgence to let her dance apart from the temples and sanctioned styles. Let the silk weavers believe her to be crazy. They treated her as if some unspeakable tragedy had happened to her in Romnai before her return to the Silk City. Most probably believed her dalliance with the low-caste Ekana had made her go insane. Others maybe blamed the death of her mother, though she'd already been performing her unconventional dances long before then. Maybe some thought she'd always been somewhat odd, blaming the gods or the fire or the luck of the mumblers.

Let her stepmother think she was impious and too quickly

indulged. For all Tupti's understanding of other women in difficult situations, she probably agreed that Indima was gods-touched in some way that changed her sanity.

Some of those who met her eye would know the truth, though. Or at least they would guess the part that mattered, that she was someone who knew things. That she had the secrets to find the way to Chaitanshehar.

She wanted to remember their faces when they did seek her out. And she wanted to drive home the image that she was a wise one who had seen far more than others, something the right kind of unblinking stare could impose.

As she looked from person to person, their dark skin and eyes and fine, high-caste features reflected the lanterns that were just coming on. One was suddenly familiar. Her father.

He frowned wryly, dropped his gaze, and turned away to head home.

***

The Silk City did not have the kind of drinking places Indima had known in Romnai. People were more likely to meet at each others' homes to celebrate. Or else to drink alone. Maybe it was because so much of the city belonged to one of two jatis, the high-caste silk weaver jati, or the slightly lower caste cheetah jati who were their servants. Beyond those two were a mix of low-caste laborers and soldiers, but they kept themselves apart. If you dared venture beyond the silk weaver jati's parts of the city, you could find some halls that more resembled the bars she used to know.

Some days she went to such places to dance. Back before she'd begun to dance in the streets, those places were the only ones she dared to dance in. Today she wasn't in this establishment to dance, but to find out who would speak to her so she could pass along what information she knew.

As with everything in the city, the place was tight, the walls close and the spaces between patrons minimal. How had she ever found the space to dance? It was only a brief question. The people moved aside for her now, just as they had back then. An aura of otherworldly authority gave her whatever space she needed. A table near the back cleared as soon as she approached it, and she took her seat.

The proprietress brought out her usual drink. It was in the small glasses the bar usually used for fire liquor. The image of her sipping from the hard liquor suited what she wanted people to think, but the proprietress, as always, had filled this with tisane instead, sweetened just slightly. The woman, whose name Indima deliberately never learned, was one of various people in the city with connections to Datri, a part of that woman's spy network. She had reached out to Indima even before her first time dancing there, offering the bar as a good place for both dancing and clandestine meetings.

The first people to approach her tonight were two women, wallahs who worked in the city. Silk weavers were never interested in Chaitanshehar—what had they to gain by losing their status in some distant city? And the city's porters who transported goods from beyond the city were their own jati and seldom sought her out. It was the lower servants who found themselves curious.

Indima still spoke obliquely while she judged how trustworthy they were.

"There is a way to that city, a city declared pure by fire. Not pure because all the people in it are identical, but pure because they are undivided." Might as well make it sound like a metaphor in case anyone grew suspicious. "Would you like to know more?"

They both looked scared, but the shorter one bit her lip and nodded.

"Then the first thing you'll need is food. Lots of food, as much as you can carry. Not just for your own sake while traveling, and not only so you have some food when you get there. But for them, too. A peace offering as they allow you to join in with them."

The taller one glanced away and then spoke low to her companion. The only word Indima overheard was, "hungry."

"Save up to buy as much as you can. Get a horse and wagon even, if possible."

She gave them some more information, speaking mainly to the shorter one who demonstrated more interest in the idea of actually traveling to the new city.

After those two, she met with a cheetah jati servant. Rare for one of them to consider leaving their high ranking life, but Indima knew that he'd been recently unlucky in love, rejected by the one he'd sought to court.

She doubted he would end up following through with any plan that took him away from his powerful family and peers. The cheetah jati were servants, but far above others. She gave him enough of an idea of what he faced and then sent him on his way. If he decided he wanted to learn more, he could find her a second time.

A woman from the small, local soldier jati came later in the day, after a few others that blurred together. She needed to escape, needed somewhere, some kind of hope that she might be able to get away. She wouldn't say everything that was happening, but enough for Indima to guess the woman's fear and the treatment she faced among the people who were supposed to protect her.

"I...there's only so much I can do to help you." She wished she could find a dance that would carry the woman to safety. "I will tell you what might help. There is a place where you would be safe, but it's a hard journey and long, and it takes time to prepare." The woman didn't look like she had that kind of time. "I can't promise that you'd be able to get away safely."

Did she know anyone who might be able to help her get away from her jati long enough to escape entirely?

Tupti.

"Don't say that I sent you or what you plan to do in the end, but you should speak with my stepmother's assistant." She kept her voice so low that the other woman had to lean in with her ear almost to Indima's lips. "They know how to help someone in your situation, find you a place to escape for a time. It's not so different from what they do officially. And then you can decide if you want to make the bigger journey."

"How will I find them?"

Indima gave her directions and explained how to contact them. When the woman left, Indima lay her head back against the seat back and closed her eyes. Helping others could be so draining. She battled between wishing she could do more and wishing someone had been there to offer an escape to her, when she'd first been forced to come to the Silk City.

When she opened her eyes, someone else was already waiting to speak to her. "I was about to leave. I should return another day soon, so we could talk then." She rubbed her eyes to see better in the gloom.

"I'm not sure you will."

Indima squinted. The taller of the two women she'd spoken with to start the evening stood there, but she wasn't the one who'd spoken. It was a middle-aged man dressed in the robes of a priest.

There were few priests in the Silk City, only enough to keep the small temple going. She knew this one, Chiray, who oversaw her dancing in the temple.

"Tisrah," she said. "Why have you come to this place? Am I needed for a dance?"

Chiray didn't answer her directly. "I have been informed that you encouraged this woman to steal a horse and wagon."

What? Of course she hadn't. She'd encouraged them to get a horse and cart if they could, but she'd said nothing of stealing. "I have never instructed anyone to attempt thievery." She stood and stretched her back. "You have been misinformed."

"I think you'll need to leave with us," he said as she made a move to escape past them. "I continue to have questions about your judgment."

To let herself be escorted away from there? Not a chance. Indima lifted her arms above her head and began the dance of the goddess Gouwind, faithful wife and ruler of her well ordered home.

The priest interposed himself so she couldn't spin past. "Don't make me have my soldiers escort you out. We both know how bad that would look, for the temple and for its most famous dancer both. I only wish to speak to you further."

A flash of anger blazed through her. Let them arrest her, if that's what they were going to do. Let them do whatever they would, it wasn't as if anyone would stop them. Priests and soldiers, everyone bowed to their wishes, even in this city where neither jati was especially large.

But as she snapped her arms into a new position, she pictured the people she'd tried to help earlier that day. This woman standing before her had been false, and some would probably decide against ever leaving the Silk City. But some were truly in need of her help.

She thought especially of the last woman, desperate to escape her family or lover or jati for some reason Indima had never questioned directly. As careful as she was to be discreet, this was a public place. Someone who knew that woman's real story would have seen them together.

If she let herself be arrested in such a public way, it would only make things worse for that woman and the others. And make it more difficult for her to help anyone else in the future.

She lowered her arms and gestured for the priest to follow her, as if she were still the one in control. The same calm and otherworldly waif she had always been.

Inside, her heart beat an uneven rhythm, like the time she was caught by her jati with Ekana, a pattern that said she'd already lost control.

And nothing remained for her except to go along and hope the punishment wasn't too much.

If only she dared reach out to someone like her stepmother so she could be rescued herself.

CHAPTER 13

The Dream of the Forgotten South crashed against the rocks before an ice covered land, far north of where they'd put to sea, the weak sun low toward the horizon. A shipwreck made it sound dramatic, but by the time Harkala heard the first crunch of timber on rocks, they had been caught in the current so long that they were weary to their deepest level and prepared for the worst. That they were in sight of some sort of real land when it happened made it feel like a cosmic joke, with the gods themselves stooping to mock them as they drowned in the freezing water.

Ekana and one of the other crew members had to carry her into the lifeboat by force. What good was a little boat when the big one had failed? It wouldn't bring them south. It would only save them so they could freeze, if it even managed to reach land.

The icy breakers sending up flecks of sleet and snow all around them made her doubt it was worth the attempt. But they got her in, got everyone as secure as they could. And hoped.

For all the good it did.

Neelar fell from the lifeboat as soon as they dropped into the breakers. He was lost from sight before anyone could react, lost to the pounding waves.

Harkala cried out to save him, but it turned into a cry of pain. The cry he never even had a chance to utter. They had no choice but to focus on rowing the rest of them to safety through the rough sea, or they would all suffer the same fate. Ice formed on the oars as they lifted from the water, a filigree that reached farther each time, closer to the boat's inhabitants, until the rowers plunged them back into the waves, erasing the ice so it could begin again.

The boat scraped bottom, and the sailors in front jumped into the knee-deep water to drag the boat as far up the shore as they could. Sembaari helped Harkala onto the beach. As soon as she was clear of the boat and the people trying to secure it higher up above the water, she scanned the breakers where the treacherous rocks were. No sign of Neelar bobbing in the water. No sign of him clinging to debris or struggling shoreward. She had hoped, even though she knew it was in vain.

Beyond them, *The Dream of the Forgotten South* had not yet sunk. It listed heavily to one side as the waves battered it against the rocks. It taunted her, a relic of the excitement she had felt when they set sail, floating just out of their reach.

"We need fire, quick," someone called. She still hadn't torn her eyes away from her ship by the time she heard the roar of flames. She moved toward the light and put aside all thought. What was there more complete in the world than flames? They created the cosmos and destroyed its constituent parts. They burned away dreams, proved all things mere illusion. She sank into the shale beside the fire, her legs curled up beneath her.

Some time later, she woke to Ekana shaking her shoulder.

"We've put up a bed for you, Harkala. And a little bit of shelter. A roof, anyway. Close enough to the fire to keep you warm."

She stared at him blankly for a moment, her mind back on the ship, back when he'd reluctantly given the wheel to her. He'd apologized later, stiffly, and Sembaari had tried to explain to her some of Ekana's life before he'd come back to Jarnur. She'd been too numb to understand most of it, and what did it matter by then anyway? They were stuck in the current.

No, not anymore. She rubbed at her face and tried to see in the darkness, tried to remember, tried right away to forget again. They were stuck on some frozen land, and he was showing her a place to sleep. She stumbled after him to the other side of the fire. They'd made a rough tent out of a paulin from the ship. The heat from the fire funneled into the tent, and would until the wind changed significantly.

Unable to form thoughts into words, Harkala climbed inside and lay down. Only as her eyes closed did she sit back up and ask, "But what about everyone else? You'll make another tent for you, right?"

"Hush. Sleep, captain," Ekana said. "We'll tie up some other paulins and get to sleep too. None of us has any interest in freezing to death."

Harkala laid her head back down and slept.

***

A thundering snore woke them all. Harkala crawled halfway from her tent and saw a herd of strange creatures gathered on the beach. Was herd the right word? A pod? A pride? They were gigantic things with long, tapering bodies and flippers for arms. Whiskers around their faces gave them a comical look, but the growls and grunts of their noises promised something more like violence. Some of the crew members picked up the weapons they'd managed to salvage from the ship and arranged themselves as if to fight the animals off.

"Leave them be," Harkala said. "We don't know what they are or how to hunt them or even if their meat is good for anything."

They ate some food while they watched the beasts. Harkala wandered a short way up the beach away from the herd of animals, where she found Neelar's body, tapping the shore and pulling a short ways away with every lapping wave.

They dragged him out of the water and piled stones around his body. Harkala spoke of his bravery in joining their expedition and his efforts to get them this far.

It sounded hollow to her, since *this far* was not at all where they wanted to be. Still the crew murmured their appreciation as they laid the final stones.

Maybe he was the lucky one, to die so quickly. Harkala saw a future for them, one of slow starvation, but it would be the cold that killed them first.

The land was barren, as far as they could see. The beach was littered with driftwood, and that made for an easy fire, but wherever those trees had grown, it wasn't anywhere within sight. There were rocks on the shore, long strands of seaweed, and the pebbly sand—and little else. Maybe they could find a way to make the seaweed edible or find a way to hunt the animals that came to that barren shore. Maybe there would be seabirds or seabird eggs they might poach.

Beyond that? She tried to see anything to break up the monotony inland, but all there was that way, in the dim light of the low sun, was ice. It came down as far as the beach, leaving no gap in between for edible plants to grow or any animals worth hunting to live.

While they made their way back to the makeshift camp, the giant creatures on the beach snorted their honking noises and jostled with each other. One smaller one slipped into the water and swam down and out of sight. Two of them tangled heads and flashed their long, tapered fangs at each other. Harkala watched, expecting it to turn into a fight, and fighting between such colossal beasts would surely be impressive.

Instead they each shifted out of the other's way and settled back in to bask in the weak sunlight. Her notebooks were lost, still on the ship, so she satisfied her scientific curiosity by merely observing their behavior.

Something moved on the beach near the beasts. Harkala froze and watched movement that didn't resolve into anything in particular. Just a sense of the beach becoming fluid for a moment. She nudged Ekana and pointed.

Ekana stared for a long time without reacting. Harkala began to question if she'd seen anything at all. Then she saw it again, and much clearer from this angle. It was a person. Or several people probably. They wore some kind of clothing that made them blend in with the shore, so it was hard to get a read on how many.

Ekana swore under his breath. "Have weapons to hand," he urged the others in a low voice. "They're not coming toward us yet, but there's no way they'll ignore us for long. Once their hunting is complete."

Hunting the great creatures on the beach was exactly what they were doing. That would answer the question of whether the animals had meat that was safe and worth eating. And the island being inhabited meant there was a chance they could survive after all. But not if they angered the people who already lived here.

"Weapons to hand, yes," she added to Ekana's instruction. "But do nothing threatening. If there's any chance of us surviving on this island, we'll need them to take us in and show us how."

She shivered as a blast of cold air blew in her face.

The hunters closed in on one of the beasts that was a little apart from the rest. The hunters froze, and again Harkala could scarcely see them. The animal lifted its whiskered face as if sniffing the breeze, and then laid it back down. The hunters resumed their approach, slow as a funding request from the university.

All of a sudden they sprang forward fast, and the change in speed left Harkala unsure what to focus on. Before she or the animals could react, the hunters' prey had three spears in its side. The whole herd of creatures took up a cry of alarm that made her cover her ears. Most of them spun around and swam for deeper water. A few made a deep-throated croaking sound that pulsed, each of them together. They closed in on the hunters and their wounded prey, their bodies wriggling back and forth as the water grew shallower.

Harkala's hands clenched as she watched. As most of the hunters continued to concentrate on the wounded animal, one hunter held up a horn with a long bell. They blew into the horn, and a vibrating note countered the animals' croaking. The beasts drew back and shook their tusked heads. The biggest gave one last bellow, and the wounded one tried to lunge forward to meet up with the herd, but the hunters held it back with a net cast over its seaward side and the thrusts of more spears. The horn player blew a final, toneless note on the horn, a bleating, ear-splitting antithesis to music, and the rest of the animals fled into the safety of the water.

The hunters made quick work of butchering their prey.

When they were carting the last of the meat and bones off the beach, Ekana waved his arm. "Wait, help!" he called. He repeated something similar in a language Harkala didn't know.

The hunters didn't respond or even look over their way.

They'd been seen. No doubt could change that fact. So what did the people of this land think of them?

What did they intend to do to them, obvious castaways that they were?

Ekana scheduled the crew into shifts who explored the area around their little camp, searching for anything useful as well as further signs of the local people. The shore provided an open route around this portion of the land. There were some boulders and rock formations that stood in the way, but it was easy to circle those and gaze a long way around the shore. They explored a good ways around to the east. The way it curved to the north led them to guess that it was an island of some kind, or perhaps a peninsula of some distant, frozen mainland. There was open sea to the east of them. No hope of traveling home that way by land.

That sea was full of ice. In fact, even if they were on an island, Harkala supposed that somewhere not too far north the ice must form a solid connection to the mountains north of their own homes. But then those mountains would be as impassable from the north as they were from the south. Trapped, no matter what way she looked at it.

Closer by, a glacier came nearly to the sea. That was the bulk of the ice she'd seen earlier. There were no plants growing there, no inland relief from the cold sea spray. The sun set so early, before she had even finished trying to take everything in. No sign of the locals while they were exploring, not even a hunting trail heading inland for them to follow. They decided to explore to the west the next day.

Dusk lasted a long time, as if the sun was only a short way below the horizon for hours after it had set from view. Sometime before the light was entirely gone, three figures left what seemed to be solid glacier and came down the strand.

This time Sembaari greeted them. He'd been teaching her words and phrases of his mumbler language, but she couldn't follow what he said exactly. Probably something like, "Hello and welcome to our camp."

The visitors shook their heads and said something else she couldn't understand. Neither could Sembaari. "It's not any language I've heard," he said. He said something else, slowly and carefully.

The others responded. The sound was completely different from what Sembaari said, a quick language that went from sound to sound without any apparent pause. Sembaari tried again, even slower. The mumbler language had, to Harkala's ear, a more fluid, up and down rhythm to it, with words that rose in pitch and trilled downward. Nothing like the relentless drum beat of the strangers' words.

Whatever they were saying, they were repeating it over and over, the same sounds, the same rhythms. Not trying different words in the same language and not offering a different language for them to communicate.

Harkala spoke aside to Ekana. "Are they not mumblers then?"

"I don't know. The mumblers are lots of different people with lots of different languages. But usually they all know the trade pidgin."

It wasn't polite, or at least it wouldn't be polite in Jarnur—who could say with an unknown people what was polite and what wasn't?—but Harkala leaned closer to stare into the faces of the strangers. Sembaari had dark skin and features not terribly different from her own or Ekana's, proof even there that the mumblers were actually a number of different peoples. But most mumblers had much paler skin—an *unnatural* shade she'd always been taught growing up—and much wider features. Less refined, was what people in the cities taught each other, as if the mumbler's faces were not as fully formed. A people cast from the ovens of the cosmic fire before they were fully done. That idea was surely an insult and a simplification.

The strangers kept their faces well bundled. Their eyes were farther apart than her own, and both were a light ash-brown that would have stood out as uncommon in Jarnur. But not unheard of. The skin around it looked brown. Maybe. Not the same as her own, though. There was a hint of something else she couldn't place, of the brown tusks of those sea creatures, of the wood of *The Dream of the Forgotten South* before it had been smeared in tar and placed into the sea. Not mumbler pale, certainly. But not a color she'd seen among her own people either.

How many peoples filled this wide world?

As a scholar she knew there could well be hundreds, even thousands of people groups around the world. The best thinkers had calculated the size of the world, a vast ball of rock and water, shaped by the Cosmic Fire. And they knew there was a Forgotten South somewhere with other people. Or at least, so the stories told. So the idea that there could be many lands, many valleys warmed by sea air and lava, many homelands where the sun itself was sufficient to keep them warm—it wasn't so strange when she thought about it. Not strange in her head.

But strange in heart to meet the proof face to face.

Sembaari made little progress communicating with the strangers. They did a lot of pointing. Often they gestured out in the direction of the wrecked *The Dream of the Forgotten South*, hands cupped as if to mark out the shape of the hull. Starlight shone on the water and the dark bulk out there, still mostly on the surface. Still utterly destroyed in Harkala's mind. They pointed along the shore to the west frequently as well, making scooping gestures with their hands. Were there other ships there?

Harkala felt closest to understanding in one particular sequence. One stranger pointed to sea and made the scooping motion. Then he made an exaggerated turn of his body to face west, and his pointing seemed to imply that it was some ways in that direction, not just around the curve of the beach. But then all three of them broke into the scooping gesture, and they repeated it several times.

Many ships?

A flicker of hope lit inside her. Could it be possible they would find many ships? A functioning port? Even if they couldn't get straight back to Jarnur, their dream—her dream—might not be ended.

She quickly extinguished the thought. She couldn't let herself get excited for something she might be interpreting wrong.

The strangers ended up leaving some meat behind. Walrus meat, Ekana said. It was an animal fishermen claimed to have seen, near the northern limits of their fishing voyages. They cooked it over the fire after the strangers had left. It tasted oddly sweet and had an unfamiliar texture, part squid and part something she couldn't identify. If she hadn't been so hungry, she wouldn't have stomached it.

The crew decided on their turns for watching the fire, burning the plentiful driftwood, which gave bright flames but less heat than they would have liked. Where Harkala lay, the flamelight shone brightly into the makeshift tent and right on her face. She tried to turn away, but there was no good way to escape it. She squinted, then squeezed her eyes tight, sure the light would keep her awake all night.

Within a few deep breaths, she was sound asleep.

***

The sun rose over the ocean of ice. Overnight much of the sea had frozen, making the waves along the shore into permanent shapes of some deity's imagination. The frozen waves squeezed the hull of *The Dream of the Forgotten South*. Some four or five of the creatures, the walruses, sat on the rocks that had wrecked the ship, as if overseeing its steady destruction in the new morning.

The crew had no wish to dawdle. Exercise would warm them better than their bright but powerless fire.

As they headed west, Ekana voiced the question Harkala had been wondering ever since the night before. "What were our visitors trying to tell us last night? There's something important off this way."

"A gap in the glacier?" someone suggested, their voice too muffled by wraps to identify them. "Maybe there are steam pools where we can get warm."

"Could be a valley of some kind," Sembaari said. "A depression in the land, and that's where they have their village."

"I thought it was a warning," one of the crewmen, Yashek, suggested. "Their hands looked like they were making waves rising up. Maybe the sea comes in on the tides and floods the beach up here. Some danger like that."

And what of ships? No one mentioned the possibility, and Harkala didn't dare voice it. She'd no doubt been mistaken when she tried to understand the scooping motion. Hope was a dangerous emotion.

This stretch of beach was a rougher path than the route had been going the other way. When the tide retreated, it left piles of ice, sharp peaks that looked likely to slice through their furs and boots if they walked too close. So they had to weave up and down the beach like drunks.

Yashek scampered onto the leading edge of the glacier and tried to make better time there, but the footing proved even worse. He jumped back down and came behind them, a ship's length back. They didn't wait for him to catch up.

Sembaari decided to try the other way, going down to the very edge of the water. There the ice had dissolved back into the waves. Harkala didn't like the way the shingle seemed to give way beneath each of his steps. Just once losing his footing, and he'd fall flat into the freezing water. With the only fire now well behind them and likely reduced to ashes at best.

She stayed with the main group, cautiously avoiding the beach ice by circling around, up and down. Sembaari pulled ahead and soon reached a curve in the shoreline.

He stopped as if he'd seen something worth paying attention to. Harkala watched him for any sign of what it was.

He turned toward the group and pointed up ahead. Then he cupped his hands around his mouth and shouted, "Ships!"

Harkala's heart skipped a beat. She stumbled on a shard of sea ice and caught herself on Ekana's back. Ships? Was her hope not in vain after all?

Oh, hurry, hurry.

Harkala pushed to the front of the group just as they caught up with Sembaari.

The beach ahead was full of hundreds of...not ships, but shipwrecks. The corpses of a hundred dreams—dreams of a forgotten north, a forgotten east, a forgotten west—littering the strand.

Harkala let out a wail of disappointment.

Ekana wandered down to the nearest one. He touched the timbers that had been bleached by the northern sun. "So many ships in one place. I bet that current we caught usually carries wrecks to shore here."

The current she'd steered them into. The thought was a weight on her mind, on every one of her inner organs. "I guess we were lucky enough to end up wrecked in a different location." She could hear the flatness in her own voice but made no effort to add any emotion when she felt so little of anything. "Or unlucky enough."

Sembaari shaded his eyes and looked inland. "I wonder why they insisted so strongly that we come here."

Harkala forced her mourning aside, buried it so she could dig it up again at some future time. As any good archaeologist does. Then she tried to see the beach full of shipwrecks from the eyes of the people who lived in this land.

So many wrecks meant they were used to castaways ending up here. Castaways who didn't stay. She didn't know that for certain, but the strangers hadn't understood a word they'd said—not surprising itself, if they were the first ones to sail away from Eghsal—but also hadn't seemed to expect to be understood, hadn't tried other words or languages, as far as she noticed. It had all sounded the same, and accompanied by many well practiced gestures.

It led Harkala to only one conclusion.

"They want us to build ourselves a new boat and go away."

Ekana rubbed his cheek and moved from one wreck to the next. "You might be right. And with all this timber to choose from…"

"It won't do us any good," Harkala reminded him. "If the current drives ships to shore here, how would we get away?"

Ekana strode to the edge of the water and gazed out toward the horizon. "Currents change," he said over his shoulder. "The seasons change, and the current changes with it."

History changes, too. Doesn't mean she could rely on that change to help them. "Of course it can change. But can you predict the timing well enough to get us away safely?"

"It's possible. If it changes just right, it may be a perfect trade route to and from the Forgotten South. North in winter, and maybe a little sooner would avoid the dangers we found. And south again in the spring."

A dream built of the pieces of shattered dreams of hundreds and thousands of others. Something fitting in that, she supposed. History was built of similar pieces and fragments. But it sounded too hopeful. If the currents were good for trade, why was there no sign that the local peoples were used to trading with others? Not that there appeared to be a lot of trade goods on this barren shore, she supposed.

Harkala sat on the beach. The shock of her disappointment was still too much, overwhelming any energy she might use to help the crew identify ships and parts of those ships that were worth repurposing.

They exclaimed over some timbers, digging into the sand for buried planks they could turn into a new hull and masts. And they discarded others that were too dried by the open air or infected with rot. All of it washed over Harkala. Excitement or disappointment were just differences of scale on a scale she couldn't find it in her to reach. Emotions were too taxing, and she was tired beyond any ability to pay.

The crew kept at their scavenging until late in the day, pulling together a great pile of wood they hoped to use. They were just about to turn around and head back to their camp along the beach when Harkala noticed figures approaching them. At least a score of them, probably twice that. She called out to Ekana.

As if to confirm their suspicions that this shipbuilding from refuse was exactly what their visitors had wanted, a group of the strangers who lived in this land trooped over to them from the direction they'd left behind. They carried a great deal of gear with them. Harkala recognized many things they must have recovered from the wreck of *The Dream of the Forgotten South*. Food and trade goods and supplies she'd given up for lost, including her notebooks and writing supplies. And timber from the other ship, enough to double the pile they had already gathered. Without any word to Harkala or her crew, the strangers reassembled the makeshift tents and built them a driftwood fire, well away from the dried wood of the shipwrecks. They left another portion of walrus meat beside it.

Then still silent, they faded out of sight into some path in the ice that Harkala couldn't see, just as the sun fell below the watery horizon. The flames of the fire they'd been given licked greedily at the firewood.

CHAPTER 14

No twist of arcist magic and no clever way of weaving a spell had the least effect on freeing Pavresh from Kamlak's power. Maybe he was right and power was all there was to the magic, and Pavresh's way of insisting on understanding the stories—which had been his mentor Chaitan's way as well—only weakened him in the end, blinded him to the reality of the magic beyond those images.

Pavresh tried tweaking his spell for preserving himself, making it faster, practicing casting it even when Kamlak was nowhere in sight. If he happened to pick just the right time, maybe he could evade Kamlak's control.

It was never just the right time.

Pavresh spent hours with the spell working—or he hoped it was working, at least—with no sign of Kamlak, and then just as he let his focus down, Kamlak would enter. Or he'd show up just too soon, when Pavresh was considering making an attempt but not quite ready.

Pavresh analyzed what Kamlak did to try to turn it against him, but that never bore fruit either. The exact spell escaped his grasp. He could create the idea of wanting to follow someone's instructions, of compelling a person to obey. It was similar, but it lacked the precision and power of the way Kamlak controlled him when he showed up.

For his part, Kamlak took great pleasure in parading Pavresh around as his marionette. His own pet arcist, performing entirely at his whim. Pavresh thought he sensed some loneliness in how Kamlak needed to show his power to Pavresh, needed to gloat and be appreciated by the only person who understood what he was doing, how impressive it was.

Taking Pavresh to a street-side balcony, he forced Pavresh to watch the workers entering the nearby factory. "See, this could be your people in that other city of yours." As if he'd forgotten the name.

The workers marched in perfect unison. Another shift of workers marched out right as they went in, perfect coordination between the two groups. No jostling, no arguing, and no complaints.

Even the workers that left, as they separated to go their own ways to sleep, kept themselves in time to the drums that beat all over the city.

Pavresh despised them. He despised the martial beat and trumpet sound that directed their footsteps and controlled their actions. But he felt it, too, felt the impulse to join in and do his part for the leaders' great plans.

Was it different from his own spell in Chaitanshehar that pressured people to work for the good of the city? It was. He had to believe that it was. But when he felt and heard the drumbeat of Kamlak's magic, he couldn't express how it was different.

Pavresh lost track of the days. Kamlak would visit, some days to brag and other days to simply talk about arcist magic, as if they were two colleagues trying to puzzle through a difficult problem. Pavresh suspected that he might be studying Pavresh's attempts to unravel the magic as well, watching him and improving his spell as Pavresh sought for any weaknesses.

Even so, he couldn't stop trying.

At some point Kamlak stopped showing up in his room. For nearly a twelve-day, he didn't stop by. Someone slipped him food, but always while he was asleep. How they knew when he was actually asleep, he couldn't decide. There must be a window of some kind that let his captors watch him.

On the second day of Kamlak's absence, he scoured the walls to figure out where the window was. There was nothing obvious. His best guess was that the grate high up one wall was not for ventilation, or not only that, but for keeping an eye on him.

Pavresh tried to stretch up as high as he could, tried to brace himself into the corner of the room, but he couldn't get enough purchase to climb. The grate remained out of reach.

He created around himself the image of a prisoner falsely imprisoned. A victim of injustice who cries out for assistance. An animal baby in need of rescue. Then he projected that image, as well as the magic allowed, through that grate.

No one entered to rescue him.

When Kamlak finally returned, he came inside Pavresh's room full of an anxious energy. "You can't imagine the sight, Pavresh. I wish I could take you to see the tunnel, but the journey is too far. Several days' travel to get there, and the same back. But the work is progressing so well. I want everyone to see it."

Pavresh couldn't move his arms from the awkward position he'd had when Kamlak arrived—his right elbow cocked sideways and his left arm tucked in tight to his side.

"Progressing fine while you're there," Pavresh said. He probed the boundary that let his mouth move to speak but kept everything else stiff and separate from his thoughts. "Now that you're back, you think they'll keep working so well?"

Kamlak offered Pavresh a dish of winter berries without freeing his hands to be able to accept the offer. When Pavresh didn't—couldn't—take any in his fingers, Kamlak smiled and gulped a mouthful straight from the bowl.

The scent of the berries, sharp and clean, filled the room.

Before he'd finished chewing, Kamlak said, "You had your school. I can have apprentices too, wouldn't you say?" He tilted his head back as if to listen to some music outside the walls. "And tools, as well. Ways you haven't even considered, to cast an arcist effect when I can't be in a place."

Pavresh often likened the martial effect on the city to a drumbeat. But it was the trumpets he sometimes heard distantly, through the walls, that he suspected played the major role in Kamlak's spell.

He made a half-hearted attempt to free his body from

Kamlak's spell. It didn't work any better than he'd suspected it would.

"The tunnel," Kamlak continued, able to ignore Pavresh's magic as if it were just an insect to be brushed off the table before mealtime. "The tunnel will carry our power deep into the mountains. We found a pass that gets us farther south than I had even hoped. And my miners dig. Oh, do they dig!"

"That's wonderful."

"I would show you if I could."

He jumped up and was gone before Pavresh could respond. The scent of winter berries lingered for most of the day.

***

Kamlak's visits with Pavresh resumed, and he often spent the time vaunting his success to Pavresh. It wasn't the achievements of his miners that he focused on. He'd outrun the news, and nothing new was expected from that way for some time. So for now he bragged instead about arcist magic and how much better his approach was.

"You're a brilliant man, Pavresh, but still only on the surface after all. Underneath, you're trapped by the same narratives you try to manipulate. You have to break free from the way you've imagined it. Take all those great ideas and push them farther."

Pavresh had no answer, as was often the case when Kamlak started talking about his own way of seeing arcist magic. Kamlak made his theories sound so believable, but Pavresh didn't know how to translate those claims into magic.

Maybe his thinking was still too superficial after all.

One day, Kamlak set him marching out of the room. They left the seminary entirely and crossed along the lower edge of the city. The martial beat pervaded everything he saw, prodded every person who happened by. Kamlak directed him into a building near the mudpots. It stank of sulfur on the outside, and within was even worse, the smell concentrated and amplified by industrial processes.

Pavresh knew little about welding, but he recognized it

happening in that metal shop. Smelting and casting metal in one section, and welding the pieces together in another. Great, ball-shaped things of some dark gray metal.

"Planning to create a new sport, Kamlak? I will coach the red team for you. If you just set me free to do that."

Kamlak's laugh was dismissive. "Again you fail to understand what's going on right before your eyes. I have stopped blaming you. It is simply your nature."

He brought Pavresh down to the sunken, cement-lined floor. Heat from the furnace grew oppressive. Pavresh tried to roll back his sleeves, but Kamlak's magic gave him no chance to do so. His back grew wet with sweat.

"Steam engines have such potential power," Kamlak said. "Have you seen them up close?"

Power, of course. He'd recognized the power in steam engines ever since he was young and saw the way his father's mine used steam to carry loads of ore up to the surface. But had he ever studied the way an engine actually worked? "No," he had to admit. "I've never looked that closely."

"A true steam engine requires much greater precision than this shop can give, but it isn't a steam engine we want. Have you seen what happens when an engine fails? I suppose you haven't, if you haven't looked closely, but they don't just stop—"

"They explode." Pavresh had seen the wreckage of two locomotives, still dangerously hot from crashing. Almost twenty years ago, when he'd first come to Romnai. The images were still fresh, seared into his mind. Their engines had fused in the heat of their collapse. Metal melted into the rocky ground, coating the twisted remains of the track. "Oh, I know what that means. Destruction."

Kamlak rubbed his hands together. "Exactly. But what happens when we can control that destruction? Your miners have known it for ages and used violence to dig through the ground. But they never put it all together like we have today."

"What exactly have you put together?"

"These steam balls." Kamlak gestured with a sweeping

motion at the metal spheres being cast and formed and fused together throughout the shop. "Each of them a steam engine inside. Well, not really a real steam engine, but think of it that way. Roll them down a mine shaft, add some heat as they strike each other, and boom! We create a tunnel faster than anything you can imagine."

"And collapse the tunnel you've already built onto your miners."

Kamlak wasn't about to be dissuaded by anything Pavresh could say. "We have it all calculated out. Our miners will take shelter at a sufficient distance. We've worked out how far it needs to be, exactly where to place the explosions and how many to use. Soon we'll set the plan in motion, and our place as heroes of the city of Pashun will be secured."

Pavresh had the sense that when Kamlak said, "our place," what he meant was, "my place."

The workers placed some mechanism inside one half of the metal balls. Across the floor, the completed balls each had a distinct opening on one side and a cap waiting to be sealed over whatever reaction they initiated. Heat pulsed the air, turning Pavresh's sight wavy.

Kamlak watched him as if waiting for him to say something. Waiting for a reaction. Why? Pavresh thought back through the statements and looked around at the steam engine bombs. That was a lot of energy, a lot of power for a tunnel that would likely lead nowhere.

A lot of destruction. What if he gave up the plan to head south, turned that destruction somewhere else? Or even if they didn't change the plan, but returned from the Forgotten South to use the explosions against Chaitanshehar?

That was what Kamlak was hoping to see, Pavresh's horrified reaction as he realized what Kamlak had planned.

Well, he could turn that perverse wish around. "I hope you have good protection to keep them from exploding too soon. Imagine what would happen if these ones here were to go off right where they are! That's a lot of damage to your seminary and your fancy houses up above."

Kamlak's frown passed almost before Pavresh could note it. He recovered and pointed at the pieces. "You have to build up the steam first. They're harmless right now."

"Streets torn apart, buildings collapsing slowly toward the geysers below. I know, I know." He moved his shoulders, as much as the magic allowed, in mock protest. "You're not going to let it happen. Not to Pashun, your own city. Still, what if Mahendri sees some advantage in that happening? He might order something along those lines." What would be Kamlak's worst fear in this situation? "Or even wrest them away from your control entirely, turn them against you. He's used you for what he needs, so after all authority's under his power, then you're just another bomb to toss out and see what it destroys."

"This is what I get for letting you use your voice." Even an overpowered magician could sound petulant. Pavresh tried to think of any folk stories that fit that mix of arrogance and childish peevishness. The haughty ruler, perhaps, though so far Kamlak kept his power publicly subservient to the other leaders.

Maybe that was why he felt such a need to show off his plans and spells to Pavresh.

"For your information, Mahendri has left on his own tasks and will be away for a long time. And guess who has all the power necessary to control matters while he's away? With my control of the magic, I'm so much more than a useful, temporary tool." Kamlak made a tiny motion with his hand, and Pavresh felt a change in the spell. It felt like a pair of shears that had been tensed around a string suddenly closing. He didn't even bother trying to speak. He knew already that he wouldn't be able to, that his mouth and vocal cords had been cut off from his control.

"This is a new thing." Kamlak punctuated his words with emphatic hand motions. "How often is there something truly new? A twist on an old way, that happens all the time. But these balls of destruction, they change everything. They change the power in the valley."

Kamlak droned on about the future he envisioned and the authority he would one day command. Pavresh only half listened. Most of his focus was on the magic that bound him. Kamlak had made a mistake, changing the spell like that while he was aware of it, while he was paying attention to how the magic affected him.

The change in control, from his body but not his voice to everything, both body and voice, had been abrupt. But the difference in how it felt opened a wrinkle in the spell. He probed that point, examined it from every angle. How did that change mean the difference between words and silence? He ran a mental line from that wrinkle of magic to his throat, to the part of his mind that controlled speech.

A deeper pattern teased at the edges of his mind.

He kept probing, kept rearranging the pattern, as Kamlak showed him the various stages of the metal casings. Such things mattered on a practical level, maybe mattered more than anything. But to the bigger picture of what Kamlak was doing with arcist magic, those questions were pesky nothings, insects to be waved away with a single sweep of his arm.

When Kamlak marched him back into his room, he probed the arcist block that Kamlak put on him, felt it change as soon as Kamlak let him go.

So that was the spell. Pavresh contemplated it the rest of the day, arranging and rearranging ways to free himself. If he could just unravel a little of it, the rest would come apart with little effort.

Alone in his cell, he'd already been freed, so that meant examining the spell by guess and memory. When he'd done what he could by memory, he turned to examining the trumpets and drums of the city, hoping to find a pattern of weaknesses to help him not only free himself but break Kamlak's hold on the people of the city. He waited impatiently for Kamlak to return.

***

When Kamlak brought him his next meal, he didn't even bother with arcist magic. He set the food down, looked around as if making sure Pavresh wasn't attempting any escape, and then left without a word.

So much for testing the pattern.

A few days passed before Kamlak clamped his magic around Pavresh and marched him out of his room. Pavresh didn't try to resist anything at first. If it were him in Kamlak's place, he'd be more cautious at the beginning. Let things play out a bit, and Pavresh might find it easier to loosen the spell.

They left the seminary and descended among the volcanic fields below the city. Pavresh had never spent time there. He couldn't even turn his head to take in all there was to see, but he took note of the way the mud boiled in the pools and the layers of chemical deposits that gave the rock formations a fantastical look.

It felt like a different land from the geysers near Romnai, a danger hidden by child-like colors and otherworldly shapes. He added those images to his store of magic. Another land, an impossible place, an unspoken betrayal by nature itself. If arcist magic was only power, then such images didn't matter, but he still felt better trying to interact with his magic in the ways he always had.

The noise of the gurgling mud soon covered over the sounds of the city. A group of people had gathered in a cleared space a short way into the volcanic field. They were a curious mix of people, some with paper and writing chalk and looking glasses, as if they had come to observe something that needed careful study and exact measurements. Roughly equal in number, the other portion wore fine clothes and had the look of princes along with their high-ranking servants.

A large pool of mud curved around two sides of where they stood. Waves of heat came from a hole in the ground a good fifty paces away, opposite that mud. Pavresh peered toward it but the distance was too great to see inside. All he could see was the steam rising up into the cold winds high above. The cloud sheered off toward the west in those winds. If only it could carry him as well. He wanted a sail to catch the wind, a craft that could float over the volcanic field and deposit him in Chaitanshehar far away.

Two figures made their way out toward the hole in the ground. They wore blacksmith clothing, thick and padded. Or perhaps it was more like that of a furnace tender on a locomotive. Pavresh hadn't spent the time he should with such people, learning their stories. He'd been too afraid of the steam engines, back when he might have had the chance to learn more.

With long rods of some kind, they pushed an object closer to the hole and then let it fall inside. Pavresh braced himself—mentally, as he had no control to prepare himself physically. He recognized the object as one of the steam engine balls Kamlak had shown him, his grand plan for forcing a way through the mountains with massive explosions. There was no impact, no reaction of any kind.

Someone spoke to the crowd. Pavresh didn't recognize the man, but he spoke with authority. A prince of some kind. Likely the former mayor, Prince Hrisha, or one of his allies. No sign of Mahendri, so Kamlak had likely spoken the truth about the shadow mastermind's absence.

"This is the future we are observing today. The way to open up the mountain passes to the south. The way to subdue discontent. The way to establish our city as preeminent, in Eghsal Valley and beyond. Watch, feel the earth's response, and dream of the future that awaits us."

A thrill spread through the crowd. Arcist magic, and not just the ever present martial drum beats that filled the city. This was a story of the future and progress, of power and success. It built both personal and city-wide images of what that success meant, climbing with excitement as the furnace tenders levered a second object toward the hole in the ground.

If Kamlak was creating this overwhelming sense of pride and promise with his magic, did he spare any attention to the spell he placed on Pavresh?

Quickly, Pavresh worried at the magical edges of Kamlak's binding. He found a weak spot and imagined himself loosening a rope that had been tied poorly, unraveling a weave that had begun to fray.

There was some noise to the side and a little behind him. He turned, saw it was only the people there edging away from the front. They were anxious to see, a feeling bolstered by Kamlak's magic, but still frightened. They strained their necks. The two furnace tenders had pushed their object to the lip of the hole and backed as far away as their poles allowed them. The people beside Pavresh also backed away, bit by bit.

It took a moment for Pavresh to realize that he'd moved his head on his own. On instinct, it was true, but even so it was a break from Kamlak's control.

Where was the *power* now? He tried rolling his shoulders to stretch the muscles. No, he couldn't make such a deliberate motion yet. He continued picking at the edges of the spell.

The speaker raised his voice into a crescendo. "Watch and feel the first proof of the glory of Pashun!" At the same moment, the arcist magic reached its own fever pitch, and all hesitation faded from the crowd. They leaned forward. Even Pavresh strained to see, affected just like the rest by the magic.

But inside he still told himself a different story, one of the lone hero escaping the villain, of the captive finally finding a route to freedom. And with Kamlak's efforts all focused on the effect of the moment, Pavresh finally broke free.

He threw himself down to the ground behind the others, and they ignored him, so intent on the spectacle before them.

Kamlak didn't ignore anything.

"No," he cried, an anxious cry echoed in the magic. "Stop him!"

The second ball rolled into the hole.

Whether that was what the furnace tenders had meant to do,

whether it went differently because of Kamlak's cry, whether it would have played out the same regardless, Pavresh didn't know.

He knew only that he was free and scrambling away when the explosion shook the whole world.

At first bits of rock flew through the air. Pavresh thought the entire ground was dissolving, flung into the air at the same time their footing sank into an abyss. The rocks above would compete with the rocks below for who could bury them first.

Then the flying rocks stopped, replaced by dust. It coated them. Pavresh had to flick a live ash from his sleeve.

Had to flick… And he'd done so as well, had brushed the ash away without thought. He was still free. He had to remember that, had to act while he could. At any moment, Kamlak might manage to trap him again.

The small space out among the mudpots was a chaotic jumble. Bent over, Pavresh dashed away toward the nearest part of the city. Others were running away too—toward the city itself and simply from one side to another, blocked and confused by the boiling mud and treacherous ground. Among the chaos, he was just one more dust-covered figure fleeing for his life. Would this be how he finally escaped Kamlak's power?

At the lowest level of the city, a street that merged with the volcanic fields seamlessly, Pavresh looked back. A sense of order was returning already to the crowd that remained. They'd formed a line, several deep, and begun a calm retreat from the hole in the ground.

Had there been any casualties? The two tenders would have been in most danger. Maybe the prince who'd been speaking had been injured. That would be a sort of justice. He thought he glimpsed a form lying beyond the group, unmoving, but the distance made it unclear.

Not only the distance. Pavresh squinted to see better, but the sun dimmed, turning the land into shadow. A cloud of steam was approaching, growing wider as it spread.

No, not steam. Steam would have been grayish white, if

it had any color. This cloud was a yellowish brown. A smell of sulfur and something sour, acidic came over the rocks and pools of mud.

It had already swallowed Kamlak and his crowd of spectators. It billowed into the streets. The same construction that funneled heat up from the volcanic fields drew the fog upward, filling the city.

Pavresh pulled his shirt over his mouth and nose and ran.

He couldn't outrun those gasses.

As tendrils of the fog reached for him, Pavresh wove a spell and anchored it tight to his own body. He was an innocent in need of care. A kind man on the run from an unfair opponent. A person who must be hidden and tended to, for as long as necessary.

As the gas from the explosion rose through the streets and Pavresh felt himself losing consciousness, his last thought was to wonder if there would even be anyone left to do the tending, to hide him away.

To save his life.

CHAPTER 15

Jaritta was rolling a ball, wound out of stringy cypress bark, to Nataravi on a crisp morning when Chandri came climbing up the street from the wall below. Sheela leaned against his shoulder as if wounded.

Jaritta would have said she was beyond jealousy. His separation from his first wife hadn't been devastating to either of them. They'd simply grown apart and decided to go separate ways, and he'd never seemed to wish to go back. To see him so close to her now sent a pang through her, but it melted at the joy in her husband's eyes as he saw Jaritta and Nataravi. No matter what else had happened, his happiness to see his family was palpable.

Jaritta ran toward him, but Nataravi, who'd had a head start, beat her there. Chandri had to release Sheela to one of the others as he scooped up Nataravi and swung her around. He set her down and gave Jaritta a long hug.

"It's good to see you. Look what we brought." He stepped back and pointed at the base of the wall. They'd piled up what looked like some two dozen large bags. They bulged with something Jaritta could only guess was food.

"The trading was good, then?" *Please let them not have promised too much fighting on the mumblers' behalf.* "A lot of villages willing to send their supplies?" They made their way over to the bags as they talked. Sheela had to hop, using her companion's shoulders to balance herself.

Chandri shook his head, but there was still an infuriating smile on his lips. "No."

Jaritta's heart sank. They weren't willing? Or there just hadn't been many?

Sheela answered before she could ask. "He means this isn't from the trading. We've made arrangements for supplies to come. It should be brought to the upper side of the city as they gather in what they can find and spare."

"And this?" Jaritta gestured at the bags beside the wall.

"The mines," Chandri said, a touch of pride in his voice that seemed to Jaritta out of place.

"They're abandoned," Sheela explained. "The one we found, at least. And from the looks of it some others as well. No workers, no work being done. But they left behind a fair supply of their emergency food."

"Miners' emergency food?" Jaritta opened one bag. She couldn't identify the stuff inside, but it looked tempting even so. The twelve-days empty of food and full of hunger lent an edible air to anything remotely food-like.

"Some kind of bread and dried out bits of other food wrapped in with the bread. It stores well without spoiling. Doesn't taste particularly good, but edible."

"We had to eat some ourselves in the mine," Chandri said. He had crossed over to where Ovitiva slept in a basket in the shade and was gently rocking it. "While Chhayasheela's ankle healed."

"Are you badly hurt?" Jaritta peered down at Sheela's leg. The injury was covered by her wraps.

Sheela shook her head. "Climbing up the slope just now made it sore again, but it's healing."

She should sit down with Sheela and learn all about their journey. What supplies to expect, and what promises had been made. All she wanted was to head back to their own place with her husband and the girls and just be together for a while, not thinking about the city or food or anything beyond that moment. Not worrying.

"Why don't you find a place to rest, then. Get some medicine if you need it, prop your leg up, whatever else it requires." Jaritta was using Sheela's ankle injury as an excuse. She admitted it to herself, but at this moment she didn't care. "We'll meet late this afternoon to go over your trades and plan what's next."

Back in their chambers, the girls played with Chandri while they talked—as well as the girls let them. She could have just watched them playing together and been happy for a long time. Ovitiva fussed some but cooed and babbled most of the time. She.....mumbled. That was why her ancestors had chosen to call the original people of this land "mumblers," after all, because to them the mumbler language sounded like a baby's nonsense babbles.

Nataravi climbed on Chandri's shoulders and slid off over and over, which made any conversation next to impossible.

Finally she settled into Chandri's lap, and asked, "Daddy brought food?"

Jaritta laughed. "I've been telling her that's where you were. Getting us food, so I guess she does listen to what I'm saying."

"I did," Chandri said, his face very serious but a twinkle in his eyes. "Have you been hungry?"

Nataravi only nodded.

Jaritta took the moment to ask, "So, it's not too long before I hear the official report, but anything you want to say first? You're so good at noticing the details other people miss." She closed her eyes and took a quick breath before adding in a quiet voice, "Please tell me it was worthwhile."

Chandri nodded, but his pursed lips told a more nuanced answer. After a moment he said, "We did what we could. We found villages willing to trade, arranged for a steady supply of food. But..."

"But what? Did you over-promise what we could give?" She imagined them pulled into years of endless fighting against the soldiers of Pashun, drawn ever more into defending mumbler villages and hunting grounds. "Are we going to be a city of mercenaries?"

"No," He gave a light laugh. "If anything the opposite."

What did that mean?

He must have read the question in her frown. "The mines empty, the miners marching off to the southeast. I don't know what's going on, but the villages might need us even less than they think, at least in the short term. No, the real problem is that I don't know if it's enough. The villages don't have that much extra food to trade. We have a lot of people here. A lot of people who are already hungry, and it's a long time until we can harvest anything."

Jaritta leaned back against her floor pillow. "Yes. We do have a lot." A good thing, a testament to how attractive her dream was becoming. And yet, each person was one more to feed. She looked away, not wanting to ruin the happiness of being reunited with Chandri. "We'll make do. A little here, a little there. Winter gardens, plundering the empty mines, food from Azheeran's travels, and food from yours." That plus the blessing of the gods, but when had *they* ever granted good luck to Jaritta's plans? "It'll add up," she insisted, to convince herself as much as to convince him.

Chandri picked up one girl in each arm and came close to share her floor pillow, leaning in side by side. "It will. And we'll make do." He kissed Ovitiva on the head before adding, "Somehow."

***

In the days that followed, Jaritta worked side by side with Chandri to distribute the new food.

It did not go far.

Even so, if everyone rationed carefully, the food from that one mine might get everyone through an extra few days, even half a twelve-day if they were stingy. It was something, and already the first delivery of game arrived from a hunting band of mumblers. That would bolster their stores, get them another day here, another there.

"This was all one mine, right? We should raid the others too, see what we find."

"I suppose I'll have to." Chandri's voice was resigned.

"Well, you might not have to go next time. We can send Sheela out with her other traders for the food. As long as she's not setting up new agreements on the way, you don't need to be there."

Chandri stretched and smiled. "That sounds like a good plan to me."

Indeed. It was good to have him around again. Good for herself, good for the girls, and good for the city. She thought about what else had happened while he was gone that they hadn't discussed. "Did you notice the earthquake when you were out? Maybe a twelve-day or two before you got back? It wasn't strong here, but it seemed especially loud for some reason."

Chandri picked up a bark doll their daughter had dropped on the street. "There was a loud noise once. It was a little after we'd left the mine, loaded with all those bags. But I didn't think it was an earthquake. I remember wondering if a mine shaft had collapsed somewhere. Or else there was some kind of explosion in one of the mines that wasn't abandoned. A steam cart exploding, maybe, except it was too loud for that. Glad we'd left our mine by then."

"Oh, it was an earthquake. At least, it felt like one here. We used to have them in Romnai too, and it felt just like that."

Chandri shrugged in the peculiar mumbler way, with his hands but not his shoulders. "Maybe it was. It sounded like it was pretty near us, I thought."

After a moment, he said, "Come to think of it, it reminded me of a—" He used some mumbler word that Jaritta didn't know.

"A what?"

He repeated the word. "You know, water shooting from the ground. Great big noise all around. The earth probably shakes a bit with that, too."

"A geyser?" She thought she knew the mumbler word for that.

"Well, yes, like that. But our word geyser is smaller, something you see all the time. The other is for a bigger one. You can't predict it, you only see it once a decade or so. But it changes the lava fields every time." He gestured with his hands to emphasize how big it could be. "You mean you use the same word for both?"

"Yes. I guess. I mean, I didn't know they were something different."

"Strange." Chandri shrugged. "Well, that's what it sounds like. I wouldn't be shocked if the mud flows differently somewhere in those lava fields. New geysers spouting and new gullys cutting open the ground."

"Maybe Sheela can look into it when she goes back to the mines." Jaritta picked up Ovitiva to nurse her. "What was it like to travel with her again?" Had to keep her voice level, casual, to ask that.

He looked at her sharply, and she turned her head down, as if needing to focus on Ovitiva latching.

"Strange," he said at last. "But nothing too awkward. I was just one of the group for most of it. Carrying packs of food, letting her lead the way."

"Is she a good trader, do you think? Trustworthy for that kind of a task?"

"She was here at the start. So even when she's out there, she's faithful to the city. I can't imagine anyone else doing a better job as far as trustworthiness."

He left out something. "But not as far as making the best trades?"

"Oh that's fine, too. I don't think she'd promise anything except what you've instructed her." When she didn't answer, he added, "She'll make the bargain she can. That's not the issue. I just don't think she fully grasped the urgency of our mission. I can't blame her for hurting her ankle—and it was hurt very badly at first. I was afraid we wouldn't be able to save her foot at all for a while. But even at other times, we didn't hurry like I wanted to. We wandered, didn't always take the direct route."

No hint in any of his responses for anything to be jealous over. So she pushed that aside again and answered, "Well, it was good that you were there, I suppose." Except that they'd already discussed him staying in the city the next time.

Ovitiva stopped swallowing and fell asleep. Jaritta gently placed her in the cradle, and then said, "I'll be sure to insist on Sheela being quick the next time I send her out. Is her ankle healing well enough yet?"

Before Chandri could answer, the city of Chaitanshehar shook. Jaritta grabbed hold of Chandri then let go to steady the baby's crib. As she swayed away from him, Chandri picked up Nataravi and shielded her with his body.

It was Eghsal City again. It was the geysers threatening houses, the ground opening and untrustworthy. Their home turned against them. She fell, landing hard beside the cradle.

That wasn't supposed to happen here. She gritted her teeth and sat up, placed her back against the cradle to steady it. Ovitiva woke with a crying wail that sounded even over the shaking. Chandri slid in next to them, adding his body, his strength and presence to keep them all steady. Jaritta reached over and took Ovitiva out of the cradle so she could hold her.

Whatever happened, at least they were all together.

A bowl fell and shattered, and in the other room something clattered around until it stopped rolling. *Let it not be a lamp or lantern*, because the last thing they needed was a fire tearing through these houses. Even though she didn't have a free hand to spare, she touched the burn scar on her cheek with her shoulder, remembering the flames in her parents' chapel, imagining a fire burning through her new home.

The shaking subsided.

"Are you all right, Jaritta?" Chandri's voice was shaking. He pulled his cloak away from Nataravi and examined her.

Jaritta looked down at Ovitiva. She was crying, but the noise didn't yet pierce the ringing that blocked out all other sound. Crying was a good sign in a baby, right? "I…yes, I think I'm fine. Let's…" She had to take a deep breath to control her voice. "Let's go check on the others. On the rest of the city."

She held the still crying Ovitiva against her while Chandri picked up Nataravi, and they headed outside.

Dust was everywhere. That was the first thing she noticed. A coating of dust as if the city had been abandoned for centuries. There was a strange smell, as well. Not the smell of sulfur that often rose from the swampland and mudpots, and not the smell of the active volcanic fields that were swallowing the old Eghsal City. It was a unique smell, sour and sharp at the same time.

She listened for any cries of pain or alarm. The ringing in her ears was subsiding at last. As it faded away, it was replaced by shouts of concern, people checking on their neighbors, asking what had happened. No sound of crying except her own baby, whose cries were also calming away as they walked.

"Think this was one of your monstrous geysers?"

Chandri looked like he was going to correct her with the right word, but then just shook his head and said, "No. Bigger than that."

The other leaders of the city were converging in the dusty street. "Any major damage?" she asked Azheeran when he arrived.

"Not up where I was. Seemed like it might be worse down lower."

Even as he answered, Poorma came up from near the wall, her death jati robe flapping in the wind. Jaritta wasn't superstitious, but the sight of her gave Jaritta a moment's pause. Somewhere inside she flinched away from the thought of Poorma's death jati touch.

"I saw a cracked wall in one house down that way," she said, after they'd greeted each other and asked about any injuries or damages. "We'll want to check the wall itself first, the city wall. Make sure that's still sound."

The wall looked to be intact still, when they had a chance to examine it. Below it, the path to the fields was damaged, both the switchbacks and the more direct steps beside the river. They couldn't tell from above how bad the damage was.

As they came back down the wall into the city, Jaritta said, "We'll have to send someone down below to check on things. Azheeran? You know—"

Before she could finish, a new rumble shook the wall. Jaritta stumbled forward and fell, curling her body around her baby. She might have caught herself if she hadn't needed her arms to protect Ovitiva, but instead she landed hard on her shoulder.

That arm went numb.

Chandri helped her to her feet with Nataravi grabbing her numb arm as if to help that way. Jaritta tried to snatch it away, but it wouldn't move. She awkwardly cradled the baby with her good arm while finding her footing.

"There may well be more," she said between gasps of pain. "More aftershocks. More damage. Let's send some people around to…" She had to stop as a wave of pain spread from her shoulder. "Sorry. Around to check on the city and a group to try to see what damage there is below. Where it was centered."

"Valni should pick some guards and head down." Chandri began guiding her back up the street toward their home. "But you must rest. And the girls, too. They're tired out and scared."

Jaritta nodded through another wave of pain. "Help us."

Chandri gave his suggestions to Azheeran and Poorma and then walked with her the rest of the way to their chambers. In their room, he gave her some medication, a twisted piece of root. It had a bitter flavor, a taste like wood and raw acorns, but she chewed it as if she could take out her frustrations on that bit of root, and the walls faded away from her thoughts. Chandri faded away. The girls faded away. All that remained was a vague sense of the world trembling as it shook her to sleep.

***

Datri came out from her hiding place a few days later.

Jaritta greeted her with one arm in a sling. Her shoulder didn't hurt, but the medicine she was taking to keep the pain away meant she didn't feel much of anything. Cold, heat, other aches—she needed Chandri to tell her what to wear for the weather and to watch her closely so she didn't gash open her foot or scrape an elbow to shreds.

He always saw the dangerous spots before she could and steered her away.

"Do you think your spies can tell us anything about this?" Jaritta asked after the barest of greetings.

Datri held up her finger and whispered something to Nataravi, who laughed before hiding shyly behind her father. Then she lifted the blanket over Ovitiva's cradle and clicked her tongue at Ovitiva. Jaritta tensed, ready for the baby to cry, but she cooed in response and then was quiet again.

"Have to fulfill my auntly duties."

Jaritta had to think twice to remember that Datri was their aunt. She'd never claimed the role, and Jaritta seldom thought of her as her sister-in-law. Maybe if Jasfer were still alive it would be different.

"Too soon to learn much of anything. Travel is disrupted, that much I can tell."

"In which direction?" Chandri asked, his Eghsal Valley voice heavily accented with the sounds of his own language.

"Everywhere, but I think east is worst. No one from Pashun has come through, even someone who should have been on his way here and getting close. I hear Valni found some signs in the swamp?"

"Not much to go on, but yes. Some wetlands drained. A shift in the path the water takes through the swamp. But she didn't dare get too far away from the city just now."

"You'll need a team to go learn more."

"Your spies—"

"My spies aren't fit for joining an official anything, much less working as a team." Datri waved the idea away as if even the suggestion was ridiculous. "You'll need a real team, like the one you sent out for trading."

Jaritta pursed her lips. Sheela *was* champing at the bit to get moving again, but Jaritta wasn't sure her ankle was sufficiently healed. She looked at Chandri for his reaction, but he had the look on his face that he got when he was struggling to follow a conversation in the language of the Eghsal Valley. Datri, she realized, made no effort to speak slowly or clearly.

"Sheela," she explained to him. "Is she healed enough to go on another expedition?"

"I haven't spoken to her, so I'm not sure. She claimed it was already getting better when we came back, but it didn't look great when we climbed up here."

"Someone bring her," Jaritta called to the attendants nearby. "Chhayasheela. She'll be bunking with a mumbler family probably. With some of the trading scouts."

After an attendant left, Datri said, "That's not what she's good at, though, you know." She picked up Nataravi and held her comfortably on one hip, making faces to get her laugh.

"What do you mean?" Jaritta felt Datri leading her toward an answer, but wanting her to say it herself.

"Chhayasheela." She pronounced the name with perfect pronunciation and switched to a fair attempt at the mumblers' trader pidgin. "She is a good trader. A good leader in the wilderness. Too hasty at times, but a quick thinker."

"Yes, I suppose those points are all true." Must she be forced to praise her husband's former wife? She squeezed her nails into the palm of her hand.

"But she is not skilled at noticing the kinds of details we may need to know. The movement of the troops, if there are any. The damage from the earthquake and what it means for us here. The origin of that quake, if there are any signs to be read."

It dawned on Jaritta what Datri was getting at. Chandri was skilled at those things. Chandri, who kept her safe and sane… Even through the medicine that muted all feeling, she felt a rise of panic.

"No, I need Chandri here at my side while I recover. He needs to help me with the girls. He needs to protect me from injuring my shoulder again. From scraping open new wounds."

Datri opened her free arm as if in a mock hug. "What are sisters for, dear?" she said in the language of Eghsal, her words sliding together in a way that Chandri no doubt wouldn't be able to follow. She bounced Nataravi on her hip to make her laugh. "I didn't leave my cellar for the fresh air. I left it to get to know my nieces and to help my convalescent sister."

"Ellechandran," she said in pidgin before Jaritta could answer, "the city has a need of your services once again."

Sheela walked up at that moment. She limped, but not enough to slow her down.

"You need to investigate the earthquake, figure out what has happened, and report back to Chaitanshehar as soon as you can."

Jaritta felt too stunned to respond. How was it that she was a leader of the city, the one who'd had the dream, yet when the city's needs became difficult, she froze? She couldn't speak—for herself or for him. Chandri looked at her, a perplexed look on his face. He would argue. She would, if the medicine gave back a portion of her energy without also giving back all the pain. Maybe the other leaders would side with her. But it didn't matter.

When Datri spoke that way, she got what she wanted. Her calm certainty would turn aside any argument as she brought her lifetime of authority to bear.

Jaritta knew she had already lost—the argument and her husband both.

CHAPTER 16

Harkala named the ship *Illusion of a Dream*. She almost refused to board it at all. Was it mutiny if she refused her own orders? The rickety ship inspired no great visions of discovering the Forgotten South, learning the true history of their people, or establishing any sort of link to the people who had remained behind so many centuries ago. The only image it gave her was of crashing again into the rocks.

This time she didn't expect any of them to survive.

The locals came down to the beach, though. They had visited periodically while her crew built their ship and even showed them the shoreline where pitch could be harvested out of the sand to make the ship watertight. A score of their men and women now stood on the beach, all dressed fiercely, their faces impassive. They turned the prow of *Illusion of a Dream* to face farther west and made sweeping gestures toward the sea in that direction.

They weren't about to let Harkala change her mind, no matter what fears she had.

After the boat was facing the right way, they took their positions in half a ring around Harkala and her crew. Their arms were bare as if untouched by the cold, and crossed over their chests. Any one of them looked more fit than Harkala's sorry comrades. The women wore their hair up, pulled high to keep their vision unimpeded. The men cut theirs shorter and bound the ends into two braids that touched their shoulders. Not one of them ever came close to smiling or even acknowledging Harkala as she and the crew prepared the ship for its voyage.

"We're only going to wreck again, aren't we?" she asked Ekana when they were all aboard. "The current will just dash us into the rocks."

And no extra life boat this time to bring them to shore. They had needed to use the pieces of that boat to make their ship seaworthy. The pitch on the bottom of this cobbled up vessel glistened, holding timbers both old and new together in what they could only hope—and doubt at the same time—would be sufficient.

"You might be right," Ekana said, his voice resigned to their necessary plans. "They seem to be indicating a current that will take us south, though. At least, that's how I understand their motions."

"Taking sailing tips from our questionable interpretation of an unknown people's hand signals. What has our grand expedition come to?"

Ekana tested a rope that held down one corner of a sail and shrugged. "Survival, that's what it's come to. If we can even manage that much. We've put our hands to the wheel, though. I don't think there's any turning back."

Such a lesser goal than their original. But if that was the task, then she would make every effort toward it. They still had many of the goods they had set out with, salvaged by the locals from the old wreck, now packed into the rough hold of this new vessel. They would have to do what they could with that, hope it wasn't too damaged by the sea, hope they found someone interested in trading. "Very well, first mate. Then that is my command to you."

"The tide will be drawing us out soon. If you want to address the crew before we leave…"

Harkala nodded her thanks for the reminder and took a position in the center of the deck. "Crew of the *Illusion of a Dream*, I won't pretend that this is what I had in mind when we set off from Jarnur. But you are true sailors, and a sailor doesn't waste their time complaining about the waves. They know the waves change, and they know the sea is never tame."

They were watching and paying attention, but she knew she couldn't hold their attention much longer. They were not scholars attending a lecture but her crew ready to sail the ship as well as they could.

"So now we set out and learn where the sea will take us. Not back home. We do not give up so easily! Still toward our old destination, if we can make that happen. Know that I trust in your skills, and we must trust in the gods or the Sacred Fire or simply the sea itself to take us to where we are meant to go."

She gestured for Ekana to take over and get them moving. He barked out some rapid commands. As soon as the crew pulled up the repurposed anchors, the ring of locals closed in on the ship. Using branches of driftwood, they pushed the ship away from shore, a nudge to set them on their way. The retreating tide pulled them rapidly away from the frigid land.

Here, where the locals had gestured for them to go and directed them with their pushing, there was a deep channel. No treacherous rocks or surprising currents to end their journey before it had begun. A wind from the north tried to push them away from the channel, but Ekana kept them on their southwesterly route.

Harkala watched for any signs of a current gripping their ship. The waves didn't change directions, and the ship kept on the course Ekana set all day. The island fell into the northern mists, and nothing else was visible in any direction. Only water, waves, and hints of great beasts swimming below the surface. At night they watched the stars to check their route and kept a lookout for any obstacles as they sailed onward.

When there was still no change the next day, Harkala asked Ekana, "Where is this current they indicated we would find?"

"We may have misunderstood." Ekana waved one hand up at the sails. "They probably meant the winds. Those have been steady since we left, so we're making good speed, as well as I can reckon. I was thinking about the current that carried us to the island in the first place, and that probably made me misunderstand."

"How long do you think we should stick to this course?" She was the captain, and the choice would technically be hers, but that didn't mean she wanted to make the decision all by herself. "We'll want to head back eastward at some point, right?"

Ekana tilted his head back and peered from side to side of

the horizon. "Thing is, we don't even know where the Forgotten South was. Due south from home, only cut off by the mountains? Or was it south and across this or some other sea? I don't suppose there's anything in your history studies to guide us?"

"No, nothing." She was silent for a moment, mimicking Ekana's studying of the horizon. "Let's continue this way until tomorrow, as well as we can judge. If we still see nothing at sunrise, angle southeast. How do sailors state it, some ten or fifteen degrees to port? The farther we go without seeing anything the more I want you to curve us toward the east. That will bring us back toward whatever landmass lies south of Eghsal. We'll have to run into some land eventually."

"Yes sir, captain."

The look in Ekana's eyes told her she was making the right choice in his eyes. For herself she had to add the words, *for now*.

***

On the fourth day a storm gathered to starboard. Harkala watched it build, the clouds growing as if alive, growth adding to growth and expanding to heights beyond sight. Lightning lit the darkening sky as the clouds swallowed the setting sun.

The clouds stayed the same distance away. Every time Harkala looked, she was sure they couldn't grow any bigger without breaking, rushing forward to find their scrappy ship in the open sea. Surely such a storm would sink them in its first surge. But every time she could see it building more—higher, bigger, fuller—without breaking. The ocean sky seemed to ache with holding it back.

But *Illusion of a Dream* scudded along in parallel to that danger, pushed by winds that felt like mere tendrils of the storm, brief breezes that pushed them a little toward the east.

Ekana let them curve that way, as they'd already planned anyway, and the storm fell away behind without ever striking their ship. She heard distant thunder one night as the clouds finally broke well to the south of their little boat. The waves kept her awake for some hours before they calmed down, but it never brought even a drop of rain.

Their water stores could have used some fresh rain.

When they woke in the morning, brown seaweed filled the ocean before them. It scraped against the side of the ship, a gentle, calming sound. A sense of peace filled Harkala. The soft scraping of the seaweed and the illusion of never moving made her sleepy and calm.

But they *were* moving, and quite fast from what Ekana estimated. He reckoned their speed and said they should be coming even with Jarnur within a day or two, only much farther south. How much farther he couldn't guess. The current that had pulled them north had wrecked any sense he had for such a reckoning. But the air felt warmer than it ever did in Jarnur, and the waves that splashed up were cold, certainly, but nothing like the frigid waves where they'd begun.

There was little for the crew to do except for keeping a lookout and caring for the salvaged ropes they'd used for rigging. An almost never ending task, but when they had a breather from that work, Harkala spoke to Sembaari. "Could you snag me some of those pieces of seaweed? I want to study them."

When he drew up a bucket, Harkala tasted the water first, touching a cupped handful to her tongue. It tasted no different than seawater did back home, the familiar mixture of salt and seafood. She'd been right about it being warmer.

She sketched a picture of the seaweed into her log book, which the people of the frozen land had salvaged from the wreckage. A drawing of a seabird and its egg was opposite, too lacking in detail for the kind of scholarly work she intended to record on this journey. She would have to do better work from here on out.

The seaweed had clusters of tiny bladders around the stem, with leaves that had sprouted out beside them. The weed itself had a vine-like body that cut off after almost as long as her outstretched arms. She peered over the edge to guess how much deeper the plants went in the water, but it was impossible to judge.

Everything was brown, the color of leaves in fall. Did this seaweed follow a seasonal pattern? She pictured the sea turned light green with living leaves. The seaweed didn't remind her exactly of autumn. Probably simply because it was wet. Fallen leaves that color would be brittle.

With a knife that was too big for such delicate work, she cut open the bladders. There was nothing inside but air, but she drew the structure anyway. She cut open the vines and peered close. There were lines that might represent some kind of internal structure. She did her best to record those markings as well, wishing for an eyepiece to let her examine them more closely. She tried using the telescope, since it let her see things far away over the water, but the image didn't come clear like she had hoped, and the light was insufficient.

When she was done, she was surprised by the setting sun. Most of the day was gone, and the sea of brown and blue still spread on every side.

When they left the mats of seaweed behind a few days later, the ocean grew choppier again, and the water a deeper blue that looked colder than the spray felt.

After another day, they spotted land straight ahead. They were going almost due east by then, still a little south because of how the wind blew. Over that day and the next, the land took over the horizon, not only straight ahead but curving around to the south as well, and extending north out of sight.

This was what they were looking for, a land that surely touched their own somewhere to the north, a South—whether the Forgotten one or one completely new and unknown. Harkala stood at the prow, knuckles white on the gunwales as she watched the land take shape.

***

There were no rocks along the coast they came to. It was a grassy place that tempted them to simply come ashore. Run the ship right up the beach if necessary. But Ekana wasn't sure they'd be able to get *Illusion of a Dream* back to sea if they did so.

"What if the locals are even less friendly than back north, and we have to flee to the ship?" He pointed at the edge of the sea where their ship would presumably be. "It's such a gradual, shallow waterfront. We get back in, and the mud has a hold on the hull. Or small rocks tear the salvaged wood to shreds. We don't want that." He scanned the shore as they turned further south to parallel the land. "Watch for a river where we can drop anchor. Or a cove where the water is deep right up to shore."

They found nothing promising as the afternoon wore on. They skirted the coastline, and many small creeks wended their way through the grass to the sea. None was wide enough or deep enough for their ship to pull into. The land beyond was empty of any sign of humans. Grasses blew in the wind, long and light green, unlike anything Harkala knew. The soil beneath the grass appeared to be sand.

A few trees grew but not many. Farther from the water, rolling hills rose up, and trees grew there. Birds sang, a counterpoint to the harsh cries of the seabirds that circled the ship. Once, Harkala thought she heard something different, something that might have been caused by humans. She strained her ears, trying to pick out the noise from the sound of waves and breezes. Something chattered loudly for a moment. It reminded her of squirrels only much louder. Squirrels grown to human size or humans who had regressed into life among the trees.

Probably not a human noise after all, only some animal, likely one that didn't live in the north.

Thinking of the north, she turned around and looked off the stern through her telescope. The land to the northeast looked much the same. Toward the horizon it appeared to turn more rugged, with what might be rockier hills and even the hint of mountains far off. The mountains that formed the southern edge of the Eghsal Valley, surely. Or was that only her mind trying to create those details? She sketched the lay of the land, the types of trees she could make out, and the shape of the clouds over the distant peaks. If they *were* peaks.

It was like history, with clues that wanted to be turned into a story, but she could never be sure how much was really there and how much she was adding herself, because of what she wanted to see, because of what she thought she should find.

They passed some small coves, but none would serve as mooring. The grade was still too shallow.

"Looks like a spit of sand ahead." Ekana pointed at something in the water in front of them. "We'll have to pull away from shore a little."

Everything looked so different from the sea near Jarnur. How did he even recognize that spit of sand as something to take note of? The hard rocks of the north were replaced by soft grasses; the cold light, pale and always in danger of disappearing, turned to warm sun that flooded everything with light, as if it would never disappear. The colors—blacks and grays and cold blues—turned to greens and yellows and a blue that really deserved its own different name, it was so unlike the color of the sea off Jarnur.

The ship tacked out far enough to avoid the sand. Ekana strained to see the shore beyond it as if expecting a mooring place on the far side. Nothing came to view.

"Night will come soon," Ekana said. "We'll anchor, and in the morning we may have to be less picky about where to stop. At the least we need to stop at one of those streams and refill our water."

"Not that we've seen any sign of dangerous people living near here anyway," Harkala answered. "Or anyone at all for that matter. I suppose we'll be just fine going to shore for a brief time."

In the morning they'd only sailed a short way when they saw the jetty. It was made of wood, built on top of piles of rock and debris, and stretched far out into the sea. The near, northern side looked inaccessible, but there appeared to be berths for ships of many sizes around to the other side. Masts and rigging made a backdrop to the structures. They dropped their sails while deciding how to proceed.

"It's big," Sembaari said what they'd all been thinking.

Ekana nodded, looking between the structure ahead and the empty land beside them. "I wouldn't have been surprised by some small dock first, other hints of…of people, of civilization. This…"

People were moving along the jetty. Harkala tried to guess what they would be like. Like their ancestors? Had these people driven her own ancestors away, so many centuries ago? Did they still tell stories of a group of people who left, never to return?

More likely the Eghsal ancestors were forgotten entirely. Who told stories of the losing side, of the ones who tucked in their tails and fled?

The size of the jetty wasn't merely in how far out into the sea it extended. Ekana had to swing their route out to pass the tip of it, but what drew Harkala's eyes were the buildings right there on the structure itself. Near shore, the jetty might as well have been a city street lined with houses and shops. They squeezed together, built upward several stories above the water.

Eventually the buildings grew shorter, a single story for a long span of the jetty. And only near the end did the wooden structure stand alone. She filled pages with notes on everything she saw, not even trying to understand yet, but simply to observe. Waves broke over the wood. Figures moved through the waves—or beyond the spray, perhaps. They walked between the last of the houses and the squat, red building at the very end. A lighthouse, but it didn't resemble the lighthouse she knew from home. Jarnur's light was a simple, steady lantern magnified by mirrors. This one flashed a light over and over in a pattern that appeared deliberate. Like they were sending a message to someone. Summoning their soldiers? Warning the *Illusion of a Dream* away?

Didn't matter. At this point they had no choice left except to come around the jetty and find themselves a berth. What came from that would come. As history or the gods and the great Cosmic Fire decreed.

There was no sign of panic or urgency at the end of the jetty as *Illusion of a Dream* circled it. The light flashing in the lighthouse appeared to be nothing more than a signal of where the structure ended. Then why the pattern? Did it convey meaning that she and her crew ought to know?

A message to the ships of what goods were needed, what welcome they might have? Maybe there were other piers along the coast to the south, and each one had its own pattern.

Ekana brought them around and along the other side of the structure. Harkala peered through her eyeglass at the people.

They wore trousers with divided legs. Sailors often wore similar clothing in Jarnur, as did horseback-riding messengers who traveled between cities, back when communication between cities was more common and less likely to be martial. But Harkala found it odd on the men and women simply strolling along the jetty. Surely in the city—and this conglomeration of buildings certainly qualified as a city—robes should be the more decorous option.

The trousers were plain-colored. The shirts they wore were anything but. Most wore striped shirts, the colors were bright and clashing. Had to compete against the sunlight, she supposed.

What Harkala really wanted to know was whether they looked more like the people of Eghsal or more like the mumblers. That would be the final evidence in deciding what story they would tell of the lands they found when they returned home. If they returned home.

The spyglass gave her no quick answer. There were people with much darker skin than her own, a deeper brown than she'd ever seen. There were people with skin a similar russet shade of brown to her own but with wider, more blunt features like she associated with the mumblers. And there were those who looked like the island people who had driven them away from their home, brown with pink undertones unseen in Eghsal—but unlike those islanders, these people had reddish-yellow hair that set off their skin color, making it look darker.

Maybe they were different castes. Maybe all those who had looked like the people of Eghsal did now had been their own caste and had left, leaving these other people behind.

Maybe.

The more she watched, the more she grew to doubt she would find anything she could easily understand or explain in a satisfying way.

The other side of the jetty looked much like the first except for the berths for ships. It widened as it neared the shore, making room for a good number of buildings crowded in together. But the shoreline looked much as the north side had. No river, as Ekana had suggested they might find. And very few buildings on the land itself. Did they fear the land? Was it dangerous somehow? Harkala searched for signs of volcanic activity or similar dangers and saw nothing. No rising columns of steam and ash. No expanses of land where plants couldn't grow.

Ekana brought them close and into an open berth.

Harkala's heart raced. She forced her hands to unclench and her breathing to be even, giving herself an outward look of calm. She was a scholar, curious but up to the task, and she would show the proper sort of intelligent certainty that her role required. That facade hid a volcanic geyser of emotions ready to erupt at any moment, but it was her job as historian and ambassador to make sense of this meeting. Whatever would happen.

Sembaari led the way off the ship. He spoke more languages than the rest of them and could carry himself with the bearing of a messenger for someone important. There were dockworkers all around them, but no hubbub. Strange ships coming in must be a common enough sight. The workers ignored them. Were even strange, bedraggled people disembarking such a common sight?

A woman with a fancy-looking, green-and-gray-striped

shirt sauntered over. She greeted them. Harkala guessed it was a greeting of some kind.

Sembaari spoke in one language. The woman frowned and shook her head. He tried something else.

Again the woman didn't appear to understand. She began talking to them, very slowly emphasizing each word. Harkala strained for any familiar words.

She heard one. The woman had said, "ship." it wasn't the usual word for ship, and her pronunciation sounded strange, but Harkala recognized it.

"It's our language," she said, cutting off whatever Sembaari had been trying to say. "I recognize that word. They speak an old version of our words." Was this, could it possibly, finally be the Forgotten South that she'd dreamed of?

To the woman, and matching her careful and slow way of speaking, she said, "You speak our language, don't you? You speak the same words we do."

The woman frowned, shook her head just the same as she had for Sembaari.

"It's changed," Ekana said, as if she hadn't known that all along. "But you've studied old documents. Maybe you can piece it together."

The woman spoke again, and Harkala did her best to listen. This was what she was here for, what all her studies had prepared her for. She matched the sounds to old writings, imagined how not only her own language would have changed in six or more centuries but how the language here would have changed as well.

Nothing became clear. Bits of words that hinted at something familiar, but when she tried to put it together, the meanings fell apart.

Ekana must have seen the frustration spreading over her face. He touched her arm and said, "You can figure this out, Harkala. I'm sure you're capable of it."

Harkala gestured for the woman's attention and pointed at their rickety ship. "Our ship," she said, as slowly as deliberately as possible, using the less common word she'd thought she'd understood. "Ship."

The woman shook her head and pointed at Harkala, Ekana, Sembaari, and the rest and said her version of the same word. Then she pointed at the ship and said something entirely different.

Not *ship*, Harkala realized. *Crew*. The word was the same but its meaning had changed as well as its pronunciation.

If every word could do the same...her head spun with the implication. A change in pronunciation here in the south, a change in pronunciation in the north, and a change in meaning in each... The possibilities dizzied Harkala's mind. There were too many ways things could diverge, too many routes a language might take. What good were her studies in the face of infinite variations?

"You can put it together, Harkala. You're a scholar. You've studied. You can—"

Her grasp of what she knew and what she might need to know slipped away from her fingers like streaming water, away from her mind. "No, I can't Ekana. History is bigger than understanding, and languages change more than you can imagine." More than she could imagine. She felt herself losing her balance and grabbed Ekana's shoulder to steady herself. "I don't think anyone can ever understand but the barest sliver of learning. And this place, this language, is so far beyond my sliver."

Harkala sank down onto a coil of rope and let her head fall into her hands.

CHAPTER 17

The ground below Pashun still shook now and then. Whatever Kamlak and his masters had intended with their explosive demonstration, it had set off some reaction within the volcanic field. Pavresh couldn't be certain how frequent the rumbles were during his recovery—he was in and out of consciousness too often to be certain of much of anything—but he often woke with the feeling of having felt the quaking in his sleep.

The other thing he felt was Kamlak's horns, strident and controlling.

The horns came several times a day, and he could feel the arcist magic swell in power each time. Shielded by the walls of his caretaker's cellar, he resisted their pull, but he felt the magic tugging at him. It made him contemplate how Kamlak was using them.

Send a trumpet along with the miners, and they could be controlled. Kamlak probably had to make sure someone who knew some arcist magic was playing the flourishes, but he didn't have to be there himself, not once he'd established the spell's hold on the miners. It gave the magic a lot of flexibility that Pavresh wouldn't have imagined, a lot of *power*, as Kamlak would insist. And yet here in the city, it was a weakness as well, because the horns had to be played over and over to renew the magic. Maybe Kamlak hadn't anchored the martial spell as solidly in place as Pavresh had done with his spell in Chaitanshehar.

Or maybe arcist magic itself resisted the way Kamlak was using it.

He liked that idea. There was comfort in imagining that Kamlak's approach went against the essence of the magic. If so, it promised an end to Kamlak's efforts, promised that it was doomed, someday, to failure as he got distracted with other events or moved his efforts on to something else.

Of course that was a story. And probably a false story in many ways, an illusion that threatened to lead him astray. Kamlak would mock him for falling into the same old patterns. He couldn't let the comfort it promised distract him from more active attempts to undermine Pashun's actions.

Power. It came down to the power of the magic and how that power was wielded. And throughout his captivity, he'd been observed by Kamlak, so the next spell Kamlak cast—if he'd survived the explosion—might well draw on the depth of Pavresh's approach and prove even stronger than the current one.

Pavresh saw his caretaker seldom. She was an older woman, and her hesitation to ever speak to him told Pavresh most of what he wanted to know. It was dangerous for her to care for him. Kamlak or *someone* was still looking for him. But, perhaps most importantly, the arcist spell he'd anchored to himself before he passed out was working. It forced her to see him as harmless, as someone to care for no matter what other voices were saying.

As he began to walk back and forth in the small cellar where his caretaker hid him, he decided it was time to learn the things she couldn't tell him without words. He confronted her the next time she brought food and an herbal tisane to help him recover.

"Thank you for caring for me."

She dipped her head and tried to move away, but he touched her hand to forestall her.

"Tell me what's going on in the city. Please. I need to know." Telling her too much about why he needed to know might break the spell, and even if it didn't it would put her in more danger. "What are people saying in the streets?"

Too much speaking at once. He cleared his throat, and it turned into a coughing fit that doubled him over in bed.

She was scared, scared simply by talking to him. Her eyes darted up the steps and out the dirt-darkened half windows up near the ceiling of the cellar. The fear came from the martial horns, though, from the magic. Pavresh could see how it twisted her, how her caring for him was because of the person she was underneath, uninfluenced by magic.

Or maybe he merely wanted to see that in her, and it was his magic that was pulling her from her own inclinations, forcing her into actions she wouldn't have taken otherwise. Who could say?

For now, saving Chaitanshehar was all that mattered.

When his breathing was normal, his caretaker finally spoke. Her voice betrayed neither fear nor hesitation. "People are saying there is work to be done. People are doing the work, working harder, fulfilling our roles."

"And who's telling you those roles?"

Her brow furrowed, and she didn't answer. Probably something she couldn't answer, something forced on her by Kamlak's magic, but she wouldn't necessarily recognize Kamlak himself.

"I was injured when you rescued me. There was an explosion, like a geyser. Do you know of anyone else injured?" *Anyone else coughing?* he could have added, but the coughs themselves implied the question.

"Someone died. Maybe more than one, I don't know. Others were injured."

Kamlak? But how could he ask that without risking the spell that protected him dissolving away?

"Anyone important? It didn't…change anything in the city, did it? All your work to be done is still happening, right?"

She shook her head. "No change. There was a funeral, but I must have been needed at work then." Her memory seemed vague, which Pavresh supposed was a side effect of Kamlak's magic. It made the people of the city into hard workers but left them dazed and unable to focus well on something like the past. "Someone's servant, I think."

Not Kamlak, then, most likely. Pavresh wasn't surprised. The magic, bolstered every few hours by the horns, still felt like his work. When Pavresh started coughing again, his caretaker slipped away.

***

The coughing would make it difficult to pass through anywhere unnoticed. For the most part Pavresh was feeling recovered, tired of being cooped up in the basement and ready to get back to Chaitanshehar to let everyone know what had happened.

Rashul, dead. He still could hardly believe it.

Rashul and the rest of them, and only the one survivor, himself.

He needed to relay the news, let them know what Kamlak and Mahendri had in mind for their magic-controlled followers. The proposed tunnel to the south might be a distraction that gave Chaitenshehar time to prepare, but soon Pashun would command a massive force of well trained and perfectly, inhumanly obedient soldiers. What would they manage to do against that?

Pavresh had always been able to rely on his magic to help him blend in. He became almost invisible with the nudge of arcist magic, a forgettable and quickly forgotten figure who happened to be in whatever space he was when someone saw him. The magic deflected their attention. But a coughing fit would drag anyone's attention right back to him.

He practiced pacing back and forth in the cellar to build up strength and hoped his coughing would improve.

The horns continued, but there was a change in the magic. It felt weaker, a hesitant version of the power baldly claimed by the martial horns. Maybe Kamlak was sick, lying in some seminary room dying.

A good time to escape. Outside this cellar he would be more vulnerable to the magic, but he could wrap himself in his own magic spell to resist the horns, slip out through the edge of the city where there was a path leading along the north side of the mudpots, and be far enough away before the horns sounded next. It wouldn't be an easy journey, alone without full supplies. But he'd spent years journeying without a lot more.

He managed to beg some supplies off his caretaker and he thanked her profusely for her care. Her eyes slid away as if already trying to forget he'd been there.

Before he left, he wove one spell for her, a spell that he hoped would protect her from Kamlak's magic eventually. Breaking her from it entirely probably wouldn't be much of a gift—it would put her in more danger as her actions would differ from everyone else in ways that might draw attention to her. But if he'd planned it right, the spell he anchored to her would slowly open her eyes to how the arcist compulsion was manipulating her, and the more time passed, the more it would open the eyes of others around her.

It might not free her—or anyone—entirely, but he hoped it would loosen the grip that the magic had.

He waited for the lull that always preceded a summons of horns, when the magic would be weakest. He should have almost an hour to get out of the city and far enough away that they would have no effect on him.

He'd only gone a short way, though, when the streets quaked and the buildings shook. He fell to the cobbles. Dust rose up and filled his lungs, setting off a fit of coughs.

The shaking continued for what seemed a long time. Pavresh crawled to the edge of the street, thinking the building offered better protection. But the wall itself swayed, so Pavresh scrambled farther down the street as pieces of wood and plaster fell around him.

He huddled beside a stone fence until the shaking was over.

Even after that, he couldn't think about what had happened or what to do next until his coughing subsided. People began moving along the street, checking on each other, on the buildings, while he was still doubled up.

Someone checked on him. Out of common concern or responding to the spell that encouraged people to care for him, he didn't know. Pavresh didn't even look at them, only waved that he would be all right and kept coughing. His lungs seemed to be closing up. As much as he tried to breathe in, he couldn't get a full breath of air before the coughing would resume.

He got up and stumbled along the street, still coughing. The fit would pass eventually, surely. He had to get on his way while he could. But which way was he supposed to even go? He seemed to be turned around.

An old man, walking with a soldier's erect gait, came up beside him. "You need some yellow tisane, cadet. Come with me."

Pavresh had no strength for anything but to follow, and when his fit grew worse, to let the man support him.

Inside a small room, the man boiled water and briefly steeped some kind of leaves in a cup. He left it inside and handed the cup to Pavresh. "Don't chew the leaf. Just leave it there in the cup. But drink the rest."

It was bitter. Pavresh's throat closed around the taste. But almost as soon as he'd swallowed, his lungs opened up as well. He breathed without coughing, and it felt like the first time he'd ever breathed fully.

"It's not perfect," the old soldier said in the silence that followed. "Sometimes helps fast, sometimes not at all."

"Thank you. How did you know to use that?" Another cough tickled at his throat, as if in revenge for him daring to speak. Pavresh took another swallow of the tisane to ward it off.

"My jati spent years helping restore order in the mines," the man said, puffing out his chest. "Hard work, and important. But a lot of them got bad coughs afterward. So we learned a few tricks to help them through."

He might well need a supply of that tisane until his lungs recovered. If they ever recovered. Talk of mines made him think of his father's mines. Old miners there often ended up with a cough so bad they couldn't work any more. Even when the coughing subsided, they could take a breath but not release it fully, and the bad air stayed deep in their lungs. Often it never got better, the rest of their lives. Why had no one brewed the drink for those workers? As soon as he thought it, he knew the answer. No one cared. If they got sick, there was always some new miner who could be sent down in their place.

"Is it an herb? I might want to have my own supply."

The man nodded. "We called it swamp grapes. Here." He stood and pulled a large bundle of dry sticks from a cupboard. They were covered with small, dried leaves and what looked like tiny berries, all of it a light yellow. "Those of our jati who needed it are no longer with us. You may have these. And look for more in sandy places."

"Thank you, again."

"There was another one, but I don't have more. The leaves of a flower. We called it naga's trumpet, because the flower looks like that. Put it on the fire, and breathe the smoke."

Pavresh nodded. It wasn't much to go on, but he could picture a flower that the healers in the mumbler villages used that might be the same. There seemed something right about finding healing from the fire and its smoke. It fit his Enshi religion.

"When we go, if I see any, I will point it out to you."

"Go?" Pavresh tried to think of anything he'd said about going anywhere.

The man nodded. "South. To see the tunnel. We've all been summoned." In the silence that followed that word, the sound of trumpets came. Loud and close by…and Pavresh unprepared to protect himself. "And there they are." The man stood upright, ready to march all the way to Kamlak's tunnel.

"Some are staying behind," he said. "But not us soldiers. A soldier is never too old to answer the call." He turned his head, a sharp, parade-like turn, and looked Pavresh up and down once. "I imagine you have been summoned as well. The project will need people like you, even with your coughing."

And with that, Pavresh felt the tendrils of the arcist magic tighten around him, turn into iron shackles. He struggled, tried to slam down his own counter magic, but it was too late, and this time the magic came with more power than ever before, a more solid anchor along with the overwhelming need to comply. All he could manage was to protect a tiny portion of himself deep within, as if huddled within a shell of arcist magic.

He rose to attention beside the old soldier, the yellow swamp-grape sticks clutched in one hand.

***

They moved south en masse. Everyone knew what to do. Everyone including Pavresh. He simply grabbed a sack of food, added his bundle of swamp-grape sticks, and joined the crowd.

When he coughed, the old soldier nudged him and pointed at the leaves. But how could he stop to steep them when the march was so important? He stifled the coughs and marched on, dizzy and nauseated with the effort to keep himself breathing. When the others sang in soaring unison, he couldn't join in, but he listened and kept up the pace all the rest of that day.

In the evening, he managed to brew himself some yellow tisane, and it eased his breathing enough for him to sleep. In the morning he found a flask among the supplies and filled it with the medicine to carry with him. The drink was tepid and bitter but still able to ease his lungs.

There were ample signs of the earthquake. Tumbled walls in the city they left behind. Cracks in the pathway. A massive rockslide coming down from the mountains and ending just shy of their route. Would they have taken a different way if that slide hadn't destroyed other routes and other paths?

Pavresh could just bring himself to wonder, but he couldn't bring himself to speak his thoughts aloud or investigate. No one spoke of the earthquake or the rockslide or of anything except for the task at hand. Where to go, where to set up camp. how far they hoped to get the next day. With perfect efficiency they prepared food for everyone, ate, and prepared for sleep. Breaking camp in the morning required so little time they might as well have been setting out from a home they would return to.

Kamlak's horns sounded their ear-catching ditty each morning and night plus three times during the march. They weren't his only tools. A drummer set the pace. Several drummers, more likely, though Pavresh only ever saw the one. She kept her beat going throughout the whole march, another way for the arcist magic to keep them in its thrall.

Was the drummer an arcist herself? And each of the trumpet players, for that matter? Or had Kamlak crafted a form of control that worked even when no arcist was anywhere nearby?

The magic prevented Pavresh from investigating either way.

Over the next days he knew he should try to escape. He'd managed to escape Kamlak's direct control, after all. He should be able to escape this. The shell of his own personality struggled to open, to push away this terrible control and set him free.

Only he couldn't.

The way Kamlak had created his effects was more powerful than before, working in more complicated ways. It placed a weird division inside his own thinking. A part of him was aware of who he really was, what the magic was capable of doing. It was aware that he needed to get away, that he needed to warn Chaitanshehar what was happening. But that part of his mind couldn't piece together thoughts into a real plan. Whenever he tried to concentrate on what he might do, that part of him went silent.

The rest of his thinking was given over to drumbeats and horn blasts, and the step by step of marching through the mountains away from Pashun—and Chaitanshehar, and the valley of Eghsal itself. He thought only of those things and of breathing through the coughing fits, catching up when he fell behind. It had no room for plans or escape or awareness of any real kind.

The days blurred together, but he thought it was the third day when the soldier pointed out a flower to him. "Naga's trumpet," he said. "Take the leaves."

Doing so didn't interrupt his task of marching, so he pulled off a few and found more throughout the day. That evening the soldier showed him how to place it on the edge of the fire and direct the trickle of smoke it gave off toward himself. The smoke was foul and made him cough. But afterward, his lungs were more open, the air passing in and out fully with each breath instead of only in part.

The snow on these mountain peaks had come rushing down recently. They marched over the aftermath of avalanche after avalanche. The lines of one path met the lines of another in a mass of confusing patterns directly over the snow.

The route across would be a challenge, at least for those at the front. By the time he came through, a path was established and felt no different than any other way through those mountains. Hard trampled snow was as solid as rock, as good a road as any other.

Whatever route they were taking, others must have come through prior to the avalanches. Had anyone been on these paths when the snow cascaded down? An advance group who'd left Pashun early? A group sent back from the miners to guide the people through? If so, the mass of pilgrims trampled those corpses.

Cold winds blew. It was summer, but out here in the mountains, far from the heat of the volcanic fields, that only meant the cold was less bitter than it might be. Snow fell around them, but the drums and trumpets kept them marching steadily through whatever weather came their way.

Every day there were loud noises up ahead, at long intervals. Pavresh pictured the explosion in the volcanic field, wondered what they might be destroying up ahead. A hole straight into solid rock, for all he knew. He tensed as much as the magic allowed him to for the explosions to trigger new avalanches. In one place, a rockslide had come down after an avalanche, burying what had been freshly disturbed snow in rocks and boulders.

They detoured around that instability and came at last to their destination.

Pavresh knew it was where they were headed, though he couldn't say how he knew. Maybe it was in the flourishes of the trumpets as they gave their regimented blasts. Maybe it was in the drum pattern. Did it speed up ever so slightly as they got closer? Or maybe Kamlak's presence up ahead made the magic stronger and left an impression that he could sense without understanding. A magnetic lodestone to other arcist users.

They came around disturbed snow and rocks to find a path that led sharply downward. Miners were at work clearing rubble from the slope.

Pavresh's divided mind meant he hadn't entirely put together their pilgrimage with Kamlak's grand plan of blasting a way to the Forgotten South. It finally fit when he looked down the path into the opening of a tunnel. Here was Kamlak's route through the mountains. The face of the mountains above were clearly impassable. They rose sheer into a bank of wispy clouds, and even the earthquakes hadn't dislodged the mass of snow that shrouded these peaks.

Here was where Kamlak had set the exploding steam engines, a series of explosions that apparently triggered a much bigger quake than anyone could have guessed. Pavresh pictured the people at the demonstration with their papers and lenses, the way they'd seemed to be taking measurements of the explosion. No doubt they—those who hadn't been injured or killed—had used those numbers to calculate where to place the explosives and how to open the way into the mountain.

He hadn't put those two events together before, either, but now it was clear even to his divided mind that the explosions and the quake went together. The event beside the mudpots in Pashun had only hinted at the power of the devices Kamlak and his people had invented. The use of them out here had caused the quake that had traveled as if along some line deep in the earth, through the mountains and at least as far as Pashun.

And here the miners were still at work.

Which meant, at the least, that his plans hadn't failed completely.

What more it meant, Pavresh wasn't quite sure.

With the rest, he marched right in and took his place clearing his portion of the rubble. He was one of a crowd, an unknown figure among the workers, blending in by his own innate nature, by the dust and dirt of travel, by Kamlak's attention elsewhere. Unnoticed, but he still couldn't escape from Kamlak's control.

The way into the mountainside was clear enough to pass through on foot, but the entire mass of people from Pashun spent the rest of the day clearing a road fit for horse-drawn wagons. They camped just outside the mouth of the tunnel. When their trumpets sounded to signal the end of the day, the same sequence sounded from far within the mountain—or maybe from the far side.

Muffled by distance and rock, it still amplified the magic's hold on them as they drifted... or rather, *snapped* off to sleep, minds switched off as if a part of a vast steam engine.

***

The tunnel had sustained damage. The walls bulged in places, and a ceiling collapse at one point blocked more than half the tunnel. Kamlak must have hated that effect of his more recent explosions. His observers had surely calculated that such damage would be likely as the leading miners continued blasting their way into the mountain. They still hadn't seen Kamlak, but Pavresh could sense his magic growing stronger as they got closer to the end.

With the experienced miners directing them, the people of Pashun shored up the remaining weak spots and built a large wooden support beam and structure to make the ceiling secure. Rock dust made everyone cough, not just Pavresh. They pulled cloth up over their mouths like they used to in Pashun—though there it had served to block out the smells of the mudpots.

They camped inside the tunnel. How long must the tunnel be, to get through that last wall of impassable mountains? They'd kept an impressive pace outside, through foothills, mountains, rockslides, and avalanches. Their time marching through the mountain had been, if anything, at an even faster pace, though the work to secure the tunnel had certainly taken a significant portion of their day.

As they fell asleep, Pavresh fought to stay awake. He found a weak point in the magic, a slight gap that he could push and give his mind a small space to feel whole. His labored breathing, a curse in so many ways, actually gave him the opening to resist—ever so slightly. He didn't think he'd be able to resist sleep for long.

While he could, then, he thought of stories of tunnels, stories of being buried and coming back to the sunlight world of life. Staying so long in the tunnel felt like a sort of death. It was a tomb that weighed heavy above their snoring faces. A stony reminder of their mortality.

And in death came its own variation on freedom.

Pavresh wrapped himself in that, in the sense that no story could hold onto anything or anyone beyond death.

It didn't free him from Kamlak's control. It didn't overcome the trumpets that still seemed to echo softly off the rock walls of their mountain grave. But as he fell asleep, it gave his mind room, a little room, enough for the inner shell to open and his divided self to begin to come together.

He needed sleep, When he woke, perhaps his mind would be whole enough to make whatever plans would be needed to get through one more day.

They woke early. Another fact he knew without knowing how. There was no more maintenance to complete this day, only a fast march in the darkness. He joined in, but it felt more like his choice so he could learn what was happening than the simple compulsion of previous days. This portion of the tunnel looked more recent and very rough. It must have been where the actual final explosions had been, and the focus of the experienced miners as the rest of them made their way from Pashun. The pace through the rubble tested Pavresh's breathing. He drank yellow tisane, long since cold, and did his best to stifle the coughs that came.

Late in the day, they saw light up ahead. The dim light of the above ground world, a westering sun shining down at the end of their path.

The tunnel opened abruptly. A huge hole had blown outward in the south-facing side of the mountain. Pavresh shielded his eyes. Below the opening, the blast area of pebbles and broken shards of rock led down toward a small mountain river.

Other mountains were before them. They looked little different from the mountains they'd been traveling through. Snow-covered and rugged. There was no hint of vast southern plains, as Pavresh had imagined, even as far as he could strain his eyes to see. There were no long lost cousins standing there to welcome them. A huge column of smoke rose from the rubble, out of the debris from the blast. He felt no heat from it, but the smoke rose into a serpentine shape high in the sky above them, a naga's shape. A distant glimmer of arcist magic touched the smoke, but it was weak and vague. An impressive sight with just a touch of something added to it, as if the smoke were a sign from greater powers that their journey had a purpose. Somehow, and he could think of no arcist spell to create such an effect, the winds did not tear it apart.

Maybe this was all there was to Kamlak's scheme. A tunnel to nowhere, but a people forged to become soldiers. A hint of meaning that was little more than smoke. Even that much would suit Kamlak and his masters just fine.

As someone, dressed like a prince, stood to speak to the gathered masses, Pavresh took a second look at the river.

It flowed *south*, racing down and out of sight.

An ideal pathway out of the mountains.

"Welcome all." The prince's voice echoed off the blasted rock, a voice augmented by powerful arcist magics. "Welcome to the Forgotten South."

CHAPTER 18

The beggar's dog growled at the stranger who approached them. The woman stared at him for a long time. The beggar kept his eyes lowered and nudged his begging bowl closer. When she still didn't move, he mumbled, "Sorry about the dog, tisrah. Protective is all. But I won't let her bite you."

She finally tossed in some money and turned away. The beggar tipped his head toward her retreating form in an unseen bow.

Only after she was gone did he look into the bowl. The coin had the flash of a stylized flame etched on one face. The beggar caught his breath and snatched it out of sight. That coin alone was worth as much as he'd received begging all year.

Not that he would ever find someone to believe he hadn't stolen it.

Turning so much money into food might not be easy, but he would worry about that later. He spun the begging bowl and waited for the next generous passerby.

He hadn't received much more when he picked up his bowl and mat and walked away, the dog at his side.

The mourning women passed by. He'd seen them often in the streets, soldiers who marched without weapons or armor. Except now they'd taken back their fighting staffs and struck the cobbles as they walked. Maybe their mourning was coming to an end. One wore a headpiece shaped like the beak of a bird of prey.

The beggar shied away, as he always did. Further on, he came back to the same street and then slipped between houses to rest in his hidden space behind the bushes.

It wasn't empty.

A group of people had gathered beyond the bush, his bush. He should back away. He could always find a new place, could always sleep on the street itself if he had to. It was downright warm outside at the moment, these days growing longer and sunnier to make up for the winter days when the sun scarcely crested the southern peaks. The piles of snow that were left were more slush than snow and more dirt than either. He would—probably—survive.

That was the benefit of being an untouchable. No possessions but what he carried. No house or manor to preserve and pass along to the next generation. When a place became too dangerous, it was simple to cut out, to leave for a new place to call home—for a few days.

The beggar told himself this even as he approached the bush.

The people there, a dozen or so, were putting on masks. A ball? No, only the most wealthy had time for masquerades these days, and they had sufficient places to dress themselves in their own residences. The masks *were* colorful, and some even had feathers to add to their aesthetic.

But the eyes that caught his were full of steel and glacier ice. No glint of an upcoming party, but the glimmer of violence in store.

"He's seen us," someone said, their voice steady and their finger pointing accusingly. "Grab him."

He couldn't move. The masks reminded him of something, but he couldn't place a dirt-grimed finger on what. It bubbled into a terror that kept him rooted in one spot.

Masks leered close, surrounding him. Clean fingers grabbed his dirty sleeves, his thin arms underneath.

"He can identify us. Throw him in the sewers."

"No." The others listened to this voice. "Put a mask on him. Let him lead the way."

Someone slapped a mask over his eyes, and a string behind his head went tight as they tied it. The dog whined at them, but then was quiet. He caught a glimpse, through the eye holes of the mask, of someone tossing food to the dog as a treat. So much for it trying to protect him.

Then the last voice said, "Welcome to the Sons of Ryo. You get to go first today. Isn't that a high honor?"

The hands spun him around and propelled him back toward the street. The jostling moved him along with no chance to escape. The evening crowds were out, such as they were—those with nothing to fear from soldiers, those with no choice but to hurry through the streets to their homes. Five years ago such a small number of people, few and scattered, would have made the city feel eerily empty. Now they were the life of the city, what it had left.

The beggar's captors rushed through the streets, yelling slogans the beggar didn't know. He knew of the Sons of Ryo. They hadn't been as active recently, but a few years ago they'd caused a little trouble in Romnai and a lot in…somewhere else. What they'd wanted wasn't always clear. Violence. Stirring up people against other people. A return to old traditions, most of which hadn't ever been real but made up by the angry mobs. They weren't trying to fight for the untouchables. Of that he was certain. There had been other people doing that… No, he couldn't quite remember that part.

Was it some other sort of revolution? The Sons of Ryo hadn't tried to overthrow the princes, from what he could remember of that time. They hadn't liked certain princes, though. Especially in that other place. Or maybe that was all pretend, like their costumes here. They'd wanted stronger princes, stronger soldiers—they'd wanted rule by fear and violence.

He hadn't wanted that. What he'd wanted, he wasn't sure anymore, but he hadn't liked these people.

A short way away they came to a shop. From the view on the street, it appeared to sell clocks, though anything beyond the front window was lost to the beggar's view. Inside someone, probably the shopkeeper, moved about. The Sons of Ryo smashed a window and pushed the beggar inside.

He stumbled against the broken glass. A shard stabbed through his thin pants and cut his leg open. He lashed out, knocking the remaining glass pieces flying, and landed on the floor of the shop.

Hands wrapped in their robes to protect them, the real members of the Sons of Ryo climbed in behind him. The shopkeeper shouted something and then disappeared in the back—to hide or to find someone to help. They would want to be gone from here soon.

"Well done," one said, clapping him on the back as he tried to find his wounds and slow the bleeding.

There was a large water clock near the window. It was a fancy clock, one designed for a wealthy merchant to buy. Or maybe simply one to keep in the store to draw people in. An empty bowl with a small hole in the bottom sat in a larger, decorative bowl filled with water. Every hour the smaller bowl would fill just enough to sink to the bottom. Then the shopkeeper could take it out, drop one kiwan stone into a shallow groove cut into the larger bowl's outside to mark the hour, and begin the process again.

It looked like the keeper, or a succession of shopkeepers, had been here for nine hours that day.

The Sons of Ryo scattered the kiwan stones and swung the smaller bowl against the floor until it cracked. It wouldn't do much good if water filled it too fast. Then they poured the rest of the water onto the floor.

Others had found a row of different clocks along another wall. These were incense clocks. The stick of incense was precisely crafted to burn at a steady rate. The beggar remembered using such timepieces before. When he... No, that must have been someone else, a story he'd overheard in the streets. But he knew the sticks would change their scent throughout the day, marking the morning with one fragrance, the afternoon with another, and falling away to ash at the close of the day.

In fact, those sticks appeared to be the main product of this shop. Once, only the upper caste kortru houses would have used such incense. So many sticks offered for sale in a common—though fancy—shop meant that the merchants and other middle caste families were beginning to buy them as well.

Had he once bought incense in this shop or one like it? He tilted his head to ponder the images that bled through from *that time*, from before. He didn't think he had. But if not, how did he know so much about them? Had he been part of—? Thinking about it made his head hurt.

The Sons of Ryo threw incense sticks on the floor where the water spoiled them in an instant. They snapped others and tossed them around the shop. Then they shoved handsful into the beggar's fists, into his ragged pockets, down the neck of his great coat.

"Down with the upstarts!" someone shouted.

"Lord Ryo condemns this shop!" another answered.

The beggar tried to speak, but he didn't know what to say. What were they doing to him?

They climbed back to the window, and someone produced a flame.

Fire. Here?

The beggar threw the sticks from his hands and covered his head in terror. Too late. The sticks in his pockets were burning. The sticks shoved against his neck ignited as the Sons of Ryo fled into the street.

The beggar screamed and beat his arms against the fire.

Falling to the floor, he rolled back and forth through the water. It put out the flames in his great coat, but the smoke in the room made it impossible to see. A memory of smoke as the greater danger than flames paralyzed him. He lay in the puddle as the cloying smells of many kinds of incense filled the room, lower and lower.

There was a different noise suddenly. A dog's bark. The beggar's head lolled to the side, and he saw the dog up on the window ledge. It whimpered in pain, as if the jagged edge of some glass had cut its paw, much as the glass had cut its master's legs and hand. But still it jumped down, into the puddle surrounded by flames and clamped its teeth on the beggar's coat and the layers underneath.

It pulled.

Probably would tear the cloth into pieces with how ragged some of the beggar's clothes were. He scrambled in the direction the dog was pulling to save the cloth.

Heat bathed his face, and his legs cramped up as if with remembered pain. But he kept going, letting the dog half help him and doing as much as he was able to on his own. Flames filled the space where the window had been, fed by the air outside into a frenzy.

The door. Someone had left through the door, so it couldn't be locked. He couldn't leave this all to the dog. He stood partially upright, put a hand on the dog's neck to keep it with him, and rushed to the door.

It fell open. Fire licked around its frame, flames that tried to start the beggar's clothes on fire again. They sizzled at the touch. Soon the water would be dried away and powerless. A spark smoldered in the dog's tail. He swatted it away and held damp cloth against the fur.

Covering his mouth and gripping the dog's neck, he ran through the doorway and into the street outside.

Neighbors were coming with buckets, and the soldiers would likely arrive soon to help. He careened past them into a bank of slushy snow and lay down, scooping the dirty slush over himself and the dog while the people fought the fire under control.

"Hey, wasn't that man one of them?" a voice called out as the buckets and drizzle combined to put out the flames. "He helped start the fire, I think."

The beggar didn't even bother to open his eyes. Some people approached him. Their footsteps scraped on the damp cobbles.

"You. Were you one of these vandals? What do you have to say?"

The beggar half opened one eye. The sight of the people—three or four—leaning toward him was blurry, so he closed it again. His dog growled at them.

"You look like you're in pretty rough shape." That was a different voice. "We should get him some help."

"Help? He started the fire. We tie him up and march him to jail or leave him for the soldiers to deal with. Either way."

"I don't know." Another voice. "Probably just some untouchable who happened by at the wrong time. Don't touch him, or you'll need to have a priest cleanse you."

Someone leaned in closer, despite the dog's increasingly frantic snarling. The beggar felt their breath on his face, but the person didn't touch him. "Though, not sure he'll last that long regardless." He peeked out, saw a figure holding the dog off with an arm around its belly. Too far away to be the one who'd been speaking.

"Ah, just leave him be. The fire's out. If the soldiers want him, let them. They'll be here any minute."

They let go of the dog, and it bounded over to lick his face.

By the time the beggar managed to sit upright, no one was in sight. The melting snow had quickly extinguished the fire, once the flames burned through the outer walls. The smell of wet ashes made him retch at memories that wouldn't quite form.

No one in sight didn't mean the soldiers wouldn't show up. Pushing his back against the wall of the nearest house, he rose to his feet.

Couldn't go back to his hiding spot behind the bush. He found his way into the sewer tunnels and slept near a boiler that warmed him as he dried.

***

The beggar needed his bowl and his mat. The Sons of Ryo had grabbed him without letting him take either one—not that he would have been able to keep them in the confusion of their vandalism anyway. He might get by without a mat this time of year. A beggar without a mat in winter would find the cobbles cold beyond enduring much too soon to receive enough for the day. For now he would end the day sore, but he could endure that.

A beggar without a bowl would receive nothing at all. Where

was there to throw a coin or an end of a loaf of bread if there was no bowl?

The sewers gave him a way to sneak back to his former hiding place. That was how he found it in the first place, after all. It took him a day of wandering, of wading through wastewater and groping along dark walls to finally get to the right section of tunnels. He waited until the next morning to climb up.

The light revealed an empty place. No Sons of Ryo waited for him, and only on seeing their absence did he realize how he'd dreaded them standing right there, gathered for another day of violence. Both the space behind the bushes and the paved path between buildings on the other side were unoccupied.

Unoccupied by a beggar's bowl and mat as well as by people.

The beggar cast around as far as he dared—beneath the bush and into its branches, along the walk, even a short way down the nearest street in either direction. No sign of either of his few possessions.

He returned to the sewers.

A mat shouldn't be too difficult. People threw out old blankets often enough. They might be worn through in places, but doubled up they could serve. He might even find one down in the sewers without too much searching.

A bowl, though. A broken bowl might be thrown out, but when a bowl broke, it usually shattered beyond use. There was no doubling up the sides to fix the pieces, while a bowl that was merely chipped would continue to be used.

The memory flashed through his mind. A bowl that surely wouldn't serve its original purpose any longer. It was probably lying in the ashes of the fire that had turned the clockmaker's shop into a shell of a building.

He would have to go back there at night.

Hunger gnawed at him by the time darkness fell late into the night. The lights of the city bounced off low snow clouds, so it never got as dark as he might have wanted, but waiting wouldn't make it any darker. His great coat, wrapped tight and collar turned up, hid his face.

The shop remains were dark, at least. The streetside lamp that might have given some light had also been destroyed in the fire, and nothing had been done to replace it. The beggar watched for other people for some minutes, and when no one came, he rushed into the shadows of the burnt out shop.

The smell of incense and char filled the air, made damp by the firefighting and the drizzle that had fallen since then. The dog sniffed at the ashes and sneezed. The light was too little to find the bowl by sight, so the beggar kicked the ashes, hoping to stumble across it.

More incense ash rose, choking him. He covered his mouth with his sleeve and kept searching. He kicked the big bowl, stubbing his toe. He swallowed his cry of pain and turned around, widening his searching feet.

When he kicked the small bowl at last, it skittered across the ashes and hit a remaining portion of wall with a distinct clang.

Everyone would wake up. He ran over and scooped the bowl up to muffle the sound. Then he stood perfectly still. Waiting for the echoes to die, waiting for someone to come and investigate, for cries of alarm and authority.

No one showed up.

When he was sure the shadows weren't hiding a dozen soldiers waiting to arrest him, the beggar slunk off, the bowl clutched to his chest.

***

The first day begging with the new bowl, he received more coins than he ever had. He hoped this second day would be as good. He chose a spot at the edge of one of the larger markets. Many people of all castes came and went. He was far from the only beggar here.

Beggars used to be far more common. Back before… When… Anyway, he used to see them, when he wasn't one. They'd be along the steam baths near the volcanic fields. They'd gather at the base of the Bridge of the Forgotten South and anywhere there were likely to be people. The crowds of them around markets had always been especially thick.

What more was there to do when you were an untouchable? You still had to eat somehow.

But so many untouchables had left. Had gone away...somewhere. Now it was rare to have more than a few in a single location. So the beggar felt self-conscious with there being other beggars nearby. Did he beg in the wrong way? Was he making some mistake that would get someone else in trouble? Some behavior that would turn the people of Eghsal against the untouchables even more than they were? He hadn't been born knowing these kinds of things.

Even here among other untouchables, therefore, he set himself apart, choosing a spot near them but not among them.

These other beggars were the least of the untouchables, the most in need of help, any help. The sickly and old, those who had lost some ability to move about freely. Had lost the ability to flee Romnai and go where the others had gone.

The beggar imagined a better society, a city where they were cared for, where they weren't untouchable.

Imagination was a dangerous thing, though. His mind shied away when he began to picture exactly how that might work, exactly how someone might force such a change on a city like Romnai or even devise some new city, far away from here. Where such a new city might be founded. Dangerous thoughts and treacherous imaginings. He forced the ideas away and let himself be mindless, a part of the marketplace and nothing more.

His thoughts floated, and his body was no more than a husk that was part of the bustle.

People gave him coins. He dropped back inside himself long enough to thank them. Even the noise of the coins hitting his new bowl was like the bells of the priests to help their followers imagine the mysteries of the gods and the sacred fire, to set their minds free.

One pinging coin was sending him back to contemplation when hands grabbed his shoulders and pulled him fully into himself.

"What..."

There was a small, wiry man pulling him upright. The other beggars ignored the disturbance.

"Get off me." The beggar's word slurred. "What do you want?"

"It was you!" The man pointed at him with one very long finger. "You set the fire, didn't you?"

"I didn't set—"

The man lunged at him again and grabbed him around the neck with one arm. "You have my bowl. You robbed my shop for a bowl? After burning it down?"

The dog growled and tried to get between the beggar and the man, but the man blocked it with his shoulder and pushed the dog away. He grabbed the bowl from the ground, dumped out the coins, and began beating the beggar with it.

"No, I, that's not it at all." The beggar slipped from the man's grasp. Covering his head with one arm, he reached around on the ground for the lost coins with the other. "I found it, but I didn't start any fire."

The man backed up and dropped the bowl but then snatched at the beggar's sleeve, yanking it upward. His bare hand revealed the small, still healing cuts on his fingers and the back of his hand, red with infection.

"Then what is this? A glass cut, and another. Looks like you've been breaking windows."

The beggar pulled his hand back away. The dog jumped in again, this time placing itself firmly between the two men, snarling up at the shopkeeper.

"Help!" the man called as he took another step away. "Soldiers! Arrest this man. A vandal, an arson, and a thief."

He kept repeating it while the beggar snatched up his new, makeshift mat and what coins he could quickly grab. He hesitated then took the cracked bowl as well.

He should run. His body was long past being able to outrun anyone. He made what speed he could, but it wasn't a run.

And it wasn't enough.

The shopkeeper shadowed him, still calling for help. And within half a block, soldiers marched down the side street and intercepted them.

The beggar made no effort to resist, but the captain still grabbed him by the lapels of his dirty coat and gestured for two of his soldiers to hold his arms.

"Get that dog away from here," he growled.

One soldier drew his long knife, but another one had already kicked the dog and picked up a stone in case they needed to make the mutt go farther. It whined but kept its distance.

"A thief, are you? Let's see what else you have that you're stolen."

"I'm just a beggar. I found the bowl, I swear."

The captain was already patting him down. He stopped at an inside pocket on the coat's sleeve.

"What's this, huh?"

It took the beggar a moment to remember what he had hidden there. The coin the captain withdrew from his pocket flashed in the light, turning the flame etched into its surface for a moment alive. Fire, again. He should have seen the coin as an omen. It should have been his sign to stay away from... No, his mind faltered. It should have been his sign to burn down the whole city. To let even bigger flames consume everything, because there was nothing worth saving.

Nothing except his dog, which the soldiers had chased away.

"Pretty expensive nothing." The captain paused, glanced around at his soldiers, and pocketed the coin. "That bowl, that is. Even cracked, it must be expensive."

He stared at the beggar, as if daring him to speak up about the coin. The beggar said nothing.

"Take him in. This one may be more than a simple beggar. A liar, as well. So warn anyone there not to trust what he says."

The captain flipped the bowl in his hand as if studying it for a moment. Then he tossed it to the shopkeeper. "Won't be needing this as evidence. So take it."

"Sirs. He destroyed my shop. Isn't there some way—"

The captain growled at him. "Take the bowl. Apart from that I don't want to see you again, or else we end up dragging you in for thievery too."

The shopkeeper clutched the broken bowl to his chest and ran away. The dog followed the beggar and his captors from a distance, whining but doing nothing to save him.

CHAPTER 19

The vision of creating a new kind of city was ending. Was over. Jaritta could feel what remained of Chaitanshehar slipping away through her fingers, like clay that's too wet to throw.

She served up a mash of tasteless food for Nataravi and forced herself to eat some of it as well. Swamp wheat, though it was an insult to real wheat to call it that. An insult to swamps as well. It was a weed that grew thick along the edges of the swamp. Its seeds resembled wheat seeds, and didn't even require threshing. When cooked it expanded until the transition from water to swamp wheat became meaningless. Everything in the pot was a diffuse continuum from water to seed and back.

They added what flavorings they could to make it edible. To make it through one more day.

Nataravi used to complain, but they were past that. Now she scraped her bowl clean and then licked what was left. Jaritta did the same with her own.

The mine food was long since gone. Azheeran's forays for food from the old ruins had brought a supply of dried fish and what wild crops hadn't been eaten by animals. It was doled out bit by bit, to give the people of the city some variety. And mumblers brought game that scarcely fed a tiny fraction of Jaritta's supposed city.

Her family's turn to have a portion of any of those other foods was not today, so they swallowed the swamp wheat without lingering over it. No pleasure in eating, no joy in the flavors, but energy to get something done, at least to survive. Maybe.

Datri arrived while Jaritta was putting the dishes into the tub for washing. As she usually did. Jaritta suspected she must have some way to spy into Jaritta's chambers so she could know exactly when they were cleaning up their breakfast dishes.

"I see you've eaten. Good. There is much to do today."

Having something to do was Datri's way of getting through this time of hunger and fear. Probably better than Jaritta's impulse to hide away in her chambers while the dreams she'd once had for the future dwindled bit by bit into nothing.

But that didn't mean the thought of hiding away even from Datri wasn't an attractive option.

Datri scooped up Ovitiva and knelt beside Nataravi. "Do you want to learn to be a good spy?"

Jaritta snorted but then grew somber. She wouldn't really use a child as a spy, would she? Knowing Datri, it wasn't a foregone conclusion. "I'm not sure she has the skills you're after. Yet."

"There's more to spying than you might picture, sis." She said it with a wink, but there seemed to be a bite beneath the words as well. "But anyway, do you have any urgent tasks at the moment? I actually could use some help from you." Turning her head as if to include Nataravi in a joke, she added, "And Nataravi as well."

What was there to do? A thousand tasks. Find food. Make sure everyone who was left had at least something to eat. Check in on those who'd gone down to the fields early in the morning. Save the city. None of it demanded her immediate attention.

"Nothing urgent, I suppose. How can I help?"

"Let's go up to my home. I want you to understand what I do."

Jaritta cocked her head at her sister in law. Why did she want that?

Datri didn't wait for Jaritta to ask. "In case something happens to me. In case some new information comes in and I can't attend to it right away."

"Are you well?"

Datri's mouth cocked upward on one side, amused at the question. "I'm not sick. But the arcist wasn't sick before he disappeared. Your husband wasn't sick before circumstances changed, and he had to be absent."

As if she needed the reminder, twisting its blade through her thoughts.

"Azheeran wasn't sick when we sent him looking for food from the mumblers to the north. What if we decide that I should go there next time or visit Pashun or travel back to my parents in the Silk City? I wouldn't want all my work to be wasted unless and until I return."

The Silk City. That place hadn't really played into her thoughts of the future. Romnai had its Thirty Princes, Pashun had a portion of the city claiming to follow Romnai's princes and another faction claiming their own Thirty. Or they used to be split that way, before whatever lunacy had sent them abandoning their mines and apparently marching off southward as one group.

Even Jarnur had its own, completely separate circle of princes that had sprung up in the last five or six years. But how did the Silk City fit into that? Its leaders were silk weavers, not princes. "Is there any reason for someone to go to the Silk City? They're not directly allied with any of the self-proclaimed princes, are they?"

Datri shook her head in mild exasperation. "That was not the point I was trying to make. But you can see what I know as we sort through the letters and other information I am always gathering."

Jaritta conceded and gathered up what she'd need to keep the girls with them up in Datri's place.

The climb brought them through the familiar sights of the city. Of a city emptying. The vacant structures stood side by side with well kept little homes. One house had burnt recently. When had that happened? She couldn't remember any talk of a fire being put out. The old scars on her cheek twinged in sympathy with that fire. The city was scarred, much like she was.

Datri's home was near the upper edge of the city, and its low door faced outward, into the wilderness above. The better for spies and travelers to enter unseen.

Jaritta had to duck to get through the doorway.

It wasn't the first time Jaritta had been there, but she'd never once been invited beyond the tiny sitting room at the entrance. A curtain cut the room off from the rest of the living space beyond. This time that curtain was pulled off to the side.

Jaritta felt like she ought to tiptoe through. But Datri ushered them along as if she frequently hosted visitors. The room beyond was utterly ordinary for Chaitanshehar. None of the fanciness Datri must have known in the family manor in Romnai. Or from growing up in the Silk City, for that matter. It contained a simple kitchen, several chairs, and a plain table, covered in carefully arranged piles of paper.

Was this the heart of Datri's vaunted spying network? Surely it was only a part of it.

As Jaritta looked around for a safe place to let the girls play, her eye caught one thing that wasn't common in Chaitanshehar. A portrait. A portrait of someone she knew. For a single heartbeat she thought it was her father. He looked younger than he'd been when the priests had forced him to kick his daughter into the streets, but the shape of his face was the same.

Or almost the same, because now she recognized her brother. Over six years since he died, or went missing. If he was still alive, he might be unrecognizable. It had been another six or seven years before that when she'd last seen him. But as soon as she noticed the wry twist in his smile, she could hear his dry chuckle in response to one of his own jokes, his earnest voice so cautious and considered.

"I had Yatim bring it from Romnai," Datri said. "No one has tried to claim our old house, did you know that? Kalavendi is still keeping it, while people believe I've gone off to the Silk City to visit my parents and never returned. But might, any time."

Our old house didn't necessarily imply Jaritta's as well, but it had been hers once too. And deep within its rooms was a chapel with a steady flame that would easily burn a young girl's cheek. For all she missed of earlier days, she had no wish to go back to that place.

Datri went on, "We had the painting done shortly before he left, and I hadn't even hung it up anywhere before I fled here. But it was still sitting against a wall in his old office."

"Did he know you had come here, before he was arrested?" Before he was killed.

Datri nodded. "Yatim was with him, remember? He got some of my coded letters. So he didn't know everything, didn't know all my reasons or what things were like here. But he knew I'd come and joined you."

And did he approve? Or did he still believe Jaritta deserved execution? She didn't ask those questions. Too much had changed since then for the past to matter here and now. Beliefs changed fast when the world's whirlwind swept through a person's life.

She tore herself away and settled the girls down at one end of the room, near another door that probably led to a bedroom. There were other hints of Romnai in the place. Some were little items that had come from the family manor, but mostly it was the feel of how Datri had arranged the room. It was the manor house condensed and translated into a new, more rustic place. It felt like home, but that had been a house she'd been forced to leave as a teenager. Which meant it wasn't a *welcoming* sense of home, so much as one that left her off balance.

"What do we do first?"

Datri gestured at a chair. "Have a seat. Let me show you how I arrange the letters I get, and how easy it is to remember."

The table proved to be a stylized map of the Eghsal Valley. The careful piles each lay where one of the cities would be, more or less. Romnai had the biggest pile. Or rather, several piles all arranged on the same part of the table, each pile connected by topic or key figure within the city. The pile from Pashun looked like much older letters, little that was recent. An ink stamp on the back of each note or letter told her which pile any note belonged to, in case something happened to the piles.

In fact, she'd been recently going through a number of notes from a variety of locations, and the letters lay in a mess on an unused chair.

"Do you think Nataravi would like to help with this part?" Datri asked.

Jaritta looked at her daughters. Ovitiva was looking sleepy and could probably do well with a nap. She was no longer nursing frequently, but she might let Jaritta cuddle her to sleep. Then Nataravi could help her aunt while Ovitiva slept in Jaritta's lap.

If only she could let herself fall asleep as well.

"I bet she would love to learn, if you make it into a spy game." Datri nodded as if that were obvious.

While Jaritta gathered up Ovitiva, Datri said to Nataravi, "You have good eyes, I think. Do you think you can spy the right pattern?"

Nataravi's eyes grew big, and she nodded without saying anything.

"Great. See this flower? Can you find all the letters that match that picture?"

Nataravi nodded, and while Jaritta rocked Ovitiva to sleep, Nataravi searched through the pile for the right pictures of a flower. When she had a hand free, Jaritta scooped up the notes from the Silk City and paged through them.

There was a lot about new fabrics that weren't silk but felt like silk. And there was family news, mundane and of little interest to the future of Chaitanshehar. Unless…

"Are these coded?"

Datri glanced over. "Some are. I'll have to teach that to you, too. But those mostly aren't. Just details to help me keep track of the big picture."

Jaritta flipped one over and stopped. "Indima?" The waif-like dancer who'd been at Chaitan's house. Ekana's former lover. Jaritta could picture her, the way she moved on the stage, the way she hung on Ekana's arm. Until they were caught and she was gone. "Is this— "

"The one you knew, yes."

"How do you know her?"

Datri laughed. Datri's laughs always had a touch of cruelty to them. "Same way I know Pavresh, really. We were on the train to the Silk City together. Our families knew each other before that, so I'd known her somewhat even earlier. But there we were on a train to the east. Indima crushed at being forced to leave Romnai. Pavresh pretending to be a cheetah jati servant for our silk weaver families and struggling with it. Well…" She closed her eyes as if seeing the inside of the train car. "No, I guess he did a fair job there. It was in the Silk City that he struggled more. But he was half in love with Indima, or thought he might be. And he was spying for the man who would be my husband only a year or so later. Funny how these things line up."

Jaritta stared at Datri. She'd never known this part of the story. Pavresh always turned awkward around Datri, but she had chalked that up to the way Datri had pushed him out of Jasfer's household when she arrived. That there had been a longer history hadn't occurred to her.

"And Indima? You've been exchanging letters ever since?"

"No. Only the last few years. She's a dancer now, a temple dancer but more than that. And her dances are coded to send people our way."

"Maybe she should dance some food our way as well." Jaritta continued leafing through the letters until Datri needed her to learn some other part of the system. They spent several hours in her house, going through what Datri knew and how she kept track of it. Jaritta's mind was spinning when she and the girls finally left to return to their own chambers.

***

There was still so much more to learn. Over the course of the following days, every time Jaritta could get away from other duties for a few hours, she went up to Datri's home to learn what she could. Sometimes the girls came with her. Sometimes they stayed with Poorma or one of the other leaders of the city and their families.

She returned one day and picked the girls up from Bhurat, a former miner who now taught many of the younger children. He had a way with the young ones, a grandfatherly sense of playfulness and joy. Half a dozen small children were in his house at the moment, and all were eating yet more of the watery swamp wheat paste. He smiled and began to tell her how the morning had gone when Datri burst in behind her.

"Sorry," she said without seeming especially sorry. "One of my contacts just arrived, and I think you should come back up there with me."

But she'd just left. Jaritta caught Bhurat's eye with a question in her gaze.

"Oh, they'll be fine with us. Don't worry at all."

She pursed her lips but nodded. She might want nothing more than to gather her daughters and hide away with them for the rest of the day. But the city's needs came before her own. "Nataravi, Ovitiva, give me a quick hug. I'll be back as soon as I can."

As they climbed back to Datri's place, Jaritta asked, "What makes it so urgent? Is the news bad?"

"I never said the news itself was urgent. I don't even know what it is. They needed to rest first. But I wanted you to know how the reports can go."

"Who is it? Where's the news from?"

"Patience. I'll let them tell you. But it's a contact I had in Pashun. It's been so long since I've had any reliable information at all come from that city."

Jaritta's heart picked up. Pashun. Would this help solve the mystery of the fate of Rashul and Pavresh? Would the spy know anything of the earthquakes and aftershocks, anything that would tell of what danger her husband was in?

She quickened her steps to hear the spy's report sooner.

The woman lay sprawled on Datri's low couch in the sitting room and didn't stir when they entered. Should they wake her? Jaritta wanted to hear what she would say. When she caught Datri's eye, the younger woman shook her head and said in a low voice, "We'll give them a moment to wake up. They're weary with traveling."

Quiet as they were, these words were enough to rouse the spy.

Jaritta had thought of her as a woman, but as the spy sat up, that impression changed. There was something about them that could pass as either man or woman, almost in the same way that Pavresh had been able to pass as any caste or jati.

She blurted out, "Are you using arcist magic to do that?"

The spy cocked their head and shook it, not as if to say *no* so much as out of confusion.

"This is Jaritta," Datri said. "My sister-in-law. She's trustworthy. If I'm ever gone when you report, you may need to report to her instead."

The spy nodded, stretched, and settled into a more comfortable position on the couch.

"So what do you have?" Datri finally asked when the spy looked ready to answer questions. "I haven't heard from you for a long time."

"It's a mess." They shook their head as if sad. "Pashun is not the city it was." Overwhelmed by the memories, perhaps, the spy fell silent.

"Who's in charge?" Datri prodded.

"Same factions, really, but they've reached some sort of truce. Prince Hrisha leads, as far as being visible. He's been the face of the Romnai Thirty ever since the coup, but he hasn't really left Pashun in all that time, as far as I've noticed. So he's visible."

"Mahendri?"

They shook their head. "Maybe behind the scenes. And someone else too, behind the scenes with him. A magic user."

Jaritta froze for a moment and then leaned close. "Magic? Who is it?"

"No idea. But definitely magic. That's the real thing that's causing the mess there. And the reason I couldn't make it back here until now. Magic controlling people, magic binding everyone into one mindless effort." They fell silent as if remembering.

This time Datri let them take their time.

Finally the spy said simply, "I was caught in the magic, too. Once you're part of it, there's no real escape. The only reason I got away at all was that I was sick when they marched, and they left me behind. When I could get up again, I was free from its power."

With that confession off their chest, the spy launched into a much more detailed account of the city, of the magic that bound the people and the constant sounds of military drums and the horns calling them to arms in a war that never took shape. "Every day is so closely regimented. We listened to the horns and knew what to do. Craft weapons and tools here, fix a broken wall or a steam engine that isn't working, bake bread there."

Oh, bread. If only they could have some here. Jaritta tried to picture being there. The pull of a magic that erased identity and thought, that was the most frightening part. She imagined tendrils of that magic snaking out into the foothills, ensnaring Chandri, turning him into someone she no longer knew.

The singular effort was not toward them, at least, but aimed at some kind of tunnel to the south. The spy had never seen it but knew its size and location from the reports they had received.

"But that's not the real goal, I don't think. Or maybe for some of their leaders it is. But the real result is they're turning the whole city into soldiers." The spy glanced around at the walls— and seemingly through those walls at the city below. "And I don't think the leaders have any intention to send an army south. It's aimed straight at you, here. Eventually."

As if there would be any *here* left soon enough.

They heard the rest of the spy's report, the details mixing with the information from the letters that Jaritta had been reviewing. When the spy was done, Datri asked, "So what can you do next? Back to Pashun?"

The spy grimaced.

"I understand," Datri said. "You don't want to be captured by that magic again. It makes sense, now, that I hear so little from my other informants I have there. Or used to have there."

"There's not even anyone left there, really. Not in the city itself. So there's nothing I could spy on."

They should conquer the city, then. Let the soldiers return to find she'd claimed their own homes. After a moment's thought, Jaritta shook her head. They wouldn't have the people to defend it, anyway. Their ending would be just as grim and hopeless there as here.

"Did they leave any stores of food behind?"

The spy shook their head. "Doubt it. They needed all the food they could transport to march, I imagine. I saw the wagons heading out, even as sick as I was, and there couldn't have been much left behind. The individual houses—maybe they have some ends and scrapings in their pantries. But nothing significant."

Not worth sending a force there to scavenge, then. But if they could get word to Chandri to sweep through the city on their way back here… "You know anything about food?" Jaritta asked. "Growing it, hunting, scavenging?"

The spy looked at Datri before speaking, as if weighing how to answer. "Preparing it. I can make a little food go a long way, if that's what you want to know."

"Final decision isn't up to me," Jaritta said with a shrug. "But if you wanted to stay here for a while, rest, recover, give Pashun some time to settle into whatever they have planned. That wouldn't necessarily be a bad thing."

"Except for one fewer contact in the city." Datri rubbed her jaw. "Not the city itself, actually, but it would be good to have a contact with their army."

"Not if they just end up under the army's spells," Jaritta said.

Datri assented with a small hand gesture. "Well, we should hear back from Ellechandran and Chhayasheela soon, and that will give us some idea. There's no real sense in sending you there to be a pawn of their spells." With a definitive nod, she added, "Get some more sleep. I'll help you get settled for a time in our city, until I need you somewhere else."

Datri's manner gave off an odd combination of comfort and duty. Of welcome rest in the city her spy was serving, but with that steel reminder that Datri would decide if the spy had to serve in some other way in the future. Jaritta had to wonder how Datri had established such loyalty from her spies in the first place…and more importantly if she would be expected to command spies someday, because Datri couldn't be there. She wasn't sure she would be able to mimic her sister-in-law's demeanor.

***

It was some days before Jaritta had a chance to make her way up to Datri's place again. This time she came with the girls in tow.

She regretted their presence when they were midway up the city and began hearing shouts and cries and the sound of violence. It was a noise she knew from Romnai as an untouchable, but a noise that was foreign to Chaitanshehar.

She hugged Nataravi against her side as they climbed around the sloping curve of the street. There was a brawl. Nataravi stared, round-eyed. People were swinging fists. Someone fell to the ground. She thought she saw someone kicking the fallen person as she turned her daughter's eyes away from the scene.

The city guards were already moving in to break the fight up. Jaritta lingered, wanting to know what had happened but not wanting her children exposed to it any more than they already had been. The guards quelled the fighting quickly. It still tore at Jaritta that they'd had to break up a brawl at all.

When she saw Azheeran walking away from the cluster of guards, she came back around the corner to talk to him.

"No one seriously hurt," he said, rubbing his hand against his cheek. "They might have some sore heads, but nothing more."

"What was it about?"

Azheeran shook his head sadly. "Food. They were arguing that one of them stole food from the other. Words got ugly. I think they were different castes before coming here. Different jatis, anyway. That set them fighting."

Fighting over food. Fighting over castes. Two things that shouldn't happen in their city. They were a city without castes. And they were a city where everyone was committed to the idea of the city itself, a mere feeling but one enhanced by Pavresh's magic.

What if his magic was weakening in his absence? What if he never returned to fix it?

Jaritta pushed down the panic she felt. She could save those worries for another time, have Juishika look into shoring up the arcist magic, if necessary. "Well, I'm glad the guards brought it under control so quickly. Please commend them for me, let them know I saw their quick actions."

Azheeran nodded as she passed by, continuing to Datri's place.

What was happening to her city? People getting lost and never returning. People starving. People fighting in the streets. Husbands, her husband anyway, sent off and returning, only to be sent away again. It wasn't what she'd dreamed of, wasn't the city she had tried to mold. Where had it all gone wrong?

She was floundering, letting it slip away, failing the ones she most wanted to please.

And the only answer she could find so far was to learn the surface details of Datri's spy network and hope things improved. Somehow. Someday.

Yatim stood at the entrance to Datri's house. He held a walking stick that was taller than he was and carried a bulging bag strapped across his back. Seeing him always brought Jaritta back to her days in Romnai, to sneaking in to visit her brother in his manor back when he did what he could to support her. Yatim had been Jasfer's closest confidant and the one responsible for keeping him safe.

Until he'd been arrested by the princes of Pashun and carted off to be sentenced in Romnai.

Jaritta forced the memories of the past aside and said, "Datri sending you out for some information?"

He shrugged and gestured her inside. Jaritta frowned. He usually at least spoke to her.

Datri met her just inside the door. Her hair was a wild tangle as if she'd been in too much of a hurry to even pull it back. "Oh, I'm glad you're here. I'm leaving."

"What?" Jaritta felt her body freeze. She couldn't leave Jaritta alone with her failing city and all the people she was letting down.

"There are some new letters. You know the codes now. You know how to organize them. Help save the city."

Datri's gaze wouldn't stay still. She darted a look at all corners of the room, at Jaritta, at the girls. She collapsed against the wall for a moment then bounced back upright.

Jaritta wasn't sure whether to grab her shoulders to make her stand still or just get out of the way.

Datri went down onto her knees and held out her arms to Nataravi. "I will miss you, Nataravi. Help your mom with the letters. When I see you again, I'll introduce you to your uncle Jasfer."

Jaritta caught her breath. Did she really mean… Dizziness made her lean against the wall.

Nataravi returned the hug but clearly didn't know what Datri was talking about. Then Datri stood and took Ovitiva and held her for a moment as well. Ovitiva had outgrown being cradled, but Datri held her that way anyway. Briefly. After quickly handing her back to Jaritta, Datri picked up a bag and headed out the door.

"What do you mean, *her uncle?*"

"It's Jasfer. He's been found. He's alive." Datri took a deep breath as if to still the battle between hope and disappointment before it could start. "Maybe. It might be him. I need to know."

And when it wasn't him? She would come back here, right?

Or return with him at her side, still ready to help Jaritta with this failing city? More likely it would have collapsed before Datri could return, whether alone or not.

Then Datri was out the door and away, walking side by side with Yatim.

Jaritta whispered, "Safe travels. Sister."

CHAPTER 20

How to dance in a jail cell? Indima contemplated the moves she might make, the allowances to carve out for close walls, a cramped cot, the shackles the guards sometimes left on her feet. Contemplated, but she made no move.

Waiting drained the dancing impulse.

Waiting, wondering what the priests would do to her, wondering what the leaders of her own jati would do.

When she'd been caught having an affair with a low caste laborer, her jati had exiled her from Romnai, sent her to this city, a city that still wasn't her home, no matter how many years had passed. But where could they send her now? Was her subversive dancing worse than being found having sex with someone from a lower caste? Or would they simply scold her, warn her to change her ways, and set her free?

She lay on the rigid cot and contemplated.

Her father came to visit.

"Oh, Indima. How many…" He rubbed his eyes and changed what he was going to say. "How are you? No one's treating you poorly, are they?"

Indima shook her head and slid back from the edge so her father could sit. The cot squeaked as he sat.

"I don't know if I can get you out of this one." He was a respected man in the city, a silk weaver who was developing a new silk-like fabric that could, possibly, be made here in the north. Indima had no doubt that his position had kept her out of serious trouble many other times.

But maybe not this time. It wasn't as if she hadn't known the risks. It wasn't as if she didn't consider it worth the danger, if she could help even a few people escape. What was the life of a lone dancer worth, after all? Might as well spend it on something more valuable and lasting than her dances.

"It's not your job, Dad. Protecting me. I'll find my way through somehow."

"They're throwing around words like sacrilege and treason. You don't...I know that's not what you mean to imply in your dancing. You're not against the gods. You're not against the princes." He let silence fill in, as if waiting for her to confirm his beliefs about her—or to deny them.

She did neither. How could you be against gods when they were as empty as thought? But, on the other hand, how could any thinking person not be against the princes and their grip on power everywhere? She despised them.

And that meant she despised the priests, for whom she danced, as well, for they were the equals of the princes, members of the kortru caste and rulers of this valley.

Which implied that she despised her own jati, too. The silk weavers, wondrous keepers of the ancient silks who preserved history with something the outsiders called magic and they called science. A valuable part of their culture, no doubt, but just as powerful as the other two jatis, just as responsible for the terrible things the people beneath them had to endure.

But how could she express any of that to her father?

She didn't despise him. He was a good man, if sometimes blinded. And she didn't always despise the priests she served or even the few members of the princely jati she had met over the years. It wasn't the people themselves she hated, but the idea of them, the way their actions built Eghsal Valley into what it was.

Instead of saying anything, she forced herself to sit upright and leaned her head against her father's back.

When he left, she stayed sitting upright. Maybe she could dance herself to freedom. Maybe the gods, empty and lost in the rigid strictures of many generations of priests, would take pity on her and open a way. Or maybe her dancing was a form of magic and would let her walk right through the walls. That would be a fitting, storybook ending to her captivity.

She stood and held her arms out as if to begin a dance. Her

elbows were cocked just so, her fingers loose yet ready to snap into the precise figures of a dance.

When she reached inside herself for any music to dance to, her form withered away. What was the purpose? To dance to nothing was to evoke nothing, to summon a nothingness that would come as no relief. She dropped her arms first, then her shoulders and chin, and she sank down to the cot.

Indima lost track of time but it seemed both a short time and many eternities later when a group of people entered her cell. Two were silk weaver officials, a man and a woman who ruled the town—or as they might claim, helped to guide it.

The third one was unknown to her. He did not wear silks. His robes were fine, or what would be counted fine in other cities—the clothes of a high ranking servant perhaps or even a prince who did not wish to stand out as one. He stood behind the other two without seeming to be in a servant role.

"Indima," the woman said. "Your actions have raised many questions. About your own values." She leaned forward and drew out the words into an accusation. "About your dancing. About your contacts elsewhere."

Contacts elsewhere? She was cut off out here, exiled to the Silk City for that very reason. Or had been cut off until Datri reached out to her.

She'd expected this to be about complaints from the priests, about dances that weren't part of the temple tradition. It looked like she might have upset someone else instead. Either way, she made no effort to answer.

"This is Prince Mahendri. He is here on other business, but when he learned we had arrested you, he requested an audience."

Indima stared blankly at a point just above the woman's head, ignoring the stranger entirely. Prince or no prince, he had no claim on her attention, no right to it.

"It is an honor to meet you," the man said. He had a mouse's voice, a weak, speaking-from-behind-a-curtain voice. "I saw you dance some years ago, in Pashun, and you created a stunning effect with your movements."

That drew her notice enough to condescend and look directly at him. He stood with his hands clasped across each other before her, as if a supplicant.

"There have been some rumors," he went on. "Rumors that have even reached us in Pashun, that you know something of the refugees who are encamped near our city."

Indima snorted. "A *refugee* camp?" To hear it described that way shocked her from her silence for a moment.

Mahendri nodded. "Yes." As if it were the accepted way to describe Chaitanshehar. "I need you to tell me what you know of their so-called city, and how you know it. Who are your contacts? How do you communicate?"

There was something odd about his voice. On the surface it sounded completely reasonable, and it seemed to promise that he would remain blandly reasonable as long as she complied. But a more sinister note echoed beneath his words, a warning that the reasonableness was a thin facade, one he might cast off in a moment if she tried to resist in any way.

Good luck breaking through the steel shields Indima had erected around herself since coming out here. She prided herself on those. Only dancing could wear them down, and they snapped back around her thoughts and identity as soon as she finished.

When she didn't answer, Mahendri said, "I know you know more, and I *will* learn that from you." He made a show of brushing dust from his hands—though he'd touched nothing in the cell to have given him any dust—and turned toward the door.

Just before he left, he said over his shoulder, "We know about your past in Romnai, with Chaitan and that crowd. Make no mistake. Soon we will know everything you know about Chaitanshehar, and its reach in other cities as well."

The two city leaders followed him out of the cell.

Mahendri was back—alone—the following day. Demanding

the same thing while she stared fixedly out the window, high in the wall.

"We know about Ekana."

Everyone knew about Ekana. Maybe not by name, but they knew her disgrace. It was no threat to bring him up.

"We turned him against Jaritta."

That made Indima catch her breath, the shields shivering for a moment. Ekana's betrayal was still painful, and that memory not completely shielded away.

"We paid him. I forget how much. Not much to people like you and me. To a laborer like that, though." Mahendri shrugged as if Ekana was something beneath the level of a true human being. "He snatched it from us and turned against your old friends as if they were nothing to him."

She didn't answer, but it took effort this time. She had to prepare herself for other surprises, for Mahendri to find ways to pry open her shields. Because she couldn't afford to let them down for anyone.

Later that evening, he said, "Do you know what happened to Rashul? He was in the refugee camp, but we got him."

Indima took a deep breath through her nose.

"Killed him. Right on the street. I think it was one of the streets you danced on."

She couldn't sit still for that. She stood abruptly and was gratified to see Mahendri flinch away. Let him fear her attack. She wasn't built like a warrior, but a dancer's muscles were strong, and he was no warrior himself.

But Rashul dead? It had always been a possibility, of course. Any of them could die. And Rashul had courted retaliation from the princes even back when she was with them in Romnai. That he'd survived Jaritta's coup was only because he'd been arrested before they could take action. After his arrest, he'd spent the next years cowered away from his former friends in fear. Until, from what Datri told her, he'd gone to the new city.

She heard his voice in her mind. His urging them to imagine

a better society. To imagine Chaitanshehar, though that city didn't exist yet, not even in name.

The shields slammed back into place to protect her from anything Mahendri would say. Rashul was dead at the hands of this mouse of a man and his servants, Ekana turned away by the same circle of enemies. And Chaitan was dead of the illness he'd had since before Indima met him. None of that mattered if their ideas lived on.

For their ideas to live on, Chaitanshehar had to survive as well.

That night Indima danced.

The cell gave her no real room to move, but she found a way to dance, moving her arms and sweeping her legs and turning back and forth with a music only she heard. She danced a memory of Rashul, his stirring visions and powerful words. She danced a memory of Chaitan, which became more about his house and the people who gathered there. Some now dead. Some scattered like she was. And some together in Chaitanshehar trying to make it—not the refugee camp Mahendri insisted on calling it, but a true city. She danced of Ekana, inspired by the same things, the same words and ideals, but turned bitter and apart. Spreading false stories of the Forgotten South last she saw him, torn between wanting to be at the forefront of something new and wanting to tear things down to spite the ways he'd been excluded.

And she danced of herself. Alone, apart, in exile, and now under arrest. But shielded as well, and not about to give in to any pressure Mahendri tried to bring against her.

She finally fell onto her cot exhausted, and was asleep even before her pulse had slowed down.

***

Mahendri's visits soon wearied her. What good did staying silent for so much time do for anyone?

So instead she spoke of Chaitanshehar's secrets. "The

southern face of the city has a hidden wall. No one makes it through that alive."

"What do you mean, a hidden wall?"

"I guess you'll have to find out. On the eastern side, their defenses are magical."

"You're making this up."

"If you send a force that way, it triggers an arcist response. Pavresh's magic will sweep down and knock you off the mountainside."

"Oh, I forgot you knew Pavresh too. Did I mention that he's been captured by us as well? Our arcists are working to turn him against Chaitanshehar."

That gave Indima a moment's pause. Pavresh captured? Certainly shouldn't surprise her. But Pavresh turned to their ally? Never.

"But even he doesn't know the things that you do."

She forced her voice back to the easy lies she'd been making up. "They have a group of soldiers they've trained to fight with frying pans and tattered silks."

"I'm not going to be satisfied with childish fancies and silly lies. I want to know about your spymaster. About his network and how far it reaches"

His? Well, Mahendri didn't know as much as he thought yet. "Their training would make the jatis of Pashun cry out for mercy, but they've figured out how to turn that pain into a formidable fighting style. Face them, and your soldiers will be thrown back down the mountainside. But I know their weakness."

"Oh? I suppose it's a rolling pin or a sewing needle?"

"A particular shade of yellow they can't abide. It's because of a part of their training that uses wands of young wood of that specific color. They have to thrash each other to perfect their moves. Not a one of them who doesn't turn weak as a baby with fear and remembered pain when they see that color."

Mahendri headed for the door.

"Wait, I wasn't done. Because up at the back of the city,

and curving around the perimeter of the city toward the north, they have enslaved a naga. It is the real spymaster and protects that swath of the city from any attack, no matter how perfectly planned."

"I *will* learn the real secrets from you. Just give me time."

***

Time was what Mahendri lacked. Indima had all the time she could want, sitting in her cell and dancing when no one watched. But Mahendri couldn't stay in the Silk City indefinitely. He was here for some other reason beyond pursuing her, and that task would surely drive him away. Maybe he'd give up, release her to her own people's judges and be done with her.

Her father's connections could keep her from too severe a punishment.

Of course she should have never let her hopes grow.

Mahendri arrived one night, his small contingent of guards or soldiers or whatever they were—about a dozen men and women who seemed trained to both fight and serve tisane—crowding in through the door.

Indima shot upright in bed and backed away against the wall.

"You still have not told me the secrets of Chaitanshehar. Yet I must leave, so that I am in Pashun when—well, the next piece of the plan falls into place. You will come with us."

Indima offered no resistance. What purpose would it serve?

But as she let herself be shoved out the door, she wondered about how quiet this building was. Why was Mahendri leaving in the quiet and dark of nighttime? A prince like he was, shouldn't he have some kind of farewell. A fancy dinner or a parade through the streets so he could assure his superiors that the silk weavers would continue to serve.

An official of his standing shouldn't sneak off in the middle of the night.

Unless he was trying to do something unexpected, something his hosts would not allow.

Something like stealing away a daughter of the city without the permission of the city leaders.

Indima shouted for help at the edge of the street. The cry was swallowed by the walls, by the heavy, chemical-smelling air that rose off the lava field and carried her shout away into the sky.

Mahendri gestured with his head, and one of the attendants clamped a hand over her mouth. She struggled, and another attendant picked her up, held her like a bale of cloth to be carried through the gate to a waiting wagon. The first person still held a hand over her mouth, and a third helped to carry her, their hands unyielding bonds.

What good were shields of steel if the enemy could simply pick her up, shields and all, and cart her away?

Her struggles were no more effective than her earlier docility. They carried her as if she were an afterthought.

Through the gate, a carriage was waiting. Not the wagon she had pictured for the bale of cloth, but not all that different. Before she had time to take in what was happening, she was pushed into the carriage, and they were riding away. They caught up with a line of other wagons, carrying a variety of supplies that were destined for Mahendri's city. Supplies and people as well. A surprising number of attendants rode along with those goods, driving the wagons, even simply resting as they went.

Was he expecting to be attacked? It almost felt like they rode with an entire battalion of soldiers instead of mere porters.

Riding straight south. That was unusual. Goods came from the south frequently, on a rough trail that connected to the end of the rails beside the river. But travelers usually took the more comfortable route westward by carriage or sleigh and boarded the train in that direction. The eastern end of the rails were supposed to be rough and unsuitable for travelers.

But the people of the Silk City might try to overtake them if they had gone the other way.

So Mahendri still feared being stopped or at least wanted to avoid the hassle. That was good to know. Perhaps she could use it against him.

Indima let herself try to catch some sleep in the bouncing carriage. It was disjointed and far from restful. When she sat up, she tried to beat a rhythm on the bench with her fingers, but the rhythm was never even. They stopped periodically through the night, to rest the horses and allow them all a chance to relieve themselves. The women who were among Mahendri's attendants kept a close eye on Indima. As if she would have any hope of making her own way back to the city on foot ahead of certain pursuit by Mahendri and his porters.

Back at the carriage, Indima found herself beside one of those porters.

They were an old jati, one that had served the silk weavers of the city for many generations. Indima kept her voice low and said, "The leaders of the city don't want me taken away. Do you know that?"

"Of course I know that. Else why do you think we'd go this way?"

"And you do *his* bidding instead of the Silk City's? Aren't you a part of Silk City? We're more alike than this Mahendri will ever understand. People of the eastern valley. That matters."

The man snorted. "Silk weavers and porters are alike?" He put his hands back to back as if to separate two entirely different ideas. "Not how you all act back there." He dropped his hands into his lap.

The derision stung through her careful shields. "Closer than some prince from Pashun."

"Not Mahendri. He's been the porters' friend for years. Helping us. Letting us see the cruelties of your stuck-up jati. Supporting us, so now it's our turn to support him." The man's face was set in an expectant smile, a look both cruel and satisfied, as if he looked forward to some way to take out his anger on others. As if anxious to join a fight somewhere.

So much for getting the porters' help in escaping her captors.

The days blended into one after that, the rest of the journey south, the rickety train ride westward, the switch to a smoother train, and crossing the river to ride in a carriage again. Southward toward Pashun. Other porters and people of similar jatis joined them as they went, swelling their numbers into a significant force. More and more of them carried weapons openly, and when their stops were long enough to allow it, they practiced marching and swordsmanship.

Not like a soldier jati that was keeping their skills sharp, but more like some other group trying to turn itself into a soldier jati.

At every turn she looked for a way to escape, a dance she might perform to open up a magical door, a way to sneak away and disappear into the treacherous wilderness.

But dancing wasn't magic, and no chance opened up for her. The gods were as neglectful as always.

Still a bale of useless, inert cloth, she came to the city of Pashun just as a flourish of trumpets sounded to wake the city. The streets were nearly empty, but the people who remained marched from their houses at the sound and set about their varied tasks.

CHAPTER 21

The people of the south had no trains. It wasn't only that they lacked the word or that some other word had come to mean trains, like the word for ship. They had no rails leading away from their city-on-a-pier. And they had no steamships in the berths of the jetty. No sign that they knew steam power at all.

"I thought they would be more advanced than us," Harkala mused out loud to no one in particular as they sat on the deck of the ship. "That we would come down here and find a civilization as far beyond ours as our cities are beyond the villages of the mumblers."

"What you call advanced, I'm not sure I would," Sembaari answered.

But of course he would say that. He came from one of those villages. No surprise that he would want to defend them. She made no effort to answer.

Ekana shaded his eyes from the intense sun with one hand. "A train isn't the only way to travel. You think we've made enough of an impression to fund a trip overland?"

The people here took a long break from trading when the sun was high and hot, but the crew from Eghsal had been at work since early morning finding trades for the goods they'd salvaged from their earlier wreck. Some of the goods fetched what seemed to be a high value, or would have been at home. Some scarcely earned a second glance from the traders. Which was all as Harkala had guessed. What was valuable in one place wasn't necessarily so in another.

They'd managed to get food for themselves, at least. And water was free for the taking from the shallow river that trickled toward the sea, ending in an expanse of wet sand just before it could flow into the ocean, a short way south of the jetty. Warmer water than Harkala preferred to drink, and no good way to cool it significantly in this warm land, but there wasn't even the slightest hint of sulfur in the flavor of the water. She'd never tasted water so pure before.

When they tried to indicate their wish to travel inland, to trade their goods for land passage to the mountains in the north, they ran into difficulties.

The people of this place seemed to rarely leave the coast, except to go out to sea. So the idea of guiding strangers the other direction... Either it simply wasn't done, or the idea was so strange that they couldn't interpret each others' hand motions well enough to come to any agreement.

"No passage by train to be bought," she said in answer to Ekana. "And what boats they have to go upriver aren't much more than rowboats, since the river's so shallow. But we think we reached an agreement on horses, right?"

"If we understood right, and they did as well. It still seems awfully cheap for that many horses."

Harkala tapped the wooden mast for luck. "A more primitive people sometimes finds different things valuable than we do."

"That's what I mean." Sembaari sounded almost angry, and Harkala couldn't think why or what he was referring to. "No trains doesn't mean more primitive. No steam engines but ships that are better for sailing. No rails, but maybe the land beyond the coast isn't fit for rails. Wet sand surely can't support a railroad well. Or maybe the metal for your engines isn't to be found here. That's worth knowing, for trades. But I bet they're more advanced than you in other ways. Just look at these ships, and the people who must travel from many lands to trade here!"

"Well, maybe," Harkala said. There was no real way to divide societies into less and more advanced after all. "But either way, we have no easy way to head north. Only the mounts we think we've been promised. What we need is some kind of guide."

"I've tried to find someone," Ekana said. "Either they don't understand or no one is interested."

"Then I guess we're stuck with what we can manage ourselves. We'll sell the ship too, hopefully get some wagons or a carriage of some kind. But I'm not sure they'll be willing to offer much for it." She touched her knuckles to a driftwood plank that formed part of the deck. Good to be rid of the piece of junk, and yet it had brought them here, brought them where no one of their people had ever gone.

"If we sell the ship, how do we get back home?" Yashek asked. "What happens when the mountains turn us back?"

Hadn't this choice been obvious from their trading? But looking around at the stiff way several of them sat, they hadn't all accepted that it was necessary yet. "We'll never make it north in this ship, anyway."

The sailors looked around at the ship as if already missing a dear friend. *Illusion of a Dream* was not a fancy ship, but she had to admit she felt some attachment to it. Not exactly nostalgia, but a sense of leaving a part of themselves behind. It was probably a much stronger feeling for true sailors.

"Maybe someone could hold it for us," Yashek suggested. "Let us buy it back if we return."

With how little they'd been able to communicate so far, Harkala doubted they would be able to be understood enough to make any such agreement. No harm in answering as if they could. "We can try, perhaps."

In truth she did wonder what the seas looked like hugging the coast here. If they found a better ship and made their way cautiously northward, knowing that there was something, a real destination and not only vague stories and promises... They might remake the drogue they'd used on their first ship, find some way to pass through the difficult stretches.

But no. They had taken the route they had, and now they would try over land. Knowing there was something to be found beyond the mountains, and coming at it from the other direction, could they find the way through that had eluded everyone—Eghsal and mumbler alike—for centuries?

Neither route had a high probability of success.

But if they were here, then Harkala might as well learn what she could of the land, might as well be its scholar and outside observer. And maybe one day her notebooks filled with what she learned could find their way back north and establish her fame among future scholars.

"After this rest, we'll head for shore and see what there is to see."

***

Yashek stayed with the ship.

A true sea captain would have insisted he join them, would have forced him off with the sword if necessary. Ekana wanted her to do as much. Declare him a mutineer, run him through if he would not submit to her justice.

Harkala didn't have the heart for that. Nor the desire to face the city's authorities for murder, if it came to that. She was a scholar, not a sea captain. Her expertise was in old documents and dusty shovels and creatively interpreting ancient figures. Not in sea captaining.

She left him behind to find his own way among people he couldn't understand.

She sold the ship, anyway. Yashek could work out with the new owners whether she'd sold his services as well. There were no carriages to be bought, and not even a cart, but they bought enough mounts to carry all their gear and few remaining trade goods that were left.

The mounts were a mixture of beasts. Horses to ride. A half dozen mules carrying bulky packs on either side. And then four taller, hump-backed beasts that the people here called *camels*. The people they'd traded with had insisted the camels would be needed as they went, though the language difficulties meant Harkala wasn't sure why.

They climbed up from the shore, on the bank of the shallow river. A rustic road meandered inland, away from the river. Proof that the people of the jetty didn't completely ignore the lands beyond the shore. But meager proof, given the dune grass that grew not only beside the road but right across it in many places. They followed it northeastward, over the dunes and into a thinly wooded land.

Why did no one live out here?

The trees ended shortly, a rim of vegetation that separated the shore from the inland, like a balding man's fringe of hair. If she extended the image, then the bald pate above was a grassland filled sparsely with sharp grasses and little else to be seen.

When they stopped to make camp over the following days, the animals made no attempt to eat the grass. It had long blades that rose from sandy soil, and looked like it would cut the animals' mouths if they tried. Instinct made them too smart to try. No doubt that was a part of the answer to her question. No pasturage, no herding. They fed their mounts from their supplies.

Maybe the lack of rails and locomotives was because there was nothing in that land, no reason or need to transport goods and people across those barren distances. Beyond the trees, there was no sign of even a hint of a road. But also no obstacles to prevent them from simply setting their mounts in a direction and letting them go.

"What is that?" Sembaari pointed far in the distance at the mountain peaks. There was a cloud of gray and white hanging over a particular peak. It didn't look like a normal cloud, but more like the steam of a geyser.

Only, not quite the same. It looked like a cloud that had lingered in one place for days already, its edges beginning to fray with the winds but not yet blown completely away.

"It looks like a naga." Ekana pointed to trace the outlines of the smoke. There was a bitter note to his words, as if he blamed the nagas for some of the pain of his past.

There was something snake-like in the way it coiled up into the sky. For a moment it felt like a sign. A shiver ran down her back. She tamped that feeling down. A cloud could look like anything, and how often did one look vaguely like a serpent?

"I see it too," Sembaari said, "and my people don't even tell tales of those creatures. You can see the way it curves up from the mountain. Like a snake."

"Maybe it does now. But clouds are always changing shape. Still…"

She studied it in silence for a moment. Could it be a geyser, telling them which way to go? No geyser ever spouted off that high into the sky, surely. Even if there were geysers on this side of the mountain range as well as beyond those peaks. It could be a perfectly natural part of the world, regardless, and still be a sign of sorts for them to follow. It wasn't mere superstition to wonder.

"Let's angle toward that for now and see how it changes in the coming days. Maybe there's something worth investigating in that direction."

The cloud didn't change all that day, not enough to lose its shape at least. Maybe there was something to the superstitions of sailors and mumblers. She grew more uneasy throughout the next day's travel and found herself staring at the ephemeral shape more and more as the day went by.

The landscape changed, but she spared little attention to those changes. More rocky, that much she was aware of. She should be writing such details in her notebooks, but when she made time to record her observations, she found that few of the details seemed worth mentioning. Their route toward the distant plume of naga smoke didn't change.

Only when they stopped to water the mounts—though the camels never seemed to need the water—did Harkala look more closely at their surroundings.

The rocks were buildings. Old buildings long since fallen. They led their mounts past ancient foundations and along what might have been streets. How far back had the landscape changed? Harkala looked back. They had surely been moving along these ancient streets for so long that the city must have been massive. The city that once stood here would have dwarfed any of the cities of Eghsal. Would have been bigger than all the cities of Eghsal put together. Add Jarnur to Romnai, smash Pashun and the Silk City against it, and it would have been just a neighborhood here. Even bringing in old Eghsal

City when it was a city and not mere ruins didn't change much, nor would the so-called city of Chaitanshehar, from the descriptions she had heard.

A city so big the people on the coast shunned the land all around it, centuries after it had fallen.

A city so big a tiny portion of its refugees might have sailed northward and founded the civilization of the Eghsal Valley?

Oh, to stop and set up a dig site! She sketched a section of ruins and furiously recording everything she could see—how high the foundations rose from the ground around them, how thick the sharp grasses grew in the gaps.

She shook her head sadly when she saw her sailors taking shelter in the shade of those foundations. They were not scholars. She couldn't ask them to stop. She was the captain of the expedition even if they were no longer on a ship—maybe even more so now that they'd left the sea that was their expertise—so she could demand they stop. But she wouldn't.

They commented on the ruins as they continued their journey, but they were weary comments, devoid of the curiosity Harkala felt.

Beyond the ruins, a dry river bed sloped down, away from the sea. That surprised Harkala, when she thought of the comparison to the Eghsal River, but with her eyes she followed the route it once took. It would have watered a shallow valley on its way south to the other river that came out beside the jetty.

That valley was all sand now, looking loose and empty. Not even the sharp edged grass of the dunes grew there. The same valley stretched away in front of them, climbing as it went north. The naga cloud stood above the sandy desert as if some kind of ancient god.

"I suppose this is what these animals are good for," Ekana said, patting the neck of one of the camels. "I'd still trade it for a steam locomotive and some rails."

"That's a long way through sand." Sembaari shielded his eyes from the sun. "And we don't know if there's any water or where it would be."

But was that any different than setting out into an unknown sea? A desert was simply a sea of sand, and the saltwater of the ocean was no more thirst-quenching than sand, anyway. A sea captain would wonder which way the wind was blowing and allow that to help them steer the ship.

When Harkala gazed across the view to figure out the direction of the wind, she realized how much the naga-shaped cloud had blinded them. The desert spread wide between them and the mountains, but it was narrow just below them toward the east. And beyond its edges was other land. A patchwork pattern, green and inviting. She stared through her telescope. The lines of cultivated fields were perfectly clear. Fields that surely required water.

"We'll head straight across first." She pointed in the direction of the fields. "Then we can make our way north on the far side of the desert."

Ekana took his eyes away from the naga cloud as if pulling a hand away from a ship's bucket of tar. Only after he'd turned his full body to face east did his eyes light up in understanding. "Oh, that's a route we can manage."

She had to repeat herself to break the hold the naga cloud had on the others.

Most of the water of the ruins had dried up, but they found a small spring still alive in the base of a set of steps. It tasted of rotting leaves but not sulfur, so they drank and refilled their water jugs.

Then they set out down the ridge into the narrow arm of the desert.

From within, that stretch of desert did not seem narrow. They camped in the trough between two dunes of fine sand. Harkala spent the entire next day convinced she'd led them wrong, that the landscape had tricked her into heading north into the depths of the desert, that they were wandering and would continue to do so, in circles, until they gave up.

But late in the day, they finally came across a narrow

irrigation channel cut into the soil. The water within was carried by a ceramic irrigation pipe, cunningly crafted and laid.

The people of the shoreline had been uninterested in their arrival. Strangers seemed to come frequently, and Harkala's crew were not more strange than most.

The situation in this inland realm was quite the opposite.

They had only made their way between two fields and started along a third when a contingent of mounted guards accosted them.

They looked like mumblers.

Harkala couldn't stop herself from staring. Perhaps not entirely like mumblers, but their pale skin and broad faces were much the same as the image Harkala had in her head for a mumbler. They wore their hair, mostly dark brown with a few lighter browns mixed in, long and pulled to each side. The men had beards, trimmed short. Their weaponry looked formidable, more advanced than the slings and swords of Eghsal, and the gear on their horses betrayed a high level of craft, much *unlike* the primitive villages of the mumblers up north. Still, the facial resemblance was uncanny.

Harkala held her hands open and stayed silent. Sembaari must have seen the same resemblance—though he, an actual mumbler, looked nothing like them—because he started speaking in what Harkala had come to recognize as the mumblers' trade language.

The guards shook their heads, and one answered, but it wasn't in the same language. Sembaari frowned and tried again, presumably in a different mumbler language. He got the same uncomprehending response.

Harkala said in her language, "We're only travelers, traveling through." What was the old word for a traveler? She tried to say that, and then changed the word in ways it might have changed in the centuries since, while pointing northward toward the mountains.

More shaking of heads. At least they hadn't drawn any weapons. One guard used her hands and arms to show them they should follow a few of the guards, on between the fields. The rest of the guards fell in behind them.

The fields simply led one into the next for what felt like a long time. At the intersections of the fields, there were elaborate wells and pipes, extending in different directions, but little else to be seen. The crops were too small for Harkala to identify. At last there was a real road between them, though still merely hard-packed dirt. The produce of those fields, even if this land had little else that would be valuable in Eghsal Valley, would be a good potential for trading. If they could ever find a way to get through.

The road finally came to a cluster of buildings. It wasn't a city, as Harkala would have defined a city. Perhaps it rose to the level of a town. She knew of towns from reading old documents—there had been some smaller settlements in Eghsal's history, but they had either failed or been subsumed by the bigger cities. The harsh conditions of the valley, the need for warmth from the lava beds or coastal air current, and the threat of mumbler attacks meant the early settlers had needed to consolidate their resources.

To her this seemed like little more than a hunting camp made out of permanent building materials. Even so, it had an official looking building at its center.

A fountain stood before the building, where the cities of the north would place some kind of small flame. Did these people worship water, as hers did fire? Already she had seen evidence of the wonders they created to move and use water throughout their land.

The building itself was little more than a three sided shelter, no matter how fancy the woodwork appeared. The leader of their guards herself took position on the throne-like leather chair in the center. She spoke at length, but they couldn't make any sense of her words.

When she paused, Harkala said under her breath, "Sembaari? Any chance you recognized any part of that as a mumbler language?"

"Not the least bit sounded familiar."

Harkala nodded to say she'd heard, then she strode forward toward the woman on the leather throne.

"We bring goods to trade." She pointed back at the packs on the animals and held out a pelt she'd retrieved from one pack. Then she repeated "trade" several times, slowly, emphasizing it differently in case they knew the word from trading with the people of the coast.

No reaction from the people, so she added, "And to pass through your land, to go north." She mimicked them going through the fields and then pointed toward the mountains beyond their land. "North, past your land. It's where our land lies."

"North," the woman repeated, pointing the same way. "Your land."

Harkala's heart skipped a beat. Was she understanding them? As the woman repeated the words again, Harkala felt her surprise crash back down. She was simply repeating the sounds. For all Harkala could guess, the woman might think "north" meant the mountains and not the direction. But did it matter, if they could at least get a sense of their meaning across?

"North," Harkala said again. Then she gestured to take in all her crew and animals and pointed north again, repeating the word.

The woman nodded and said some other word they didn't understand. Then she pointed at the animals and said something else that sounded like she expected them to understand. Harkala shook her head and looked at the others. The woman rose from her chair and pointed at the pelt in Harkala's hands and then at the animals and repeated the sound.

"I think she's trying to say 'trade,'" Sembaari suggested.

Oh. "Trade," Harkala repeated. "Yes, you want to trade?"

"Trade." This time the guard got the pronunciation correct.

Harkala unpacked some of their goods and laid them out

before her in what she hoped would be an obvious invitation to barter goods.

***

They spent two days in that tiny town, camped with their animals outside the simple buildings. What people lived there avoided them, heading out into the fields early and returning to their own homes in the evening. The guard, whose name sounded something like Elsh, proved eager to learn their words for the things they were trading and even managed to puzzle out some other words as well. They communicated with many gestures still, but Elsh's curiosity was a big change from the attitude of the people back across the desert.

Harkala suspected that she had interacted with others before, people who spoke different languages. That she understood how to communicate in those situations and had also learned what she could of those other languages each time.

It wouldn't have been the people of the jetty, or else they would have encountered trade roads and some idea that this other civilization was out here. No doubt there would be other peoples in this vast land, cities and nations to the south or further east with their own trade routes and alliances, ignored by those sea-faring people on the jetty.

The trading felt awkward, like Elsh was always offering much less than what Harkala thought things were worth. The goods she offered were fine items, fancy and intricate works of metalcraft and even cloth that looked and felt like real silk. How the silk weavers would grow jealous at that! But the amounts offered bordered on an insult. When Harkala tried to push her on the trades, though, Elsh would shake her head and then point to the north.

After several times of this happening, Harkala realized that Elsh was saying she would accompany them toward the north, that she was willing to trade for some goods, but the real price would include the escort through the local lands.

After two days they were ready to continue. Harkala pointed

toward the mountains and said, "We'll go *north* now. You understand, right?"

Elsh nodded as she gathered her guards to surround Harkala's crew. "North." Then she got a questioning look on her face and pointed directly at one mountain. "North?" Then she pointed at several in succession. "North?" And before Harkala could find a way to explain, Elsh pointed at the naga cloud. It was finally losing its shape but still noticeable above a particular peak. She made a gesture as if to say *or* and then asked again, "North?"

All of those, and did it really matter? Harkala mimicked the space above and beyond the mountains as well as she could and said, "North."

Then pointing at the cloud again, Elsh said another word she'd picked up while trading. "Yours?"

Harkala didn't know how to answer.

They set out through that rich land, dotted with towns. Away to the east, Harkala could see the outlines of at least one larger city. Canals and pipes connected the land in ways she couldn't entirely understand. Wondrous devices hinted at an advanced society, even if they had no trains.

Other people, officials of some sort perhaps, came to meet them, but no one tried to speak with Harkala. Elsh talked to them and sent them on their way as if she commanded significant authority.

They veered toward the northern edge of that city they'd noted. Buildings soared many floors above the streets, creating a jagged profile against the hazy horizon. How did they make their buildings so tall?

It was a land of wonders, an advanced people who delighted in water and architecture. A civilization that could prove a good trading partner, if they could only find a way through the mountains ahead.

Maybe the naga would show them the way after all. The remains of the cloud beckoned them closer.

CHAPTER 22

Leaving Chaitanshehar wasn't easy. Datri gripped Yatim's arm to keep from turning herself around and going right back to her home. The pull of the magic felt impossible to break on her own.

How did her spies do it? She always told them to remind themselves over and over that they were spies, that they were leaving for a reason, for the good of the city.

With Yatim's help, she took more steps, quick and small as if by their quickness she might break free. She was a spy, a spy master in fact. And what she did was for the good of the city.

But was it?

What she did was for the good of her husband, if he lived. For the good of her own mind's ease. That part could be rationalized as good for the city. Not that she needed the rationalization herself. She only hoped it was enough to overcome the magic spell.

Yatim gave no sign that he suffered any struggle to leave. He had his purpose—to help her, to possibly save his long-time master and friend. Chaitanshehar had no masters and servants anymore, but he still fulfilled his role.

He was an easy read. Often Datri had to peer beneath the layers of people to find what made them behave as they did. She was skilled at picking those layers away, finding the hidden shame, the secret fear, the desperate need. Yatim needed to do the job at hand, nothing more and nothing less. He had a few different lovers over the years, in Romnai and in Chaitanshehar, but no scandals. He had never needed more money than he had available to him. Maybe it was good that Jasfer had always paid him well in his early years serving the family. But greed was no motivation.

He guided Datri now from one tree to another, and each tree they put between them and the city helped to lessen the magic's pull. Her steps lengthened without slowing down, and they soon reached the top of a crest. The magic still beckoned up here, but Datri could walk without gripping Yatim's arm so tightly.

After crossing a rock shelf to another climb, loose scree held in place by the ice underneath, they came to a tall pile of rocks. Human-made. It revolted Datri.

"Come around to this side," Yatim said as he pulled her arm.

She wanted nothing to do with *this side*, with any side of that thing. Just get her away from it. Even knowing that it must be magic, recognizing her revulsion as part of that magic, she had to grit her teeth and duck her head. As if that would hide her from the beacon.

Once on the other side, though, she took three quick strides away, and felt both the beacon's power and the city's completely opposite one release her.

"Wow." She let the word escape. "The others didn't put that there, did they?"

"No, that was us. Me." Yatim brushed his hands together as if removing the dirt that came from moving it. "Pavresh found it, and I asked him if I could move it up here instead of them destroying it. Helps with making the escape."

Pavresh. Datri still didn't know what had happened to the arcist or Rashul or the people who'd gone with them. Her spies in Pashun, what few had been able to break free from that city's magic and report to her, had heard nothing about them, but from what they told, she had low hopes of ever learning the truth. They were as lost as her husband had been these last six years.

Yatim pointed up the slope a short way. "The stable is just around the bend."

Calling it "the stable" conjured images of many horses, attendants, feed. This was nothing of the sort. The city couldn't afford to feed so many animals, even if it could have arranged for the rest of that. A lean-to against the rock had space for three animals but at the moment had only a single donkey. It also had a room full of traveling supplies, though precious little food to get them all through.

Yatim would have to hunt, and Datri would tighten her belt. She needed so little food these days. Her need to know what had happened to Jasfer made food an afterthought.

They put the bundles of supplies across the animal's back, and began their trek up and over the mountain pass above the city.

This route had been unknown when the city was founded, until Pavresh had come this way with his pilgrimage of beggars and untouchables. Now they followed it back, and if her rumor proved true, it was to find her husband, once a powerful prince, now among the untouchables who remained in Romnai.

She pushed their pace, only let Yatim stop for the night when he insisted that they needed to rest and wait for the light of the next day. Bitter winds and snow squalls—even this time of year not rare—were merely hassles to press on through.

***

They came to Romnai as a warm wind was building up over the geyser fields. It made the city heavy with heat, and the smell of the lava beds was thick, sulfur and old onions and something that smelled like human sweat.

Datri's stomach growled. The storms had slowed their journey more than she could have guessed, and their travel food had barely kept them going. The city might stink, with its smells both human and volcanic, but it meant real food as well. Even a beggar in Romnai ate better than the people of Chaitanshehar did these days.

They went to the family manor first.

Jasfer had never been declared officially dead. He was no longer a ruling prince, but that by itself didn't mean his family lost the title to their manor. Datri had used that fact as well as her network of spies, to keep any other princes from trying to claim the building—and to keep her own involvement with Jaritta's city a secret. As far as anyone knew, she was in the

Silk City visiting her family, waiting to return. The money she'd hidden away when she left the city kept the manor from falling apart and her network of spies in place. Some of the servants still lived in the manor, keeping in communication with Datri.

They were surprised to see Datri and Yatim walk in.

Kalavandi, still the chief steward of the manor despite her age, sketched a hasty bow. "Tisrah, we didn't know. Or we would have prepared—"

"You didn't know. That's sufficient. Bring us some food now. Whatever is ready. We'll have some other errands before nightfall. You can prepare the rooms then."

They ate warm bread, and Datri wasn't certain there was ever anything better. The cold chicken and wedge of cheese they shared between them were most welcome as well, but the bread was what filled her and told her body that she really had returned to Romnai.

"Now we can figure out what to do next."

Yatim pushed back his empty plate from the edge of the table, a gesture more in keeping with the servant quarters than this fancy table, but in perfect keeping with the hurried food they'd eaten. "Your contact?"

There were spies to connect with while they were here, people to press for further information, but Datri's mind was still moving too slowly to tackle those tasks. "That's probably all we'll have time for today. We can let them know that we're here and then see."

They walked into an adjacent neighborhood. Smaller houses lined the streets, the homes of lesser princes and upstart merchants. She and Yatim walked openly. No better way to bring attention to themselves than to be furtive. Walking openly, in unremarkable clothing, she might be anyone. Few people who weren't her own spies would recognize her as the wife of a missing prince.

This place felt so different from Chaitanshehar. The streets of Romnai struck her with their nostalgia, with a thousand memories of her former life, of her former power among the princes. But she missed the chaotic jumble of Chaitanshehar as well, and the sense of everyone working together to build the city toward its future.

The soldiers were an ever present sight. That was different from both Chaitanshehar and her memories of Romnai. The capital city had always had its share of soldiers, as long as she'd lived there, but their overwhelming visibility was new. She instinctively shied away from them as she walked.

Her reports from the city had said the falcon jati women marched in mourning, heads shorn and traditional outfits put aside. She saw no sign of them, only the fierce and wilderness-hardened wolf jati soldiers and the members of smaller jatis who looked like they might break in a real battle but wouldn't hesitate to wade into a street fight and take out their anger there.

At a certain point, where the front stairs of one house jutted out almost into the street, Datri feigned a fall. She held her ankle as if she'd twisted it.

Yatim leaned in as if to help her, and she waved him away. When he stepped back, he carefully dropped a simple card into a gap in the stairway, where the masonry was cracked. Datri made a show of wiggling her foot about, cautiously attempting to put her weight on it.

Again Yatim came back to help. Now that he'd dropped the message off, there was no need for miming anything, except to keep any observer from guessing it was mimed. She let him steady her while she took a few steps. Nodding, she said, "It should be fine."

They continued on, with her favoring that leg for the first few blocks. When they reached a small street market, Datri lingered over the bundles of cloth for sale and bought a length of red dyed fabric that might be made into a decorative sash. She pretended to dither over some of the other offerings—a single piece of cloth was a weak excuse to come all this way unless she proved herself to be especially picky—but in the end she left with only that one. Such excess. The smells of roasted meats and spices made her mouth water. If they could only transplant it into the hillside city she now called home.

"It's getting late, isn't it?" she asked Yatim.

He nodded.

No time to contact any of her spies, even if her head was starting to shake off the travel fog. That would have to wait until she'd spoken with her contact. They made their way back toward the manor. Instead of going inside, they walked past the entrance and turned a corner, leaning in the shadows against the granite blocks of a nearby house.

She'd been seen. No surprise. She had assumed they would be noticed at some point, if not immediately on coming into the city, then within the first day or so. They'd probably been reported already upon entering the manor. She was sure of it now. The figures in the shadows near the house were no coincidence. The soldiers stationed at the intersections were only the most visible part of their surveillance.

They could ignore the soldiers, hope her careful arrangement of lies gave her enough cover for a few days here. In fact a part of her wanted nothing more than to just go to their rooms and sleep. But she needed to know more about what these soldiers expected and how they would treat her sudden arrival. Ignore them now, and she might miss her chance to learn that.

Datri considered where she'd seen the figures. Their commander wouldn't be out on the streets watching. He would be inside somewhere but still nearby. The question was where.

There was an empty pub a short way up the street. The commander might take refuge there. But seeing the numbers and arrangement of the soldiers, Datri suspected he would choose someplace closer.

"The Tharekh manor has a solarium up front." Probably not Tharekh anymore, after the new Thirty was formed, but whatever jumped-up family had taken the manor away from them. "That's where they'll be."

Yatim nodded and led the way back and around another

corner. They crept along the edge of that street toward what had once been the Tharekh manor.

The side door to the solarium had a guard stationed in a chair outside. Wolf jati soldier, a bare blade lying across his thighs.

Datri simply presented herself to him, easing out of the shadows directly before him. "I'm here to see your captain."

The soldier jumped to his feet, his sword held at a low angle before him. "Who are you?"

"I'm the one your captain is here to watch. And all the other soldiers out there, they're here for me."

The soldier stared and took a small step backward. Was she such a spooky figure? She laughed inside but on the outside she kept her calm composure, a particular self-confidence that had always served her well at getting people to simply accept that she had whatever authority she claimed.

"Go on, let your captain know I'm here. If you won't let me right in myself."

Not a chance he'd let her and Yatim in on their own, but the suggestion was enough to get him to lower his sword and go into the solarium. A moment later he returned and beckoned for them.

The captain was seated where she'd guessed he would be. And drinking something. She sniffed. Tisane. Alas. A slightly inebriated captain would have been easier to handle. She sashayed through the dimly lit solarium and took a seat opposite him before he could offer her a chair.

Yatim had let himself be detained near the door, but in sight of Datri.

"You're a bold one," the captain said.

Datri leaned back and studied him before answering. He was a wolf jati soldier. Middle-aged, which meant he'd probably spent many days in the snowy mountains that circled the valley, protecting the cities within. And now he was here. Was the comfort of the city a welcome relief to him, or a trial? Did he long instead for the harsh conditions of an assignment?

No, he looked like a hard-edged man, but Datri was a good judge of the truths people kept secret. This was a man who'd served his people and now enjoyed the chance to leave those difficult labors to others.

Good.

If it had been the other way, this would be more difficult.

"Bold, you might say that." Datri gave a girlish shrug. "Or a fool, maybe. I guess I'll leave that determination up to you."

"If your thought is to seduce me, you aren't going to succeed. I'm not tempted in the least."

A bold claim. It could mean several possibilities, but knowing what she did of the wolf jati's mystery religion, she suspected his attraction was toward those who challenged the fire in their rites. Anyone, man or woman, outside that rite was no longer an object of his lust.

She built her image of him quickly in her head, as an artist might use rough strokes to sketch a subject. If she were meeting a prince or silk weaver, she would have filled in more of those details in advance, but she wasn't going to have the time to do more than this rough sketch. She could feel him itching to be done with her.

A soldier watching over a shady character wasn't supposed to have the object of his surveillance burst right in on him.

"Captain." She gave the word a Silk City accent, drawing out the first vowel. "May I call you Captain. Or if you tell me your name—"

"Captain is fine."

Prickly about his status, but cautious as well.

She dipped her head in acknowledgment. "Captain, I have no intent to seduce you. I am simply here to introduce myself. I noticed your soldiers and decided to meet the one in charge of them."

How to use the mystery religion against him? What other clues could she find to use as a lever? Outwardly she kept herself calm and unconcerned. Inside, her mind was racing.

No affairs, it would seem. Or nothing that was likely a closely guarded secret. He came across as an open, stiff-backed officer.

"I don't see the purpose in that. But now we have met."

A part of her regretted trying to put herself in this position. Maybe it would have been better to simply ignore the soldiers keeping watch on her movements and hope that they didn't cause her problems.

But if they did create unnecessary hassles…

"And a pleasant meeting, it is." She had no mug of her own to toast him, but she raised her hand as if she did. "Your company is a delight."

"I suppose I will have to arrest you now, rather than simply keep you under surveillance."

"You know as well as I do that you won't. I'm not a dangerous criminal, only someone your superiors are curious about. If you needed to arrest me, you would have done so already."

The captain raised his mug to his mouth and sipped through the metal straw. The motion drew Datri's attention to the man's face. To the scar that disfigured the side of his nose and the edge of his upper lip.

A fire scar. It was much smaller than Jaritta's. But it was caused by fire, nonetheless. To the priestly religion that venerated the fire, that scar made him suspect. To a mystery religion that challenged the fire, it made him weak, a lesser figure than his status as captain implied.

Datri leaned into that tidbit. "But I know you would love to show your superiors what you're worth. Prove to them your value."

"My value is in following my orders."

Not to a high-ranking princess, it wasn't. Datri recalled the power she'd once had as the wife of the second most powerful prince and put that over her face like a mask. "Your value can be so much more than what some people might guess. The fire chooses who it will." That sounded too much like the priests. Lean too hard on that, and the mystery religion's tenets would pull him right away. She bent over the table and stared into his eyes. "And those with the will, they choose how they will measure against the fire."

The captain's knuckles stood out on the hand holding his gourd of tisane. "I am the servant of the sacred fire."

Spoken as a faithful adherent of the priests, but what he didn't say was what Datri heard. That he still longed to be the fire's equal, to master all that was uncontrollable.

"To serve the fire is to defeat it," she said, as if it wasn't the most shocking sacrilege. "I know how that is, the paradox of the soldier."

He slammed his gourd onto the table, but he didn't order her arrested.

Might as well press her advantage while she had it, but she had to present it in the right way. She gave her voice what she called the mystic's edge, the eerie tone of one who knows uncanny truths. "The fire burns in unexpected ways. To defeat the fire now, you may have to ignore some of the actions I take. Watch *me*, if you wish. But those who come to visit me, allow them to come and go, away from your soldiers' eyes."

He picked his tisane back up, withdrew the straw, and then drank straight from the gourd. The bitter leaves would shock his tongue, but he didn't cringe.

"Only for a few days." After that, it wouldn't matter. She'd have found Jasfer or learned his true fate. "Then may the fire consume all who are not equal to its heat."

The captain refused to meet her eyes. She stood, let him see the knowing smile on her face, and walked calmly out of the solarium. Yatim joined her, and though inside she wanted to break into a run and get safely into the house, she forced him to shorten his strides to keep to her steady, certain pace.

Only inside the manor did she collapse onto the floor and release the shudder that had been growing and pulsing within.

***

The next day they had an invitation to Samatrit's house.

Datri slipped out to peek in at the solarium across the street, but it was empty. There had been two possible results of her meeting, and either one suited her. Either the captain had accepted her suggestion to leave them alone or he'd chosen a new place as his base. Probably in his head it was a combination of the two, a new place and a lack of attention for a brief time.

Even if he didn't think he was giving in to her demands, he would think he ought to focus more on visitors coming rather than her own movement, since she had suggested the opposite. The gap between his duty and her suggestions should provide her and Yatim just enough space to slip away.

Back at the manor, she told Yatim, "My husband liked to wander. Show me how he would get out unseen."

He led her down to the family chapel and then out a side door. "When he was younger, Prince Jasfer enjoyed exploring back passages and other routes." Yatim said. "He and his sister did so before I arrived, and she used to come back to visit as well. Before her attempted coup. This was one of the ones I learned from her visits." Strange to picture Jaritta haunting these same halls and passages, now that she'd come to know her sister-in-law in a very different setting.

The walkway outside was open to the sky but in such a tight space between the manor and the wall next door that it felt more like an indoor passage. They took that walk back toward the steam beds.

A rough trail trickled along behind the manors. No one on the streets would guess it was there, and even most of those who lived in the manors were unlikely to know of its existence. The princely families rarely spent their time staring out toward the forbidding geyser field, and what windows they had looked beyond the rough land below to present a view of the geysers and the mountains far to the south.

Yatim bent forward as he hurried along, so Datri did the same, crouched in a way that made walking awkward. After a couple of blocks, Yatim turned sharply between two other manors. On this path they could walk upright. They had to cross the street out front, the Avenue of Geysers, to get anywhere. That was where the soldiers had been, but Datri saw no one watching them as they strode quickly across. Wrapped in cloaks against the drift from the steam beds, they could have been any two people, out on an innocent errand.

They returned to the neighborhood they'd been in the other day, where Yatim had dropped off the message. This time they knocked at a side door. A servant ushered them inside to a small room just off the kitchen.

In a manor house it would be the room where the head of servants might meet with a merchant to agree on prices for the next month's food or other supplies. Samatrit would have had his own, fancier office in another part of the house, where cheetah jati servants attended to him.

Samatrit was no longer as powerful as he'd once been, though his family's rights and title had been restored. They did not have the wealth of a true princely family. So it was Samatrit himself who met them in the business office.

He was not one to smile.

After she took a seat, she said, "Thank you for honoring our message, cousin. And for contacting me in Chaitanshehar in the first place."

"It wasn't for your sake that we did."

No, of course not. It was because he didn't like the new Thirty. Because she and Jasfer had been the ones to restore him from his shame in the first place. And because of what she still knew about him and his family that he didn't want anyone else to learn.

"I understand. But I appreciate it nonetheless." When he didn't say anything more, she prodded him. "Your original message said you saw…him. That you saw Prince Jasfer." She could hardly keep her voice level when she asked.

"Not me. Mashunri says she did."

And… Why wasn't she here? Datri gripped one hand with the other to keep it from shaking.

Before she could ask, Samatrit continued. "She'll come in a

moment, but first I wanted to make sure. This is it. We can't be your informants, your spies. We only want to live our lives here, ignored by the princes and everyone else."

The Datri of six years earlier would have sneered at his bluster. Done? With what she knew, she could burst right in at any time and make a demand. How much more could she squeeze out of him and his family from a wish to keep their secrets quiet? But now, all she wanted was to learn what she could about Jasfer. She would have agreed to almost anything.

"Yes, that's fine. I have no interest in holding you beyond today."

Samatrit frowned and chewed on the insides of his lips, as if wondering whether to demand some kind of proof. But what did she have left to give him? She was an exile, and what power she had was built on subterfuge and secrets and lies. She composed her face so that none of her inner turmoil would be visible.

After a moment, he gave a decisive nod and went to a side door.

Mashunri came in without him a moment later.

Datri gave her no time for pleasantries. "You've seen him? You've seen Jasfer?"

Mashunri nodded. "I think it was him. A beggar near one of the markets. He had a squint-eyed dog with him. I gave him some money. A…it was a valuable coin. Enough to get him food until we could contact you and for you to get here, too."

Why not take him in off the streets themselves? But she knew not to ask that question. Samatrit wouldn't have accepted his cousin hiding in his house, wouldn't have dared anger the other princes when his own status was so fragile. Datri's arm shook, and the old scars on her back pulsed with remembered pain. "And you've kept watch for him since?"

"I did, at first." Mashunri refused to meet her eye. "I can tell you where he was sheltering at the time. He got mixed up with some dangerous folk, but we kept an eye on him, and he managed to get away from them. We kept watching his movements for a little while after."

A little while? "What happened to him, Mashunri? I came here for my husband. Where can I find him?"

Mashunri let out her breath. "I don't know. He disappeared shortly after that. Probably before our message ever reached you. I think he was arrested outside a market, from what little I could learn."

Disappeared again. When she had come so close. Datri let loose the shaking that she'd been suppressing. Her whole body quivered with tension, anxiety, the need to find him, the fear of what had been done. A cry of anguish built up inside her lungs.

No. She clamped it down, stilled her body. "Who arrested him? I've come this far. I will not be turned back now."

Mashunri told her everything she knew.

It wasn't enough. She knew that, knew that to anyone else it would have been time to give up. But as she left the house, she stiffened her back and began to lay new plans.

Jasfer was gone again, out of the reach of normal human knowledge. But she was equal to the mystery, and her knowledge of the secrets people hid extended far beyond what anyone else might consider normal.

It all came down to the same question as before. Who knew the truth? And now that she had narrowed the answers to that down, she could apply her own manipulations to force that truth out into the open.

Let her enemies try to keep her away.

CHAPTER 23

Ellechandran wished the girls could have seen the mountain slopes they passed through. The frozen waterfalls, the filigree of ice on pine needles. This was mumbler country, the country of their heritage, though they didn't know it yet.

A beautiful land, even in its harsh dangers.

They made their way over snow-covered slopes and beside ice caves that probably hadn't melted in hundreds of years. They restocked on food in an abandoned mine before they melted away themselves—into the pines and stony crags that could hide an army.

Not that they were an army, by any means, only a small group of mumblers gathered together from different villages and peoples, searching out what they could learn about the plans of Pashun's leaders and what it would mean for Chaitanshehar.

The land was not Jaritta's by inheritance, not the same way that it was for their two daughters, but he wished she could see it as well. Maybe someday, with the problems with Pashun solved and Jaritta herself fully healed from her shoulder injury, then he could take her on a tour of the villages in the area.

When the girls were old enough to appreciate it, they could all travel, the whole family, and see the mountains he'd once called home.

Those familiar mountains were now cut by an unfamiliar road. In some places, the road had suffered extensive damage from rock slides and avalanches and been repaired very recently. They could see the fresh dirt packed down, the recently moved rocks. The treads of many feet passing through. How many people had left Pashun? And what for? He longed to learn the answers so he could return, but so far they'd learned little worth bringing back.

The band led by Ellechandran and Chhayasheela cut along

above that road, watching the people passing by below. It was not a crowded way, but neither was it empty. For several days, they kept note of how many people they saw, even as they shadowed them from above.

A heavily laden wagon drew their special attention today. Might be food they could redirect toward home. Or supplies that would fill in some clues to explain what was happening. They matched their pace to the wagon's, lighter on foot than the foot soldiers and others escorting the wagon, but traversing a ridge that was more challenging.

And increasingly familiar.

Their old home lay only a short way ahead. Ellechandran felt an anxious flutter as they approached. They'd avoided the village on their last excursion, avoided it and all the neighboring villages. But now the new road led directly below it, and their destination lay on the other side. If they wanted to know what was happening with the earthquake and the people of Pashun, they had to pass directly by their former home.

This time they came, not as the exiled scions of the village who'd been forced to leave in shame—though they were that too—but as representatives of another village, another people, a city of both mumblers and the city dwellers of Eghsal.

Not easy to remember that fact, the nearer they got. Ellechandran remembered fleeing in shame—himself, Chhayasheela, and her late mother. As he recognized more and more of the landscape, that part of him became prominent. Just a shamed exile, returning where he didn't belong.

"Well," Chhayasheela said, pointing at a rock formation that had always been the guidepost to find their way back from a hunt. Or a tryst. "I guess we really are coming home."

"Not home," Ellechandran said. The ridge they were on led up between the familiar rock formation and a smaller, no less familiar shoulder of stone. A mountain goat jumped over a fissure in the stone and ambled on. "But I suppose we can't turn back anymore."

The road below climbed steeply until it was only a short

way below their own path. They rested, hiding behind whatever shelter they could find, while the wagon slowed to a crawl up the incline.

"That looks like food," Chhayasheela said in a low voice from where she lay, belly down on the lip of the ridge. "And only a dozen—"

"No, we're not attacking them. Even with the surprise, we don't know that we could overwhelm them fast enough. There may be other wagons coming. Other people on the road."

It was definitely a group from Pashun escorting the wagon, and closer to two dozen people, he guessed now that the road came up closer to them. Some of the people walking beside the wagon had the look of real jati soldiers.

As the wagon neared the next curve in the road, Ellechandran noticed movement among the rocks and bushes. A city dweller wouldn't have seen a thing, but there was no question to his mumbler instincts and upbringing that there were people on the slope above that curve.

He kept his voice low but could hear the note of urgency in it when he said, "If you were trying to set up an ambush near our old home—"

"Yes, I see it, too." Chhayasheela strained forward. "Wearing their battle masks. They have the numbers to overpower them. Especially if we—"

"No, we aren't here to fight."

"Well, if it were me I'd start the attack right…" she paused, following the wagon's path with her finger, "…now."

Just as she said it, a cry came from one of the wagon attendants as he fell right in front of the wagon wheel. The wagon butted against him—against his body, more likely—and came to a stop as the mumblers jumped from their hiding places and attacked.

The wagon attendants did not react how Ellechandran had expected. They didn't scare or break into separate groups but instead formed into a unified, though tiny, fighting unit, protecting each other as they waited patiently for the mumblers to attack.

Ellechandran knew the fighting style of his people. And he knew how the city soldiers fought as well, knew how they could overwhelm the defenses of Chaitanshehar, knew how they could defend themselves when cornered.

The villagers still had the higher ground, but that was their only advantage, and it would not protect them for long. They were descending without discipline, without the careful coordination they would need.

"Maybe we should…" They could *try* to help. Their numbers would be a boost, and they were familiar with Pashun fighting. But they were scouts and wanderers, not soldiers either. Ellechandran bit his lip, trying to decide.

The first assault proved his fears right. The mumblers flung themselves against the soldiers as if their only thought was to overwhelm them, and not one of the soldiers fell down. Several villagers, though, had fallen already.

Studying the scene from above, Ellechandran noticed something that wouldn't be as obvious on the road. The wagon stood at the beginning of the curve, and where the curve was sharpest, the far side of the road fell away to a lower part of the slope. It wouldn't take much to get the wagon to fall.

No wagon to capture, and the villagers would call off their attack. No wagon to defend, and the soldiers would retreat or hurry back to Pashun to replace those supplies.

"Get them to call off the attack," he told Chhayasheela. She spoke the same language as the fighters, with a perfectly native accent, so he hoped she could figure out something. "Give me a moment, but when you see me by the horses, get them to stop and retreat."

Ellechandran ran, crouching, back the other way and then down toward the road. He made no attempt to control his descent, letting his arms cartwheel as he raced past the road and into the brush below it. It was scant for hiding in, but the soldiers would be too busy fighting off the villagers.

He hoped.

The sounds of fighting were so close he thought he might stumble into them. He kept low and ran as well as the steep angle of the ground allowed. The fighting fell behind him, and he climbed up to the edge of the road.

The driver was among the soldiers in their tight fighting formation, and they'd moved their fallen comrade away from the wagon wheel. Ellechandran sprinted and vaulted into the driver's seat. He cut halfway through the traces even as he urged the horses to move.

The soldiers in the rear of their formation turned toward him. Too late. The frightened horses had taken off. Before it was going too fast for him to escape, Ellechandran jumped off, back into the brush below the road. As he did so, he managed to cut one of the leather traces the rest of the way through.

The wagon pulled sideways on its remaining trace. The horses pulled as hard as their collars allowed, still terrified at the noise and movement and the strange way the wagon was drifting.

Then with a snap, the last trace parted, and the wagon veered over the edge and into the darkness below. The horses galloped around the bend, slowing to a trot just before they were out of Ellechandran's sight.

The brush where he landed had scratched his legs and side enough to sting, but it didn't keep him from crawling up to where he could see the result of his actions.

Some of the soldiers had broken for the wagon but seemed conflicted over chasing the horses or trying to retrieve the fallen goods below the road. Others were still in formation, swords out to defend themselves. Above, Chhayasheela's voice carried over the other noise, calling for a retreat that only some of the mumblers were heeding.

Ellechandran found a rock he could loosen from the ground, and he heaved it as far as he could down the road, beyond the soldiers who were standing there uncertainly. Then he dropped back down, hoping the soldiers would investigate the noise. He heard sounds of people heading that way but didn't dare look up to see if it was everyone. His body was tense with the fear of discovery as he made his way again through the brush back toward where he'd crossed. No one came after him. The climb up would be more difficult, and leave him far too vulnerable. So he found some shrubs even lower down the slope that offered real cover, and he lay down to wait for what would develop.

The villagers soon retreated up the ridge. He could hear the soldiers discussing, but not well enough to know what they were saying. Someone jumped down from the road into his view, but it was far enough away that he wasn't worried about discovery. The soldier was checking out the wreckage of the wagon.

He hoisted a sack of something up to the road, but after some more words with the others—with a superior, perhaps?—he left it lying on the road. They probably wanted their hands free, in case any mumblers chose to attack as they.

It was dark by the time they departed. Ellechandran was about to leave the brush when someone dropped in among them. "Sheela?"

"It's me." Her passage in among the shrubs broke twigs and branches, a sound loud enough to make him cringe. Surely the soldiers, no matter how far they'd gone, would hear that sound.

When nothing came in response, he said, "Well, how's the village? Have you spoken to—"

"No. I...well, I hid after everyone retreated. I put Venthaian in charge of the others and sent them in. But I couldn't, not without you." A good choice, Venthaian was a solid and steady member of their group, though his ability to speak pidgin was less than some of the others. He could manage things until the two of them had a chance to rejoin the rest.

What *would* happen when they introduced themselves? They were exiled, forced to leave the village out of shame because they'd let themselves be seen by some earlier group of people from Pashun. Had those people been passing on the same route that was now a road? His memory was crystal of where he and

Sheela had been, where the strangers had suddenly appeared. They might well have been on the road, heard a noise, stepped off to investigate. And found a young couple lying in the clearing.

To be seen by the city dwellers was shameful. A person of their tribe could only be seen while wearing a battle mask.

That alone would have been enough for them to have to go through a purification ritual, but not enough to be sent away from the tribe.

But they hadn't merely been seen, glimpsed through the woods. They'd been caught, together, in a meadow apart from the village, wrapped only in blankets. And the soldiers who had found them, vulnerable and terrified, had tried to speak to them.

It was the city dwellers' words that brought them such shame. Words were dangerous, a poison when they were spoken by the people of Pashun. They were too young to hear such things, had not yet gone through any of the rituals that would protect them. No member of their village could risk the infection that Eghsal city-words might cause.

If they'd had a powerful family, they might have found a way to stay. Certain rites or rituals for purification, a minor punishment for their dalliances as well. But he was an only child and orphaned, and she had only her aging mother. Maybe that was why they'd found themselves drawn to each other, their lesser status to begin with, their powerlessness that was only exacerbated by their shame.

And so they'd left.

What words *had* those soldiers spoken to them? Were they scouts of some kind, already planning whatever it was that was happening through the mountains in this direction? Or were they merely asking for directions? Or asking about the hunting?

Now that he spoke their language and its thoughts and patterns affected him, he wondered what it must have been. They couldn't have known that speaking to the embarrassed young lovers would condemn them.

No surprise that Chhayasheela hadn't wanted to face their former fellow villagers alone.

Ellechandran released his breath. "I suppose we should go there now, then. Be done with it, learn what we need to, and leave."

She nodded, unable to speak.

Together they headed toward the gap between the towering rock formation and the smaller shoulder of stone.

"What happened in the fight back there?" Ellechandran asked after a moment. "Many dead?"

"One of the city dwellers. Maybe another as well, I couldn't really tell."

"And the villagers?" Anyone they would have known? But of course they'd been masked, so she wouldn't know that.

"Your trick ended it pretty quickly. I saw them carry someone up. Might have been only injured. Several were injured enough to need help. Not sure if any died." Even an injury could end up being deadly, up here in the mountains. Anyone injured—or killed—would be someone they knew.

A path led up into the rough mountainside above. Each turn of the trail was as familiar as a childhood routine; the rocks that jutted above the dirt, the bends in the tree trunks showed aging but not *change*, not really. Here and there the slight differences only emphasized what was the same.

"There used to be a big tree there," Chhayasheela commented on one turn.

"It was dying already, I think." Ellechandran looked at the gap where the tree used to block the view of the peaks above. "There was a rock here we all used to jump from. It rocked but never came free."

Chhayasheela laughed. "I don't remember that. But I do remember these stones up here. They look like three people huddled over a fire."

The trail took them to a flat space on top of the ridge, a small tabletop that was just big enough for the forty stone houses with roofs of hide and fur.

A village guard stopped them, still wearing his battle mask. They knew him, even with the mask. Semuthian had been some five years younger than them, but he hadn't recognized them yet. In the trade pidgin he said, "Who are you? Are you the leaders the others said were coming?"

A short way beyond him, the rest of their band sat in a circle around a fire—not welcomed enough to be given a place inside, but welcomed enough to be fed. Venthaian had made sure they were settled, though as for that, the villagers would have done most of the work. Welcoming strangers was a sacred duty for their village. Making sure they weren't enemies first was even more sacred.

"Hello, Semuthian," Chhayasheela said in their own language. Her voice sounded tired, resigned to whatever would come to pass. "You know us. We are back, but not to stay."

Semuthian squinted at them then pulled back as if afraid.

"We won't bring you shame, Semuthian." Ellechandran made his voice as scornful as his tight throat allowed. "Just take us to Naathurai or summon her here. So she can let us sleep in safety. We'll be gone in the morning."

Semuthian scrambled backward and retreated into the village. A little later, Naathurai hobbled out. She was older than he remembered, her step slower and less steady. She stopped several paces away.

"You are not welcome in this village. You are unclean."

Chhayasheela lifted her chin. "I am Komelmagai's daughter. You would say this to her daughter? You would dishonor your late friend in this way?"

Naathurai's eyes were sad, but she said only, "So she has died, then? I knew it would happen someday. And yes, I would say it to her, and she would have understood. The strangers' words are dangerous to the young. Their eyes and their ways of seeing the world can infect us through our children, unless we are properly prepared to face them." She looked them each over and added, "As I see they still infect both of you."

Could he deny it? He was changed from the villager he

had been, changed in ways that their appearance only scarcely touched. The young man who had snuck off with his lover was a different person entirely. And much of that change was because of the outsiders they had met and befriended.

Because of words in the languages of Eghsal, pidgin, and mumbler—words spoken together, shared.

He could see that Chhayasheela still wanted to argue, wanted to claim that time had healed them of any shame and the elder's treatment of them was unjust.

Ellechandran agreed that it was, but this wasn't a time to argue. "Whether we are an infection or not doesn't matter. We're not asking to join the tribe. We're not asking you to house us in your homes or welcome us as long lost children returning. We're asking to be *guests*."

It was a peculiar word he used, not the common one for someone welcomed to the communal fire or hosted in any way, but a specific term that rose from their most sacred ceremonies. A guest had a sacred right. It was not the right to impose on the village, but it did mean they must be allowed to remain in the village, or at least at its outer edges, and not suffer any kind of harassment.

Switching into the pidgin of traders and travelers, he said, "Please, is there a place in your village where we might stay?" Would this village have food to bring to the city? That was no longer their primary purpose here, but they could try. "And trade?"

Naathurai was silent, frowning as if she wanted still to send them away but knew that she couldn't. Finally, she said in pidgin, "You may set up your tents here, but no farther. You are not to enter the village or seek out anyone inside. As soon as the weather allows, you are to be gone. We will build you a fire and bring you the guest food. Food taken from the miner-folk below, likely."

Back to their own language, Ellechandran said, "Please, Naathurai, we have no wish to see our former friends. Not to say hello, not to infect them in any way. But we do long for news of the region. We need to know, to have some questions answered. Until we have that, we cannot leave, no matter the weather."

In a soft voice, Chhayasheela added, "And training to offer in trade, so that next time you fight the miners, they don't defeat you so easily."

Naathurai leaned back, contemplating. She did not look inclined to give in, but finally she said, "Set up your camp. I will send someone to speak with you. Someone unlikely to be influenced by your words and actions."

With that, she hobbled away, back in among the stone buildings.

After the tents were set and the food sizzling over a warm fire, a figure approached them, mask-less. Even after the fire lit his face, Ellechandran didn't recognize the man. Most likely someone from a neighboring tribe who'd married into the village in the past few years. Was that Naathurai's solution? Outsider status, so it would protect him from contagion? Or already an outsider, so they could go on shunning him afterward the same as before?

He spoke in the trade pidgin. "I will answer questions."

"How strong was the earthquake here?" Ellechandran asked first.

"I will answer questions, but not from the two outcasts."

What a childish way to protect the village. And yet…if it pleased them, what did it matter? He could play along. He and Chhayasheela fed questions to the others and listened to the answers and learned all they could of the earthquake and the presence of the people of Pashun in the area.

The quake had been strong here, but caused little damage within the village itself. An avalanche had damaged one of their hunting grounds further up the mountain. The worst damage had happened farther south and east, in the same direction that the road led.

They pushed for more details, trying to pinpoint the exact

location and nature of the explosions that had become frequent as they traveled.

"I don't know much more than that. There were a lot of smaller explosions with it, though. It didn't feel like a normal earthquake."

That road had been a trail for the miners and their people for years, though seldom used. It had been over the past year or so that the miners had begun to widen it into a real road. A month or so before the earthquake the numbers of people coming this way had grown, heading toward something unknown. Several days after the quake, an even larger mass of miners had passed through, such a vast grouping that all the mumblers in all the local villages wouldn't have numbered as many.

"Who?" Ellechandran burst out, then let one of the others pick up the question. "What did the people look like going through?"

"They weren't people."

What? After a moment's silence, Ellechandran realized he wasn't the only one staring at the stranger. And that the stranger was letting them stare, drawing out their attention.

"Not really people," he finally said, and added a word that didn't sound like either their native language or pidgin. "They were bodies, but not people, their spirits cut off as they marched. And very fast, too. A pace that normal miners could never keep up."

Ellechandran released his breath. What did this image mean? Nothing good for Chaitanshehar, he was sure. If these spirit-less bodies were ever sent against that city, what could they possibly do to stop them? They needed to get this report back to Jaritta so they could lay their plans. But was it enough new information, no matter how valuable, for them to turn back now? Or did they need to learn more?

None of the other mumbler tribes in the area, the stranger went on to say, had any idea what the people of Pashun were doing. All the more reason why they should keep going, so that the report they would bring back was a complete one, one they could act on right away.

"Will you speak with us to trade?" Ellechandran asked. When the stranger said nothing, he prompted the others to discuss the possibility of trade, food for training. The man wouldn't commit to anything. His mistrust was plain, and no surprise, if even trading would require them to wear ceremonial masks. Trade with other mumblers was one thing, with a city of the valley people was entirely different.

Finally they got him to agree to send a letter back to the city with as much food as two or three people could carry. They would work out the trades with someone in the city, but only if they could find someone who spoke the trade pidgin fluently.

As they concluded the arrangement, Ellechandran noticed an odd quirk in the way the stranger used the pidgin. He pronounced the words with an accent, the vowels twisted just enough to be different without being unintelligible. It reminded him of the way Azheeran and some of the other mumblers talked, mumblers who came from north of the river.

"You aren't from here," Ellechandran said in the language of this village when there was a break in the conversation. "I hear it in your voice."

"Of course he's not," Chhayasheela said. "Otherwise we'd know him."

"Not from anywhere near here," he insisted. "Are you?"

"I'm not supposed to talk to you two, except to answer questions." He clearly struggled with the local language, but pride or something made him stick with it, in response. When no one answered him, he glanced around and said, "No. I came south to join *your* city. But I couldn't…couldn't find it. Couldn't accept the idea of joining."

Arcist magic, one way or another. The Pashun arcist's beacons driving him away, or something inside making him unwilling to commit to the city's bigger purpose and Pavresh's spell. Either way, he'd clearly become committed to this village, in his own way.

"Well then, I wish you peace in your new home. May you fill the roles we might have filled if we had remained."

The man dipped his head in answer and made his way back in among the buildings.

***

In the morning they packed up their tents.

"Do you still miss it sometimes?" Ellechandran asked Chhayasheela. The smells of the mountains were so familiar, of the frozen dew on the pine branches beginning to thaw, of the campfire they had just put out and the lingering scents of their hasty breakfast. "Do you wish we were still back here?"

Chhayasheela put a hand on his shoulder. It sent an electric jolt through him, another kind of reminder. He met her eyes and felt his breath catch.

"No." She turned away "I miss some of it, sure. But no, I wouldn't give up any of what I have today for those things."

Without waiting for a response, she led the way down to the road below.

A different set of eyes flashed before Ellechandran's mind. Nataravi's. And then Ovitiva's and Jaritta's, the puckered skin of her scar surrounding one eye. No, he wouldn't give that up either.

But that didn't change the strange way he felt like he was half a different person when he was back here in this place. As if a part of him had never left, and if he could just reunite with that part, then he might feel completely whole again.

People were watching from the village. Eyeing him, waiting for him to leave. If the villagers were trying to remain unseen, they were failing. Let it shame their watchers, to be seen. Or better yet, let it force them to realize that it was no shame, one way or another.

He followed the others down to the road, where they picked through the spilled goods from the wagon. Much of it was feed for horses, but there were sacks of food as well, and even one bundle of weapons that they might use in their trades with the mountain villages. Or for the city's protection.

These supplies would be useful back in Chaitanshehar. Ellechandran looked back to the west along the Pashun road. How long would it take to get home, their new home? They could even skip the message he'd given the stranger, see if anyone from the village was willing to travel with them for trading instead of hoping the villagers followed through with their agreement to send someone.

But there were still too many questions about what the miners and city folk were doing and what it would mean for the city of outcasts. Their march into the mountains did not leave Ellechandran feeling like the city had escaped danger. Whatever the people—or not-people—of Pashun were doing, it was sure to spell trouble for Chaitanshehar in the future. They needed to learn what that was.

And to learn that, as an outcast already, he must exile himself again from what he knew and loved, and leave such thoughts behind him. Entrusting the rest to the vague hope that he would make it back someday, that the city would still survive, that there would be food and welcome and safety when he finally was able to return.

Home, safety, welcome, return. The farther away he went, the more those words blurred into meaninglessness. No matter the language.

CHAPTER 24

Pavresh was swept along with the masses, beside the river and down the southern mountain slopes. His lungs burned at the effort it took to keep pace. Smoke from the colossus in the sky above drifted downward, and gusts brought the smoke coursing through the crowd. Its shape seemed to bless them, to urge them onward in their journey, yet Pavresh crumpled in on himself, coughing.

He managed to escape the current of people and sat on a rock to recover.

He should be joining them. The magic summoned him onward, downward, into this new land. There was a desert far below them, but what was thirst to the magic? Its draw overcame the need to drink, and it should overcome the need to breathe as well. But when he tried to stand up again and obey the call, the coughing fit forced him back down.

There was no road for the crowd rushing downward beside the river. That fact didn't appear to slow them, and by the time the end of the pack marched through, a fresh road had formed, trampled by so many feet.

With the dust settled, Pavresh's breathing became easier as well. He still felt like he couldn't take a full breath, like he was constantly one good, deep breath away from being able to function normally, but that breath never came. At least he didn't feel like he was dying. Each breath was a disappointment, not quite satisfying enough, but it got him through until the next one. And the farther the main body of people moved away from him, the more freedom he found from the magic. He could think clearly sometimes, though the urge to join the rest would pop in now and then, almost enough to keep him moving.

As he sat against the rock, a smaller cluster of people descended from the tunnel above. He could hear their progress, the sound of a score or two of feet as well as several horses, even while the turn in the rough trail hid them from sight. They had a drummer with them as well, setting a beat that stirred him to motion.

He should be marching, should be a part of the bigger group. They needed him among their mass to achieve their purpose. He could recognize the magic as it pulled at him. That was a good first step, and the less energy he had to put into just breathing, the more he might have to resist it. Full freedom from its power was not yet within reach. He staggered to his feet and took a few awkward steps down the new road just as the others came around the bend behind him.

Caught, shamed, a failure to the cause.

When he tried to explain himself—before anyone had asked because they were still a fair distance away up the road—his words were cut off by another coughing fit.

"Are we sending sick men with us, now?" one of the mounted people asked. "He should have stayed back in Pashun." It was Prince Hrisha, the former mayor of Pashun who was among the current Ruling Thirty. Part of *one* of the Ruling Thirties. Pavresh had seen the man at times since his capture, but never interacted with him. Was his the voice the horde had listened to, announcing their arrival in the Forgotten South? "If he heads back now, we'll surely catch back up with him soon. On our way back, to destroy the untouchable city."

"Unless we choose not to turn around right away." Dartak's voice was still strong, much as it had been in the Grand Assembly of the Princes in Romnai. "Here is a new land. Surely that merits some investigation."

Pavresh glanced between the two but kept his face lowered in modest submission.

"Maybe." Prince Hrisha's voice was a clear dismissal, a reminder that Dartak was an outcast in his own way, and his words came from a past that no longer mattered. All contained within a single word. He turned from Dartak and spoke to someone else. "Blow your arcist horns, Kamlak. Maybe it will stop his coughing and inspire him to move, one way or the other."

"I don't need trumpets." By then the cluster of people had reached Pavresh. Kamlak addressed him. "Old man…" Kamlak must have recognized him at that moment. He pulled Pavresh upright. "Or not so old."

Kamlak's ear and the skin around it looked scalded in a way it hadn't before. His own scar from the explosion at the steam beds. It hadn't slowed down his planning in any way that Pavresh could see. If it had been caused by fire instead of steam, would the priests have cast him out as they had Jaritta? Maybe, though the scars would never be as bad as Jaritta's were.

Pavresh tried to protect himself, as he had every time Kamlak had taken control of his body. His efforts achieved nothing, and Kamlak made no attempt to do anything. After studying him a moment, he said with cruel humor, "You're caught in the magic already, aren't you? You escaped only to be caught again. That's so fitting it makes me want to believe your narrative ideas about magic are true."

Letting go of Pavresh's shoulder, he said to the gathered leaders of this Pashun expedition, "This is the great arcist who protected the city of the untouchables. I may need his help with whatever we do down here. He will come with us."

After a flurry of movement, Pavresh found himself sitting in a saddle and riding alongside Kamlak. He had no water to make the yellow tisane, but he chewed a piece of it, hoping it would ease his breathing, and simply went along with the others.

The horns of Kamlak's magic still beat in his veins.

***

It took them well into the next day to descend far enough to get a good view of the land below the mountains. The desert looked as impassable as any mountain range. It was a labyrinth of small canyons and barren rock. If Pavresh had to create an arcist image of a land unfit for humans, he would have been hard put to create anything worse than what spread before them. It was a place opposed to life of any kind.

The magic's hold on him felt lighter, but curiosity about the new land had an even stronger grip. What would they discover up ahead? Would there be any evidence of the old stories, any people with new stories he could learn? Even apart from the sense of discovery, he was enough in control of himself to remember the purpose Pashun had in mind for this expedition. It was to create an army, one that could crush Chaitanshehar. The longer they spent south of the mountains, the more time for something to develop to protect his friends back home.

The crowd of people, miners and workers who were being shaped into soldiers by the tasks their leaders gave them, stood at the edge of one sharp canyon drop, backs straight as if to impress the desert with their discipline. As if preparing to wage war against the land itself.

How soon would the leaders give up and direct them back through the tunnel and northward?

"You won't make it anywhere through there." Pavresh said. He could feel his voice sounding dull, but at least riding instead of walking had largely restored his breathing. "It's not a place for people."

Not a place for city dwellers, anyway. What would the mumblers see here? He stood in his stirrups and looked all around. He was far from the only person doing so, looking for other paths ahead.

Kamlak was talking, arguing that Pavresh didn't understand the power of his martial spell, that arcist magic could even overcome a desert. Pavresh didn't listen closely because he was studying the land. When Kamlak paused, Pavresh muttered, "You can tell yourself that story, but doesn't mean it'll work."

Far to the east, across a wide stretch of desert, there was a hint of…something. A hint of human habitation. Maybe, unless his mind was simply tricking him into seeing what he hoped to see.

The thought that the old stories might be real made him

dizzy. He'd doubted the supposed history of their land. Between mumblers who looked like city dwellers, cities more ancient than history could account for, and the archaeologist's discoveries about the insufficient ships of their ancestors, he hadn't known what was real anymore. But to see those buildings—were they really buildings?—to be faced with this evidence of a Forgotten South... His head swirled.

It all suddenly seemed real again, only real in a richer and stranger way than he had believed as a child.

That didn't solve the dilemma of the barren land before them. If that was the Forgotten South to the east, if there were people to meet and truths to learn, then they had to get past the desert to learn more. And it looked as impassible as the mountains ever had, with no way to blast a path through.

"I don't need to tell myself stories." Kamlak moved directly into Pavresh's face, using arcist magic to freeze Pavresh in place so he couldn't even step back. "My *power* is stronger than your stories. As I've shown you over and over."

He shouldn't be taunting this man. He should be hiding, trying to free himself. At least he could control his eyes. He gazed east along the mountains. The mumblers, he supposed, would avoid leaving the mountains in the first place. Could there be a route through the foothills?

Curiosity and delay, both drove him to help this army continue onward.

"That's your route," he said, cutting off some rambling statement Kamlak was making. When Kamlak released his spell enough for Pavresh to move, he pointed behind them to a valley between the last two lines of foothills. "If you want to get past the desert, you'll have to march them around that way."

Kamlak looked where he pointed. It was a rugged land without a tree in sight, the grass and shrubs a pale green that made the landscape look nearly as dry as the desert. But it wasn't barren. There were stands of bigger bushes that snaked in lines between the hills, hinting at streams. And even the dry grasses implied at least some moisture.

Pavresh snapped a small leaf off one of the shrubs and crushed it between its fingers. A strong aroma filled the air, wild but pleasant. He breathed deeply, hoping it might help his lungs.

Kamlak dropped his extra focus from Pavresh and sent a group of soldiers to explore the gap in the foothills. Pavresh sat down nearby to breathe in the scents. He had used up his small supply of dried naga trumpet flowers, but he still had the sprigs of yellow tisane herbs and had even been granted permission to brew some tisane in the mornings. He sipped the bitter brew, and it eased some of his discomfort. Kamlak could do whatever he wanted now as long as it carried them farther from home.

He only began paying attention to the other arcist when the people he was talking to raised their voices.

"You are losing sight of what we are here for." Prince Hrisha emphasized his words with small but forceful gestures, his hands cutting the air as if they were sharpened blades. "The miners are now soldiers. That was our aim. Now we turn around and finish the job."

"*You* are ignoring the world before your feet," Dartak said, his voice rich and compelling as always. "Forget about silly revenge fantasies and move forward."

"It is not silly revenge to conquer our enemies behind us before we leave ourselves vulnerable—"

"That is not—"

Kamlak cut them both off with a sweep of his arm. "Stop. You are both thinking too small."

Ah, now this was an argument Pavresh wanted to happen. Let them fight amongst themselves. Drawing on what little magic he could access—what little he dared with Kamlak right there, he made himself forgettable, not worth Kamlak's time. And at the same time he tried to bolster the sense of anger he felt between the princes and Kamlak. Let them be rivals. Let them be jealous.

"Stick to wizardry, arcist," Hrisha said after the shock wore off. "You are not a leader, only a tool."

It was the wrong thing to say. Pavresh felt the shift in the magic as Kamlak cocked his head, and he had to suppress the smile on his own face. "Oh?"

The sense of authority fled from Dartak's feeble, old body. The importance that Hrisha conveyed disappeared. And Kamlak spoke with a forcefulness that admitted no room for doubt. "I said you are thinking too small. Mahendri is not here, but he is on his way. He will be disappointed if he comes here to find you acting without thought. Forget what we leave behind us in Eghsal Valley? Never! Ignore the opportunity that lies before us? Absolutely not! We will press on and take what we need from this land. The foods, the goods, the people to fill up our armies if need be. Then we come right back and make sure all of Eghsal recognizes us as their leaders."

"Us? You are not—"

"Us. Mahendri and I, not either of you." He made no effort to keep the sneer from his voice. "We may allow you your roles, but don't think that means you're in charge." Kamlak forced his will onto the two through magic, and seeing it done woke something inside Pavresh, a memory of the weaknesses he'd tried to take advantage of before. The drums and trumpets had a hold on him that didn't allow him to resist. But remembering how he'd broken Kamlak's hold inspired him to look again for some way to escape the magic's control.

***

As they traveled the rough route through the foothills the following day, Kamlak had need of the horse Pavresh had been using. And Pavresh, nudged by his own spell into a discarded tool, was no longer deemed necessary by the leaders. On foot, Pavresh fell back among the older and ailing members of the throng of would-be soldiers. Even the great, lumbering food wagons passed ahead of them. Kamlak allowed one drummer, also carrying a horn for the times of day when that was necessary, to stay with the stragglers. She kept them moving as well as their various aches and sores allowed.

At first Pavresh found himself walking beside the old soldier who'd shown him the herbs to ease his breathing. Together they found more of the naga trumpets.

"If you place it in a censer, like the priests use, you might be able to breathe the smoke more easily along the way," the old man said. "You wouldn't have to wait for the evening campfire. But I don't suppose we can find anything like that."

As they walked along, their group falling farther and farther behind the main body as the day progressed, he and Pavresh searched among what stores they had for something that might work to burn the flowers on.

"This might do." Pavresh held out a flat dish, made of clay, that seemed to be a cross between a bowl and a plate. "It could hold the flowers while they smolder."

"Clay will get too hot," the soldier said. "Find something else."

"Or find some way to hold the dish," Pavresh said, though by the time he was done he was talking to himself.

It was while searching for some scraps of cloth to wrap around his hands that he saw someone else he recognized. The woman who had cared for him after his escape was with this rear guard of the old and infirm. She didn't look to be in poor health, but she didn't walk fast either.

He remembered the spell he'd given her as he left. Maybe her slower pace was because she didn't feel the drumbeat's insistence as strongly as everyone else did. And if he'd cast it correctly, those around her wouldn't feel it, either.

He came close to her and offered a familiar greeting.

She frowned and said, "Greetings to you." It was a very formal way to say hello, one not necessarily for a person in a higher social standing, but for someone the speaker didn't know.

If she needed to pretend she didn't know him, he understood. "My greetings as well," he said, using the same, more formal word. "I am wondering if you have any cloth that I might use to hold this dish safely when it's hot?"

She took the dish, flipped it over to examine it, and handed it back. "Don't use cloth. You'll need so much you'll grow clumsy and drop it. Use a fork with a wood handle, or a stick if you can't find one."

"Thank you. A good suggestion."

They had to keep moving then so they didn't fall too far behind, but the next time their group took a break, Pavresh and the soldier searched for a solution. The forks they found in the bags were too small and would have let the dish drop.

Some of the people wanted to light a fire to warm themselves as they rested. While they argued with those who said there wouldn't be time, Pavresh kicked around at the brush, wondering how well it would work as firewood. The sticks snapped easily beneath his feet.

He bent down to examine the broken branches. They were hollow, which might work for his purposes, but very frail as well. He found the strongest segment he could, one still green and pliable, and stuck one of the short forks inside. Sticking straight out, it only dropped the dish, but by angling it, he could wedge the dish between the stick and the fork, and it was surprisingly sturdy. He'd just have to watch and make sure the wood didn't catch fire.

Just as the group was picking themselves up to continue their march, he got some of the flowers smoldering in the hot clay. The smoke he breathed soothed his lungs.

This time when they continued, Pavresh positioned himself near the woman who had cared for him. He felt the drums loosen their hold on him throughout that march, felt the change deep in the blood that pumped through him.

His improved breathing made him feel like he could easily pick up his pace and leave these stragglers behind. The call of the trumpets still urged him on, made him want to try even to catch up with the rest of the force. But by staying near the woman, he could resist that urge.

He spent his energy poking at the weak spots in the magic, trying to find a way to fully free himself from Kamlak's spell.

***

The stragglers camped separately and made their own way along the route of the leaders, now a clear road cutting through the dry shrubs. There were plenty of naga trumpet flowers to keep Pavresh breathing easily. Pavresh created a counter story around the group. They were older and injured and sick, all that was true, but they were separate as well, for reasons that went beyond those facts.

He made no attempt to make it clear what those other reasons were. All that mattered was the idea of them being separate, of them having their own role that wasn't identical to the mass of people marching to the rigid drums up ahead.

They never lost sight of the bulk of the army. The main force was always, at least some of them, visible far ahead between the ridges. But the trailing end of their horde grew farther and less distinct as the next few days passed.

At one stop, when Pavresh's lungs felt especially strong, he joined a few others in passing between the slopes of the foothills to gaze beyond them, into the Forgotten South. It was dusk, though they still hoped to continue for another hour or two before they stopped to camp. The dim light made it difficult to identify if the land below the foothills was still desert or if they had made it around those barrens to something else. A flat land extended toward the south. Far away that land rose up in what looked like another line of hills.

There were lights beyond the flats. Lanterns or campfires of some sort. Definite signs of human habitation. Pavresh stared at the spaces beside those lights, hoping his eyes would adjust enough to make the details clear. He saw hints of the outlines of buildings, but little else. If that was all one city, it was far bigger than any city of Eghsal.

What would they be, coming into this new land? What was the story, the arcist image for their arrival?

They might be the glorious visitors of a more advanced people, coming with gifts and greater knowledge. Or they might be the rustic barbarians, descending to pillage and destroy a people they couldn't even understand. Or did that place too great an importance on their arrival? Whether as a people of awe or disdain, it implied that their arrival would be momentous for the ones who lived here already. Were they even beneath that, an annoyance from far away to be quickly forgotten?

Maybe the people here weren't even human. He imagined a vast city full of the nagas of legend or beings of fire. He pictured their houses unfit for humans, their artwork beyond anything humans could comprehend. For all the sense of momentous history that Pavresh—and the entire horde of the Eghsal people from Pashun—felt about their arrival, there was no reason to assume it would be a world-changing event for the people here.

No reason except for the perhaps deceptive feeling he had deep inside, and no logic or arcist magic could completely tamp that sense down.

Whatever happened when they came around the desert to that vast city ahead, it would surely be important—for themselves, if not for the world as a whole.

The stragglers caught up with the rest of the horde late the next morning. They were gathered above a route down from the foothills. A rolling grassland stood between them and the buildings of a city as vast as anything Pavresh had imagined. A city of humans or of naga, of giants or of something else he couldn't even imagine?

The leaders had taken a place above the others, on the face of the foothill. Hrisha raised his hands to quiet the people for him to speak. With a touch of magic that Pavresh felt like a brief breeze, he managed to draw in the full attention of the people below him.

"We are embarked on a grand mission, a grand future. There are those who oppose us and those who stand in our way without knowing it. But the future summons us to a greatness that is beyond what any of us can imagine. Now to speak us into that future, listen to these words from the past, guiding us forward."

Hrisha stepped aside, and Dartak took his place. From this distance, Dartak looked even older than he had close up. His hair full and silver, his dark skin wrinkled without hiding the intensity of his eyes, his back straight. He seemed like one aged into wisdom, one who hadn't lost his intelligence or strength even as the years passed.

It was Kamlak's doing. To Pavresh's senses the air fairly crackled with arcist magic. And it wasn't only in the service of making Dartak seem wise. It lay in setting the two men up as opponents. Hrisha and Dartak seemed like two old enemies, each unwilling to concede the stage entirely to the other, each with their own priorities and ideas of how to proceed. But grudgingly they came together to support the actions ahead.

How much of that was truly how the two were, and how much was simply Kamlak's magic, Pavresh couldn't disentangle. Maybe it simply reflected the disagreements they had with each other, as he himself had overheard. Maybe it was done to undermine them each so that after this mission, neither would be in a position to challenge Mahendri—or Kamlak himself—for power. Or simply to inspire the people before them to set aside any doubt or old grievance and push on ahead.

Focusing on the magic, Pavresh had missed the exact words Dartak had spoken. He'd talked about the future and the city that lay before them, that much Pavresh recalled.

Now, as Dartak wrapped up his speech, Pavresh felt a new weave to the magic. The martial power of the drums and horns fell almost entirely away as Dartak was saying, "The memory of our ancestors goes with us, and the blessing of the gods, the blessing of the Sacred Fire that they serve."

Something new rose in place of the previous magic. They were traders, but it was a kind of trading never known before. They brought goods beyond imagining. They brought promises of ease and glory, of honor and power that anyone could attain.

The spell was breathtakingly powerful. It surged and

flickered around them, as if it were a fire itself. It made speech itself almost impossible and focused all their energy on moving forward.

And yet, curiously, Pavresh felt all that only as a distant fact he was aware of. He didn't find himself convinced that he was a trader, or that any of their horde was in possession of amazing goods. He felt separate from it, aware of but apart from its influence.

Had he finally achieved his freedom from Kamlak's control? He felt around the edges of his mind, at the drumbeat he could hear even when the drums were silent, at the sound of the horns. The new spell surely took an intense focus and energy from Kamlak and the arcists he had trained. Half a dozen men and women stood around him, amplifying his spell, without its effects pulling Pavresh back within its control.

When Dartak said, "And so, in that spirit and with that assurance of the Fire's blessing, we go now to craft the future before us!" a lone horn sounded. Pavresh stiffened to attention and realized that he was still bound—even if loosely—beneath the control of the earlier spell.

What had changed was the focus of this new magic. The image of them as bringers of powerful gifts hadn't been for them at all. It was for the people they would meet—whatever form those people might take and whatever stories might have shaped their thoughts.

The sheer scope of their journey threatened to overwhelm Pavresh's senses. Kamlak's dream of arcist magic as power was vaster than any story Pavresh had ever thought to tell himself, and it allowed no room for resistance or nuance.

It was arcist magic as a conquering force. A spell to subjugate the people of this new land by force, without a single blade drawn.

CHAPTER 25

The towns and countryside that Elsh led Harkala and her crew through became a city, not one with sharply defined edges, but a city that took form gradually, coalescing out of the fragments of itself that were the isolated farmhouses, the villages, the towns.

They entered one town market and traded the camels for extra donkeys. By the time they'd left the other side of the market, it no longer felt like just a town. The fragments drew together until they were no longer crossing a space between but were on city streets proper. The houses still had only a single story, and there were gaps wide enough for an alley between, but it still felt like a city, with a bustle and urgency that had been absent farther out.

Because Elsh—still with her band of soldier-guards—guided them, no one stopped them or asked them questions. A part of Harkala wished they would. She wanted to know all about this place, these people. They didn't fit any of her previous understandings about the peoples of the world, and certainly not the stories told in Eghsal about their ancestors and the Forgotten South. Some looked like mumblers. Others like the people they'd seen back at the city on a pier. And others were different still, in the shades of their skin or the shapes of their faces. But they all belonged together in that city.

The language barrier always got in the way of those wishes. They might linger to study a shop or watch a parade, but what did it mean? There was no one they could ask. The bits that Elsh was beginning to learn were the best they could hope for.

They saw no rails or steam engines. The city was quieter for it, or noisy in different ways. The creak and rumble of cart wheels, the neighing of horses, the cries of the drivers. It all felt more distant than the sounds of Eghsal cities.

"So many people outside," Ekana mentioned as they passed

an open air space full of tables. "Or rather, so much of the city itself is outside."

"It's warmer," Harkala said with a nod. Though in some ways it wasn't much warmer than a nice day in the inland cities up north—Romnai, when the heat from the volcanic activity was right, could be considerably warmer. But it wasn't a pleasant warmth there. And when the sea currents brought especially warm air to Jarnur, they usually brought rain as well, or at least the threat of rain, so people didn't spend much of their time outdoors.

The city didn't feel primitive, even so. There was something elegant and advanced about it, a feeling that Harkala couldn't quite explain to herself. It was a people without rails, not because they hadn't advanced enough to invent or need them, but because they had chosen a different way that made locomotives an unnecessary step.

They came to a place that felt like a center of the city, or at least like it should be the place where people chose to gather, because of how the streets all led there and because of the towering buildings around it. The buildings were of stone, with parts of the walls made of some kind of clay or mud. They didn't feel heavy, like the stone houses of Jarnur did. These rose up lightly into sharp points and fancy scrollwork. A kind of artistry Harkala had never even imagined.

Here too there were tables set up along the street. At some, people were eating food off beaten metal plates or drinking from small mugs. Other tables were set up for working, like a desk in some prince's study but set out here in the sunshine.

The street widened beneath those tall spires, giving room for a few small stands of goods being sold. Nothing like the lively chaos of a marketplace in Eghsal Valley. More like a few select booths from one of those markets were transported here and allowed to remain as long as they didn't disturb the peace of the plaza. At first the space looked like a normal-sized plaza, but it kept opening up bigger as they approached. Other streets leading into it expanded into smaller, proto-plazas that fed into the central space.

A tall building on one side reminded Harkala of a temple. She wondered what deities they worshiped in this city. There was no fire out front and no view into the interior to give her any clue.

The cobbles of the plaza were laid out in circles and waves, leading them toward a great fountain in the center, just as there had been water given a central location in the first village where they'd traded. Maybe they worshiped water here after all, though the fountain wasn't close to the temple-like building. Plants with broad, dark green leaves surrounded the marble basin.

Near the edge, some of the cobblestones became glass. Thick glass and sturdy, but she could see the water coursing through beneath, leading out below the plaza and into the city itself. Elsh stopped and dismounted, so Harkala did the same.

Ekana stayed with the horses at first, but Elsh gestured him over as well, and their mounts made no attempt to wander away. Everyone gathered close. Elsh parted two leaves so they could look down into beautifully clean water. Not a hint of the sulfur of the lava beds, the strange chemicals of the natural steam baths, or the salt smell of the sea. No smell of anything, really, only the vegetation smell of the leafy plants and the powerful sense of *clean*.

Elsh said what she often did when she wanted to know a word in their language. Harkala pointed into the fountain and said, "Water."

"Watereh?" Elsh added an extra syllable when she tried to repeat the word, so Harkala said it again.

When Elsh had dipped her hand in and drank, she held the leaves aside for each of them to taste from the fountain. As Harkala did, she repeated, "Water," and pointed with her chin at the water in her cupped hands. Then she said, "Drink water," and greedily slurped it from her hands.

Harkala mimicked her. Who knew she'd been so thirsty before coming here? Who knew water could taste so pure?

"Now north," Elsh said when they'd each had a drink. "Water, drink water, and now north."

As if the water was a ritual, a blessing to send them on their journey. Sacred water. As she looked at the pipes leading into the fountain—great, arcing works of art for carrying water—and also the sluicing current beneath the glass cobbles at their feet, she knew that it was more than just a vaguely spiritual honoring. They might worship water, or worship the deity of water or something like that, but this fountain fulfilled more than a merely spiritual role.

The pipes that radiated out beneath the street were a key part of the city. How, Harkala wasn't sure. Was it simply water to drink and bathe in? Did it somehow power things in the city, the way steam engines did in the north? Harkala was a scholar, but a scholar of the past. She didn't pretend to understand such new technologies.

But she understood that the water was central to whatever strange technologies this city had, in counterpoint to Eghsal's steam.

And somehow, in Elsh's mind if nothing else, that power went north with them now as they passed through the rest of the city.

The fountain was nearer the northern edge of the city than Harkala had realized. Once they'd left behind the shadows of the tall buildings around the plaza, the city seemed to lose its grip on itself, allowing the pieces that had formed slowly as they traveled up from the southwest to dissipate. Before them was a flat land stretching a short distance toward a series of foothills. Beyond that, the mountains.

Harkala had to scan the peaks to find the remnant of the cloud-smoke naga they had followed earlier. It was well to the west now and mostly disintegrated, but a hint of its shape remained visible against the low clouds that settled over the northern sky.

Still calling to them.

"North." Elsh pointed straight across the flatland rather than toward that cloud of smoke.

Harkala nodded and turned in her saddle to face her crew. "We don't know what we'll discover out there on this side of the mountains. Maybe it will be as impassable as it seemed from the other side. Maybe we'll discover a route no one has discovered before. But here we go again to find out."

They had only just begun to cross the flatlands when a different sort of cloud rose up opposite them. "What do you think that is?" Ekana asked.

Harkala had no idea, so she let the others discuss possibilities.

"A herd of wisent might raise a cloud like that," Sembaari said. "Are there wisents here? Or other large beasts?"

"Maybe it's no more than a dust storm," one of the sailors suggested. "It rises like some storms do from the sea."

But would a dust storm come toward them, when the winds were blowing from the west, across the plain?

By late afternoon, it was clear that a mass of people was causing the cloud, a great horde that filled the horizon. Elsh stopped them, as if uncertain.

"Do you know who they might be?" Harkala asked.

Elsh didn't understand or didn't know how to answer. They slowed to a stop.

"Friends? Enemies?"

Elsh stood high in her saddle, straining to either side, and then shouted, "Back!" Whether she had learned the word from them somehow or said it in her own language and Harkala understood because of her actions, Harkala didn't know. But in an instant they were all riding the other way.

They had only gone a little when the sound of trumpets caught up with them, a piercing cacophony that wrapped around them, calling them to pause, to join the horde. She wanted to do what the music told her. The sound of those horns beat against her, with pulsing insistence. It pulled at her in a way she couldn't define, stripping away parts of her thoughts until her thinking went murky. She put a hand to her head to keep from losing her balance.

They should wait, let these others catch up to them. No, they needed to spur their horses onward, try with everything they had to get away.

They didn't stop, but they let their horses slow down as the horn blasts beat relentlessly against their will to escape.

A drumbeat added itself to the noise. The rhythm didn't match the horses' hoofbeats, creating a dissonance that bothered Harkala more than she thought it should. She wanted it to resolve into a single beat, to unify. She pulled on the reins.

The horde's few mounted members pulled ahead of the main mass and closed in on Harkala and her crew.

She looked back and cried out to see familiar faces.

Not that she knew the people riding up toward them, but their skin looked like her own. The style of their clothes would have seemed normal on the streets of Jarnur.

"Who are you?" she called back.

Her shock at seeing them was echoed in their own reactions to her words. One rider pulled his horse into rearing. It pawed at the evening sky. Another spurred his horse forward. Harkala, no longer trying to flee, waited. The rest of her crew circled around her, and Elsh and her soldier guards formed a second cluster a short way beyond.

"You speak," the man at the lead said, breathless, when he caught up with them. He was an older man, his hair white but his back straight and an air of excitement in his voice. "You speak our language. You must be… This must be… Have we reached the Forgotten South?"

"Of course we have," another man cut in before Harkala could respond. His face flushed where the skin looked like it had been burned by a spilled gourd of hot tisane. There was a strange force in this man, a magnetism that made her want to hear what he said. It lined up with the impulse of the trumpets and drums, an impulse that clamped down on her, controled her more and more as they came closer. To her group, the man said, "We have come from a distant land. A land you do not know, but you may have your own legends of us. Now we return, and we call on you to join us."

Harkala opened her mouth to answer, to explain who they were and their whole story. But she found herself unable to speak. The strange power of this figure before her made it impossible to do anything but fall in line behind him, to follow wherever he led, to give food and weapons to his horde, to go where they went so she could fight their enemies.

She felt an urge to give over whatever goods she owned and call it a fair trade, and then to take a sword and join them.

Elsh stepped around Harkala's crew and drew her sword. Then holding it out before her, she knelt before the strange leader of these invaders, these strangers that were Harkala's own people. The lack of language to understand was nothing when the man could command people with a force that needed no words.

**

A part of Harkala knew that the trading the horde did in the city over the next few days wasn't real trading. They set themselves up in the plaza with the fountain and invited the people to trade—speaking in the language of Eghsal as if the people here would understand them. But then, those under the horde's spell didn't speak. They just knew what to do.

Harkala hadn't managed to speak yet either, so she couldn't explain to anyone that her crew came from Jarnur or that no one else in this city could understand them.

And yet, none of that seemed wrong to her either. It was fine that no one spoke the same language. The trades they made were more than fair, and only made the people trading want to please these strangers more.

What did they need? How could she try to get it for them? Silks and finery? Weapons and food? The questions pounded against her mind so that other thoughts and concerns became distant, the worries of another mind.

The man she'd first considered the band's leader was named Kamlak, but it was others who spoke as if they were in charge. After three days of camping out in the plaza, drinking the sacred water from the fountain, and trading for riches unimaginable, a middle-aged man climbed onto the lip of the fountain's basin to address the people in the plaza. He was dressed like a prince, despite the long travel they had endured.

"In these days of trading, you have seen only a taste of the wonders our land has to offer you. The glories of the northern lands can be yours as well, the steam engines, the mighty mysteries. By the will of the Fire and the gods, you can enjoy the riches to which you are entitled."

Did he have any idea how few people understood what he was saying? That it was no more than a few sailors from Jarnur?

And yet… Harkala had the sense that the people of this city *did* understand him, or at least they understood the underlying message. It came through in the same force that compelled their trading and other actions.

"Now we must return to our own lands," he continued. "Some of you may be chosen to accompany us. Your mighty in arms, your trained in battle. These can come to see the wonders of our home, to fight by our sides, and to return to tell you what they have experienced."

Only some? A frisson of fear passed through Harkala. Would she be left behind? Or any of her crew? She must make sure to join them, must make sure that all of them would be able to return to their homes.

As if she had the control to make sure of anything.

"And long may our partnership endure. We will return to trade again, after we have tested the mettle of your goods, to find what is of value for us. And to bring you more of our good riches in return."

The horde cheered first, and the people of the city followed suit. Then the leaders mounted their horses and rode back toward the north, and the people rushed into the gap in their wake so they could follow.

Harkala had enough control over her actions to mount up hurriedly behind the main mass of the people of Eghsal. Ekana squeezed in beside her mount and Sembaari on his other side. She managed to look around and count up the rest of her crew as they were ushered along in the current of people. It helped that they had mounts. Most of the horde marched on foot behind the mounted leaders. The donkeys they'd been using for their gear were lost or simply taken by the horde already, making their own separate way north.

All the locals who had gathered in the plaza appeared to be going along with them. The claim that only some would be chosen appeared false from the outset. Perhaps only the chosen ones had come to the plaza in the first place. Many of them had wagons loaded with supplies as well as horses and donkeys, which was surely a welcome addition.

And most had swords. Many, many swords that had come forward in the trading, all making their way north while their owners were compelled through some uncanny form of control.

It was wrong, a part of her told herself, wrong to control others in this way. But it was a distant, disconnected part of herself saying that, a portion of her mind that couldn't affect anything. It couldn't possibly be wrong, not when it was for the glory of her own people, for the glory of her homeland.

***

The travel north to the foothills was a blur. Her crew was with her, all in the same place most of the time as they went. Elsh was also there, with at least some of her squad of soldiers, but they became separated during the journey across the plains. She rarely saw them. Many others from the great city behind them were scattered throughout the army as well. They were a gathering of many peoples, unconnected by language—but no one spoke, anyway. The strange compulsion connected them in a way no difference in language could weaken.

They turned westward to make their way through the foothills. How far away was the sea here? Much too far for any hint of salt to carry on the wind. As she sat in a stupor beside the fire one night in the middle of those hills, someone spoke to her. "I know you."

She didn't know the speaker, but he looked like someone she should know. An Eghsal face, copper-toned skin. But then almost everyone in the horde matched that description more or less. He looked like someone who belonged there, nothing more nor less.

She hadn't been able to speak freely since joining with the horde, so she didn't bother trying.

"I visited your dig near Jarnur. How did you end up here?"

Memories opened up like flower blossoms. Not new memories she'd forgotten, but a part of her history that had seemed cut off, unimportant. The archaeological site. The ship that had wrecked upon the frigid northern island. The second ship that had carried them to the city on the pier.

But what she really wanted to know first was something else. "You're talking. Talking normal. How are you doing that?" The fact that she could form the words herself surprised her to silence.

The stranger nodded sadly. "His magic is very strong, I'm afraid. I can't quite break free, either. But I was already with these people when he created it, so it doesn't hit me as hard. And I've been working my own magic against his since the beginning."

Magic. That was the word for this terrible power that sunk its claws into her. Arcist magic. She had heard scholars discussing the phenomenon but had never imagined it controlling her. "I'm talking now, though. Did you do that to me?"

"Maybe a little. I don't think Kamlak even understands the full effects of what he's done. I certainly don't. But my presence loosens his spell's hold on people. Let me ride double with you tomorrow. I may be able to help some. At least enough for you to talk freely, I hope. I want to know how you ended up here, what stories you can tell."

His name was Pavresh. Her horse couldn't take a second rider, but they were able to commandeer a donkey for him to ride, and they went side by side. Her crew ended up behind in the march, so it was only the two of them talking, in a crowd of intense but silent progress. Over the next day he told her enough that she remembered him visiting the excavation site. But mostly she talked, the whole story of their journeys spilling out for the first time. He wanted to know everything they encountered. The challenges of the sea. The ways of the mysterious island people, as much as they had guessed them. The mix of peoples on the jetty who lived out an odd sort of lassitude beside the ocean. The ruins they had passed through inland from there.

She didn't mention the sailor who'd chosen to stay behind on the coast. In fact she said little about the people of her crew, because it was the peoples and places they discovered that interested him.

She spoke in depth about the city they had just left. She told of the villages to its south and how they came together. Of the lack of Eghsal's technologies but the sense of a different sort of advanced elegance she had sensed in the city. He was curious about the place and insisted on her pointing out Elsh to him. Harkala only caught a glimpse of her, far ahead.

"And she's learning to speak our language?" he asked.

"Only a little, so far. But she's trying and getting better."

He leaned back on his mount and said, "Oh, to hear the stories she might be able to share. I can't wait."

Maybe it was being near him, or maybe it was simply that once loosened her tongue couldn't be forced to silence, but she surprised herself with how easily she was able to simply talk, and how the magical hold on her loosened through the day.

He listened and prodded, sometimes circling back to much

earlier points and other times letting her simply tell what she thought would interest him. His questions sometimes fell into a fit of violent coughs, but he waved away her offer of a drink of water. When they paused for a break, he burned a pile of flower petals on a clay dish and dangled his head over the tiny fire, breathing in its smoke. After that break, his coughs grew less frequent and his breathing easier.

Based on the questions he asked, he seemed to memorize every detail she included and appeared to be sorting those details a mental map of the route they took. The day passed quickly by.

Late in the day, he said, "You know, it was your student, Nakhil, who directed me your way before, but I haven't seen him. Was he still working with you?"

"At first." Thinking his name made her miss his quick intelligence, his enthusiasm for the remains of the ships they had found. "But he began pursuing other studies. I think he will be a great scholar himself one of these days."

"I suppose he wasn't a sailor, anyway either. But how were you sure enough to dare the sea in your ship? You weren't a sailor, were you?"

Her a sailor? Maybe now she could claim that identity, but certainly not when she began. "I had help. Early on it was just Ekana and Sembaari. And Sembaari wasn't even a sailor himself, either, though he sometimes tried to claim he was."

Pavresh had gone still when she said that. Finally he managed to say, "Ekana? I knew an Ekana from Jarnur. A fisherman and a dancer?"

"A fisherman, yes." Was he a dancer as well? He'd danced to honor the ship when they first set out, hadn't he? "And he's graceful. So maybe he was a dancer once, too."

When he didn't say another word for the space of several dozens of their mount's steps, she asked, "Why? You think he's the one you knew?"

"I suppose he might be." He didn't sound pleased to admit that. "I would like to meet him when we stop tonight."

When he said that he would like to, Harkala had the sense that he was also saying the opposite, that he didn't want to meet Ekana at all. She had no guess what their history might be, and he didn't elaborate.

They rode late that day, well into dusk before finding a place to camp. It was directly below what was left of the naga cloud.

After caring for the horse—care that was perfectly coordinated with all the hundreds of others who were riding mounts—she and Pavresh made their way among the fires, looking for Ekana and the rest of her crew.

The trumpets played them all to sleep before she'd found them, and even Pavresh's ability to resist the magic wasn't enough to keep them from immediately laying their bedrolls near the closest fire and falling almost at once to sleep.

In the morning rush while everyone was supposed to be quickly eating the food to get them through the day, they tracked down the fire where her crew had slept.

"It *is* you," Pavresh said, before she'd even recognized Ekana.

Her crew sat rigidly as they ate, not yet loosened from the arcists' spell. Ekana was able to open his eyes wider at seeing Pavresh, but he couldn't talk.

Pavresh came close beside the fire and accepted the food her crew mechanically offered him. "Do not trust this man," he said.

"I've trusted him over and over on our journey, and he has saved us from disaster. What do you mean, we shouldn't trust him?"

"He's a liar and a betrayer."

Harkala opened her mouth to defend him, but Pavresh's presence was already loosening the magic's hold on the others. Ekana stood up and for a moment held his head high. Then he let it droop.

"It's true. I have been both of those. There have been times when I was so wrapped up in myself that I didn't realize what I was doing."

The look in his face was like the look he'd had when he refused to relinquish the ship to Harkala.

He handed his food to Sembaari as if he was done, no longer hungry despite the long day of travel ahead of them. "No, that makes it sound like an excuse. I knew and did it anyway. But it isn't the full story, Pavresh. I am not a liar here. I will *not* betray anyone again."

Harkala looked from one to the other, still not knowing what to make of this revelation. Ekana and Sembaari had come to her telling many conflicting and wild tales. But nothing of betrayals, and once she'd confronted them and forced the truth out, they'd been as reliable as stone.

"Perhaps," Pavresh said. "But how will anyone know when that promise is about to be betrayed as well?"

At that moment the drums shifted into a marching beat and a cry went up. People pointed to the sky. The naga cloud had reformed. It was twisting in a wind that didn't reach down to their level.

Or maybe it was simply dancing.

The naga's body knotted on itself and then straightened to point toward the north.

"The naga summons us home!" someone cried. A ripple went through the horde, a gasp of breath as the people realized that their tongues were loosening.

Soon others took up the cry as they pointed, gathered their packs, and prepared for the day's march. "The naga will guide us." "We go home with their blessing." "The naga have promised us victory."

The horns sounded for them to march. The magic urged them to be ready to fight for their homes, their families, their lives.

Enemies waited up ahead. The people of the horde prepared themselves for battle, prepared themselves to obey orders and overcome anything that stood in the way of their leaders' plan.

Urged on by the magic, they were sure that the naga had chosen the horde's leaders, that the mass of people were doing the naga's will by following the summons and doing as they were told.

Harkala and her crew made their way to the horses, the arcist Pavresh still shadowing them. As Ekana took to his saddle, he lifted red-rimmed eyes toward Pavresh and Harkala beside him.

"If I betray anyone this time, it will be the nagas. And the humans who claim to do their bidding." Looking up toward the cloud, he said, "A betrayal for a betrayal, a simple trade."

Without time for another word, they set off up into the mountains, weapons loose, minds already conforming to the units and squads of a well organized attack.

Chapter 26

Datri tracked down the soldiers who had arrested her husband. *If it was her husband*, but she couldn't afford to let herself doubt that part of the story, not now when she was finally so close. It took time and secrecy and knowing where to look, but what did such things matter? Her watchers could wonder about her activities. The princes might hear of her presence and grow curious.

None of that mattered, if she could find Jasfer and save him.

Except it did matter, if the princes tried to stop her. She couldn't be sure how long her network of spies and informants would keep her safe, the lies she allowed to spread, the hints that should lead the city's princes astray if they tried to investigate.

Datri sat at her husband's desk and rested her head in her hands. She had to think this through carefully. All her cleverness and manipulations to find Jasfer would mean nothing if the princes caught them both and sent them right to jail.

She summoned Yatim. "The soldiers watching us need to believe we've left, and I'm not sure our path out back will be good enough. What else can we do?"

"How will you convince them we're gone in the first place?"

"Leave that to me," Datri said. "I want you to find us ways in and out, completely unseen."

Yatim left to search, and Datri began planning their for-show departure. Someone could play their parts, dress in thick wraps as they set off in a carriage. No, it would have to be a train, heading for the Silk City. That meant someone who could pretend to be her for a longer span of time. She had several informants who might manage. No one here had really known her well enough for it to be a problem. By the time anyone reached the Silk City, it shouldn't matter.

Oh, let it not matter by then. She wanted to find Jasfer and leave. The manor was comfortable and familiar, but no longer home.

In between arrangements for her feigned departure, she learned all she could about that squad of soldiers, a minor jati that were no more than glorified market guards. More than one had secrets they would want to keep that way.

She chose one who wasn't even supposed to belong to the jati—or hadn't by birth, anyway. If the information in the temple records was right, he was born to a laborer jati and lied to get his way into the squad of soldiers. Liars were always good marks. They usually had more secrets waiting to be discovered.

She sent him a note expressing her wish to meet, made it appear to be a young woman from the neighborhood, and waited for an answer. In the meantime, she learned what she could of the other members of the squad, as well as other jatis of a similar makeup and low standing, just in case.

The guard responded in less than a day. Eager. Clueless. Probably not very smart, and certainly well beyond his depth. Perfect. When she met him, in a side room of a tisane bar with dim lamps and thick smoke, she wasted no time pretending to be anything but what she was.

"I need to know what happened to a man you arrested some twelve-days ago."

"I don't know anything about—"

"As soon as you remember, then I *don't* know anything about your parents. Or the jati you were born in. Or your other secrets But if you can't remember, then I might not forget what I know."

"My parents. My jati. What do you mean?"

"I think you know. So tell me. It was a beggar. You arrested him near the Didraon Market. He had a dog with him. You didn't arrest the dog, of course, only the beggar. The dog has been seen since, but he hasn't."

"I…I suppose I might know who that was."

"I care more about where he is now, not who he was."

"I'll try to find out."

"No, you *will* find out. Tomorrow night, same place. Or I can't promise I won't let some of what I know just slip out."

When he came the next night, he came in disguise. Datri groaned inside but on the outside remained impassive.

"I can't tell you." He glanced over his shoulder and then away.

Datri leaned close. "Are you sure? Remember what happens if you don't."

He exaggerated where his hand was on the table. "I can't. Whatever you do with this, it wasn't me who told you."

Datri slid her hand over and cupped the folded up paper he released from his hand. He was afraid, afraid of whoever had taken Jasfer. That might mean someone had realized who he was just like she did.

"I understand," was all she said. No promise not to reveal his secrets. It was always best to leave people unsure if they still had to worry about you.

He hesitated, dithering over whether to ask about her threat or not, but after a moment, he got up and left. Datri waited until she was in the manor to look at the paper.

The jail was one used for political prisoners. Well guarded and too small to slip inside unnoticed. Dartak had spent time there, after his plotting that led to Jaritta's coup was revealed. So had Samatrit.

Datri allowed herself a small smile. Much more likely to find the leverage she needed in a jail for the politically dangerous than it would have been in a common jail off on the edge of the city somewhere. The guards for the powerful were almost always already compromised.

Samatrit wouldn't want to see her again, especially so soon. No matter, she composed a quick letter in code to his wife Mashunri and set in place her supposed departure from the city.

***

The beggar missed his dog. Being in a jail cell was shameful and degrading, but not much more so than being an untouchable and a beggar were already. Being without his dog felt empty.

They should let prisoners keep their dogs. Though, how many of the prisoners in this jail were beggars missing their pets he couldn't say. No one let him out to wander the halls. Maybe he was the only one.

He had food, at least. He ate more—and more regularly—than he had as a beggar. And if it was rather bland and unappetizing, well that wasn't worse than what he'd eaten on the streets most days.

Maybe the people in charge should turn jails like this into a place for the beggars to live. When and if they wanted to. Some untouchables made do with shacks and abandoned homes, and there was food for those who could beg at least a few coins each day. But others huddled on the streets, their blankets growing damp in the ever present mix of drizzle and snow that came from the geysers' steam.

Not like he would ever have the power to make a difference for people on the streets like he had been. People in charge didn't listen to the likes of him.

When visitors came, he stayed silent.

They wanted something, but the beggar could never quite piece together what. They tried to figure out his name, as if he knew what it was. Tried to figure out who he'd spoken to, who his associates were. As if he talked to anyone or had anything resembling friends in this mad, cruel city. There was no one, apart from his dog. They spoke of names he didn't know, names he shied away from and forgot as soon as the visitors left.

They were fancy men, his visitors. Dressed in silks and followed by guards and attendants. Some spoke as if they knew him. Or thought they knew him and wanted him to settle their doubts. Some as if he was a complete stranger or a fraud.

Either way, he asked only after his dog. "You look smart." Not that he ever really saw the person he was speaking to. "Maybe you know where my dog is."

They would get angry at the question sometimes, repeat themselves more forcefully, but all he could say after the buzz of their voices rose into the end of their question was, "I don't know anything about that. But my dog, it was a mutt. Her. *She* was a mutt. Mottled fur, brown and white and black. A scar by one of her eyes. Liked to steal sausages and beg for other food. Have you seen her?"

When the woman showed up, at first he hid his face. He wasn't sure why, but he didn't want a woman to see him. Didn't want *this* woman to see him this way. He covered his head with his arms and waited for her to go away.

She didn't leave.

Her voice grated on until finally he looked out at her. He knew…no, no he didn't know her. Maybe he had seen her while begging. That was the explanation. She'd given him money or food. Or maybe she had run away from him, because that was what she should do on seeing him on the street.

Why didn't she run away this time? She should.

He tried to stare at her so she would flee. Was his a scary face? He thought it must be. It had been damaged by the guards, scarred. Was that this time? There had been an earlier time, other guards, but he couldn't remember what happened and when.

She had tears in her eyes, but she didn't run. She was still talking.

So he went to his usual question instead. "I miss my dog. Have you seen my dog?"

She shook her head and asked something else.

"You look smart. Very smart. I told those other people they looked smart, but they didn't look anything like you. Maybe you can find my dog."

"Maybe I can." For the first time he actually heard the words she said.

He sat up straight and waited for her to say more.

"Tell me about your dog so we can find it."

He told her the dog's colors, told her where they used to go.

"The sewers are warm when it's snowing. May not smell good to a smart woman like you, but I think my nose is broken inside. I don't smell it anymore."

He cocked his head, thinking back to the last time he'd seen the dog. "I guess my dog's nose works fine. I'm surprised it stayed with me down there. Maybe those smells don't bother a dog. She was a good girl. But she might not be able to find her way alone. She's probably on the streets. Or someone's guard dog."

"You may have to show me. Will you come with me?"

The beggar stared at the hand she held out toward her. Hands were frightening. They beat, they punched, they arrested. When someone gave a beggar something, they didn't hand it over. They threw it, dropped it, anything to get them away from the untouchable as soon as possible.

But a hand held out couldn't be right.

He pulled back but stopped. Something about that hand reassured him. If it had been one of the men in their fancy clothes, he wouldn't have touched the hand for anything. Promises to find his dog were not worth a thing if the hand snatched the promise away, replaced it with pain. Was this hand as empty as those would have been? She had no guards, no attendants with her in the cell. Her clothes were not made of silk, but something sturdy for traveling—and well stained with the travels she must have taken already.

He ran his own hand over his face and cautiously reached out.

When she took his hand, the world lost its solidity. Gravity was meaningless when half the objects in the room wanted to rise up in flight, when his body lost any sense of up and down.

Someone was coming into the room as he teetered. Maybe she had brought an attendant after all. When he tried to follow the new arrival's approach, the beggar's legs gave way.

He swooned and fell into the arms of the woman who would find him his dog.

At last.

***

Yatim could carry Jasfer, but it messed up the agreement she had with the guard out front. The plan had been for Jasfer to wear Yatim's servant garb and leave with her while Yatim stayed behind, dressed as a guard, to leave a little later on his own. That way anyone who saw her arrive with one person would see her leave with one and not be suspicious.

Well, if the guard wanted to keep his side hustle selling fire liquor to the prisoners a secret, he'd have to find a way to accommodate the change in plans.

The guard was not pleased.

"No, no, no. That is not the agreement. I'll be caught."

"You'll be caught at this point, anyway. You think your bosses will just forget that this prisoner was there?"

"I blame it on the new guard we hired." He gestured at Yatim. "This tall man who disappears shortly after the prisoner. But how do I claim that, if I let him waltz right out with the prisoner in his arms?"

"He's passed out. Don't you have ways to bring your sick prisoners to be healed?"

"We have a doctor who can come. But mostly, when they get sick…" He made a hand motion across his neck, like someone has died. "Not our problem much longer if they don't get better on their own."

"So he died. Not such a stretch, after years on the streets. And after how he's been treated here."

"Then the doc comes to check the body." The guard shook his head and began shuffling some papers. "No, let me think. You'll just have to put him back in his cell and come back another time."

"We do that, we let slip the story of your liquor sales."

He held up his hands as if desperate to stop them. "You don't need to do that. Let me see here." Having finished with the papers on his desk, he opened a drawer.

With the speed of a younger man, Yatim let Jasfer slump

against the wall and in the same move spun around the desk and wrapped his arms around the jail guard. The guard didn't even have time to move.

"Why did you do that?" Datri asked.

"Look in the drawer." Yatim wrapped some rope around the man, securing him to his chair.

Datri rummaged through the drawer, which was full of small pieces of paper, an extra set of pen nibs, and a blotter that had been used so thoroughly it seemed more ink than whatever material it had been made of. And among all that mess lay a large, metal whistle.

"Planning to summon someone to arrest us?" Datri asked. She slipped the whistle into her pocket. If he played things right, he could claim that they were lying about his side business and might get away with it.

The guard glowered as Yatim tied the knots tight.

"Whether you were planning to or not, you have your excuse for how he got free." Datri gave him a brief sneer then schooled the look into the same calm one she'd used to convince him to let them inside in the first place. "But remember, I still know all about your jugs of fire liquor. So when they come and free you, when they ask you what you know of our identities, it might be wise to change some of the details so you don't get caught."

Yatim picked Jasfer back up from the floor, and they hurried from the prison, just as dawn was lighting up the city. The prison was near the Grand Assembly. Datri hated that place. The quicker away the better. They came in through a maintenance tunnel Yatim had found.

It was tight, with how Yatim had to carry Jasfer, an old access point for the pipes that brought water to the wealthy manors. The only access point had been around two pipes, so he'd had to knock down a wall to let them pass through. It was good enough, she thought as they let the wall carpet fall back over the opening. What did she care about dirt and scurrying creatures if it could bring her—and Jasfer—back home?

Unseen, she prayed to whatever gods would listen. Even so,

they wouldn't dare stay for long. For now all that mattered was getting Jasfer into the house and hoping no officials showed up too soon asking questions. Was it really him? The excitement of the escape had kept her from wondering. Now the full truth settled in. This was him, her husband, returned from the dead.

As soon as Yatim laid him on a bed to sleep, Datri knelt down on the floor beside him, laid her head against his caved in chest, and waited for him to wake up.

***

There was no dog here. The beggar looked around the room and then around the house, but the dog was nowhere. There was no sign a dog had ever lived in those hallways.

They were good hallways for exploring, though. The windows were all covered with thick curtains, which he liked. No light leaking outside, no way for anyone to see him. He found back routes through the house, side doors that led outside—he wasn't ready to go outside yet, so he didn't take them—and even a tunnel that looked worth investigating.

The woman didn't like him wandering. But it was what he was good at, what he had always done. When she saw she couldn't keep him in just a few rooms, she tried to stay with him. If she was there, he spent the whole time asking her about the dog, telling her what he knew, guessing where she should look.

But sometimes he wanted to explore all alone. Even a dog might not find all the places he came to.

One time the woman rushed him into the tunnel on purpose. The two of them hurried inside and then huddled there for what seemed like a long time. There were voices back in the manor, harsh voices, the kind of voices that made him want to hide. They stayed there until the voices were gone.

He liked that. Liked the tunnel, liked being there with the woman. Liked that the voices never found him.

One room made him nervous. It was the family chapel, down in the basement and near the back, where the steam beds warmed the room. It made him think of fires and burning and the scars on his legs. And other scars, too. The small flames burning in the lamps made him picture scars that weren't his own.

He couldn't think through whose or why they mattered.

When he was walking with the woman one time, she steered them into one particular room.

"This was our room. Do you remember, Jasfer?"

Jasfer? Why did she call him that? "Was the dog here? Where is it now?"

She seemed to have tears in her eyes, but then she usually did since they'd come here. Maybe this place made her sad. "Once we find the dog, we should go somewhere else," he said. Because he wanted to comfort her, because he didn't want her to cry. Where would they go, though? She wouldn't want to live on the streets.

"We should, you're right." The woman wiped a hand across her eyes. "Your sister is the leader of a new city. We should go there."

"Do I have a sister?" That didn't sound wrong, exactly, but he couldn't recall.

In another room, she lingered as if to give him more time to study it. To remember it?

"Your parents' room. You would have come running here in the night, if you were scared."

"I don't remember being scared," he said. "Except of the soldiers." A vision of flames crossed his memory. "And fire. I don't like how it burns my legs. Even after the flames are put out."

"That's a memory, Jasfer. Hold that. I was burned, too. We lay in our beds while we recovered. Do you recall?"

He frowned. "Did we have a dog then? I remember a fire in a shop. And the dog rescuing me. And a pot or bowl or something like that."

If she answered him, he didn't hear it. Maybe there had been more than one fire. Maybe that was all memory was, a burning of the past, a turning of the past into flames. And somehow those flames cut him off from the things the woman remembered.

The woman brought a dog to the house the next day. It was a kind dog, and he put his hands into the fur around his neck. And even when it growled, he didn't pull away. The dog calmed down beneath his touch and curled up to sleep near his feet.

But it wasn't his dog.

He went with her the next time to look in his old haunts. The woman insisted on him wearing a heavy coat and a hat that covered his face.

As if he would let himself be seen anyway. He led the way into the tunnel beneath the house.

After a few turns, they came to a lower tunnel that was narrower and older. She balked and asked something about it being safe, pointing at the pipes and ventways. He kept walking. There was something familiar about the tunnel, as if he'd traveled this way before. If so, it was before he had found the dog, before...before his memories went smokey and lost.

He avoided the tunnels where they would have to wade—for the woman's sake and that of her guard. They had switched a few tunnels, back and forth, and maybe passed a block or two away from the manor, when they had to climb up to the street.

The sun was setting. That made it a good time to be out. Bad time for begging, but a good time for what they were doing. Who could recognize a silhouette? No human would, but a dog might smell them, just like it would any time of day or night.

Dusk was long, but the walk was longer to the place he used to sleep, hidden behind the bushes. They kept their heads down and covered. He called for the dog, peeked into the tunnels below. This was not a good place, not anymore. He'd been found here by the strange cultists. That much he remembered. So as soon as he was sure the dog wasn't there, he widened his search.

They went by the shell of a shop he remembered. Only when he was there, standing outside its burnt out shell, did he realize it was the fire he'd half remembered before. Fires and memories, they all consumed themselves.

A dozen dogs were in the empty marketplace where he'd often begged. They were eating the refuse left by the traders and their customers, and when the beggar entered, they rounded on him, snarling. He called out like he used to, a whistling sound he'd invented, and some of the dogs stopped their growling.

He whistled again, and one dog slunk toward him. He crouched and opened his arms. The dog didn't run to him, but it did come close, circle once, and lie down right in front of him, its head resting on its dirty, matted paws.

"I guess that's our dog," the woman said.

The beggar didn't answer. He lay down beside the dog and drifted off to sleep.

***

"You aren't getting Jasfer back, not really."

Datri grimaced and wouldn't meet Yatim's eyes. "What do you mean? We already found him."

"That man in there? The one you keep calling Jasfer?" Yatim cinched tight a bundle of clothes they would be taking with them back to Chaitanshehar.

"Of course *him*. I call him Jasfer, because that's who he is. You can see it in his face. Disfigured, but it's still there. And the scars on his legs—"

"Oh, it's his body, sure. That man in there has Jasfer's body. I'm sure if we could trace its history back, we'd discover a moment when it was Jasfer." Yatim quivered as if only with the greatest effort could he keep himself from flinging the packed supplies around the room in a rage. "And Jasfer was my master, of course, but also my friend for many years. Even longer than he was your husband. I wish it was him as much as anyone, even as much as you do."

Datri opened her mouth to argue, but of course he was right. Yatim was loyal much beyond the loyalty of a servant.

"But that body is not your husband, not my friend. His mind

has gone." He grabbed the packed supplies, as many as he could load in his arms, and stomped off toward the waiting mules.

His mind was gone. She couldn't deny that fact. Would she ever get it back? With careful tending and familiar surroundings, maybe she could. But the soldiers were growing more brazen. They'd stopped watching the manor when she'd sent her spy away to the Silk City pretending to be her, and she didn't think they'd been seen sneaking back in. The curtains kept any sign of their presence or activity hidden. But that hadn't stopped the officials from coming by to look for Jasfer after his escape. Datri heard rumors from her contacts, rumors that made her wish she was already back in Chaitanshehar.

They had to leave, and the sooner the better.

So now, in the dark of night, not wanting to light extra lamps to give any clue that they were awake and moving about, she went down to the stable. Yatim was double checking that all was ready. They would take five mules—the last that belonged to the manor plus two extras they had bought with some of the wealth that Datri had once wielded without thought. They loaded them up with all the supplies they might need for their journey, and as much extra food as they could scrounge up without drawing anyone's notice as well. Each of the people would be mounted on a horse. The dog should be able to keep up with them, even as they took the rugged route across the lava field and over the mountain ridge. The other way might be easier, but it would be patrolled by soldiers.

"Maybe it would be kinder to let him stay here," Yatim said. "Kalvandi will be here to care for him. It's a familiar home. Maybe another twelve-day or a month of sleeping in his old room, of resting, of seeing the familiar hallways. Maybe it would bring his mind back."

Datri shook her head as she checked her horse. "No. He has to come with us. He is Jasfer—still, in some way. And he is Jaritta's brother and my husband. He must come to Chaitanshehar."

She sighed, a sigh that turned into a groan filled with all

the heartache and uncertainty that came along with the joy of finally finding him.

"He *is* Jasfer still, somehow. And even if he never regains what he used to be, his place is with me, wherever we end up."

When she turned around, she found Jasfer standing in the doorway to the stable, his traveling cloak already wrapped tightly around him.

"I'm ready to go," he said. The squint-eyed dog came up beside his leg, looking like a guard dog already well versed in the ways of the wilderness.

Datri closed her eyes and released a deep breath. That was the answer, then. They would leave Romnai together, leave it likely for good.

Once they had finished their preparations, Datri helped Jasfer into the saddle of his horse. He rode as if he remembered how. As she stepped away, he said something in a very quiet voice that sounded nothing like the innocent voice he'd used since they'd rescued him.

She had to lean close, and he said it once again. "Thank you, Datri.

CHAPTER 27

There was food at last. Not an overabundance, but enough for now, enough for hope. Jaritta gave Nataravi a fresh slice of pear while she gathered up the chickpeas that her neighbor had kindly roasted for them to eat.

The harvest had been good, with new, low-sunlight crops already seeded to hopefully provide some additional food through the winter. The mumbler tribes who had come hadn't only traded some moderate amounts of food, but brought them seeds of plants that could grow even later in the year. Some they cultivated up near the city, where they might clear the snow to keep the plants alive. Most of what they had needed more warmth, so they planted those seeds down at the edges of the swamp where the winter would be mild.

Jaritta still worried how they would get enough for everyone. If the harvests would continue to be enough. If the mumblers would still bring food to trade. But the urgency was pulled back, with space for them to enjoy what they had.

Back in their own chambers, a new, small pot of honey sat on the counter. Fruits and nuts and sesame seeds were in small dishes beside it, and the wealth of it, the thought she could just eat any of it anytime was staggering. Most likely she would end up using the various ingredients in other dishes, but for now she drizzled honey on some of the roasted chickpeas and shared them with her daughters.

Now she could focus her worries on Chandri. The letter they'd recently received at least gave her an update, told her that he'd still been alive at the time it was written. It had taken a long time to reach her—she couldn't help but wonder if he was still alive and safe, couldn't help but wonder what new things they were learning about Pashun's road into the mountains and what it all meant. Earthquakes and armies, and only the gods knew what else.

When they had finished eating, Nataravi asked, "Can we see the chickpea field?"

She was on the verge of saying no when she stopped. They spent far too much time huddled up here inside the city. It wasn't good for the girls. It wasn't good for herself. They all needed time to wander and see different things. "Yes, let's see what there is to see down there. It might not be chickpeas right now, but we can find out."

Juishika had done something to the switchback pathway to loosen the arcist power of Pavresh's spell as long as they stayed on the path. It didn't make descending easy, but Jaritta could manage without needing an arcist guide.

Even so, getting to the bottom of the pathway was almost too much for Nataravi. Ovitiva fell asleep on Jaritta's back before they'd made it halfway down, and Nataravi was asking to be carried shortly after that.

"I can't carry you, Nataravi. You're too big now, and I have Ovitiva on my back."

Nataravi was on the verge of crying when she saw something across the falling river beside them. "Who is that?"

Jaritta looked but didn't see anyone. "I don't know. What did you see?"

"Not what, who. A person looking at us from the bushes. But they're gone now."

Jaritta stared at the place her daughter had indicated. Children said nonsense things sometimes, and Jaritta still saw nothing. Nataravi kept walking, the person in the bushes and wanting to be carried both forgotten. Jaritta glanced back again as they descended, but there wasn't even a hint of movement. Surely just a bit of childish fancy. Oh to be that age again, when she could forget so fast.

They rested at the bottom, ate a quick snack, and drank some water.

Maybe they could relax for a bit longer. Jaritta stretched her legs out and half closed her eyes.

Not a chance.

Both girls prodded her awake before she could even claim to have taken a nap.

"Oh, fine. Let's get a look at some of the fields."

The wind was cold, even this close to the lava, and snow was falling on the peaks. But low down, there was a warmth that surely came from the ground itself, protecting the seedlings, propelling their growth.

A green blur shaded the brown soil, a hint and a promise of the crops to come. Jaritta had no idea what crop these would be. Up close, they were tiny blades with two leaves, one on each side like a hilt.

"We'll eat this someday."

"This exact one?" Nataravi's eyes grew wide.

That was a promise she couldn't keep, but a harmless one to make. "Who knows? It might well be. I'll try to find it again when it's harvested."

They wandered a little longer along the paths of the field. Jaritta set Ovitiva down so she could feel the thick soil and touch the plants as they grew. But it felt soon when Nataravi said, "Can we go back now, mom? I don't like the person watching us."

Jaritta froze, all but her eyes. A chill ran up and down her body. "Who's watching us?"

She looked carefully in every direction. Was there someone hidden in the field breaks? In among the swamp trees?

"I don't know, mom. Just someone." She pointed vaguely toward the trees, but Jaritta saw nothing there.

Kids make up stories, she reminded herself. Maybe that was all it was, a story she made up because of the shape of the trunks or a vine tangled in the bushes.

"Yes, let's get going home," she said, still moving slowly, still studying the shadows beneath the trees and other plants and anyplace a person might hide.

The city kept some farmers down here, and soldiers as well, though the earlier fears of Pashun sending its soldiers against them had eased over the past year. But neither farmers nor their own soldiers should be skulking about the edges of the field. And what about the person Nataravi said she'd seen across the river? There was no way to the city from that side of the river, so there was no reason for the guards to patrol the area.

Had that been a tree trunk and unfamiliar shadows too?

Or mumblers spying on them? They were working on good relations with the nearest villages and traveling bands, but that didn't mean all interactions with the various tribes would go well. Even a friendly tribe might want to observe them from hiding.

Even worse if it was soldiers from Pashun, returning to harass them, to finish the work of destroying them

Best not to let the girls see her fear.

"If we're speedy we can try another of the new foods we got. How fast can you run to the trail, Nataravi?

Jaritta jogged to keep Nataravi close, but let her win the race. She looked back over her shoulder whenever she didn't have to keep her eyes on the trail ahead. No person appeared among the brush. The climb took much longer than coming down had, Nataravi's legs too short and her body much too tired. Jaritta held her in front while Ovitiva rode on her back. The climb felt eternal, an unfair and unjust sentence given to her by the capricious gods.

Neither she nor the girls saw any more figures in the shadows along the way, even as dusk fell before they made it to the top.

***

They were not the only ones to notice the faces in the brush. Rumors ran through the city of strange people glimpsed at the edge of sight, of being watched from a distance. Whoever they were, they never came close to the city proper, but often at the edges there would be a vague hint of movement, of some sudden motion just out of sight.

Jaritta climbed to the top of the wall and spent long minutes at a time staring into the sparse trees to discover whatever truth there was to find. One of those times, Azheeran joined her.

"Are they mumblers?" she asked him when they'd stood in silence for some time but seen nothing.

"Possible, but I don't think so. You always comment on our pale faces. Pale faces aren't easy to hide in the shadows."

"What if they're covering their faces somehow, so they don't show up. Don't you think they might do that?"

Azheeran leaned forward for a moment as if to see something that caught his eye. When he stood upright again, he shook his head. "Some villagers will paint their faces, yes, and even wear masks. But I think your people would comment on that instead. They would notice."

"My people? This whole city is my people now. Including the mumblers." It was more reflex than arguing.

Azheeran didn't respond directly. "That would be part of the rumors, that difference, unless they're so good at hiding their faces."

Probably correct. The people of Eghsal had been trained from childhood to notice the pale faces of the mumblers. It was in their stories, the scary enemies who lived away from the cities, who might turn into a terrifying force of fighters if the people of the cities weren't vigilant. Pavresh would probably have said there was some arcist magic in how those stories influenced everyone who grew up in the cities.

"So who do you think it is then?"

Azheeran tapped a finger against the parapet. "I wish I knew."

A bird flew over their heads, a hawk of some kind soaring on the air currents before it banked into a sudden dive. No fear of the strangers, whoever those people were. The hunters were finding as much game as usual. No sign any animals were changing their patterns any more than they had since she'd brought the people here. So if it wasn't their frightened imaginations all playing off each other, then the strangers were good at not disturbing the wildlife.

"Valni might know more." Jaritta gathered up her basket and the extra wrap she'd brought when the day was cooler. She had to go back for the girls soon—Juishika was watching them, but she couldn't force her to do so all day. But first she could at least look for Valni. "Shall we see what she has to say?"

Azheeran held out his hand, gesturing for her to lead the way. Valni often spent her day on the wall, when she wasn't patrolling off on her own. She had a post inside a room in the center of the wall, the closest thing their wall had to a tower. The windows on all sides let her observe the land below with its switchbacks, as well as the city behind her, as far as the rising buildings allowed her to see.

Valni strode out before Jaritta could knock. "You're here about the people in the shadows."

It wasn't a question, but Jaritta nodded.

"I don't know. They're too elusive, whoever they are. Will you grant me leave to investigate on my own?"

A quick glance at Azheeran, and then she asked, "Where would you go? How long would you need to be gone?"

"Not long, I hope. They've most often been seen near the fields. So a day in the margins of the swamp to lay plans. If I find nothing that day, I may make myself a blind to hide in for another day at most. I expect I'll learn what I need to soon enough."

"Azheeran?" she asked. "We're two of the council, such as it is." Two of a much diminished leadership for the city. "Do we need to consult the others, or shall we make the decision ourselves?"

"She may go. That is my judgment. You decide for the others."

Jaritta glanced down the hill and saw some movement off to the side. She froze and looked closer. Only a wild sheep, climbing up from the swamp. Several others as well. They should get a hunter over to bring down one or two for food. But before she could even say anything, the herd was gone, over a fold in the hillside and out of sight.

If she left the question of the identity of the shadowed strangers to what they could see from here, sheep and birds is all they'd ever know for sure. Every shadow would seem to be the mysterious watchers, and the reports and rumors would multiply. They needed Valni to find out whatever she could to bring certainty to the city.

"Yes, do so. But put yourself in no greater danger than necessary, and report back as soon as you are able."

***

Valni found tracks of the mysterious watchers everywhere. They even came close to the city wall and into the rocks on either side. How were they not compelled by Pavresh's spell to join with the city—to unite themselves with it or to go away? Was the spell weakening? It had been more than a year since the arcist had last been here to keep it strong, but Juishika and the other students seemed capable of maintaining it. She felt its effects as she climbed downward, especially when she veered away from the switchback trail to make her own route.

Did that mean the strangers had some sort of protection? An enemy arcist might find a way to protect a band of soldiers, and Pashun certainly had more than its share of soldier jatis to choose from.

But one competent enough to stay hidden even from her eyes? Valni doubted that part.

The other way they had found to resist the spell's pull was to have a task, to focus on the role they were given and their identity within that role. It was how Valni had always been able to descend to the fields and out into the swamp. She felt the pull of the magic, but knowing that she was serving the city in descending, she was able to resist it.

So that seemed like the most likely explanation. Whoever these watchers were, they knew their role in a bigger task, and they carried it out in a secrecy unbroken by the magic.

No number of footprints could tell her who had such a devotion to a bigger task.

Secrecy was second nature to someone trained by the falcon jati, though. When she reached the fields, she slipped quickly into the line of trees and brambles that edged the first field, and she was certain that no one would be able to see her as the day progressed.

Valni caught her first glimpse of a watcher sometime shortly before midday. Someone was in the brush of a field opposite her. Valni crawled along for a better view. The watcher had chosen their hiding place well. Valni could make out their location but little else. Shadows hid any details that might let her identify the person.

It was a soldier. That much she felt certain of, simply because of how the person stood in their hiding spot, poised and alert for attack. She crawled closer to learn more. The soldier had no sword out, nor a bow. Many of the soldier jatis of Pashun placed such great confidence in their weapons, that this fact surprised her. Her admiration grew.

By the time she made her way around a thicker cluster of trees to where she could see the soldier's hiding place again, the soldier was gone. Valni froze for a long time. Had she revealed herself? No one, even a well trained soldier should have noticed her approach. But what if she had fallen out of practice, had done something silly to expose herself?

The soldier might be watching her now, might be lying in wait. Her instincts told her to flee. She backed away into the thicker brush, every sense alert for someone or something to jump in beside her, to fall on her head, to attack.

Nothing happened, though she waited almost without moving for hours. When dusk was settling over the fields, she slowly crept from her hiding place and into the field. She lay flat on the ground and listened. A swamp rail—a small, black bird rarely seen but often heard at night—made a trilling call somewhere toward the swamp.

Was it a real bird, or an imitation? She waited as the call was repeated several times—just the same as it often was. There was no flicker of a campfire off through the trees, no sound of soldiers stumbling along through the undergrowth. Clear signs that whoever these soldiers were, they were more disciplined than the Pashun jatis she had known in her brief time there.

The moon-tinted sky was too bright for her to want to stand upright. She crawled along the edge of the field, stopping often to look and listen for anything out of the ordinary. It took all night to make her way back to the switchbacks so she could climb to safety.

The sun rose to expose her on the path. She turned around and saw the figures. Twelve, fifteen, twenty women, they stood in plain view. Only one wore the traditional headgear, the brim made to look like a falcon's beak. But all wore the traditional cloaks of the falcon jati, strips of leather that could confound most sword strikes, and all carried a staff that matched the one in Valni's hand. The staff and symbol of the falcon jati.

Valni stiffened her back and placed her staff before her. Proud and unafraid, that was what a falcon jati-trained warrior should be, and so she would play that role, no matter how scared she might be. Any one of them would be a challenge for her, if they decided to fight. Against them all together, she stood no chance. And difficult to see how Chaitanshehar could stand at all if they ascended the trail, resisting the magic, bent on attacking.

The one with the headgear stepped forward. Placing the end of her staff on the ground directly before her, as if to channel its energy, the woman spoke, not a shout but her voice carried easily through the still air. "Traitor."

Valni flinched back. "No. I am no traitor. I am a falcon jati warrior."

"The High Prince is not in your city."

"I don't suppose he's out in the woods there, either. Why have you left Romnai?"

The other women muttered against her, and one took a step up the incline.

"The city you serve is not deserving of a falcon jati warrior. The woman who rules it is not a true High Prince."

No, but the current High Prince was in place because of treachery and the failure of their own jati. Valni recovered her poise and looked down at the women below her. "You speak of a true High Prince, when the man who claims that title in Romnai earned it by treachery? The High Prince is dead, and not by my failure."

Maybe wrong to taunt them. Several jumped ahead of the others as if to attack, but the one in charge held them back with a gesture. Valni took two steps upward without turning around.

"The falcon jati serves the High Prince, whoever that is. It is not our role to decide who deserves the title or not. We protect one with our lives, and then protect the next, even if he betrayed our former master. The details do not matter, only our honor. It is for this that you are declared traitor, heretic, cast out from all claims to the jati." She strode upward, her empty hand extended forward. "Now give me your staff."

"Honor?" Valni spit out the word. "No. If you had honor you would hear the call of this city and wish to join it. You would see its leaders—not one High Prince, but a group of wise leaders who fill the role he should have all along. They are the ones our jati must serve. It is the ultimate fulfillment of our vows. If it comes to betrayal, I declare you, and all who serve the pretender in Romnai, traitors."

She turned around and took two steps up, as if her words were a shield, a final statement of such power it would protect her.

She heard the staff flying at her as she took the second step and spun around. She couldn't get her own weapon up in time to protect herself as the staff struck her shoulder strong enough to make it go numb. Throwing a staff was a last resort, a fighter's move that few mastered.

No one else threw a staff, but they began to climb, looking ready to fight this time.

Valni levered herself upright with her staff and her functioning arm and took off up the path, a dozen shadowing figures rushing up behind in the sallow morning sunlight, chasing her down like a skittish prey. She gave herself to the power of the arcist magic, let it lend her what speed it could. And prayed that it would slow her sisters down enough for her to escape.

***

Jaritta helped Valni up onto the wall. The fact she let herself be helped at all told how weary she was or how out of sorts by something that had happened. Jaritta studied the switchback pathway, but the figures they had glimpsed at first had stopped pursuing Valni and were nowhere to be seen.

Jaritta waited while Valni caught her breath.

Finally she couldn't stand wondering any longer and asked, "Who were those people? Did they hurt you?"

Valni shrugged and winced when she moved her shoulder. "No, I mean, yes. They hurt me, but not life threatening. Nothing like what they could have done."

Jaritta waited, impatient.

Valni gingerly moved her left arm then pushed herself upright with her right arm and the staff. Only when she was standing straight did she say, "They were falcon jati warriors. How far they've fallen."

"Why did they stop chasing you?"

"Maybe they merely wanted to scare me. To see me run away like a coward." Valni looked back down the slope, loathing and betrayal battling in her expression. "I'm not worth it to them, not worth chasing down like a frightened rabbit when I'm already running away as it is."

She tried to shoulder her way past the crowd of worried onlookers, but when she bumped someone with her left side, she cried out in pain.

"Let's get you to someone who has medicine," Jaritta said. "Then we can see about sending soldiers down there to clear them out."

Valni rounded on her. "Absolutely not. Do *not* engage them

in battle. Do not fight them or send anyone down the slope without consulting me first."

"Sure, sure." Jaritta held up her hands in surrender. "I won't send anyone."

She walked beside Valni as they headed toward the home of a man who sold medicine. Now that the wall was behind them, Valni refused any offer of assistance, though the pain of her shoulder was clear on her face.

"Why are they here then? Should we be preparing for an attack?"

"No, I don't think so." She leaned hard on her staff to keep walking, and her voice sounded strained. "Not from them."

"Is it you they're after, then?"

Valni shook her head. Her pursed lips told that the pain was too much for her to speak through. Jaritta walked beside her in silence.

When they reached the medicine house, Valni took a deep breath to steel herself. Then in a rush she said, "Maybe they want to attack, but I don't think so. Maybe the new High Prince is out here for some reason, but I doubt that as well. They've been demoted from that role, but their masters still recognize their fighting prowess, so they'll make use of them. Or else they're out here looking for a new master. They're hoping to regain their lost honor."

She paused and knocked on the door then continued to explain her thoughts while they waited for the door to open. "And I doubt they're after me. They probably didn't even know I was here. Certainly the princes they serve wouldn't care about one single soldier when they have many jatis at their command."

The door opened, and Valni ducked her head to enter. As she stood in the doorway, she paused and said over her shoulder, "No, what I guess is they're watching us, and if it comes to it, holding us here to make sure we stay put."

As if they had any thoughts of moving now, of all times, when they had food and calm and even hope for a real future. "For what?"

"For someone to accept their service, to restore their honor. If I must guess, I'd say they're expecting a bigger force that's coming this way, some prince so mighty that he's sure to crush us."

Valni shut the door behind her, leaving behind only those words of despair.

What good was an absent arcist's weakening spell against such an image of the future? Jaritta trudged away, paying no attention to where she went.

CHAPTER 28

Ellechandran called for a halt and crouched down close to the road. He put his ear to the ground, but it wasn't sound he was hearing but a deep vibration he felt through his whole body.

"Everyone off the trail," he called. "There's something coming." *Not really people*, the words of the trader in his former village came back to him. What were they then, these empty bodies who used the road?

They'd taken some days to scout out the road from their old village, and eventually they had made it as far as the vast bore hole into the mountains. They had studied it for some time but decided not to proceed into that darkness. It was enough to tell them the cause of the earthquake. Enough to head back home and give Jaritta the information they had. They still didn't know as much as he wanted to know. Was that tunnel back there itself a threat to Chaitanshehar? What would the people of Pashun do next? But they'd been away long enough. It was time to hurry home.

And now, several days after they'd left that tunnel behind, it sounded like those not-people had passed back through the tunnel and were coming right up behind them, drawn back toward the Eghsal Valley. There was no cover close by, so they scrambled up the ridge. Ellechandran kept looking down over his shoulder for what could be making that vibration. Just as they were nearing the top, the thrumming sensation finally resolved into a sound, the echoing noise of many drums and footsteps all lined up together.

A flock of birds took off up ahead and also headed to the safety of the ridge. The scouts made it over the edge and dropped down so they could still watch for activity below.

Nothing came into view.

The noise swelled, though still far away. Trumpets and horse hooves added to the mix, but very few voices. The trumpets and drums gave him a nauseated feeling, and if he were any closer he feared he might be sick. Only the echoing mountainside interrupted their strident noise.

Why no voices? He thought of crossing the difficult barrens between Old Eghsal City and where they'd founded the new city of Chaitanshehar. Even tired, weary people spoke and sang and cheered each other on. Early on, their procession was full of all kinds of noises, the chatter of stories told, the notes of many songs. Some of that died away as the journey progressed. They'd been battered by hunger and the cold, uncertain of what lay ahead or who might be coming behind. But all those factors couldn't stop them from breaking into chants and urging each other onward now and then.

How did a group so large it shook the mountains not do the same?

Was it because they weren't people?

Keeping low, they made their way parallel to the road as well as the line of the mountains allowed, heading back toward the source of that noise to spy on it. They reached a turn in the ridge where it doubled back and took a sweeping route around a high valley. A good place for game, likely. A place where mumblers might have a village or a hunting camp. No sign of smoke rising from the jumbled rocks and low shrubs that filled the valley.

The road below cut straight across the mouth of the valley, leaving their ridge behind.

"Let's wait here," he said. Stones and clumps of dirt skittered down the slope beneath them as the source of the noise came ever closer. They made themselves comfortable behind rocks and hidden by the drooping branches of the hardscrabble bushes.

Ellechandran laid a blanket down at the very edge of the ridge so he could watch. When he lay down, Chhayasheela came and lay on her belly beside him, chin propped in her hands.

The vanguard rounded the curve. Ellechandran thought he'd been lying still, but the sight of so many people (or *not-people*) on the road made him find a new depth of stillness. He stared, moving only his eyes, as wave after wave of them came marching down the road.

When the leading edge reached their side of the valley mouth, it paused. The ones behind kept bunching in, tighter and tighter until a mass that must have numbered in the thousands poured upward into the valley. They marched in double time while the main body of the horde lingered at the road.

So much for game in that valley. Any deer and other animals would be scared away for sure.

Where there had been no smoke before, at the upper end of the valley, a sudden stream of white and gray smoke rose above the rocks. It was the smoke of a clean-burning fire suddenly put out as its tenders broke camp. The very thing he'd imagined, a hunting camp or village tucked into the edge of the mountains.

And now they were found out. Ellechandran's throat closed in horror. Why take time to put out the fire? Just run! The marching soldiers picked up their pace, racing up the valley. Closing in on the fleeing mumblers.

He couldn't see them, could only imagine the situation. Would they make it up into the mountains beyond? He hoped so, but the soldiers moved so fast. He'd never seen such an organized force, perfect efficiency and perfect violence implied in their pass through the valley. And then back down to the main group—as if the kind of mindless bloodshed that must have taken place up there was as commonplace as removing a spider from the corner wall of a house.

Other soldiers continued to arrive while the small group was clearing the valley. The thousands looked like a mere drop as it joined back into the army on the road. The whole horde continued marching north and west below them, toward Pashun.

Where it would easily overwhelm any city that tried to resist it.

The road couldn't contain their numbers, so they spilled out to either side wherever the land around allowed it.

"Home," Chhayasheela said, the word a whisper and a released breath at once.

Chaitanshehar didn't stand a chance. Jaritta and the girls didn't stand a chance. He laid his head in the dirt and contemplated the distance and how they could outflank the army and reach Jaritta before they did.

"We'll have to hurry," he said. "They're steady, but they'll follow the road to Pashun first. We can go faster if we cut across and bring a warning."

And then what? The city's paltry defenses wouldn't do much against such numbers. Pavresh's spell might give them some safety, but would even that last? Would it affect soldiers who were more like empty bodies than real people? Maybe better to abandon the city, look for some safety by scattering into the foothills.

But then he looked back at the trickle of smoke still rising from the far end of the valley below. What kind of safety would even that be?

Chhayasheela interrupted his thoughts. "I don't mean our home *now*. I mean our old home, the village. It's right on the path of this stampede of soldiers."

They had nearly returned that far, the folds and slopes of the mountains becoming more familiar. The villagers were doomed. People he'd grown up with. People who had cast him out, it was true. But still, people he had known from birth.

"We have to warn them!" Chhayasheela was standing over him, shouting the words, unconcerned about being seen from below.

He grabbed her and pulled her down to the ground. "We can try." He peered down at the endless waves of soldiers marching. "But not if we're seen first. Come on." He rolled away from the edge and stood where he wouldn't be seen.

To everyone he said, "We run. We run quiet and we run light, but we run until we can't run farther."

They dropped what gear they wouldn't need and took off

through the rugged ridges and hills that shadowed the road from above.

They made fast time at first, staying close enough to keep an eye on the army when they needed to but still out of sight. The ridge fell into a series of upland slopes, but they were mumblers of the mountains. They knew how to navigate such changes and adjust, crossing at the ideal point to make the best speed. When they took the time to look, they were already level with the vanguard, and the next time they had left the army behind.

Then they came to a ravine that cut them off from the hills ahead. Ellechandran called a halt.

While they drank water, he asked, "How should we proceed? Down and back up will take all day. If we go higher, it looks like the ravine opens up, so we should be able to get around. But I don't know how much that takes us out of our way." The path he would have chosen, before the road existed, followed the exact same route.

"We've gotten in front of the army," Chhayasheela passed the waterskin she was holding to someone else. "Let's race down toward the road, get past this ravine, and then back up out of sight. If we hurry, we can make it safely."

Ellechandran didn't like it. But they had to take some risks if they were going to warn the village in time. What would Jaritta have advised him to do?

"Then let's go. No time for resting." He picked his gear up and led the way, jumping from rock to rock down to the road.

No sign of the army yet, except for the distant, pulsing rhythm of their drums and footsteps, reverberating off the mountainsides. The scouts sprinted ahead, past the ravine, making for the hills on the far side. The landscape looked rugged, with no clear line to carry them through. The road might be faster, and now that they were in front, tempting to stay on it and increase their lead.

"Let's stay here for a little ways," he said and pointed along the road.

They eased their sprint to a loping jog and made good progress.

Eventually Chhayasheela, running beside him, said in a low voice, "How long do we dare stay on the road? I'd feel better up there with some cover."

"Me too." He looked at the slopes around them. Above the road, a series of ravines cut through the face of the mountain. Below them was equally rough. The best route, he would have said, was exactly where the road had been built. The only reasonable way around the uneven ground would take them far too long to warn anyone in their former village.

"We'll go a little farther," he answered. "Then we can leave the road once we're past some of these gullies."

The sky opened up, clouds parting to reveal a timid blue before them. The sun was still hidden, but the blue above was a reminder that the sun still shone somewhere. Ellechandran took it as a sign for them to continue. As long as the sky was open, he might dare to lead them along the road.

They made excellent time, following the curves of the mountain road. How would it stand up to the masses following behind? They must have come through before, yet there seemed something distinctly different about the army they'd seen, something that would change the very mountains. He could scarcely imagine how this land would look after their passage. Any bushes along the road trampled or cast aside, the rocks that could move thrown down into the depths below. The whole landscape transformed in ways that might last a generation. Would the animals ever return to a land so defaced? Would any mumbler tribes?

As the day dragged on, the clouds did not close around the gap of open sky, but Ellechandran looked for a route up into the highlands above the road. They'd passed the place where he'd expected to climb, but the recent avalanches and landslides had changed the shape of the land.

"There." He pointed toward a slope that came down to the road and led evenly up toward the other hills and ridges beyond. The lower edge was all scree, but they could clear that easily enough. Above that, there were bushes to hold the loose rock in place, and an incline they could take without needing to rest in an exposed location.

No one behind them yet, and the sounds of the drums still distant. At this rate they might give the village some hours to prepare and leave. The knot of worry inside him loosened.

They had just reached the loose scree at the base when an advance group from the horde came around the bend ahead of them.

Soldiers. An entire jati of Pashun soldiers, judging by the matching regalia they tied around their helmets and arms. They must have pushed far ahead of the horde as scouts, leaving behind their drums and trumpets to move quickly and quietly. Ellechandran had fought soldiers like that beside Chaitanshehar, before the spell took hold of Chaitanshehar and ended that war.

Here they had neither wall nor spell for protection. And no hope they might get away without being seen. A sharp command set the soldiers moving quicker.

"We'll be too exposed if we climb," Chhayasheela shouted. "Let's get below the road."

Down, where the land would stop their progress at once. But it was that or die in a fight. Gnalamani, who was especially agile on the steep slopes, was already far enough up the scree that it made no sense for her to turn around.

He gestured to her to keep moving. "Get out of sight," he shouted, "and get to the village, in case we can't." Then with the others he dashed across the road into the thorny scrubland below. He took a last glance up the road, saw the soldiers closing in fast, and made sure he was the last one off the road.

The arrows came before they had reached any real protection. The flight passed entirely by Ellechandran, but Venthaian fell right in front of him. He tripped and rolled down through the thorns.

He turned around to scramble back and help. Chhayasheela grabbed his shoulder to pull him further down the slope.

"Venthaian is back there. I'm not going to leave him behind."

Chhayasheela pulled his shoulder more forcefully. "Venthaian is dead, Chandri. We need to keep going."

Dead? Venthaian had always been such a steady presence, a strong and certain part of their squad. Ellechandran took another look, could just see the body lying face down halfway up the gully, caught on the woody stem of thornbush. Blood on the rocks below. He swallowed hard, and tears gathered in his eyes. Head reeling and stomach sick, he followed the others down into a labyrinth of boulders and bushes, with sharp thorns battling the hard edges of the rock at every turn.

It wasn't right that Venthaian lay back there, dead. Couldn't be. Ellechandran was supposed to protect them.

When he thought they might have some breathing room, he blurted out, "I'm no good at this part, Sheela. Leading them when we're fighting, when we're running. I need you to take over for me."

How good it would be to just let someone else be responsible. He could still be the last one, the one taking the biggest dangers for himself. But not the one deciding, not the one responsible for keeping them alive.

"I don't care what you think you're good at." She said it as if she did care, deeply, but wasn't convinced by his whining. "You *will* lead us, and you *will* be responsible for whatever happens."

The crashing sound of the Pashun soldiers came much too close. Chhayasheela glanced up, eyes wide, and said, "But I'll decide this for you. Now we run."

They were already off before she finished. The brush and rocks made arrows ineffective. Slings were still a danger, especially if these soldiers had ever trained with the wolf jati. So far no bullets had been slung their way.

So they only had to keep a small gap between them.

Not an easy task.

The land flattened, and the gully they were in widened out

into a space of scattered trees. A rivulet of water trickled from the gully, too little to carve its way through the rock. When Ellechandran turned his attention to the edges of this flatter space, he stepped into the water by mistake. His foot flew forward, and he fell back.

Whatever he hit, it made his vision spark, and when he stood, his legs ached from stretching too far and too fast. He tried to run, and it resulted in an awkward hobble.

The soldiers almost caught them. Probably would have, but Sheela noticed a route to one side that wandered off through walls of stone. With her support, he managed to get into that protection, and they stumbled onward.

The walls closed in. Were the enemy soldiers still behind them? He pictured them as mindless, relentless. Maybe they would never stop chasing. Usually gullies and canyons led downward and opened as they went. Or they might have entered at the bottom and found themselves climbing. This one simply stayed at a level...and narrowed.

"We have to climb out," Chhayasheela finally said.

Ellechandran looked around. The walls hadn't completely trapped them, but there was little sign it would lead them anywhere, either. They didn't know this area well—it was just far enough from their birthplace that they hadn't ever come here—but he knew enough to realize they needed to get farther downslope from the road. If they could get past the jumbled rocks here, there was a good-sized stream, almost a river, that would give them a path to follow and places to hide.

The sound of the soldiers no longer taunted them from behind, but they shouldn't trust that they'd given up their pursuit.

He focused on one part of the left-hand wall ahead. The two sides briefly came close enough to almost touch. "Brace ourselves there," he said. "Legs on one side, backs on the other."

"Your legs won't hold up," Chhayasheela said.

"Don't argue, we don't have time."

He pushed the remaining scouts toward the wall, and

Aagathiya climbed up first. Solid, trustworthy, just like Venthaian had been. He had a sudden fear that Aagathiya would suffer the same fate.

"Don't think you'll stay behind, Chandri. I can see you thinking that, sacrificing yourself while we race on."

She read him too well. He looked off along the narrowing route ahead. He could try to go that way. If there were any soldiers still on their tail, he could lead them off to save the others. But the image in his head of Nataravi and Ovitiva stopped that thought. He had to get through this for them, so he could at least see them again.

"Then help me up. I certainly won't make it up if I'm the last down here."

Chhayasheela and two other scouts braced him and pushed him upward, where the two who'd already climbed were waiting. As soon as he was up, he spun around and helped the remaining scouts scale the wall.

The upper edge of the ravine wasn't an open ridge as he'd pictured. It was another jumble of rocks and bushes and gaping drops into other gullies and caves that dotted the landscape downslope of the road. More open to being spied as they went, so they kept low and went slow to avoid falling.

A mountain cat slunk from a cave and dashed off at their approach.

The next sound they heard was drumming. And felt the tremors of thousands of footsteps marching in unison.

The road was far behind them, but most of their scrambling escape had been down and away from the road. Here a portion of the same road crossed the mountainside high above them. The vast army passed through, much slower than the scouts who had chased the group from Chaitanshehar, slower and ponderous. Inevitable. They blocked any possibility of them reaching the village to warn them. The sound of trumpets echoed off the mountains. The sound of war, of overwhelming force, of death.

"We can at least check on the village after they pass,"

Chhayasheela said to him when he collapsed against a boulder. "Maybe they had enough warning. Maybe Gnalamani got through in time. They might even be fleeing right now, warned by the sound of the army approaching."

Right now. Strange to think they had already failed, and yet the results of that failure were still playing out, were still in the future.

He blew out his cheeks and nodded. "Let's find a place to sleep. In the morning we'll tour the wreckage. And then across the foothills to Chaitanshehar as fast as at all possible."

***

Gnalamani lay in the dust outside the village, an arrow in her back. Outside what was left of the village, anyway. Ellechandran and Chhayasheela walked through the spaces that had been home, through fallen walls and over the trampled debris. What bodies they came across were unrecognizable.

Death and destruction hung heavy in the air. Ellechandran felt sick, but couldn't find it in him to feel much else.

"This is what, about a quarter of the number of people who lived here?" Chhayasheela's voice sounded as flat as he felt as she scanned the area where the bones lay. "Maybe the rest got away."

"What we've *found* is a quarter. You want to dig under the debris and count the bodies there?" Ellechandran regretted the harsh sound of his voice. Better to stay silent in a place like this. To show a quiet respect and leave.

He picked up a rock that had once been part of a wall and threw it as hard as he could against what remained of a building. As he threw it, he shouted, a senseless, animal cry of anguish. He wished something would break, the rock or the bit of wall, but the rock simply bounced off and fell heavily into the dust.

"Let's go." Chhayasheela took his shoulders and steered him away from the ruins.

In a field up the hill from the village, they came across

more bodies. Ellechandran winced and was about to turn away when he pictured what that field would have been. Not a field for hunting or gathering, not for preparing food or keeping animals. It was a field for playing in. He saw himself as a child running and chasing his friends in this very spot. Reluctantly he looked at the bodies again.

Several looked small, small enough to have been children born after he and Chhayasheela were cast out. Small enough to have been his own children.

Another cry of rage built itself inside him before bursting out. They were monsters, cruel and subhuman. An army of wickedness.

His cry attracted the attention of someone, or something. Noise came from the underbrush that was left beside the field. They crept close and saw a man sitting in the dust, staring at his own hands. An Eghsal man. His skin was the same brown shade as Jaritta's. His clothes were cut in the style of the people of Pashun. His hands were splattered in something Ellechandran didn't take the time to examine.

Not a person. Echoing his own cry of a moment before, Ellechandran took out a knife and threw it, hitting the man in the gut.

The man grunted but kept his eyes on his hands.

As they came close, the man spoke. It had been so long—or felt like it, at least—since Ellechandran had heard the language of the cities of Eghsal that he struggled for a moment to catch on to the meaning of what the man said.

"...didn't mean to. Most of us didn't want to. I was a soldier, a real soldier, and I didn't want this." Then he looked up and met their eyes for the first time. Whether he saw them or not, Ellechandran couldn't tell. His eyes looked haunted and empty at the same time. Sightless. Inhuman. "But when the drums go, it's impossible to resist."

He mumbled a few more things after that before collapsing onto his side. By the time Ellechandran reached him, he was clearly dead. Ellechandran wanted to walk away and leave the place, but he needed whatever weapon he could find. He reached in close to take back his bloody knife and stood up with two knives in his hands. The second one was a Pashun style knife, curved and unadorned. Its empty sheath was strapped to the man's side.

"Self-inflicted," he said to the others. "Horrified at what he'd done." And well he should be. Maybe a sense of his humanity had come back to him at the sights of that field, the knowledge of the army's actions. The bodies of the children, unidentifiable, still cried out from across the field.

"What was that about drums?" Chhayasheela asked. "He must have been under some kind of magic." She used the old mumbler word of their childhood, not the word they used about Pavresh's arcist spells. It was an ugly word, a word of evil power. "And when the drums left him behind, he felt remorse."

Maybe that was the reason. It didn't make Ellechandran forgive the man or any of them in that horde. "Let's get to Chaitanshehar as fast as we can. Tell them about the drums. Maybe we can find a way to silence them and save the city."

Or else a way to flee and forget any of it had happened—the city, the untouchables, the arcist magic, the wreckage of the village, the faceless hordes of subhuman monsters…let them all be forgotten if that was what it would take.

He sheathed his own knife after wiping it clean and kept the other knife in his hand as he led them through the mountains toward the only home they had left.

CHAPTER 29

There was nothing dance-like in the arrival of the army to Pashun. Indima tried to fit a dance to the moment, but nothing matched. The army's marching was movement with the spirit—the soul of dance—excised.

She had been in Pashun for some twelve-days, a mostly empty city until now. Throughout that time, her captor Mahendri had tried to get her to reveal the secrets of Datri's spy network. Who were the contacts? Where did they meet? How did they send their messages back and forth? She guarded her silence, no matter how he pushed.

Two days earlier, he'd changed his attempt to gloating after a messenger arrived from the road into the mountains. "It doesn't matter anymore," he said, when she again refused to say anything about Chaitanshehar's supposed secrets. "We don't need anything from you. Whatever secrets they have, they won't save their so-called city anymore."

After that he hadn't returned to her until now, pulling her from her locked room to see the army on the march.

So many people. It was like something from the old dances about the gods and the Forgotten South, the gathering of an unstoppable army.

A flourish from the horns announced their arrival. Their braying grated on Indima's ears. She wanted to dance the sound away. The drums were just as bad. In fact, they were what stripped the army of anything that might be called dancing. Their rhythm held the army in its thrall.

But it couldn't hold her. No music had ever been able to control her, only the movements of real dancing, and those rose from within.

Mahendri took a look at her to gauge her reaction, then turned away. She was no warrior. He didn't even suggest she could join the horde to fight against the renegade city. He just walked away, abandoning her. In his mind it was probably the gravest insult, the idea that she wasn't even worth his time or vigilance.

To her it was no more nor less than relief. She breathed freely and looked around.

Could she run back to the Silk City? Not a chance. Even if Mahendri truly had dismissed her from his mind, she couldn't survive such a trip alone and without supplies.

Perhaps to Chaitanshehar? That would surely test if Mahendri had abandoned her for real or only for show. Chances were he'd watch her, try to catch any contacts she met on the way. Even so, Datri deserved a warning and Indima might finally join up with the people she'd sent their way over the years. But the truth was, she didn't know the way herself, not well enough to race there ahead of the army. And that army was spread out between Pashun and Chaitanshehar already, spilling around both sides of the mud pots and geyser fields as they set up their sprawling but perfectly regimented camp.

Instead, she danced.

She chose a dance at odds with the rhythm of the drums, a languid dance of sweeping arms and jangling bracelets—though she wore no bracelets at the moment, so she would have to pretend. She let the steps carry her from the city, right into the midst of the army. They were setting up tents in every possible place, building fire pits for those farther from the steam beds, using the heat of the land to cook food where they could.

It became a busy space, with an ant hive's industry—and the silence of insects, as well. Drums like wingbeats, punctuated by the angry buzzing of the horns. But no words that weren't purely functional, that weren't for working together to accomplish some task, and even those words were few.

Language, like movement, had been stripped of its dancing richness.

The soldiers parted for her. Some frowned as she passed, their steely resolve broken for a moment by the whiff of another spell. Once she was past, the drums and horns clamped down again, returning the soldiers to impassivity and order.

The horde was massive, beyond anything she could properly imagine. There were people of Eghsal Valley, the familiar shades of brown skin that might be encountered on any city street. And she passed a knot of pale-faced mumblers, their skin marked by what looked like recent bruises and their clothes ragged and stained with blood. There were others as well that fit neither of those categories. People with outlandish clothes and shades of color in their skin and hair that Indima had never seen before. Visitors from the Forgotten South. Had Mahendri mentioned something to that effect? She couldn't remember exactly, but she was sure it somehow fit.

One group broke the overwhelming flatness of the army camp with a stilted sort of rowdiness. She steered toward them and saw a knot of people wearing carnival masks and chanting something about the gods. A banner over their tents had hand-painted lettering that said, "The Sons of Ryo." Ryo, the god of rules and social rigidity and hierarchies. No wonder they came to fight. They likely needed no magical drums to compel them.

Indima danced an inversion of Ryo's sacred dance, then spun on her heel and left them behind.

She made her way, without any particular plan, toward the rear of the force, stretched out south and east of the city. Something drew her that way, a ripple in the otherwise dreary sound of the drums.

Pavresh. She felt the way he disrupted the rhythm before she saw him, recognized his presence after all these years. He'd performed in Chaitan's house while she danced. He'd gone to the Silk City with her. She knew the way his arcist magic worked, how it felt when she danced to it. But then he'd abandoned her, just like everyone else, left her to make her own way, left her to a dance that was always rooted within the confines of her own head.

It was through his magic that he resisted the drums, but he couldn't seem to break free entirely, the way she had. The magic held him—more loosely than it held the bulk of the army, but it still kept him bound.

She was about to say something—to break her dance and speak, though it was something she never did—when she felt something else in the patterns of the crowd.

Ekana. She didn't have to see him to know. She'd last seen him in Pashun, when he appeared out of the ghosts to become real, to dance with her. Her dancing crashed into stillness, and she wrapped her arms around herself.

"Indima?" It wasn't Ekana's voice or Pavresh's.

She cocked her head and noticed the smaller man just beyond Ekana. It was the man who'd come to Pashun claiming to be from the Forgotten South. And now this mass of people coming…from the Forgotten South for real? Or was it another scam?

"The two of you are still together?" Her voice strained at the words. Better to dance than trust to words that could lie, if she only had that choice. "Are you behind all this?" She waved her arm to take in the army.

Ekana managed to shake his head, and Sembaari said, "No. This has us trapped. We haven't been able to break free."

"How are you free, Indima?" Pavresh asked. "Even my magic is caught up, as if in shackles." His voice at least came freely, unlike the others.

Instead of answering his question, she asked Pavresh, "Do you trust him? Last I saw him, I told him to speak the truth about himself and his mumbler friend and prove he could be trustworthy. I thought maybe he would end up joining you in Chaitanshehar. But I never heard anything about him in my messages from Datri." And that was something she had asked initially. "And before that, he betrayed you all."

"I think we all betray each other in some ways," Pavresh said. "Little ways and big ways, we trade the betrayals back and forth. So maybe that's his past." Pavresh made an effort to bring a hand up to his head to stroke his chin. "Truth is, no, I don't trust him yet. He was caught up in a story of betrayal before, a story of lies later, and now this story of war. In between, he proved himself trustworthy to Harkala and her crew, but not yet to me. Maybe this time he breaks away from that old story. Maybe soon we all do, if I could only figure out how to resist the spell."

Back to that question. This time she answered, though she didn't suppose he would find it satisfactory. "I just ignore it, that's how I'm still free. I notice a different rhythm, a different dance, and follow it." Certainly not something she felt like she could teach someone else to mimic.

Pavresh considered the answer for a moment before answering, "I think you've told yourself a different story, and that part of you is so strong, so sure of how you fit in, that the magic just doesn't have a place to lay hold."

Sure of herself? She wished she were. But sure of dancing as her central essence, yes, that made sense.

"So now if each of you could dance with me, I suppose I could break you free?"

She meant it as sarcasm, but Pavresh took it seriously. "No, I don't think that would work exactly. We're not all dancers. But it's possible we can learn something from you to help us all."

Learn something from her, when words could only fail to explain what she did and how she felt. She answered in a dance step, a beat at odds with the drums, a movement that slid behind the eerie stillness that bound the army.

"Keep doing that," Pavresh said. "It's like the magic I was using before that gave us some freedom, until Kamlak's spell grew even stronger. I can see some of how you do it."

Stop talking, she wanted to say. Watch, observe, study, do whatever he wanted, but no need to talk about it.

When she stopped, Pavresh softly clapped. Ekana edged closer to Pavresh, his teeth gritted as if it took all his effort simply to do that, then he managed to clap as well.

It struck her, a pang that reverberated inside. The applause of her former lover, and heartfelt as well, by the effort he put into making it happen. She flushed with the dance, with the praise of people she had known and known well, once upon a time.

Ekana strained to speak and forced out the words, "I might learn to dance. With her. Watching her."

Indima had no answer. No words, not even a dance to respond.

Pavresh answered for her. "Yes. If the two of you dance, and I try to add my magic, maybe we'll do more than free just ourselves. Can you stay, Indima? I suspect we'll travel again soon, and we might have to learn on the march."

Indima nodded and dropped into a graceful dip before giving herself over to the music that no one else ever heard.

***

Ekana wanted to join Indima's dancing, but wanting wasn't enough. How many times had he wanted something only to do the opposite? All his life had been that, time and again. The strict gods pulling him one way and the capricious nagas another, and neither of them real, and neither of them right. But people created their cities, their castes, their rules, and none of them let him do the right thing when he tried. Now more than ever, the horns and drums cast their spell on him and forced him to march instead of dancing.

Marching was all they did, from dawn to dusk and even after the sun had set below the southern mountains. This time of year, they couldn't be constrained by the shrinking daylight if their leaders hoped they would make any progress.

Half of their army headed along the northern edge of the mud pots, where the route was longer but easier. Ekana and all the others from Jarnur found themselves with the group marching around to the south. Rugged valleys and foothills made the going slow, but the geyser land in between transmitted the drums from either side, kept both halves of the army together, in snow and in calm.

Ekana tried to add an extra beat to the drum's pace, tried to turn a lockstep, here and there, into a more elaborate pass. And mostly he tried to watch Indima's way of staying with the group while creating her own, separate rhythm.

Sembaari managed to resist the drums better. He wasn't completely free or even close, but he turned his marching into a more fluid walking motion. And he could speak even when the others were forced to silence.

"He grew up with different stories," Pavresh explained when he was able to talk. "Kamlak thinks that arcist magic is about something more than stories, but those narratives still matter. I imagine if you watch the people from the Forgotten South, you'll see they move more freely, too." Then quietly he added, "But the power is still more than enough, even for them. For now."

Elsh and her soldiers seemed to have taken the northern route. Or if she was with this half, Ekana couldn't find her among the multitudes.

At Pavresh's urging, Sembaari spoke about his own childhood stories, about the legends of his village. And he talked about all they'd seen in the south, about the city on a pier, about the sharp grasses and ancient ruins that lay inland, about the water fountain that seemed to power another city the way steam engines were beginning to power things here. Indima spoke sometimes, but her dancing kept her in her own world in many ways. And Pavresh interjected his own questions when he could. Eventually Sembaari fell quiet, saying only, "It's hard to have a one-sided conversation. I grow tired of my own voice."

Occasionally through the days he would bring himself to talk again, narrating what he saw along the way when they struggled to even turn their eyes off to the side, and suggesting what he thought they could expect to happen in the coming days. Mostly he adopted the same silence that the others endured without choice.

Each day's march left Ekana so tired he had little time to talk to—or if the magic was too controlling, listen to—the others about any plans or ideas they had to break free and save the city...and themselves. Pavresh thought Indima's dancing was making a difference, loosening the hold of Kamlak's spell. At this rate it would be much too late. They marched until ready to drop, threw their tents up wherever they would fit, and collapsed within. Indima was as tired as the rest even if the magic wasn't compelling her throughout the day. He might have wished she would lie beside him, might have been jealous of where she did sleep, but he had no energy to do more than wonder, briefly, as the magic forced him asleep. It wasn't as if anyone was doing anything besides sleeping when they finally were allowed to lie down in their tents.

Eventually they came around to the swamp land on the far side of the lava field and headed closer to the other half of the army even as they approached the city of Chaitanshehar. He could see the lights of the city during the long night, shining partway up the mountainside.

***

The soldiers arrived, breaking against the slope below Chaitanshehar like some hideous wave. They were a force of nature rather than something human Jaritta could pit herself against. Not-people, as her husband had reported when he'd come rushing back over the steep pathways of the mountains only a few days ago. He stood behind her now, wearing armor like a good Eghsal city dweller, with a mumbler-style long knife in his hand.

"They just keep coming," she said, breathless.

"And it's still only the leading edge," Ellechandran said. "I wouldn't have believed there were so many people in the world until we saw them pass us on the road."

It was the end of her city. They'd done what they could to protect themselves, but this? This was a wildfire bearing down on her, trapped before its flames. A rogue wave before it's swept you away but when it's too late to run.

Yet, she didn't feel the despair of that thought. She'd mourned the city for months, been certain that it would fail. But those thoughts had been full of her blaming herself. There was no blame here, because no one could have stopped an army like this. The more soldiers that came, the more she felt her resolve harden. They would fight with all they could—for the good of the city—and when that wasn't enough, then they would fall with their heads held high.

"And I wouldn't have believed a city like ours could exist." She set off along the wall, behind the city's fighters who would protect it as long as they could. She pitched her voice so that the soldiers nearest them could hear her as she walked by. "Even if Chaitanshehar only exists for such a short time, it's a time that matters. We've set our mark in the history of the world. Nothing that happens now can erase that."

Let them pass the words along the lines of soldiers.

Valni met them behind the center of the wall.

"How are we looking?"

Valni set the end of her staff on the ground as if posing for a portrait. "As set as can be. It's a doomed, final stand, but everyone knows that and everyone is prepared to pay that price."

If there were any way Jaritta could pay that price herself and save the rest... But she knew there wasn't. It was the world itself coming to sweep them away. They would do all they could to resist, while knowing it probably wouldn't matter in the end.

When she turned her back on the view of the army, the noise didn't lessen. She climbed quickly to the rooms she and her family had lived in. Everything was still there, all but the people. The girls had left that morning with the rest of the children and a few adults to accompany them up into the mountains. No one had wanted to leave, no matter how old or sick or unsuited for fighting. To leave was to give up. But a few adults had consented to take the children above the city and flee when the time came, throw themselves on the mercy of whatever mumbler villages might remain intact.

That they hadn't done so immediately when Ellechandran and the other scouts returned spoke to the mix of hopelessness and defiance they all felt. Would even mumbler villages escape the army of not-people? Would it not be better to be together to the end? The debate had lasted until the first waves of the Pashun army came to the foot of the slope below Chaitanshehar.

A part of Jaritta wished they'd chosen differently, wished she could be with her girls as everything fell apart. It was too late for regrets.

On the wall of the rooms hung a sword that Datri had retrieved from the manor in Romnai. A ceremonial sword from the time her father was a ruling prince, fitting the ceremonial role she would play. She took it down and bound it around her waist.

As she left, she saw a small grass doll that Ovitiva must have left when they were rushing out the door to flee. Jaritta scooped it up and tucked it into her robe, beside her heart. Let it stand for both her girls. No, let both the doll and the sword stand for them, the love and the sharp-edged resolve against her people's doom.

She returned to the wall and the terrifying sounds of the army below.

***

In the morning the drums switched to a faster beat. A bloodlust beat. It made Ekana want to charge up the hill ahead and fight. Everywhere the soldiers were waking up and responding to the drums with animal-like cries, grunts, ululations. Ekana's heart pounded with the beat, responding with an anxious anger.

There was a trade-off in this more intense magic, though. Even as Ekana found himself wanting to fight whoever stood in his way, he also felt the control of the spell loosen. He had more freedom to make his own movements, to twist counter to the drums' rhythm. He tested it by dancing the opening to an old, sacred dance of Brilith, the goddess of the sea, a dance that recalled to him Jarnur and fishing vessels, things that had nothing to do with Pashun or this inland place where they found themselves.

"You're fighting it, aren't you?" Sembaari asked. "You seem more free." He danced as well, a few steps of a traditional circle dance of his village.

"This may be our only chance," Pavresh said. "Can you speak as well?"

Ekana managed to shake his head. The magic still held his tongue.

"Very well. I will do what I can through magic. Indima, have you decided what dance you will perform?"

Indima was a ghostly figure, a dance made into flesh. "Crows in Snow, but a variation on it. Sembaari knows it as well, so we'll do a three person version to tell a different sort of story. What is the story you want, Pavresh?"

"Make it a story of revolution. A story like Rashul might have told, of people resisting the powerful and bringing a genuine change for something new."

Indima met Ekana's eyes, and it felt like they were back in Chaitan's house. Namrani was playing her stringed instrument, a strange and evocative melody that was as unlike the temple music as the room was unlike a temple. Maybe it was Chaitan himself performing the magic. Or a younger Pavresh, who in the split reality of the moment was bound by the magic beside them.

With a few head shakes and gestures they figured out how they would interpret the dance, how it would change and evolve as they progressed.

Sembaari only knew the traditional one, and there was no way Ekana could convey in words what he should do, so he gestured at Sembaari, indicated for Indima how they could involve him in the complex patterns of the dance.

The army massed, ready to begin their attack while the three dancers worked out their plan. The more he planned and pictured what they would do, the more he doubted his ability to carry through. The magic was as intense and heartbeat-raising as it had been, but its power was sneaking back in to ensnare him, to freeze his dancing and force his limbs to carry him to war.

They had to get started. Ekana crouched in his opening position, praying to the gods he detested that he would be able to do this. Praying to the nagas, those supposed beings of trickery and sly wisdom who had only ever led him astray—if they existed at all. To the cursed, sacred Fire beneath and over all.

Before they could make the dance's first pass, a different movement, running counter to the drums and horns, caught their notice.

From the untamed slope, across the river from the route that led up to the city, a group of soldiers suddenly appeared, waving to flag the leaders of the army. The river wasn't far from where Ekana and the others were getting ready, and he saw the movement as the leaders headed to meet the soldiers. The army around the dancers shifted to let the leaders through, filling the space where they'd planned to dance.

Pavresh gestured for the dancers' attention. "Let's see what this is about. Might be another weakness in the magic we can use, and then we'll make space by the river for your dance." It took tremendous effort to resist the magic, but they made their way toward the river in time to watch the confrontation.

Three of the unknown soldiers left the riverbank and crossed, almost as if they were dancing, rock to rock across the foaming water.

The leaders of the army met them there. Ekana recognized Dartak, and his face burned with shame. This was the man who had promised him riches, had promised to restore Indima to him, in exchange for betraying Jaritta. What a fool he had been.

The others he'd learned by name while they were traveling from the Forgotten South, before the magic became so strong that it prevented them from even talking most of the time. Kamlak the arcist, his face burned as if in imitation of the leader of the city he opposed. He looked both exhausted by the energy it took to create his spells and at the same time exultant in the power that coursed through him . Prince Hrisha who had been mayor of Pashun before becoming one of the Thirty Princes. Another he guessed was the Mahendri that Pavresh had spoken of. Indima's eyes burned blades toward the slight man.

"Tisrae," the oldest of the soldiers said, "we welcome you to our siege of this city."

"A siege?" Hrisha said with a laugh. "It won't last long enough to be a siege."

"Nevertheless, we have held them here in preparation for your arrival. One thing I want you to know. We are here on behalf of the High Prince, and there is one in that city who belongs to us. We will take her—alive or dead—and will not forgive anyone who interferes in that."

"Which High Prince?" Hrisha pushed. "So many claim that title these days. I am one of the Ruling Thirty, though. So know that I serve the valley and the rights of the princes to rule."

Behind him, Dartak spoke up. "Last I heard, you had failed one High Prince and were begging to serve another."

The woman held her arms out as if to stop the younger two soldiers from attacking. "We serve the High Prince of the whole valley, as it is our honor to do. Ignore us, if you wish, but we will do as we have stated—and not allow any of your soldiers to stop us."

Mahendri spoke, his voice thin yet clear in the warm air that rose from the swamp. "The era of the High Princes is ended. You are welcome to fight for us, though, to bring in the new age and restore all princes to their rightful heritage."

He made a gesture to Kamlak, and Ekana felt the surge in arcist magic as it tried to force the falcon jati soldiers to become a part of their army, an overwhelming sense of power bludgeoning the women into subservience.

It failed.

Ekana was no arcist user, but he sensed the magic's failure, sensed how it faltered, how it battered against those soldiers and dropped back, unable to shake their resolve, their certainty of who they were.

Mahendri didn't notice. Ekana looked back and forth between the two factions. Surely it should be obvious. If not to Mahendri, then to his scarred arcist. But they were walking away, as if the matter were settled. The three women crossed back over the river while Mahendri called for the attack to begin. Kamlak did his bidding, summoning the power of his magic into the fight up the slope. All their focus was on the hordes of soldiers charging up the hillside toward the city, not on the women across the river from them. Mahendri's body language spoke to his certainty that the women would join them, just as everyone the army had met had joined by force.

But the unknown soldiers slipped away from the magic's grip into the darkness of the shadowed land across the river. At the edge of his vision, he noticed someone dropping down from the wall above and angling across the river to meet up with the soldiers. The figure moved with the same dance-like quality as the women across the river and disappeared into the underbrush soon after.

The leading edge of the horde's soldiers reached halfway to the wall before Ekana could think again about dancing. Rocks bounced down toward them, mowing down scores. It only increased the bloodlust in the rest, as twice as many filled in the gaps.

Indima grabbed Ekana's head to draw his eyes away from the carnage.

Just as they began to dance, a different, new beat sounded from the city above, an echoey noise of a giant drum that disrupted the martial drums and the dance of resistance both. Ekana slumped forward, and only Sembaari's quick reflexes kept him from falling to the ground as the warring rhythms tore at his insides. It was the image of the falcon jati soldiers resisting the arcist magic that pulled him back from collapse. He thanked Sembaari and positioned himself for the start of the dance.

***

Indima threw herself into the dance, knowing without thought what Ekana would do, anticipating the steps of his friend Sembaari and weaving them into her own graceful passes. It was the story Pavresh had suggested, the simple story of a small group of people who resist the powerful.

There was a surge of energy when Pavresh added his magic to the dance, a rippling sense of power reverberating and building into each other like peals of ringing bells. The broken rhythm of the competing drums gave them space to gather their wits and commit themselves fully to the combination of dance and magic.

Indima wove in her thoughts of Rashul's dreams. Stories of a caste-less origin and a future of people who are equal. Stories where taking a lover of another caste meant nothing. Her movements grew expansive, as if to embrace the world as a whole. She wove in the very idea of Pavresh's magic, of arcist magic as both big, sweeping narratives and small, individual stories. Ekana passed her by, and she swung around Sembaari as he sunk low for a fast, repeated kick.

The competing drums faded to nothing, a backdrop easily ignored. Martial drums down below, the slow and deliberately uneven drums above—they weakened the magic's hold on the army that moved up the slope, but they had no effect on the dancing. The horns seemed to turn into tone-less fits of noise without meaning. She danced a loosening of the drums' and horns' effects and felt how those near her began to stir.

Ekana's movements grew freer as they went. Pavresh was able to put more energy into his magic. Sembaari added a mumbler's touch to the dancing, opening the effects wider to admit other traditions and other stories. For the first time she understood what Pavresh had been trying to do all these years, putting himself out among the villages and other peoples of the valley, seeking to learn their stories and be taken in as a welcome guest. The dance's power grew from those influences.

The true Forgotten South made its way in as well. Their group of resistors within the army hadn't been able to speak freely for most of the time traveling, but she'd heard enough from Sembaari's stories to know that Ekana had truly reached the Forgotten South and seen and experienced things that needed to be told, things that had only been legend.

She danced for the eccentric older woman who was in no way a soldier yet found herself marching side by side with the rest of them. Some kind of historian. What had she seen in her travels? Indima brought what she knew of the woman's story into her dancing and felt the moment that the magic fell away from her.

The circle of broken magic spread outward, releasing the would-be soldiers from bloodlust, from marching orders. Instead their voices began to sound over the drums, and they spoke the language of Eghsal and the languages of mumblers, and even, Indima supposed, the languages of the Forgotten South, words never before heard in these northern lands.

Someone knocked a trumpet player down, took his instrument, and blew a blaring note of defiance. Others sought to grab the drums on their side, as they continued their struggle against the deep drumming up above.

The attackers on the slope stumbled, whether they were feeling the same freedom from the magic or simply sensing the faltering support behind them.

The battle for Chaitanshehar hung, poised in stasis.

It was at that moment that the enemy arcist Kamlak burst in among them, knocking Ekana to the ground with a punch. As he fell, Indima could feel the switch when the dance left him and the arcist magic took over, binding him utterly. The effort it took to create a magic this powerful was clear in the arcist's face. He was battling the syncopated drum, the effects of Indima's dance, the other forces that worked to undermine him. Yet he drew his power together with what must have been an extreme effort of his will and forced it over the entire army. Sembaari tried to spin away, but his feet got tangled, and he tripped over Ekana. Kamlak took control of the mumbler as well, ending their three way dance.

The arcist had no power over her, though. Even now, as she felt his magic trying to take over her movements, she danced away, felt the strength fill her from Pavresh's spells.

Kamlak made a peremporty gesture toward someone behind Indima. She moved, expecting soldiers to try to restrain her. Instead the trumpets sounded anew, harsh and braying. The sound didn't compel her to any action, but it managed to finally halt her movement.

The dance stopped.

Pavresh's magic stopped.

All that existed was the power of Kamlak's spell, controlling the masses and crushing her beneath its overwhelming weight.

Above them, the horde of Pashun renewed their frenzied attack on Chaitanshehar.

CHAPTER 30

Pavresh knew the time had come to stand up before Kamlak, pretending the confidence he didn't feel. His breaths came in quick gasps. Every other time they had faced each other, his attempts to break free of Kamlak's magic had fallen short. His only success had come through a distraction that he didn't think he could make happen this time. Now he needed to *be* the distraction, to keep Kamlak's focus on him without letting him take control.

He'd watched Indima resist the magic these past days and studied how she did it. He had seen the falcon jati soldiers keep their own identities even as Kamlak's drums tried to turn them into mindless pawns for Mahendri's army.

As the raw power of Kamlak's magic clamped down around him, he told himself a different story. But instead of simply *telling* the story this time, he *became* it in a way he never had before. He was the dancer who heard the dance so clearly that it blocked out the magic. He was the soldier who knew her role so perfectly that no other power could change that.

And he was himself—the story of an arcist master, a son of a mine owner who'd fled that life. He was the performer who only wanted the magic for the way it could create a new art form, the way it could combine with music and dancing. He was the storyteller, wandering among the supposed enemies of his people, learning their ways and their tales, making the connections to bridge them with his own people. And he was the teacher who gave those who would follow the chance to understand even more, to surpass him as he had pushed beyond what Chaitan knew.

A simple tale but each point captured him and held him in a way that Kamlak's spell couldn't quite shake. Kamlak, his former student. He added that to the narrative and deflected the spell from him.

The army moved up the slope in a terrifying wave, but he let them pass. The soldiers nearest him slowed down, touched by the effects of his spell, and fell behind the horde that set about the destruction of the city of Chaitanshehar.

As he repeated the story over and over, he made his way to a torch that was already burning in preparation for the gathering dusk, facing Kamlak as he walked. He set a naga trumpet flower to smolder on his censer and placed it on the ground before him. Then he untied his kusti, the rope belt that wrapped three times around his waist. Neither the torch nor the censer was exactly a fire, as those of his faith traditionally used one, but he moved his belt before the censer as if it were and breathed in the smoke. His breathing calmed. Moving smoothly and thinking nothing but the story, he performed his kusti ritual, trying to enter that sense of being outside himself. In Kamlak's first attack on him—before he knew his foe was Kamlak—he'd decided he had no time for the ritual, and in all his time in captivity, he'd had no chance to perform it. Or rather, he'd made no time for it, on those few occasions when he might have. Now he let the stillness of the kusti settle over his thoughts and prepare him.

He knew what he had to do. The cost…no, he couldn't think of that. It was the only way to save the city he could think of, the only story he could imagine. The story it would require took shape in his mind and took form in his movements.

Kamlak broke into his trance by grabbing the belt from Pavresh's grip.

"You've found a way to resist my magic. Impressive, but it won't save your city."

His hold was loose. Pavresh could yank the belt away, could whip it around much faster than Kamlak probably realized. Could he wound him badly enough to disrupt the magic? The strain of creating and holding such a powerful spell showed in the lines of Kamlak's face. If he died, did the spell die with him?

A tempting thought, but the story felt wrong. If Pavresh tried—even if he succeeded—he suspected that it would do little to stop the schemes of Kamlak's masters. They could be patient and find a new arcist if they needed to. They might even already have someone ready and trained well enough to continue the magic. Creating the spell from the beginning would almost certainly be beyond any of his acolytes, but maintaining it wouldn't be as difficult.

He let the belt dangle loosely between them and said, "Long ago, in the Forgotten North, there was a village." It was not a story he'd ever heard in his travels, and it started out in a way that no story ever would. The North was not forgotten, only frozen. But that was enough to make Kamlak pause.

"Your stories. Haven't you seen how powerless they are? When you understand the true nature of arcist magic, you can cut the story off before they can begin."

His voice gave no clue what he was doing, but as he said the last words, a powerful arcist force cut into Pavresh, like a blade to his mind.

He stumbled backward, dropping his kusti, but still managed to hold onto his identity. He turned the awkward backpedaling into a kusti move—though without the belt—graceful and mind-calming. Into a dance, as much as Pavresh ever danced. His breath felt tight, but he pressed on.

"And in this village, the people served their naga masters. Until the day their masters became cruel. Then they looked for ways to overthrow the nagas."

It was a simple story, a folktale like he might have heard among the mumbler villages or even from the older members of his father's household. Nothing especially profound or nuanced, but it was the magic he put into the story, each word imbued with a deceptive arcist resonance, that was important.

"Some rose up to fight, but the nagas are mighty warriors."

"I tire of your stories, Pavresh. You think it clever, and you think yourself wise. Yet here you are, reduced to the role of a nursery tender with your tale. A story of warriors who can't win. While behind me, my soldiers are fighting for real and will win."

The fighting was intense. The combination of Pavresh's magic with the three dancers' choreography still kept a large number of the nearest soldiers out of the fight, but they were merely a large portion of a tiny segment of the full horde. Beyond the nearest ranks, the remaining drums and horns fed into a bloodlust that propelled the people—of Pashun and of the Forgotten South both—up the slope to battle the few guards on the wall. *Oh, let them hold out, a little longer.*

What of Pavresh's spell, anchored into the city? He reached up toward it with his arcist senses and felt the magic, felt it calling and welcoming these visitors and strangers as long as they gave up their wish to fight, as long as they worked for the good of the city and not its ill. It was still there, and where it met the bloodlust, it created some hesitation, some confusion.

But even from down here he could sense that Kamlak's army would overwhelm his one, paltry spell. Someday, when cold winds scoured the ruins of the city that had been, travelers would still feel that brief, perplexing welcome to an uninhabited slope of the mountains—if he didn't find some way to stop Kamlak now.

"And anyway," Kamlak added, his voice sarcastic and mocking, "the nagas chose me. So I will carry on their mighty rule, if we must go by your stories. Don't you remember the smoke that welcomed us to the Forgotten South?"

"I sensed the spell you used to make that smoke. That was no otherworldly choosing."

"Exactly." Kamlak chuckled as if at a prank he had played. "And neither are your stories anything with real influence here. They're just the things you make up to pass the time."

Pavresh had to continue his story. And hope—hope might be the harder reach than mere talking. He made his magic into a precision blade, a chirurgeon's instrument for laying bare the precise location. "The fighting was brutal and short. Battle lust was quickly quenched when the blood that spilled was only their own. The nagas were impervious to their anger, to their weapons. So others decided to prove their service, to assuage the nagas' violent ways, to become the perfect servants they wanted. The servants the nagas deserved."

"I suppose you're trying to say that this is what's happening here, all these people willingly serving my vision for the future." Kamlak sneered. "You've lost sight of the real world by thinking only of such simpletons' tales, and I don't have time to listen to you anymore."

No, Kamlak was the servant as well. And Dartak and Hrisha and even Mahendri, all servants of something that was more powerful, even if it had no conscious thought or identity. But to explain that would break the story-spell he was pulling together. Had he thought of it as a scalpel? Now he pictured a fisher's hook, a barb that he placed into his target so that it couldn't be pulled free. And he needed to use it to keep Kamlak from leaving him behind. Already he could feel how Kamlak's focus ranged upward, strengthening the spell that drove the army into battle.

"It did no good. The nagas beat the perfect servants. They made sport of them and instead of punishing them for their failures, they punished them for having no faults." While he talked, Kamlak's magic was bearing down on him, trying to batter through the defenses he'd set up.

Pavresh had to pause to breathe through the assault. He bent down toward the censer and breathed in the smoke of the flowers. When he could speak again, he ignored Kamlak to continue his tale. "And so the people of the village set traps for the nagas. Not simple hunting traps—they played tricks to ensnare the nagas' minds. Three nagas wandered away and were lost in the icy waters before the other nagas realized what was happening and took their revenge."

"I could just have a guard kill you." Kamlak lifted his chin and pointed at the battle taking place up the slope. "But I don't think I'll have to." With a dramatic motion, his arms swinging down as if shutting a giant chest, he slammed his magic against the entire army. The raw power forced Pavresh backward. The aura of sheer authority made Kamlak's face bright, even as the strain of it throbbed visibly in his neck. His jaw muscles quivered with the effort.

Every soldier fighting for Mahendri kneeled for a moment beneath the weight of Kamlak's magic. No doubt many lost their lives at that moment, those fighting at the front line rendered powerless. But when they rose, no one resisted the impulse to the frenzied fighting that Kamlak demanded.

Those Pavresh and the dancers had freed were back fully beneath his control. Ekana and Sembaari lifted their blades and growled in anger at the city on the hill. Even frail, waif-like Indima accepted the bared knife that was offered to her and took her place in the ranks of soldiers heading for the city above.

Only Pavresh remained free from its effects, but what did it matter that he did? He couldn't free the whole valley on his own, no matter what he tried to do with his child-like story. It would end like Rashul's dream, an illusory image of a future that could never be.

The mountainside crawled as if covered in marching insects. The bloodlust no longer drew growls and cries from their voices, but only a determined, terrifying silence punctuated by drums beating and horns blowing. A predator's focus on the enemies above.

Pavresh's censer had blown out. The flowers still smoldered slightly, so he could breathe the ashy remnants of smoke for now and find some relief, but the fire was gone. The Fire was gone, was what it felt like, the sacred Fire that he'd grown up worshiping. He was not particularly devout in his thoughts, but he'd always felt like that Fire, in some way, was the source of his stories, the deepest layer that all other narratives played off of.

Stories were powerful. He'd seen it over and over. But they fell short against a world that bowed only to power.

There was a cracking noise, the sound of rocks falling away as the lower wall of Chaitanshehar tumbled down. Screams of pain and anguish sounded over the crashing of rock...for only a moment and then cut off suddenly. Pavresh bit his lower lip.

How many must have surely died as that fell—on both sides, but those below could afford to lose a hundred for each one who died within the city and still conquer it. How many people Pavresh had known, beggars he'd led to Chaitanshehar from Romnai and others he'd worked with to build the new city?

The off-kilter drumming still sounded within the city, for now, but it was as weak and ineffectual as a folk story.

Into the monotony of marchers surging upward came a sudden sideways movement, a dancing that leaped over the soldiers, around their strict routes, past their raised blades. The falcon jati soldiers must have resisted Kamlak's spell. And had they betrayed the princes to join the side of the defenders, or were they after their own purposes? Kamlak turned to watch this anomaly within his spell. Again Pavresh felt the urge to make a physical attack, but instead he took the respite to restore his sense of purpose against Kamlak's spell and prepare for the rest of his own counter attack.

But what were the falcon jati thinking? It seemed likely they would only end up wasting their lives to… He couldn't even see a purpose to their attacks. Maybe they would manage to assassinate a few superfluous leaders. Even if they killed Kamlak, Pavresh doubted the army could be stopped now, anymore than if Pavresh killed him.

They moved too fast and unexpectedly, darting back and forth in a weaving pattern, so that no one was able to anticipate where they would go or stop them. Maybe if Kamlak's spell had given them more freedom, someone would have stepped into their way at just the right time, and the mass of fighters would have overwhelmed even those legendary warriors. But instead Kamlak's control made them too predictable. As long as the women didn't stop too long or keep a straight path, they avoided any real fighting.

Even so, and no matter how peerless they were as warriors, they couldn't avoid the masses entirely. He watched one avoid a crowd only to run into a different knot of soldiers and be cut down. Another fell, whether hit by a sling bullet or a blade from behind.

Stay among the horde, and they would all soon fall, one by one.

The sounds of the army had grown almost silent before he realized what the women were doing. They had destroyed the drums, cut down the drummers or their instruments or both, as they raced across the current of the army.

By the time he'd realized this, the only drum anywhere on the battlefield came from within the city, the rhythm directly at odds with the spell that still bound the fighters. It felt as if that magic might soon fray.

If one defiant drum could keep beating even as the wall fell, and if those soldiers could give their lives to destroy Pashun's drums, then he could tell his story. The surviving falcon jati soldiers retreated up toward the city.

He took a deep breath of ashy smoke that trickled off his censer, stifled the cough it triggered, and spoke as loud as his voice permitted. "Many died when the nagas sought vengeance, those who had laid the traps and those who were innocent alike. The nagas were too powerful to resist." As he said the word "power," Pavresh took all he'd learned from watching Kamlak and studying those who succeeded in resisting him. Then he turned his spell with a sharp, sudden thrust aimed at Kamlak. "But the nagas failed to recognize how power so quickly rots. When those who were left resisted, the nagas found their power crumbling into dust, their strength sapped away."

The arcist spell struck directly at a part of Kamlak's skull, at the place where Pavresh imagined the connection between a person and the magic must exist. There probably was no such specific place, no organ within the brain that allowed a person to perform arcist magic, but it was the story he told himself, and it gave his own spell a focus.

He hoped to disrupt Kamlak's spell with some sort of turbulence, create enough confusion to let him pull something more together with his story.

The effect was far greater.

The spell that held that whole vast army ceased.

People cried out in pain, in anger, in dismay. They pulled away from the rubble of the wall and dropped weapons from their hands. No doubt some would be quick to resume the fight, with or without Kamlak's magical compulsion, so Pavresh had to be quick.

The abrupt change left him out of breath. It was so much more than he'd expected. While he gathered his thoughts and voice to speak, Kamlak responded, dazed with the end of his spell.

"You…you could have done that all along. Why did you wait until then?" He shook himself and looked behind him at the path to Chaitanshehar.

Pavresh wasn't going to admit that he hadn't known he could—and wasn't sure he would be able to do so again. He shifted the focus of his arcist powers back to where they'd been and tried to resume his tale. "And so the servants were able to overcome the nagas. They cast them—"

"Not that it really matters." Though clearly weary, Kamlak had found his normal, cocksure voice again. "Do you think it will take me long to get them back under my spell? Once I have someone take care of you, I won't even have to worry about losing it again." He turned around to summon guards toward him. Fortunately for Pavresh, so many of the nearby guards had been acting as such under compulsion. Kamlak had to search for anyone to come to his aid.

While he did so, Ekana returned, his sailor's sword still in hand. He placed himself directly before Pavresh. Sembaari joined him with the mumbler-style knife he'd picked up, and Indima danced behind Pavresh, danced a form of strength that surged into him and helped him to stand.

Pavresh didn't fool himself into thinking their protection would last long. Others came, some to surround and protect him but others to add themselves to Kamlak's plans for the army. He had to finish the story now before it was too late.

"They cast the nagas aside, into the crevices in the ground that surrounded the village. And those crevices became a new sort of power, one that was the antithesis of the bodies of nagas that lay within." The barbed hooks of the magic also sank into the crevices of the land around them, into spaces too small to see and beneath the entire rumbling might of Kamlak's horde.

"Wait!" Kamlak tried to interrupt him, and when Pavresh continued, Kamlak grabbed a horn from one of those near him. He blew a blast on the horn, so loud that his own people covered their ears, and Pavresh had no choice but to stop. His story would be meaningless without listeners.

Before the reverberations of the trumpet had died away, Kamlak said, "You aren't trying to cast your spell on me at all, are you? That's why you didn't try to stop me before. You're... What are you doing?" He stared at Pavresh and looked around at the land around them.

Pavresh reached out as far as his magic would allow. He imagined it stretching to the snowy peaks beyond his father's mine, up the river to the mumbler villages Pavresh had visited, to the sea beside Jarnur and beyond it to the lands that Harkala and Ekana had described for him to the west and south, through the tunnel in the mountains and the long, monotonous road that wound beyond it all the way to the Forgotten South. He placed his barbed hook as deep as he could into all those corners of the world, into the imagined lands that none of them knew but that might lie even farther beyond them.

"The power of those crevices wafted up to weaken any nagas that might return, or any other creatures that might come, creatures of fire and saltwater, creatures of dune grass or fields of ice. It was a different kind of power to make the village safe—"

"What do you think you're doing?" Kamlak pushed past his own people and right up to Ekana's sword, as if he could sweep the fisherman away as easily as swatting a fly. "Don't you understand what will happen to you if you do this? To arcist magic itself?"

Pavresh brought up his arms, though it wasn't necessary, and as Kamlak shouted for him to stop, raised his voice as loud as he could and said, "And ever after, the land and all the lands were protected from the power of the nagas." He snapped his arms down and felt the world grow poorer, felt a thinness creeping over him and over all the land he could see and picture and imagine.

Dizzy, he spun in a slow circle as if it were the closing motion of an elaborate dance, and fell in a heap on the ground.

***

When Pavresh came to, he was in the same place. Someone had laid him out more comfortably and covered him with a field blanket, and there were people nearby to keep him from getting trampled, but it looked as if not much time had passed. He found the sun, heading toward the southwestern mountains but couldn't remember what time it had been when he and Kamlak had their odd standoff.

Before looking around for the other arcist or for anyone to ask questions of, he reached for his magic.

It was still there. He hadn't destroyed arcist magic, at least. He wove a spell over himself of a wounded hero, a wise wanderer, and last a performing fool. When he released the images, they dissipated right away, fluff on the cold west winds.

"What did you do, Pavresh?"

Ekana leaned over him, and Pavresh flinched away. Ekana had stood before Pavresh when Kamlak threatened, but that didn't change his past. A coughing fit overtook him, and when it had passed, there were several faces looming above him. He closed his eyes and shook his head, hoping it wouldn't trigger more coughs.

When he dared look again, the others had pulled back, so he peered beyond them to figure out what was happening.

There was no sign of any fighting. The Pashun drums were still silent, and its horns as well, but the lone, dismal drum in the city still beat its irregular rhythm. "Kamlak?" he asked.

"Arrested," Ekana said. "Along with Dartak." He spoke the name with a reassuring bitterness. "And the other leaders from Pashun as well."

As if they could ever be sure. "How do you know you got them all?"

"Maybe not all of them, but this man and woman came down from the city and helped us identify the most important leaders, the ones who might prove dangerous."

Pavresh pursed his lips. Who would that be? Before he could ask, an entourage from the city announced its arrival among the soldiers at the base. No grand carriages, just a cluster of what passed for high-ranking people in the city, descending on foot. Trumpets announced them, but it was a sound utterly unlike the anxious intensity of Pashun's trumpets. Pavresh struggled upright, and someone set a pillow behind his back for him.

Jaritta led them. She looked older, her face so gaunt it made the fire scar stand out on her cheek, her hair turning to gray, and yet there was an iron strength that showed in her face. Beside her was Ellechandran, carrying his two little girls. They were noticeably older than they'd been when he was caught in Pashun as well. They looked stately and completely at home among the pomp, their skin color and facial features a mixture of their mother's and father's, beautifully melding their heritages.

Juishika—once a beggar, once his student in magic—stepped around them and strode straight up to Pavresh and asked the question that Ekana had asked, the one he hadn't been able to answer. "*What* did you do?"

He looked around at the battlefield. The wounded were being tended. There was peace, of sorts, but it was a weary peace, a peace that rested uneasily on powerful anger and betrayal. The betrayal of people torn from their homes in the south, of local people whose leaders had proven greedy and cruel, probably also of people who *had* believed in their purpose and still wanted to tear down the city with its heretical social structure.

He reached up toward Chaitanshehar, to his former spell anchored deep into the rock beneath. It was still there, pulsing but faint.

Meeting Juishika's confused eyes, he said, "I gave up our magic. I made it impossible for Kamlak to do that again, to compel everyone into his army."

"You *gave up* our magic? What does that mean?"

He took a deep, calming breath through his nose and wove around himself the earlier image of a wounded hero and wise. It settled very loosely around him, not the overpowering image he used to create. But it still should have some effect.

"I made a new spell, one anchored to the whole valley. For those within it, and probably well beyond its edges, arcist magic is diminished. It will still summon a vague sense, maybe even a relatively powerful one, but not one that can control anyone." He added in the sense of a kindly teacher and let that magic replace the others. "Go ahead and use the magic you've learned, Juishika. It isn't gone, only changed."

While she worked with wisps of arcist magic, Pavresh greeted Jaritta. "I am glad you survived. And that Rashul's dream may still live on." He saw in his mind the image of Rashul cut down and killed before him and he pursed his lips. "I want to honor his memory."

Jaritta nodded. "And I will need your help to do so. The city is in dire straits, but it seems we have you to thank that it still exists at all."

"Me, and your drummer up there—"

"One of your students, in fact. Haysha."

The girl who'd been born in Eghsal City, who'd been a refugee as a child when she came to this new city. He'd known she had a special feel for the magic. Hearing that she had played a role filled him with pride. Perhaps she would be one of those who widened the understanding of arcist magic even further, despite how he had dampened it by his own actions.

"Some of your other students helped her make the drum," Juishika said. "Alarmelai knew something of mumbler drums, and Sagak put aside his fire liquor to stretch the skin over it. But Haysha was the one who kept its beat going throughout."

"It's good to hear that. And the falcon jati warriors played a role. Not to mention our dancers." He had to twist around to find them. "Sembaari is a mumbler. And you will remember Indima and Ekana."

Jaritta's face froze at the name, but with the grace trained into her as a member of the princely jati, she turned to them and dipped her head. "I thank you for the parts you have played. And Indima, I would be honored to speak to you more, up in the city when we have the chance." Then to Pavresh she said, "You are weary, I am sure. We will continue our tour of the field and speak with you more when you have rested."

After they left, he asked those still around him, "But who was the couple who helped identify the leaders?"

Indima answered, "Datri. And the man she says is her husband, Prince Jasfer, though I certainly don't recognize him anymore."

Alive as well? He pushed himself even higher as if to walk away and find them, but it made him dizzy. He fell back against the pillow, had enough strength to rearrange it so that he could lie down, and fell into a deep and healing sleep.

CHAPTER 31

Pavresh took his place at the side of the open-air stage. The rubble of what had been the wall still surrounded their space, with memorial markers along one side, the names of people he would miss. But today was not a day for mourning but celebration.

Even Datri had been unable to track down Namrani, the soft-spoken musician who had created the compelling music in Chaitan's house so many years earlier. Haysha proved a worthy musician, though, and not only on the gigantic drum she had used during the invasion. She played a stringed instrument with a long neck and kept a much smaller drum near one foot to add an ever-changing mix of rhythms to her music. Her training in arcist magic helped her catch on quickly to the ways the performers combined music, dancing, and magic.

Indima and Ekana stood on the stage, naturally. Of all the dancers who had been a part of Chaitan's household gatherings, they were the ones who captured the full range of what the performances could achieve.

From the side of the stage, Pavresh added his magic to the others.

Arcist magic still worked. It was a beautiful and nuanced part of the performance, powerful but fleeting. There was no lingering effect, except in the way any artistic performance might stay with its viewers and listeners afterward.

Indima danced of being locked away, kept apart from the world, and as she danced, she became free, leaving her cell of a home behind to join with the world at large. Ekana danced of leaving a place behind as well, but his dance was an exploration, a journey into a new land. They danced together, and their steps and claps and passes intertwined, yet in many ways they each danced a separate story, unconnected to the other.

Pavresh played with the themes their dancing suggested,

enhancing and adjusting the ideas to create the most meaningful performance. Haysha's music tagged along, sometimes leading the others in new directions, but mostly content to let them lead.

When the dance ended, the people of Chaitanshehar applauded. Pavresh had to take a moment to breathe deeply so that his lungs wouldn't seize up as he walked away. The performers gathered beside the memorials afterward, and their enthusiastic congratulations became more solemn.

Valni had been among those who fell when the wall collapsed. She had played a key role in the founding of the city, especially in its defense when the city had been threatened. Her sense of duty toward the city's leaders had been equaled only by her well justified belief in her own fighting prowess.

The falcon jati soldiers, when they discovered she was there, had intended to capture her. But something she had said or done—their leader wouldn't elaborate on what it was—coupled with Mahendri's dismissal of their prestige had convinced them to help the city. And something Ellechandran and Chhayasheela had learned in their surveillance had brought about the idea of targeting the army's drums. Valni had brought that information to her former jati sisters when they withdrew from Mahendri's words. And then she'd returned to the wall to defend the city and die.

It would have been good for Valni to have seen the success of that foray.

They noted the others who had died—those who had been identified so far—and then moved on, away from the stage and the crowd.

Ekana walked close beside Indima. "It was good to dance with you."

Pavresh didn't mean to listen to what sounded like a private conversation, but they were in too close proximity for him to ignore it.

"We dance well together."

"I...would you have me stay, and...and dance together more?" Ekana's awkwardness made Pavresh feel embarrassed.

Indima showed no awkwardness in responding. "My sweet dancer. I will dance with you whenever you wish. But I'm not looking for a life partner or even a bed partner. Only a dance partner, and no one will ever equal you in that way."

Ekana nodded sadly, as if her words confirmed what he'd expected, as if they helped him make up his mind about some other matter. Pavresh avoided looking their way to give them privacy.

Jaritta and her family joined them as they walked the rest of the way to the town hall offices. She was looking well, though the struggle to bring in enough food for her city had left a haunted look in her eyes. Even so, this was where she proved herself, in the uncertainty and chaos of the aftermath. She had taken charge and helped to arrange everything that needed to be done. The success of those efforts, so far, had restored much of the vitality she seemed to have lost during the months of hunger and fear. Ellechandran stayed close beside her, and the girls went back and forth between them, with Nataravi sometimes daring to approach one of the others in the makeshift entourage.

In the city chambers, they sat around on the floor, leaning against pillows, while sharing the food laid out on a blanket before them. It wasn't an abundance of food—they had recovered a good deal from the stores of the Pashun army to add to what they'd managed to scrape together over the past year, but they couldn't just leave the released soldiers to starve as they returned to their homes.

Pavresh chose a bowl of swamp fruits, preserved in some kind of liquor. If he coughed while eating those, he wouldn't accidentally breathe the fruit into his lungs. Bread made him wary—several times recently he'd aspirated on a crust of bread. The liquor was faint but added a pleasant bite to the sweetness of the fruits. He drank normal tisane with a dose of the yellow tisane added to control his coughing.

Ekana sat as far from Jaritta as he could, not because he seemed to have anything against her, but no doubt he could read her reactions to his presence. He took a scoop of figs into his hand and paused before eating.

"I wish to return to the Forgotten South," he announced. "I can help the city create a trade arrangement with them, if you would have me do so."

From the edge of his sight, Pavresh caught Indima's reaction, a look of sadness but understanding that refusing him earlier meant she would have to dance alone.

Jaritta, on the other hand, looked only relieved. "That would be useful to have, and I'm sure there are others who might wish to accompany you."

Pavresh expected Ekana's mumbler friend Sembaari to go as well. He sat near Ekana, at the back of the room, but when he noticed several people looking his way, he shook his head. "I played at being from the Forgotten South, and then I visited the real version. Now I wish to forget it." He said it with a wink at the play on words, not as if the memories were so terrible. "I will return to my own village for a time, but I may come on a later expedition."

Pavresh had visited Sembaari's village—when Sembaari wasn't there. A flash of desire to revisit the place came and went. It lay within a beautiful wood, hidden in a pocket of the mountains where there were tall pines and good hunting, tucked among the harsh peaks. Their people, looking like the people of Eghsal but acting and speaking like the other mumblers, were his first proof that the history his own people told of the founding of the valley was not the complete truth. To visit them again, even to visit others, to enjoy the rugged journeying itself—a part of him longed for that again.

"I would accompany him," Harkala said. "Ekana, that is. Elsh, our guide, was injured in the battle but should recover soon, and she is anxious to return." She paused long enough to give a slight shrug. "At least, I think that's what she's trying to say. But I'm not interested in trade. I wish to study the land, to learn what I can across the language barrier. There are ruins I wish to excavate, if I'm given leave by them. And I would share that knowledge with Eghsal as well." She looked at Ekana and added, "And if we're establishing trade, then we do owe something to Jarnur for funding our journey."

"Have we heard anything from Jarnur?" Pavresh asked.

"A cautious response." Jaritta fed bits of bread torn off a bigger piece to Ovitiva while she talked. "They were no friends of Pashun these past six years, but no friends of ours either. If we can work out a trade route that benefits them and us, they'll come around, I think."

"And Romnai?"

"They're terrified." It was Datri, walking through the doorway while supporting the shell of the man who had once been Prince Jasfer. "Their leaders know many people don't accept them as the rightful princes. They know the falcon jati has come over here and pledged itself to our city. They know one of the most powerful princes from before the current rulers is here with us." She looked with a rueful fondness at Jasfer. "Though maybe not what his condition is."

Jasfer sat down and began eating, offering some of the food to the dog that rarely left his side. He didn't respond to anything they said or seem to notice, though when people asked him direct questions, he could answer.

Datri sat down beside him, opposite the dog, and took some food herself.

"It's good to have the soldiers here," Jaritta said. "I wish we didn't need them, but I suppose there may still come a time when we will. The other cities still won't like the way we discard their caste distinctions. And welcome mumblers. Pavresh, your spell won't protect us as well anymore, will it?"

He shook his head quickly. "No. It's still there. It should help the people who live here to work together more readily. But it won't keep enemies away like it used to."

"Should we send some of the soldiers along with the traders heading south, though?"

"I will accompany them," Chhayasheela said, speaking the trade pidgin. Pavresh translated for her by instinct, though many in that room understood both languages by now. "Some of the other villagers might wish to as well."

"Not I," Ellechandran said, to which Jaritta murmured, "Good answer."

When they had finished eating, most of them dispersed to various tasks around the city. There was always something to accomplish, some work that needed immediate attention.

Pavresh stayed, not sure yet how his lungs would respond to him moving. Jaritta hovered behind her brother.

"I hope you can remember me someday, Jasfer. Maybe not everything."

He cocked his head and petted the dog with one hand.

"Maybe you can remember exploring tunnels and alleys with me when we were little. And I hope you discover the memories of the years you helped me survive, when I was on the streets alone. Now we've each been scarred by fires." She touched her face, where new wrinkles pulled at the edges of her scar. "And we've both been outcasts, living off what we could beg."

A look came into Jasfer's eyes that reminded Pavresh of the former prince. Whether it was a full memory or only a lingering hint of the man who'd been lost, Pavresh couldn't guess.

"There are other times I wish I could forget," Jaritta continued. "A lot of pain and hurt, but it's past now. Maybe losing some memories isn't a terrible thing." She leaned over and kissed his forehead. "I'm glad you're back, brother, at least part-way back."

With a wrist to her unscarred eye, Jaritta rushed from the room.

Datri sat down beside Jasfer and took his hand, but her eyes were on Pavresh.

"And what will you do, arcist? The last time we were alone together, I helped you save Jaritta, and then you fled."

Had he spent so little time with her in the years in between, when they were both here in Chaitanshehar? But then she had kept to herself, except for the contacts with her spies, and he had been focused on his students and their place in the city.

Pavresh held wide his arms. "I'm not fleeing anywhere this time. Here is where I am, and here is where I'll stay."

"Always? You can't tell me you aren't tempted to go south and learn the stories of new peoples and distant lands."

Was he? Sure. The idea of exploration was a powerful part of his identity, an arcist image he had built up over the years, and no weakening of the magic would take that away. He found himself attracted to the idea of traveling there, of seeing that strange southern city without someone controlling him. But he didn't *have* to go. Not at once. Maybe not ever.

The idea of staying in the city for a time, of helping it recover and grow, that was the image—arcist and otherwise—that he wanted to build on.

"I'm not saying I'll never leave. Only the Sacred Fire can say what any one person will or won't do, and maybe not even it can. For now, though. I will stay and help rebuild."

Maybe someday he would have the chance to travel the South. His lungs might recover, or some new cure might exist beyond the lands they'd yet found. Or maybe he would leave it to a student or later generations to travel back, to add the stories and traditions of other peoples to their understanding of the magic. He longed for it, yet knew it didn't have to be him who heard those stories first.

"Good," Datri said, as she helped Jasfer to his feet. "The city needs you, I think. Jaritta needs your guidance, and I wouldn't want her to lose that. The way Prince Jasfer lost your guidance so many years ago." She gave a curt nod as if she'd said something she'd been hoping to say for a long time, an apology long delayed and spoken of only glancingly. Datri guided Jasfer out the door.

Finally feeling his lungs were ready, Pavresh stood as well. He lingered over the blanket of food, took one last sesame cake, and headed out for his own home up the slope, among the houses where many of the beggars he'd led from Romnai had established themselves.

Just let him be one among them for a while. Not a returned hero, not a wounded leader, not a prisoner freed at last. Not even the wise teacher sharing exotic wisdom. It was time to remind himself that he could be a part of a group of people, a common part and not set above or outside the rest.

***

Pavresh wanted to see the lava fields below. The rubble where the wall had been was too crowded, too busy with both people and memories. Ghosts, gawkers, and nostalgia. He wanted none of those, so he headed along the ridge north of the city. Valni had often patrolled here, rugged and largely inaccessible from below.

He climbed over rocks and through narrow defiles until he found a spot with a view.

Steam rose near the horizon. That would probably be the extent of what he could see from this distance. The Pashun fields had few geysers and those only rarely blew. The mists off the nearer swamps rose and merged with the steam, as if it were all one. But even so, the trees that stood out from the mix of swamp gas and lava-heated steam were impressive in their own rights, and the meaning behind the steam, the *power* that explained it all was a reminder of the stark nature of their northern valley.

It was a harsh land and not welcoming to humans. Bare rock, weather-blasted bushes, and snow were the key features of most of the valley's unsettled regions. Only the threats of volcanic eruptions, scalding water, and foul airs made some portion of the land habitable. Still humans had found a way to make those dangers work. Not only his own people, but the mumblers before them as well.

Now it fell to them to forge a new way of living and make it work, casteless and equal. The threats were no smaller than those their ancestors had known.

He would do what could be done, what portion of it he could accomplish.

Pavresh slept under furs on that ledge and watched the sun rise over the swamp the next morning. The mists and steam scattered the early light into a thousand hues Pavresh had no names for, no words to describe, and no arcist magic to fully capture. It left spots of strange light and color in his eyesight that forced him to walk carefully away from the edge.

Returning to the city, he still sensed the lingering colors of the sunrise in his vision, transforming the buildings for a moment before they returned to their usual daytime appearances.

Indima danced through the streets, alone. He watched her as his lungs forced him to rest, catch his breath. He had been in love with her once, from a distance—or thought he had. That felt like a different person. He still loved her in his way—and Jaritta and his students and the city as a whole, but that adolescent ache of longing had turned to steam, dissipated much as the power of arcist magic had, after his final spell.

He lit the naga trumpet flowers in his censer and rested on a rock. Indima's dance captured the loneliness of the city. Maybe just the loneliness of growing old, the memories of good friendships, the connections that were stretched thin by time but still there, in their own ways. She was probably thinking about Ekana leaving, of many people going different ways. Or maybe it was only that he was thinking of that.

Then her dancing changed, became celebration. What she celebrated, he couldn't decipher. Maybe defeating the army, maybe her escape from Mahendri, maybe her freedom from the Silk City. But it was a wild celebration, her leaps like flames of a newly lit fire.

When he could breathe deeply again, he created a counterpoint to her dance with arcist magic. There were no flames, but a calm and certain joy that lay within the land itself, deep within the city they were working to create. He entered the city, plucking the imaginary strings that were the source of arcist magic. And if his magic didn't linger long after he passed, and if it couldn't force everyone who felt it to embrace that same joy, well, that was fine. Let those who felt the same be reinforced, and strengthened for the times ahead when they wouldn't feel it—within themselves or outside.

Pavresh bowed to Indima as she slid past. She gave him no reaction, only continued her dance, and that was as it ought to be.

Pavresh breathed deep. There were the smells of food cooking, but beyond that, he breathed in the ideas of the city, the way it would feel as it moved forward without castes, the way Jaritta and Azheeran, Datri and Jasfer, and others, along with him, would guide that progress, no doubt toward something he couldn't yet fully imagine.

The city was too far from the volcanic activity for real steam baths, but someone had created a passable imitation with water heated by fire in one of the abandoned houses. Pavresh made his way there to recover from his night under the stars.

EPILOGUE

A Letter from Harkala.

To the leaders of Chaitanshehar—and to all its citizens

Greetings from the Forgotten South, from the city of, as I have learned to call it, Thiluru. I am sending this letter with Ekana as he returns with the goods for trade. It is not a formal report of my findings, but rather a quick letter to you in Chaitanshehar. I will be sending a real report to my colleagues in Jarnur at a later date.

Ekana is returning with many goods that he hopes—and I hope—will be valuable to our people. And he has learned the things that will earn a good return when he comes back. I miss good fish. They have something they call fish, something that resembles fish in appearance, but it is bland and tastes foul. I have urged Ekana to look for a way to transport fish here. Surely it would fetch a good deal in their markets! But even packed in ice, it's difficult to imagine them arriving before they spoil.

They have a fruit that grows here, from trees as tall as our tallest pines. The fruits are fittingly large, and people are cautious about walking beneath when it is time for harvest. When they fall, the fruit is bitter and bland. Prepared right—and there are various ways to bake or cook it right—it has a savory, bread-like taste. Will it travel to the north or spoil on the way? I do not yet know.

Thiluru is a vast city, unlike anything we have back north. I am digging into its history, and there is much to uncover, but I can state with certainty that it is not the origin of our people. Or at least that it is not the Forgotten South of our stories.

It may well be the origin of the mumblers. Or that the ancestors of the city's founders are the ancestors of the mumblers as well, at least. Where they may have come from and when and why they went separate ways is part of what I am studying. As well as how the mumblers reached our valley in the first place, if my understanding is correct. Perhaps further inland there is a route. Or there once was, before mountains shifted and rivers moved. I do not yet know.

Some of those questions will need to be answered by those who come after me.

Elsh is an able guide and learns our language as fast as I learn hers slowly. She thrills to guide me through Thiluru, to show me its sights and wonders. They have no rails or anything similar, yet it is no backwards and uncivilized place. They will have much to trade with us in the future, I believe, including ideas and new technologies. Their curiosity about our land is boundless, as is their appetite for stories.

In fact, the tale of our fight against the bound Pashun army has become a part of their stories, though it is not always easy to recognize the familiar parts we have known. In their telling, it was a battle between two great wizards, fighting in the air, while the mortal foot soldiers stood in wonder below them to watch.

The right wizard won, at least. It would be more difficult to build trust—not to mention trade—if they thought that the wrong side had won.

And what of the Forgotten South of our stories? Did our ancestors come from the city on a pier, across the desert from here? I have found old maps in Thiluru. They show other cities that are no longer there and named regions where no one now lives. When I have learned what I can of the city, I will establish a dig site at one of those locations.

Maybe I will find the truth we have longed for all these years.

Maybe I will find other mysteries instead of new truths.

Either way, it is the searching that pulls me onward more than the certainty of finding.

Ekana is ready to lead his caravan of goods northward now. So in closing, may the Sacred Fire and all the gods of history *smile on your city. May the trade between lands prosper both cities and all peoples involved. And may your city stand as a beacon and symbol for all to see.*

> *Sincerely,*
> *Harkala,*
>> *scholar and caste-less emissary of*
>> *Jarnur, Eghsal Valley, and Chaitanshehar*

THE END

About the Author

Daniel Ausema is a stay-at-home dad and a former educator. His short fiction and poetry have appeared in many publications, including *Strange Horizons*, *Daily Science Fiction*, and *Diabolical Plots*. In addition to the Arcist Chronicles, he is the creator of the steampunk-fantasy *Spire City* series. He lives with his family in Colorado, at the foot of the Rockies.

More Fantasy novels from Guardbridge Books.

The Silk Betrayal
by Daniel Ausema

Volume 1 of The Arcist Chronicles.
A young man travels to the city to study magic, but instead he finds intrigue and revolution.

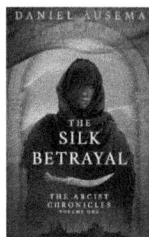

Drakemaster
by EC Ambrose

A desperate race across medieval China during the Mongol conquest to locate a clockwork doomsday device that could destroy the world with the power of the stars.

The Elephant & Macaw Banner
by Christopher Kastensmidt

Muskets, Magic, and Monsters!
A pair of brave adventurers face dangers in the wilderness of colonial Brazil. Based on the mythology and history of Brazil.

All are available at our website and online retailers.

http://guardbridgebooks.co.uk

Milton Keynes UK
Ingram Content Group UK Ltd.
UKHW042001281024
450365UK00003B/72

9 781911 486916